At
End of
Day

ALSO BY GEORGE V. HIGGINS

GEORGE V. HIGGINS

At
End of
Day

Eleanor Steele Blocher
Endowment Fund

North Manchester Public Library

HARCOURT, INC.   NEW YORK · SAN DIEGO · LONDON

Requests for permission to make copies of any part of the
work should be mailed to the following address:
Permissions Department, Harcourt, Inc.,
6277 Sea Harbor Drive, Orlando, Florida 32887-6777.

Many of the places mentioned in this book are real. None
of the characters is. There are, I believe, actual people
who have done, and said, some of the things that the
characters do, and say. It is a story, and I try to make my
stories credible. If the reader finds some resemblance of
its characters to persons now living or dead, then
perhaps it is a good story. But it is still a story, and
that is all—I made it up.—GVH

Library of Congress Cataloging-in-Publication Data
Higgins, George V., 1939–1999
At end of day: a novel/George V. Higgins.
p.   cm.
ISBN 0-15-100358-0
I. Title
PS3558.I356 A8 2000
813'.54 21—dc21   99-046414

Designed by Ivan Holmes
Text set in Minion
Printed in the United States of America
First edition
A B C D E F G H I J

At
End of
Day

1

"DERELICT," NAUGHTON'S KID HAD SAID to Rascob on the evening of the third Tuesday in March at the Getty station, collecting $31.50 for an oil change and two new filters he said the old grey Lincoln Town Car badly needed. "Air and oil both," he said. "Took a chance and did it. Old ones're both shot. Air filter looked like a gorilla wiped his arse with it. Oil filter—rollah toilet paper, brand new. Saved 'em, case you wanna see them—show you both of them, you like."

"Take your word," Rascob said. "Damn thing's gotta run."

"Didn't think you'd mind," Naughton's kid said. He'd finished in the top fifteen percent on the police exam and was waiting out the next list of appointments to the academy.

"*Oh*-kay," Rascob said. "Gonna hafta get a new one. But the Uncle likes it. Know how he is."

"Long's ah radio works," the Naughton kid said, laughing. "'Don't care ah fuckin' thing looks like—runs anna radio works.'"

"Right," Rascob said. "Radio. So—I'm covered. The radio works—it runs. Work McKeach, drive his kindah of car."

"Inconspicuous," McKeach had said. "Only way to travel. Al Castle says, way things're goin', Supreme Court, everything, pretty soon a bad *excuse* to stop you'll be enough. Then if they find somethin', courts're gonna let 'em have it. Know your car, guys aren't with us—know what we're doin', too. So, they know what you got in it. Give 'em half a chance, drag you down and search, knowin' what they're gonna find? And then when they find it, put your ass in jail? Not if you got half a brain. All you gotta do is tell 'em, 'Hey, I didn't put it in there. Didn't know I had it—don't belong to me.' Won't lay a glove on you.

"What they'll do's keep the money. 'Unclaimed propty.' No one claims it for a year? Forfeit to the state. I go in and say 'It's mine,' *I* go to the jug."

"*Best* thing can happen, we lose a lotta dough. Worst thing— they figure out some way to tie it to me. Don't like either thing. Make sure everything works. Turn signals. Brake lights—bulb above the license plate. And *whatever* you do, don't go over the speed limit. *Nothin'*—give 'em nothin'—that way you should be all right."

Rascob tried his best to be on time for his weekly meetings with Dominic Frolio. Dominic was his last appointment of the morning, but meeting him took patience—and at least twenty-five minutes. Dominic joined him no less than eight minutes after he arrived and he would not hurry business. "Rushin' does no good," McKeach said. It still made Rascob nervous; one January morning the trunk of the Town Car had held more than $817,000 in cash. The New England Pats had had a bad Sunday, losing the AFC Championship to the Denver Broncos; the Boston books'd done well.

When Rascob had started meeting Dominic, in the early eighties, the house on the corner of Apthorp Street had been a neat and modest white five-room bungalow with green trim, a screened sun porch added on the front. Genevieve had been making noises about moving to a larger place, a better neighborhood.

Dominic said he wouldn't. He and Genevieve had lived there since he went to work as a spot welder at the shipyard. "Endah World War Two—forty years ago. Yard's really busy then. Anyone who wanted, wasn't dead, could make a buck. Everybody building boats. Naturally—most the merchant fleet got sunk."

Then the shipyard went under. His job went away. "Anyway, my back was shot, killin' me by then, workin' onna stagin'." But he had the Beachside, at the traffic lights. "So it was okay. Made it good. Took up my time, you know? Kept me occupied."

In the Beachside he ran the action that Brian G. had watched over years before for a fee and McKeach now kept provisioned and protected, as he protected the old grey Town Car full of currency on its way into Boston and the back room at Flynn's Spa, Beer & Wine, Superette, at Old Colony and B.

"Once they knew who you were with: that was all they hadda know. No one bothered you. Safe's you'd ah been in your dear mother's arms."

Things stayed the same after Brian G. went down and McKeach took over. So Frolio could say now, as he did: "Nothing bad's ever happened, me and Jenny, we bought that fuckin' house. It's a lucky house, I think. Didn't know it when I bought it but I think that's what it is."

Jenny did not share his contented trust. After every hurricane season and severe winter she had to replace the azaleas killed by the salt water, muttering forebodings that some day the roaring storms would wash them and the house away. He did not listen. He never left the protection of it until he had made as sure as possible that it was safe to go outside.

"Always try to take a piss, 'fore I go out. That way I don't hafta look around, find a place to take a leak, ten minutes after I been out. An' naturally I never leave it—any morning, whatsoever—'til I've had a good shit for myself." Then he put on his cap and jacket, regardless of the season. On very hot days in August he didn't zip the jacket. On very humid mornings, he sometimes wore the Bermuda shorts he put on before he went to sit outside on his green-and-yellow aluminum folding lawn chair in the early afternoons.

"Take a little sun, you know? Don't believe that cancer stuff, sun is bad for you. Father always liked the sun—he died, he's ninety-two. What happened, all a sudden? Now it's bad for us? Everybody's trynah scare us. I figure it can't hurt."

Leaving the house on the mornings Rascob came, Dominic would pick up the same small, dark-blue canvas gym bag with black plastic handles Rascob had noticed the first day McKeach had introduced them. One day, several years later, Rascob mentioned to Dominic that the bag had lasted well, and Dominic had said, "All my things do. They should. I'm not hard on stuff." The last minute-plus was for walking out to meet Rascob.

Fourteen years had passed since Nino Giunta went to what was then MCI Walpole with twenty-to-life in front of him, and Rascob succeeded him as Dominic's contact. Thirteen and a half had passed since the first and last time Rascob had suggested that Dominic forget the eight-minute delay.

"Yeah," Dominic said. "Never did like Nino. Most guys I've done business with, I have got along with good. Four of them so far, you've lasted the longest—and that's not even counting you. The three before Nino, and then him. And then you.

"When something's happened to them—they got careless, trusted someone they shouldn't've; did something they're not sure of? Then they hadda go away? Or they just disappeared, during all the trouble here? I been, you know, sorry for them. Hoped whatever happened to them, not . . . too bad. They didn't have much pain. Nothing I could do—'cept wish they'd been more careful. But still, I did feel sorry. Bad they hadda go away.

"Nino I did not. Very careless man. Loud about it, too. 'Look at me, everyone, oh ho, I'm the big cheese inna thing. Everybody kiss my ass. I'm a great big city man.' Full of the big talk. Now Nino's in Walpole—I'm right? Will be a long time. Don't wanna be there with him. Always figured him for trouble. Never liked the guy."

In the rearview mirror this March day Rascob saw the grey aluminum storm door open at the front of the first-floor front room with the picture windows that had been the screened-in porch before Jenny's compromise conversion. Dominic emerged and shut the door securely with both hands, the right one on the knob and the left, holding the gym bag, pushing on the wood above it. Those who live in the wind respect it.

Dominic disappeared from the mirror when he reached the right rear quarter panel of the Lincoln. Rascob sighed and slouched, reaching forward with his right hand to shut off the ignition and remove his keys from the lock, then unlatching his seatbelt. Dominic appeared at the right front window, bending only slightly to peer in, raising his bushy grey-black eyebrows under the visor of his black leather cap, rapping with the knuckles of his right hand. Rascob nodded and slipped the seatbelt over his shoulder, in the same movement opening his door and getting out. By the time he had the door closed, Dominic had sidled around to the driver's side through the narrow space Rascob had left between the seawall and the front bumper, shifting the bag to his right hand and steadying himself with his left on the warm hood. He left three hand prints that would remain visible in the obliquely angled afternoon light of late winter until the next downpour.

Rascob went to the back of the car and used the key to open the trunk. Inside there was a black ballistic nylon duffel bag. Rascob reached in with both hands and unzipped it. It contained several brown paper bags with hand-written figures in green or black Magic Marker. Dominic put the gym bag into the trunk and unzipped it. He removed four brown paper bags with numerals hand written on them in blue Magic Marker and put them in the suitcase. He stepped back with the gym bag and Rascob closed the duffel. Increasing to $147,800 the running total for that day he kept in his head, for the amusement of learning later from his actual count how accurate his quick mental tallies had been, Rascob stepped back and slammed the trunk shut. He returned to the driver's door, ready to use the ignition key. "You want to leave the bag?" he said.

"I think so, Max," Frolio said. "Cold today. Forgot my gloves again." He opened the left rear door and put the bag inside on the seat. He closed the door and put his hands into his pockets. Rascob locked the car. "Nice tah see you. Should take a little walk. Clears the lungs out. And—things to talk about."

"Dom," Rascob said, nodding once, "by all means. Always look forward to it."

They went north along the seawall until they came to a flight of four cement steps with green iron railings leading up to the platform at the top. To the right a flight of five more cement steps led down to the beach. Dominic went first, clenching the railings with his liver-spotted hands, assisting his leg muscles with his forearms.

Rascob had once asked McKeach how old Frolio was. McKeach shrugged.

"Dunno," he said. "Brian G.'s his original rabbi—unless it was Moses. He's where he is when Brian got whacked, same place he is today. Doin' the exact same thing, same way he does today. Knows from nothin', anything that's going on. Ask him something and he'll tell you, he just owns ah liquor store. All that's on his mind. Already'd been doing it for years back when

I first run up against him. How many? Dunno. How old he's then? When he got started? Who brought him in? Dunno that either. Didn't ask him. See, by then I'm over thirty and I knew a couple things. Things you didn't fuck with; you just hadda deal with—unless you liked a lotta grief. And so that was what you did. He was one of them, so you dealt with him.

"Not the only one. Lot of guys to deal with. Same kind of position. Never really heard about them—how they wanted it. Never looking to move up in anything, never lookin' to branch out. And also never took a bust. Not really that involved in things—what's goin' on in town, pickin' sides or anything. Just trynah stay in business, you know?

"For them the war was an inconvenience. Same as 'The power's out. Fuckin' Edison fucked up, house's dark, and now *fuck,* it's gettin' *cold*—no way to make coffee.' People dyin'? Brian G. goin' down, Rocco, all kinds of guys—to guys like Dominic it was all an inconvenience. Didn't *care* who controlled things.

" 'Just gettah damn thing fixed, all right?' All they cared about back then; all they care about today. Doesn't *matter* how it comes out, far as they're concerned—work with anybody. Will, too. Sit tight 'til it's over with—that was all was on their minds.

"So I decide I oughta have a talk with Nick. Go and see the Frogman, all right? We always been all right. Find out which way he's leaning; what he thought that we could do.

"First I call. Those days, hadda be careful. Someone doesn't know you're comin' and then he looks up and sees you? Might get the wrong idea. Could get dangerous, things got straightened out. So, I go and sit down with him. Back room down the Lamplight. And we talk, you know? Saw things the same way I did. This was something we could do, try to get things straightened out. Middle sixties, this was.

"An' that's all it was, all right? Not like you may've heard some guys, we just come in, took over. Wasn't what we had in mind—all came afterwards. No, it was just—we would see what we could do. Sort of date it all from then.

"By then Dominic's gotta be pushin' eighty. Hasta be eighty, now. Bastard doesn't look it. Tougher'n a pail of nails. Hate to be the guy who stiffs him. Dom takes care himself."

Brown kelp and bleached-out cardboard packaging washed ashore by the severest winter storms lay against the base of the seawall. Ragged lines of weeds and rubbish marked off the beach at intervals of about a yard leading down to the clean dark sand exposed beyond the high-water mark. A faded white sign with red lettering still attached to the broken end of one white post warned that diving and shellfishing were hazardous and therefore prohibited. Idly, as he had each week since he had first seen the sign, Rascob wondered who would have wanted to wade in water too polluted for safe swimming.

"Things're too good," Dominic said after they had walked about forty yards north of the steps. Ahead of them a woman in a blue hooded sweatshirt and sweatpants with white piping sat red-faced and breathing heavily on an overturned brown milk crate, staring out on the bay. To the north beyond her the Boston skyline rose indistinctly silver in a light haze, the sunlight approaching midday flat on the glass towers. At intervals of about two minutes big jets disturbed the air around them, then roared past, descending on their right.

"President's got problems," Frolio said. "Nobody gives a shit. Everybody's all got work, much work's least they need. Bringing paychecks home. That's what they care about—should, too. Things're good for them, their families. That's why it doesn't matter, what he does, this one or the other one. Wife catches him again? Still stands up for him. She knows—all know—long's she does this for him, he's her fuckin' *employee*. Must do what she says. President, United States. Slave to his pecker."

Rascob did not say anything. Frolio said: "No women, ever, on the job. That's where he went wrong. Cannot mix pussy and work. Women stay home, take care of babies.

"All this equality and shit, we hear all the time? Absolutely for it. Known a lot more smart women'n smart men. And I've known a lot more men—you know what that means. Only two women I have known who made big trouble for themselves by not thinking before they did something with sex, and that is all. Many men? Can't count 'em. So that is why it is my rule—no women onna job I run.

"There's a woman inna building, matter how ugly she is, some man will lose his head. His woman'll find out. Then you will have trouble."

"I see," Rascob said, not seeing at all.

"Ford," Dominic said. "Charlie Ford."

"Yes," Rascob said, "the builder? Excellent prospect, I should think. He needs financing?"

"Not him, no," Frolio said, "unfortunately. For him I would say Yes, at once. A good man, old Charlie Ford. This his son, young Charlie Ford. He came to me. I didn't go to him. He was the only one."

"Well, even so," Rascob said, "he should be enough to do it, if what he's got is big enough.... Which wouldn't be unusual, in that kind of thing. And even if he couldn't use the whole of it, you know, two-forty or three hundred, well, we could live with that. The other sixty, someplace else—it wouldn't be that hard."

"He asked me for a million six," Frolio said. "He asked me, could we do that."

Rascob whistled. "Quite a lot," he said, "but still, it would be doable, I think—he still reliable?"

"Has been before," Frolio said. "Not that he has that much himself that he can get it from, but if a deal went bad for him, he could make it good. The thing is that the first time it was a little thing, a small matter of forty large for a little union problem. And the other time we did some business with him, the much larger matter. He was doing something else. That time for the fishing boat, taking guns someplace—Ireland, I believe.

"Gut said No. Too many people; sentiment involved. Bad combination, sentiment and money. Coast Guard... we were lucky. Buyers paid—advance. Two anna quarter. Young Charlie's father would've covered him, the nature of that deal, if the money hadn't been there.

"This time, the father wouldn't. Not a business of this kind. Cocaine. Father would turn away."

"Would the father have to know?" Rascob said. Two helicopters skittered in before the tallest buildings on the skyline, heading for the airport.

"He would," Frolio said. "The risk is big. His plan is not to use the planes again." He made a small gesture with his right thumb toward the sky above the water. "Too risky. To have the transporters swallow the condoms the day of the night that they come here from Puerto Rico, Mexico, whatever.

"I say to him that I agree. 'Won't work. Ever since the time the rubbers burst inside the people, they got sick. At least one died. Now they watch the airplanes, getting on and off. Profiling— kind of people who they know would do such a thing for pay. You try a thing like that again and you lose all the money— drugs and people too.

"'Besides, we do not do that. Family rule—we do not conduct such business.'"

"Well," Rascob said, drawing the word out.

Dominic looked grim. "'The man is dead,' young Charlie says to me. 'The son is dead. The boss in jail.'

"'*Viva la Famiglia,*' I say to him. 'And the Family's not in jail. The rule is of the Family, not the boss, who is in jail, or the son and father, dead.'"

Rascob gazed straight ahead and said nothing. The wind gnawed at the back of his neck and he reached back with both hands, awkwardly, to pull his hat down on his head and tug up the collar of his trenchcoat.

"You don't agree," Frolio said.

Rascob said, "Oh, I agree. The Family rule is as you say—of course we honor it. But as you know there's been an exception made in recent years. Many times, in fact. For money to be made. The business has become so great—if we don't participate we will lose control. So—conducting it is not allowed, but financing is permitted.

"As I've understood it now to be arranged."

"I have not," Dominic said. "If you go to McKeach and report what I have said, and he tells you I am wrong and the money should be given, then you tell him I said that someone else must take it—put it on the street for this forbidden business. This one—if he decides to do this one, he does it himself. That is all I have to say."

2

As casually as a regular visitor with an interest in the three-story leasehold, Nick Cistaro just before noon the same day opened for the first time the low gate in the black iron fence on the sidewalk and walked onto the brick patio of Imaginings at 73 Newbury Street in Boston. He wore a black calfskin single-breasted safari jacket, a white merino turtleneck, custom-fitted stonewashed blue jeans, black Gucci loafers. His head was large, well furnished with carefully tended silver-grey wavy hair, the face below it expressionless behind the blue-lensed wraparound Vuarnet sunglasses. He latched the gate behind him and scanned the facade—half a flight of stairs led up to a portrait studio with a display window on the elevated first floor—before crossing the patio and descending the three flagstone steps to the Imaginings door. It was forty percent grey-tinted glass invisibly hinged at the left of the display window. The window contained a life-sized stuffed-toy tawny lioness posed resting but watchful under a broad swatch of gilded cat-o'-nine-tails, a small ivory card with black calligraphy reading "STIEFF COURTESY F.A.O. SCHWARTZ" lying next to its left haunch.

The door opened and closed silently when he entered. The shop was deep and narrow, eighteen feet across, carpeted with beige rush matting and illuminated by baby floodlights recessed into the ceiling. Along the right wall there was an elongated grouping of oversized green and gilded bamboo furniture— two wing chairs, a trunk, three tables, each with two straight chairs, a chest of drawers—arranged in front of a triptych screen depicting a porticoed walkway facing on a North African marketplace long-shadowed in late-afternoon light. An audio source played a Bach piano suite arranged for guitar; he did not recognize it. At the rear of the shop were two unoccupied kidney-shaped birch desks and tan chairs facing four beige leather director's chairs and a love seat with beige hopsack cushions. Under the overhang of the mezzanine were four two-drawer brown-metal file cabinets set against a cocoa-colored wall decorated with shiny chocolate-brown masks and crossed spears festooned with beige feathers. In the center of the wall a dimly lighted narrow corridor opened into gloom. Steam rose from a squat brown mug on top of the file cabinet at the left of the door.

To the left of the desks was a stainless-steel semicircular staircase with narrow black carpeted treads; it led up to and continued along the mezzanine above. There was one black arched door off center to the left beyond the top of the staircase and another about twelve feet farther over to the right. Cistaro sniffled, pushed the sunglasses up and back on his hair and started up the stairs. At five feet eleven, 218, he made the staircase flex and creak. He tried to rest his weight lightly and no longer than necessary on each tread.

On the balcony Cistaro without knocking opened the first door. He found Crawford in the eight-by-twelve grey tweed cubicle behind it, recognizing him by the small Florida-shaped port-wine birthmark on his lower left cheek and jaw. Cistaro went in immediately, shutting the door behind him; it was hollow anodized aluminum and clinked like play money.

Crawford, talking on the phone at his cluttered desk in shirt-sleeves, had been looking down through gold half-frame granny glasses and doodling fairly good Snoopys with a hexagonal gold automatic pencil on a foot-square pad of bright yellow paper. He looked up, vexed and puzzled. "Uh huh, you're Crawford," Cistaro said, nodding. "You're Crawford and you're late."

In the corners behind Crawford were two aluminum easels displaying hand-painted one-third-scale copies of paintings by Claude Monet, one sunset-golden-orange of the facade of the cathedral at Rouen, the other evening-blue of the Thames side of the Houses of Parliament. Crawford sat between them also carefully fashioned, a compact man in his early thirties with rather long bleached-blond hair parted precisely in the center. He wore a lavender Egyptian cotton shirt with white French cuffs linked with gold sunbursts, a white collar with a gold collar pin, a navy blue tie with gold five-pointed stars, and navy blue suspenders with a wide gold stripe down the center. He had never seen Cistaro before and, distracted by his entrance, only half-heard what he said. Therefore he had not understood what Cistaro had said—but instead of saying that, he scowled. He held up his right forefinger irritatedly and shook his head. Then, looking down, he nodded. "Yes, I know it is, Dee," he said into the phone, "and I know it's annoying. And I know just what to do. But it's like everything else—won't take any time at all to do it, we go back out there together and I show you how. But I can't go out there today, and if I try to describe it to you it'll take me a while. So I'll have to call you back—someone's just come in." He stared up at Cistaro. "No, very *un*expectedly." He frowned. "Yes, then, all right. See you."

He replaced the phone in the black desk set with his left hand and gazed at Cistaro with exasperation. Then he said, "Who are you?" with the chill soft muted politeness that paralyzed museum-quality finish carpenters; quailed temperamental artisans who worked with tile, intaglio and metals and haughtily refused to learn English; and partially compensated clients who had lots of money, modestly realized they did not have extreme good taste but could afford to buy, regally, as much as they felt they needed (more than their friends had), and rather expected condescending insolence from its more reputable purveyors.

Cistaro smiled tightly, showing six teeth in the front row of his upper jaw. "I'm the guy you owe money to," he said. "You're late—paying me."

"I owe lots of people money," Crawford said calmly. "I've never laid eyes on most of them in my life. Nor have I wished to—there's no need. I'm sure I'm late on many of my accounts. It happens all the time. The kind of work I do? People who I do it *for,* fall behind on *me.* Happens to *them* all the time? Happens to *me* all the time. When *they* get caught up, *I* get caught up."

Cistaro said nothing.

"The people I owe money to—they always get it. So they know they can trust me. *You?* I've never seen before, in my entire life. So you have no experience to go on, and simply don't realize that. Are you pressed for cash? How much do you need? I'll see if I can help you."

Cistaro showed more teeth. "*I'm* not pressed for cash," he said pleasantly. "People like you, who owe *me*—*they* are pressed for cash. Why they come to me, the first place—get the cash they got to have, they haven't *got* no cash. That's what you did, you know it or not. Came to me referred, okay? Any other hurtin' puppy—guy you asked where you could find ninety large, right off? He said come to me."

"Oh, but I've never seen you before," Crawford said mildly.

"You seen people, work for me," Cistaro said. "You seen them when you saw my money. Didn't see my *face* then, but you seen Ben Franklin's pictures and you seen the presidents. That means you seen me.

"Six weeks ago, you fall in our laps, said you needed cash for two. Forty-five a week then, just like it is today. Which we told you, and you said you understood. *An'*—that even though it was a lot more'n you're used to paying, it was acceptable. That was what you said to Tony. Next time Tony saw me, he told me you said that.

"Kid never heard that one before. ' "Acceptable," he said.' Could not get over it. Well, what the hell, he's just a kid. Hasn't been around that much—you're something new for him."

Crawford's expression gradually changed. "Would this Tony be Anthony, the barber? The young fellow in the shop down on Broad Street? The guy that Mario took me to see, before the three-day weekend? He said he had another appointment coming in at three-fifteen, so he had to hurry."

"Look, he cuts hair—financial district," Cistaro said. "Why we took him on. Where he is, an' what he does, and who he does it to. Good location for him? Good one for us, too. Every day he's seeing people who at one time or another need some money in a hurry; so happens they're tapped out; got no place to get it. People talk to barbers. Why this is I do not know. If this guy knows everything there is to know, you know? What's he doin' cutting hair? But they do it, all the time, all his people, just the same. They got something on their minds, who they go and tell it to? To him. There he is, he's just a kid, all he knows's cutting hair—so they ask him for advice.

"Which day it was? Don't know. Sometime last month. The deal was for two weeks. All our weeks end on Friday—'til you miss one. Then all weeks end *every* day—so which day it was don't matter. Two weeks was what you said you wanted. Then, well, apparently it's taking longer'n you thought it would. Perfectly all right with us, long's you're all right. Keep it ten *years*, if you want, long's you *stay* all right.

"Three-four weeks, that's what you were—perfectly all right.

We sent a guy around, day you got the money, look you up and check you out? Here you were, just like you tell Tony—looked okay to him. But then week five—no check.

"'Fuck happened?' we think. 'Something go wrong with this guy? Well, we'll give him another week—prolly come in then. Tell us what went wrong.' But six weeks was due last Friday— once again no check comes in. Now it's seven weeks, today. Tony doesn't hear from you, see you come around? Naturally he's concerned—he calls us." Cistaro paused for a beat or two and scowled at Crawford. "Like he knows he hasta do.

"Gotta understand the kid," Cistaro said. "Position you put him in, okay? Mario introduced you, right? This's fine for Mario, but for Tony, not so fine. This's all he knows about you—Mario says you're all right. Okay, far as it goes. We'll take Mario's word on that, so long's we see it's *true*. But Mario's a *cus*tomer. He don't *work* for us. He's got no responsibility, you don't turn out all right.

"Tony works for us. He's got the responsibility—but he knows you not at all. Even after a month or so, he don't know you all that well. High-class neighborhood here and all? Kind of people you got up here, this end of town? *Look* like they got lots of money—but hey, how does he know?

"'Newbury Street? I don't go there. This guy Crawford came to me—I didn't go to him. I don't know where he comes from. Never see the guy before. What the hell I do?'

"Tony's a good kid. Wants to do what's right for everybody, not make some dumb mistake. So he asked me what to do. I told him, 'Hey, don't worry, kid. I'm over there from time to time. I'll take care of it.' So that's how come I'm here here today, all right?

"Put it to you, black and white—just connect the dots. Reason I am here today: You owe me one hundred and three thousand, nine hundred and fifty dollars. *Me*—not Mario. Not Tony. The original ninety; the forty-five hundred you owe week five, which you miss; plus the forty-seven twenty-five, week six; plus the forty-seven twenty-five you owe today. You made me nervous. Lots of guys would up you five points onna week-six ice, and five more in top of that this week, week seven, but I never been a guy saw any point in bumping up the count so high guy can't see no way out. I leave that tah the government."

He laughed, one bark. "So, you can give me thirteen nine-fifty or one-oh-three nine-fifty, either way is easiest for you. Which's it gonna be?"

"Look," Crawford said, shaking his head, "what I said originally there, about owing people money? People owing me? There's something that you have to understand about this business that I'm in. It all depends on exactly what it is that we've sold you—what we're *selling* you, I should say. That determines when it is the buyer owes the money. All right? And even then he still has thirty days, of course, a chance to see it in the home—if it looks like we expected. It's on *approval,* see? Everything we do—the kind of goods and services we deal in—it always works that way.

"And rarities, all right? Antiquities we deal in? What was involved in the deal that we got you involved in, through the Tony that we heard about through Mario, all right? That's what was involved. These're artifacts we're dealing in, genuine antiquities, one-of-a-kind things. And, well, it's *very* difficult, for *anyone,* involved in *any* of these transactions, to say exactly when or how the whole deal will be ... well, brought to fruition. Or sometimes—fairly *often,* actually—even *if* it ever will be. Brought to fruition, I mean. If you understand me."

Cistaro stared at him.

"Half the time they have to be ... well, sometimes the countries that they come from, see? We find that what we have to do is go outside regular channels, the normal export-import regulations that you have ... they ... that they would normally apply, would apply in these kinds of, ah, cases.

"These things can be sensitive. These other countries—third-world countries, really, no use pretending otherwise—they're not always keen on having them, well, having what we find *removed*. From the areas where we've *found* them—and this's *after,* mind you, someone's paid a good deal to have them prospected for, looked for. When no one even in these countries themselves was absolutely sure that they were there, even *dreamed* that they were there. And then if they'd *been* found, to dig them up. Or if they'd have any value if they did."

"*Really,*" Cistaro said.

"*Yes,*" Crawford said. "So it all can be a very delicate, and *time*-consuming, business, and therefore very *expensive,* in and of itself. As well. And then the actual process of having them removed; you have to be *exquisitely* careful about how you go about having them do that. Because these things are *so* fragile. From the *sites* where they're found, I mean—even *those*'re sensitive. Have to be careful how you dig. And then from the *countries, God*—when it comes to physically taking them out of the countries where they originate, well, it's like having a tooth pulled.

"I mean, *hell,* sometimes we have to spend as much as six or seven months, arranging transportation through *another* country, as backward as the first, maybe even two or three. The kind of provenance, a paper trail, that enables us to, you know, get them passed along, almost from hand to hand, really. Document specialists and so forth, just to get them into Switzerland, ultimately through Customs here, they finally reach New York. But once we get them as far as Switzerland, well, then we always feel as though we can breathe a little easier, the hard part's behind us now. But it's never really sure.

"Now the buyer we go through this for, we acquire these things for—none of this's his responsibility. Any of his concern at all. He's completely apart from all of this, knows nothing about it. And that's the way it has to be, as far as he's concerned—the way he wants it. That's why the huge markup. In this instance, for example, the artifacts involved in this deal that we're financed with the money that I got from your man Anthony ... well, the actual intrinsic value of the pieces, in the objective sense, I mean, is probably in the neighborhood of thirty, thirty-five, forty thousand the outside."

"That much," Cistaro said, looking interested.

"Oh, yes," Crawford said. "The rest? All eaten up by these imponderables. And the buyer that we have for them, the customer who ordered them, see if we could get them for him and's been waiting several months now for the chance to get his hands on them, these pieces, well, this is *so* speculative, *so* uncertain a procedure, that he doesn't owe the money until the artifacts are actually in his possession. In his home. That's why they cost so much, when they actually *do* arrive."

"I see," Cistaro said.

"So," Crawford said, "*as* you see, it isn't simple, this kind of business isn't. We deal in fairly large sums of money, but one way or the other, it's always tied up. Pretty well tied up. So, it may surprise you to hear this, but I don't keep that kind of cash——"

Crawford was still talking as Cistaro dragged him out of his chair by his blue tie with gold stars and drew his chin down hard against and then across the surface of his desk, not with sudden impact but irresistible force and unpleasant friction, until his pelvis butted up against the back edge of the desk, so that he extended his neck to its limit and choked, and had to stop talking.

"*Nooo*, Mister Crawford," Cistaro said pleasantly, over Crawford's head, as though disciplining a generally good dog that had oddly misbehaved, "I don't think you understand the kind of business you've been doing with us—*sir.* The only times I'm ever surprised is when I tell a broad to blow me and she says 'sure' and puckers up, no fuckin' argument.

"I don't care what kind of cash you got or where you keep it. Only kind I care about's American, getting what's owed to me. I don't get it, first I get mad. Then I get worried. Start to think. 'This gets around, Mister Crawford didn't pay me, didn't have the cash on hand, and I said, "Well, that's okay—pay me when you can. It's real convenient for you"? What if everyone who owes me hears about this, huh? And as a result he starts to think *he* now doesn't have to pay me any longer, he's s'posed to, huh? If it's not convenient for him. I won't do nothin' to them?'

"Trynah give you some idea, here—this is how I start to think when I begin to worry."

He paused. "I think, 'If Mister Crawford doesn't pay me, there is no two ways about it—I'll have to do something to him.' That's how I think when I'm worried.

"Now, Mister Crawford, I don't like bein' worried," he said, still speaking pleasantly, gradually releasing his grip on the blue tie with the stars, now crumpled. Crawford used his hands on the desk to push himself straight up, his face red but growing pale. He waggled his head around, swallowing, and ran his right forefinger around the inside of his collar. He tugged his tie loose at his collar, then looked down at it as though he'd never seen it before and couldn't imagine how it had gotten around his neck.

"But even though you got me worried, I'm still gonna be nice to you," Cistaro said. "I got some things I got to do today after lunch, which I'm gonna have first, before I do them. So I won't be back to see you again this afternoon 'til around five o'clock. Maybe a little after. But I *will* be back.

"So, do me a favor, all right? Traffic can get bad that time of day. Wait for me, okay? *Wait* for me. Be here when I get back. Don't let it slip your mind, and then when five o'clock comes, I haven't made it back, just turn off all the lights, lock up and go home, as usual. Uh uh. You don't want to do that. I won't like it, you're not here, I come back, a little after five, you're not here. Get all upset, and we do not want that. Especially, *you* don't.

"Have the money for me. Thirteen nine-fifty will be fine. Whole wad'd be even better, both our points of view, you can manage that. That way you wouldn't have to think, 'Now he's gone, I can relax, but only for a little while. He's comin' back in here next week, forty-five hundred more. Week after that, same thing.'

"Because I am—you realize that. No more sendin' checks to Tony, or not sendin' checks to Tony, dependin' on your mood or how things are in Switzerland. Every week from now on until you and me are even, you are gonna see me here and you'll have cash money for me. Or else more will happen to you than your necktie gettin' wrinkled—you should have that in mind. You might like it lots better, you could pay me off today. But anyway, the thirteen nine-fifty, that'll do it for today. That's the minimum, okay? Five P.M. this afternoon."

Crawford swallowed again and nodded.

Cistaro left the office, closing the door behind him and treading as lightly as he could going down the creaking open staircase. There was a slim woman about forty in a black dress with a gold jacket fluffing her dark hair as she emerged from the corridor beneath the mezzanine as he reached the main floor. "Good afternoon," she said, smiling but frowning slightly. "Would there be something I could help you with?"

"I don't think so, thanks," Cistaro said, and smiled. He left the shop. Outside he looked to his left down Newbury Street toward the maroon Ford Expedition idling at the curb next to the Burberry store and raised his right hand just slightly above his head. Then he turned to his right and walked west five doors down from Imaginings.

The driver of the Expedition let several cars make the right turn off Arlington Street into Newbury, and then swung out between the cars double-parked on both sides of the street, all the way up, pulling up beside a hydrant about a hundred yards from the stop sign at Berkeley Street. Cistaro moved quickly off the sidewalk to the Ford, opening the door and springing up and in, pulling it shut after him.

"Gettin' up this fuckin' street's a fuckin' bitch now," the driver said. "Been so long since I been on it here, I didn't realize." He was a compact, wiry man in his middle fifties with a blade-shaped face set off by sharply hooked nose, and his transparent skin, permanently tanned, featured dark sandpaper stubble. He had brown frightened-rabbit eyes that he knew revealed fear; they made him very plainly very dangerous, and that was why Cistaro employed him. "No tellin' how much trouble Rico saves me, lookin' like he's about to go off."

Rico drove with his right hand on the wheel and his left resting on his left thigh, his left shoulder jammed against the outer bolster of the driver's captain's chair. "Like tah know how much ah cops rip off the people, stores, not to see ah double-parkin'."

"I think it's legal now, actually," Cistaro said. "I think they got some wrinkle in the law, few years ago, says if you buy a permit, pay a certain amount of money, they can park in front your store."

"Oh," Rico said, "I didn't know that." He drove up the block between Berkeley and Clarendon streets. "Mustah pissed the cops off, though, city pullin' that shit. Sellin' allah double-parkin' places out from under them."

"Probably did," Cistaro said. "Would've me."

"Yeah," Rico said, "but you, with you wount've made no difference—kept on chargin' anyway."

Cistaro smiled. "Go the Terrace, have some lunch."

3

SHORTLY AFTER 1:00 IN THE AFTERNOON, Rascob drove the old Lincoln up to the cement berm marking off the fourth row of the parking lot near Joey's Clams At The Beach and shut off the ignition. "A little recon," McKeach called it. "Always do a little recon, 'fore you get into something. Know you're getting into, *first*, 'fore you get into it. Maybe you decide you don't *want* to—something doesn't feel right—always an option. Trust your fuckin' instinct." There were six other vehicles in the 221-car lot, all but two of them parked in the row closest to the edge of the beach and the clam shack.

Five men with yellow hard hats, puffy khaki insulated jackets and tan work pants or blue jeans, two of them smoking cigarettes and all of them drinking coffee greedily, were taking shelter from the onshore wind in the lee of the clam shack. They would be the maintenance-and-repair crew from the two vacant white, khaki and blue Bell Atlantic trucks, the big one with a cherry-picker bucket, the small one with a trailer carrying a new utility pole about twenty-four feet long jackknifed across the two rows behind it.

Through the Plexiglas storm windows enclosing the counter area of the shack, Rascob could see the short and stocky elderly owner in his grey fedora, jacket and white apron working the stand solo, moving back and forth, picking up and putting down, wiping, tidying and rearranging, never getting things quite right; as restlessly dissatisfied with his own work in the slow grey hours of winter as he was during the bright, busy days of summer with the efforts of the mouthy kids he hired out of the vast brick housing project across the boulevard.

The maroon GMC Suburban isolated in the second row had heavily tinted grey windows; Rascob assumed it was occupied, probably by three men, all wearing black foam-padded, studio-quality earphones.

The male passenger and the female driver in the silver Toyota Pathfinder with two ladders and staging planks lashed down on the roofrack were using disposable white plastic forks to eat—clams or shrimp, French fries or onion rings—from white cardboard containers they picked up and put down on a flat surface Rascob could not see. To him their diligent attention to the food indicated they were partners of some kind: parents happily married to other people, their jobs allowing them to enjoy selfishly one quiet meal a day without fussy children or a complaining spouse around; or an ambitious young couple reluctantly interrupting ten or eleven hours of honest daily work for a start-up company they owned, hocked up to the hilt and too busy now at the acquiring stage of life to think much or very often any more about the lovely bond of sexual attraction that had first drawn them together—now slowly vanishing, so that in five or six years, when there was idle time enough to notice its absence, it would be gone, beyond recovery, hardly missed at all.

In the front seat of the green Jeep Grand Cherokee a man with a blond pigtail and a woman with long brown hair sat motionless without talking, slouched against the doors as far from each other as possible, staring out at the bay. To Rascob their posture and stillness said they were dealing with an enormous and insoluble problem that they shared and he did not; he was grateful for that.

He remembered the last year with Brenda. Still technically married, in the first stages of the crisis they'd been too filled with fear and working too frantically, trying to repair what he had done at the credit union, to look after such a lighthearted thing as love. He had gone along with the chivalrous assumption made by the state police detectives and the young assistant AG: It had all been his idea, to play the regional real estate market, buying up options, doing it by "borrowing" from idle funds deposited by customers foreseeing events years away. The market went down. Since then, while doing time, he had come to believe that from the beginning she had subtly encouraged and helped him to do it.

"Our very own conspiracy," she called it, so simple and obvious it could not be illegal. "Going to be rich. What's wrong with that? Everyone wants to be rich." After the first three months or so in the Plymouth County House of Correction, he found it incomprehensible that he ever could have felt greed enough or found an emergency thrilling enough to make him forget about the sex that they'd had, what she liked him to do to her and liked to do to him, enough to risk it. "Another friendly animal in the dark," she would say and her delight would make her laugh; that was what they were and always would be to each other. So she said.

After he had been locked up for six months she had divorced him, on the irrebuttable statutory grounds that he had been sentenced to prison—his mild punishment for grand larceny an indeterminate one-to-ten but still a prison bit; to make it easier for his family to visit him (she was it, then, in Massachusetts), he had been administratively allowed to serve his time in the House. He saw one planting season through to harvest on the Farm; his specialty, root vegetables. On his way out after eleven months the corrections officer in charge of counseling reminded him his accountancy certificate had been revoked on the basis of his guilty plea. "Doesn't seem like they left you with much, I know, but do the best you can, willya? Don't want to see you back in here again. Does no one any good."

That brought it home to him. As McKeach said about Giunta's fall, "Well, at least if he hadda do it, Nino did it right—never fuck up small."

"The trouble with country music," Brenda said once when it was still a smart remark for them, "is the words're always true."

McKeach in a faded black suede tanker jacket, jeans and black cowboy boots stood alone about thirty feet down the beach with his back to the parking lot, near the fourth sun- and salt-bleached redwood picnic table in the right arm of the eight-table crescent Cozy Bartoldi had installed around the clam shack back in '74, when he bought the food-and-beverage operation from Blackie Brinkley.

Having grown up in the neighborhood, and knowing why he had been sole bidder—McKeach controlled the beach—Cozy would have known enough to ask how much if Blackie hadn't told him he should also pay $200 a week during the summer to John Sweeney before lunch on Tuesdays, down at The Curragh at the circle. In 1977, after his wife Suzanne died at the age of fifty-one—in an accident on the afternoon of July 4, driving home to Jamaica Plain on Route 1 after visiting her mother in Saugus—Cozy winterized the shack, adding insulation and electric baseboard heat without asking anyone's permission. "Hey, I got nothin' else to do now but sellah hot dogs anna coffee, and it's my ass I'm freezing off if I don't put the heat in—which *I* pay for, I might add—how's that someone else's business? Why the fuck I hafta ask?"

Rascob opened the door of the Lincoln against the wind and got out, using his left hip to keep the door open as a windbreak while he buttoned his trenchcoat and pulled his hat down firmly on his head. Then he shut the door and locked the car, making his way across the pavement and onto the beach, the wind making his eyes water. McKeach seemed to detect his approach, turning his head slightly to the right in order to verify it and then turning back again toward the bay.

This day McKeach wore the black baseball cap with the white Chicago Cubs script **C** logo and, as always, gold-framed Ray-Ban aviator sunglasses. His white hair was cropped short above his ears and the skin on his face was seamed and weathered. He was chewing while he stared out over the grey-green water whitecapped by the breeze, holding a hot dog with bright yellow salad mustard in a roll in his left hand. He had lifted it out of its cardboard serving sleeve when he took it from the counter. If someone had reminded him that the law had had his fingerprints on file for coming up on forty years, he would have said "Congratulations, bright boy—now you figured out the reason I don't leave 'em anywhere. No need to make it easy, someone prove you been somewhere." There was a can of Sprite on the table near his left hand.

"Still off the clams, I see," Rascob said, coming up on McKeach's right. "What is it now, two or three years? Wasn't that ban lifted?"

"I dunno," McKeach said. "Still got me spooked. That E. coli shit, man, you imagine you ate that? Of all the things can kill you, Jesus, think if it was that. Spend your whole life lookin' out for your ass, watchin' what you do, start to think you're pretty smart. And then some day you don't feel good, you go and see the doctor. And he tells you that you're dyin'—you ate someone's *shit*."

He put the last of the hot dog and roll in his mouth and chewed it fast. Swallowing, he picked up the Sprite can and emptied it onto the sand. "How smart do you look then?" He

handed the can to Rascob; Rascob put it in his coat pocket. Mc-
Keach started walking at a normal pace diagonally down the
beach toward the high-water mark. Rascob went along, half a
pace behind. "After that, you'd *want* to die, you'd feel so fuckin'
foolish. Ashamed of going out that way, anyone found out." He
sucked food out of crevices between his teeth, using his left forefinger to nudge at stubborn bits. Then he put his hands into the
pockets of his jacket.

"Saw Rusty," he said, looking down at the sand.

"Saw Rusty this morning, Rozzie Square," Rascob said. "Deal
with him, way it looks now, still in the real early stages. 'Just
futzin' around,' he says. So he isn't really sure, but it still looks all
right. Stage they're in right now's hotel rooms and scoutin' locations. Are there rooms available? Many as they need, and if so,
how much they cost. If there're places they could use for locations around here, and if there are, will the people let them use
them for an okay price.

"'You say "the movies," people get crazy,' Rusty says. 'All a
sudden want twelve million dollars for a couple days' use of
their fuckin' beach house—'at's worth at the very outside eighteen K, throw inna char grille inna back anna boat trailer, the
side yard. If that's where they're comin' from, Nova Scotia's
where the crew's gonna end up—guaranfuckintee it.'"

"Well, shit," McKeach said, interrupting, "they gotta be here
to do it, don't they? I diddun readah fuckin' thing, but everything I heard about it, whole thing happens here. Fenway Park
and that stuff? Shit, I mean, it's *gotta* be here, you can't do it no-
place else. You tellin' me a Sox game—shoot *that* in Halifax? A
Bruins game? They could do that—any fuckin' rink at all, all
those places look alike, now the fuckin' Garden's gone, fuckin'
rats they had in that place, dead monkey inna rafters."

"Well, some of it, they gotta, yeah," Rascob said. "Assuming
they don't change it, which they can always do. Rusty says all

they want's the title, really, story that goes with it. 'That's what people know. Not they ever read it—just they *recognize* it.

"'Man and woman love each other—love their little boy. Father takes him to the ball game? Okay—don't hafta be the Red Sox, even baseball, far as that goes. Could be basketball instead, Bulls or Indiana Pacers—difference does it make? And then the kid gets sick, all right? It's cancer inna book, but doesn't have to be, the movie. And where they take him? Hospital—that's all it hasta be, a hospital—*any* hospital. Doesn't hafta be the Dana Farber, Jimmy-Fund-thing Hospital. Can be blood poisoning, HIV or something, and he goes any hospital Chicago or LA, and then gets kidnapped from there.'

"You see I'm sayin' here?" Rascob said. "Basic story's all they need. Rest of it they don't. Inside of buildings, shit like that— well, it's like you just said. Any hockey rink, or any street or beach, you know? Don't want no palm trees inna pictures, hula girls or elephants, but otherwise, well, he was sayin', alla rest is flexible."

"Yeah," said McKeach, "but that's the whole point, what we're doin', why we're doin' this. They go to Canada—unions aren't so strong up there. They get it done lots cheaper. But all the work they hafta do there, to make it look like here—don't get that for *free*. Canucks up there may work for less, but you still gotta *hire* 'em—once you do that it takes dough, matter how you slice it. Can't tell me they work for nothin'."

"Yeah," Rascob said, "well, that's pretty much what he was saying. 'It's all feasibility now.' Can they *do* it here, workin' with us—assumin' that, of course, because that's the only way, without us they know they can't. But can they get enough hotel rooms at the time of year they want 'em? All the schools around here? Rooms already booked? For the graduations, see? If they are, then it don't matter—kinda rates we get them—they can't get the rooms.

"So, they'd *rather* do it here; makes much better sense. But first they hafta find out if they *can*. Or should they start lookin' someplace else."

"Well, but that's what I'm saying," McKeach said. "Like: *what* other place? What do they mean when they say 'other place'? They got any idea whatsoever of this? What he's talkin' about when he says this?"

"I dunno," Rascob said. "I didn't ask him that, you know? All I did was, I basically listened. I told you all he told me."

"Motherfuckers," McKeach said.

"Yeah, I know," Rascob said.

"Well, keep on top of him," McKeach said. "Rusty's a good guy and all, but every now and then he's been known to get it in his head he might do some freelance stuff. Slightest hint he's doin' that—you know, not *tellin'* us about—well, you lemme know right off. I'll go over, see the bastard. Get his memory improved."

"I'll do that," Rascob said.

"Yeah," McKeach said. "Now, that brings us our boy Jackie, everybody's favorite pinup. What is goin' on with him?"

"He's got three more trucks comin' on line this week," Rascob said. "These'd be the break-and-lunch trucks go around from plant to plant, job to job, you know? Ones with quilted caps you see outside the factories, selling sandwiches and coffee. In this case, job to job."

"Where's he *gettin'* all these jobs?" McKeach said. "Every month or so, it seems like, puttin' on more trucks."

"Construction," Rascob said. "We had this mild winter, right? Construction's startin' early. Last year they didn't finish all the roadwork. Guess once the money gets there, carries over, year to year, 'til the job gets done. Plus which, got the naval air base closin', down South Weymouth there, shopping center goin' in. Means it's just a matter ah time, demolition work gets started, and then as soon as that gets finished, they start puttin' up the stores.

"Comin' down or goin' up—all the same to Jackie. You bring those crews in, get 'em workin', gotta have their coffee, Coca-Cola, bottled water, usually three times a day. The two breaks, morning, afternoon, and then once a day they stop, let 'em have a meal. These guys make good money, want a solid meal for lunch? Lots of them don't wanna bother, bringin' it from home. They do, somebody's got to make it, right? Most of them, wives also workin', don't want to get up early making sandwiches their lunch."

"And they then buy our stuff too," McKeach said.

"Jackie says his trucks didn't have the stuff on paydays, be another fleet of trucks pullin' in right behind him, 'Pretty soon those guys'd be sellin' coffee too. It's a commodity now, like the Nabs and Drake's Pound Cake. The way you get the stops is by bein' reliable, on time, with good product. No excuses—truck broke down; the snow's too deep; your route guy's got the flu? You show up with ah coffee, Winstons and Marlboros. Fresh. Scratch tickets with the games they want. Bread inna sandwiches an' stuff is *fresh. Always.* Never missin' a beat. Every day, day in, day out, truck is there on time. Boss on the job won't be makin' calls day after day—"Where the fuck's the guy the truck? My guys're goin' apeshit here. Where the hell's your man?" If he's *my* man, his truck's *there,* and what those guys want is *on* it.'"

"Including the stuff," McKeach said.

"So he says," Rascob said. "He's sellin' benzos for two bucks a pill, his guys on the trucks. They sell three for eight to the guys on the job. Who then turn around and sell them to *their* friends that they *work* with for *four* bucks apiece. 'And some of *them* then turn it around.' This's what he can't get over. 'They buy more than they know they'll use so they can sell it onnah street for six, eight bucks a *pop.*'"

"Jesus Christ," McKeach said. "Many times I hear it, I'll never get over it."

"'Strictly supply, demand,' he says," Rascob said. "'Think about this, if you want, what the hell is goin' on. The market's not for *anything*. Nothing owns the market. It's not for crack, not pot, not heroin; not hash, not coke, not ecstasy; Darvon, Demerol, or Dilaudid; knockouts or Special K. Whatever's around—that's what the market's for, and I mean *anything*. You had a fuckin' smorgasbord, all right? As much of any kind of drugs anyone could want? Choice'd be the benzos. But if capsules aren't around, then the Darvon and Dilaudid, and the bags of marching powder. You got guys that look like they could tangle assholes with a buncha *paratroopers,* come out on the winning side? There they are takin' Halcion like housewives with the screamin'-meemies. Buspar and Xanax—made for people with anxiety, and here're these muscle builders fightin' jackhammers all day, got arms on them like trees, and they're *woofin'* 'em down, fifty and a hundred times the normal dose. Wash 'em down with a ball and a beer. CC and a Coors Light on a fistful of Valium. You don't have to fly to Florida see the magic kingdom.'"

"So, we need more stuff," McKeach said.

"From what Jackie tells me," Rascob said, "we will *always* need more stuff. No matter how much we get."

"So then this after," McKeach said, "you leave here, you hafta go and see the Box."

"You mean I got to go tah the office, count the money," Rascob said.

"Right," McKeach said, "you got to go the fuckin' office, an' you count ah fuckin' money. Don't need me to tell you that, you count ah fuckin' money. You need me for is to tell you—*after* you count the fuckin' money, then you go and see the Box."

Rascob sighed. "Mack," he said, "I hate doin' that. I hate goin' to the Box."

"So do I," McKeach said grimly, "but I'm the boss, and that's why you hafta go."

"Maybe he won't be home," Rascob said.

"He'll be home," McKeach said. "He works at home. He's in demand. You'll be lucky all he does is make you wait."

4

EMMETT NAUGHTON FOR THE FOURTH or fifth time wearing "one of my fancy new outfits"—well-cut dark grey Donegal tweed jacket, a soft wool grey shirt open at the collar and dark grey flannel pants, all purchased by his wife, Caroline, on Nassau Street in Dublin; and tasseled black Bally loafers; she bought those on Grafton Street—knew that even in good clothes that fitted, he still looked like a man out of uniform and uncomfortable that way.

Caroline had thought that the first time he wore any of the new clothes—"Oh, dear, still not quite ready to think about making the change." But she kept it to herself. The next time she talked to her sister, Marybeth, she said she realized lots of men love their jobs "just as much as Em does—they *are* what they do. So *of course* they find it hard, transitioning retirement. But he's going to be a handful. Ever since the mandatory age was knocked out, he thinks if he keeps putting it off in his own mind, the day'll never come.

"Seventy's what he's saying now, but he won't be ready when he's *ninety*, if he lives that long. He's *never* going to be ready. You know how often you've heard him say he was 'born to be a cop.'

I think he's determined to be one the day he dies—and not a *re-tired* cop, either."

To him she said that maybe he could somehow persuade Matty at the barbershop to leave his hair "a little fuller, that might help a little."

"You mean 'a little *longer,*'" Naughton said. "Fuller'd be *better,* and Matty's a hell of a barber, but fuller's not within his powers. And if he *did* leave it longer, then when I'm in uniform I'd look uncomfortable, and for the selfsame reason—then *the uniform* wouldn't look right. So I wouldn't feel right. No, day comes when I decide, let them retire me, ten-eleven years from now, more important for me to feel right in the uniform than to feel right out of it."

With Jim Dowd, some years his junior, feeling the elder's obligation to transmit wisdom he'd acquired on his own, he allowed himself to be more forthright. "Seen it happen, time and again—men I started working for. They moved up? I moved up too—no coincidence. Their time came to hang it up, they'd get this hangdog expression—tricked into havin' their balls cut off. 'Someday,' they'd always said; thinkin' *they'd* get to decide later, 'someday' ever came. Didn't mean that; meant someone else'd make that decision for them, and had, and now *someday*'d come.

"Probably true in any line of work, it's sure true in law enforcement. The more a man loves it, better he gets at it. Better he gets at it, harder it is, put it aside. For *anything*—two weeks' vacation, or a weekend with the family. Much less think about walking away from it forever; *staying* away? Sees himself getting older; pretty soon he's gonna *die.*

"Then all of a sudden, day arrives—he's *gone.* Comes as a jolt.

"Early part of his career, it's all right. Home with the wife and family. His wife's a good girl and she wants him to be happy, and he is. She sees his dedication, and it does have its rewards. Rank means more money. Seniority? A desk job. Less hazardous duty; better chance when he goes out the door in the morning, next time she sees him is, he comes back in that night. Not onna slab with a sheet over him—some young punk put a bullet in him. Or caught a breadknife in the belly from a husband and a wife perfectly happy fighting with each other, until he showed up and got between them. Plus the better hours—and, let's not forget, more pay.

"Policemen's wives—and husbands, too, *and* domestic partners as well, mustn't leave them out—fine and dedicated lot, salt of the earth. Taking nothing away from them when I say I've yet to meet a policeman's wife who didn't like to see him bringing home a bigger paycheck.

"But still, the more successful the man is in his job, because he loves it, more his wife comes to see it as her rival. Gradually, over the years, she begins to compete with it, to fight it. She *tolerates* the fact that it takes him away from her—she *says* 'all that time it takes from his family,' but she really means 'from me.' So if you see him fairly regularly doing something else that doesn't involve her—*every day* you see him doing it and he's as happy as can be—you still have to understand it's only because she's *lettin'* him. And also understand that somewhere down the line when she thinks he's had about enough fun, going off by himself, doing things that don't involve her, she's gonna put her foot down and that'll be the end of it.

"Control's what it's about. When *she* decides there's been enough of his horsin' around—stamping out crime and making the world safe for democracy, whatever the hell he's been doing—then forever and after he's going to do what *she* wants. And that's all, and that is *it*.

"Which, naturally . . . most men who've gotten used to command, exercising power over other people, been doing it for years, the idea of someone else who's not even a *cop*, a superior officer, telling them what to do all the time, when and where they're gonna do it—their own *wife*? Does not appeal to them.

"Maybe *especially* their own wife. Mere *idea's* embarrassing.

"Husbands don't like it, kind of supervision shit—and so they fight back. That's why you'll see old doctors, old dentists, old lawyers—all kinds of old men who got that way running their own businesses, forty, fifty years, still going to work every day. Money's not the issue; they've got all of that they need. They're still at their desks because they hadda close look at their older friends, retired; saw how miserable they were; figured out in *their* jobs, nobody could kick them out or drag 'em out. So they didn't leave.

"And those wives who were so keen on their husbands getting through—they don't like their men retiring either, once they've tried it for a while. That's why you see so many stories in the paper all the time, letters, all these women writing in—husbands, sick, retired, always underfoot. In the way all the time, giving orders; trying to run everything around the house—which the women always ran before any way they liked because the boys were off at work. And then the other women writing in, tell them to stop complaining—least their husbands're *alive*, get in their way and take them ballroom dancing and give them a little cuddle now and then—don't hear much about that nasty sex stuff, though, except now and then there will be one, speaks for all the rest of them—'Thank God *that's* over with,' and the day the old goat comes home with any of that Viagra stuff's the day she's out the door—because the women who're now writing in to tell them to shut up, their husbands're dead, and if they knew then? They'd be lightin' the big candles in the sanctuary every single blessed day.

"Caroline's the light of my life and the mother of my childen and I'll always love her dearly, but I'm putting retirement off as long as I possibly can. I know what it's gonna be like—I am not lookin' forward to it. Even now, still years away, every so often I catch her warming up the engine when she thinks I'm not lookin', payin' attention, gettin' ready, run my life soon's I turn in the badge. Suppose it hasta come someday, but I'm not lookin' forward to it. Could also be the day I start to see the end of my marriage comin'."

Except on ceremonial occasions, Detective Lieutenant Inspector James Dowd of the Special Investigations Bureau, Massachusetts State Police had been wearing plain clothes on the job for nineteen years. Arriving a few minutes late meeting Naughton for one of their very occasional lunches at the Terrace, on Soldier Field Road between Harvard Stadium on the Boston side of the Charles River, he thanked Eileen, the hostess, for showing him to Naughton's table. "Never would've recognized him, all decked out like this."

"Wouldn't recognize myself," Naughton said, trying to smile and not managing very well.

"You get used to it," Dowd said, sliding into the other bench in the booth. "Only time I'm in full pack now's when I have to go into a building where they've got someone freshly dead who was real important. Usually don't mind it—disliked him enough alive, verifying that he's dead makes it all worthwhile.

"Eileen, since at least in theory I'm on a day off from a case driving me nuts, I do believe I'll have a Guinness. You're not on the clock 'til eight, right, Emmett? Interest you in one?"

"Oh, might as well," Naughton said, pushing his iced tea aside. Eileen nodded, smiled and said, "Ettie'll be right with you," and put two menus on the table as she went away. Dowd took one for himself and slid the other one in front of Naughton. Soon a dark-haired waitress in her early forties, her good looks in her mind seriously marred by an overbite that could have been corrected easily thirty years or so before, brought their pints of dark-brown Guinness with the café-au-lait-colored heads of foam and set them on the table. "Hullo, Ettie," Dowd said, picking his glass up at once. "How're all belongin' to yah?"

"Fine, thank you, James," she said, working a smile around the teeth and making a small curtsey. "And those in your own household—well too?"

"No complaints, except with me," Dowd said. "And those no more'n the usual, I'm very glad to say."

She nodded. "And you, *Superintendent* Naughton," she said, inclining her head. "I trust you've been keepin' well." Three years before, the first time he and Dowd had met for lunch after his promotion, she had as usual called him "Emmett" instead of "Lieutenant," as he had requested several years previously, and Dowd had told her facetiously she mustn't do that any more. "He's no longer one of us ordinary mortals—he's a *superintendent* now."

Naughton feigned an expression of disapproval. "Still givin' a convincing impression, I'm happy to say," he said. "They haven't caught up with me yet."

"I'll be back in a moment or two for your orders," she said.

"How long has that kid been working in here?" Dowd said, after the waitress had gone away. Long ago in the aftermath of a state police captain's discharge in disgrace—"after twenty-one spotless years in the uniform," the commander's angry-grieving statement said—for being the third party in a lovers' triangle concluded by the husband's shotgun murder of the wife, Dowd had decided that only a woman who was absolutely perfect could ever bring him to risk both his marriage and career. Two or three years later he had joined Naughton for lunch and met Ettie Hanifin. It had taken him three or four more encounters to register that overbite and realize with great relief that she was "not quite perfect," so he was safe after all. He remembered that each time he saw her, silently toasting a narrow escape once again as he raised his pint and drank some of the stout through the foamy head.

"Cripes," Naughton said, having known that Dowd was tempted since shortly after Dowd had, but never having said anything about it because Dowd never had, "ever since her First Communion, I guess. When was it Danas bought the place, The Ground Round then, wasn't it? Not that I came in then."

"Danas bought it, turned it around, but then two-three years ago Harry Dana got the cancer, and seeing what was coming he sold out to Marvin Scotti, well-known Boston restaurateur and realtor with no money of his own who fronts for Nick Cistaro—who's here today, I might add."

Naughton's displeasure showed on his face. "Eileen told me he's in the back. With his rat-faced little sidekick."

"Figured," Dowd said. "Saw his ride in the parking lot, I came in. Maroon Expedition. Who's he meeting?"

"Eileen didn't know," Naughton said. "Only notable's gone through since I sat down's Al Bryson—runs that 'Stars in the Summer Sky' thing out on Route Nine there, gets all the washed-up, drugged-out rock stars to do weekend concerts by the lake. Pleasant enough, I suppose, you don't ever wanna grow up, and the night you've got tickets it doesn't rain too hard. I recall, Al was in his fifties, he went down that delinquency-of-minors charge—feeding smack to that fourteen-year-old boy-toy singer, OD'ed in Detroit after that. All slack in the belly, but here he is, mincin' through here in the gold silk shirt and tight pants, hair standing up and dyed green; like he's a rock star himself."

"Some union's getting fucked, then," Dowd said. "Nickie's selling out the stagehands and electricians for a mess of pottage they're not even gonna get to see—him and McKeach're gonna keep it for themselves."

Naughton laughed. "Most likely," he said. "What a son-of-a-whore that Cistaro is, huh? Long's there's a dollar in it, he must not give a shit what kind of trash he has to see to get it."

"No big need to, I guess," Dowd said. "'Til we catch him at something, at least."

"And how long we been trying?" Naughton said. "Eighteen, twenty years, I bet. I *know* it's gotta be at least that. Remember the first time I took any notice of him. Came in one night, line of duty, right after the Danas reopened it. Someone heard Abie Sayer'd relocated here; this joint was gonna be his new base for his loan-sharking business, we finally slapped the padlocks on the Paddock Grille for known felons in actual control and ownership—chiefly meaning him. No sign of Abie, but no trouble spotting Cistaro. Sittin' right up at the bar, in the middle—which by itself, up-and-coming young hood, not known for anything serious yet, having himself a beer and a sandwich after a long but-not-too-tiring day of wrongdoing? Wouldn't've meant a lot to me. But the guy who was with him did—Al De-Marco, FBI.

"Never thought that much of DeMarco, even though a lot of people I knew then thought he shat vanilla ice cream—old Commissioner Ferris was in *awe* of him. Course if Frank saw it had 'FBI' written on it, he was liable, bless himself and genuflect. Best investment that outfit ever made was 'selecting,' not just giving, Saint Francis Ferris twelve weeks of brainwashing at Quantico. 'There's a chapel right there on the grounds. So we were able to start each day down there with Mass and communion, just like I do here at home.'

"After that he was convinced the only reason the Virgin appeared at Fatima was because she'd been blown off course the way down, bad weather over the Azores, on her way to FBI headquarters.

"But still, if DeMarco was interested in this Cistaro kid, that meant we oughta be, too, so from that moment on, I was. He did know his bird book of hoods; if Al DeMarco thought this place was a promising place to chat up young gunsels, probably meant it was. Miss Bright-eyes wasn't here then."

"Right," Dowd said as the waitress came back. "Ettie," he said, "my friend the superintendent here was just telling me how you and he've kept your youth while I've aged terribly. He won't tell me how you've done it; maybe you will—where did I go wrong?"

She laughed, her eyes lighting up. "Maybe you've been workin' too hard," she said. "Myself, I've got so much seniority around here now I scarcely have to lift a finger anymore now, 'less I want to. Only wait on friends these days, and since I don't have that many of them, I don't have to work very hard."

Naughton pretended dismay. "Oh, I would doubt that," he said. "You must be on your feet all the time."

She dimpled and said: "Will it be the fish and chips as usual?"

Naughton pretended chagrin. "Oh, I suppose so," he said.

"And you, James, as well?" she said, collecting the menus.

"No imagination either," he said. "Fried shrimp. Skip the fries so I can have the onion rings. And a fresh Bass Ale when the food's ready."

"I'm all set," Naughton said, tapping his iced-tea glass.

"A remarkable, strange devil, isn't he," Dowd said after she had left.

"Arthur McKeon," Naughton said. Dowd nodded, hunching forward and resting his elbows on the table. Naughton nodded back. "Yes, he is that. In fact I had a woman actually tell me one night that that's who he really is—the devil, Satan himself. And she wasn't givin' me the leg, either. She believed every word she was saying about him. 'You'll never get him. He knows what you're trying to do to him before you know yourselves. He can go where he wants, whenever he wants; do anything he wants to do, to anyone he wants—*and get away with it*—*always.* He can probably change his shape, it suits him, just be some*one* else, some*where* else, if he likes. You guys're all wasting your time, trying to catch him and put him in jail. Playin' games—big little boys.' She said that to me, and she was perfectly sane."

5

Dowd laughed incredulously. "What in God's name'd he *do* to her?" Dowd said.

"Or someone dear to her," Naughton said. "I really don't know—maybe nothing. Doesn't matter—from McKeach's point of view the end result's the same. A lot of people believe he *incarnates* evil. And if enough people think like she does, believe what she said to me, she may very well be right: We'll never get him.

"We should be able to do it ourselves, no grand jury, nothing. Just go into court and say, 'All right, Your Honor, Commonwealth vee McKeach et al.: here's the deal. Arthur F. McKeon, alias "McKeach," alias "Uncle Mack," is a menace to the good order of society. He commits all *sorts* of crimes. Here's a partial list of all the wicked deeds we know he's done as of the close of business last June thirtieth; we think that's the end of his fiscal year. We'll begin with his early career.

"'We know around forty years ago he started extorting money from people; beating up people and killing people. He fixed horse races, prizefights, probably college basketball games, and at least one election each for seats on the Boston City Council and the Governor's Council. He stole union funds, diverting members' dues and embezzling their pension money. He corrupted public officials—tax assessors, cops on the beat, building inspectors, municipal liquor-licensing board inspectors, two state members of the Alcoholic Beverage Control, and a member of the state racing commission. Once he bribed a fire marshal setting occupancy limits for a dance hall. This was all back in the days when he was working for Brian Gallagher, otherwise known as Brian G., and more favorably, too, by most people—they knew Brian G. was tough, but they believed he had a heart.

"'And we're just getting warmed up here. We know as soon as McKeach figured he'd learned all Brian could teach him, plus a thing or two that Brian G.'d had no idea he was putting in his head, sometime in nineteen sixty-six McKeach, having become Brian G.'s first deputy, decided that all by himself *he* could make people do the things that he was now ordering them to do by transmitting orders from Brian. He realized what mattered when you ordered people around was their perception you had the power to hurt them if they didn't.

"'As it'd been, they'd seen him as having that power because Brian'd delegated it to him. But McKeach saw their perception *was* the power. This was before he started really reading books—mostly on electronic surveillance, I think, judging by his success in defeating it—but as a lot of people've since learned to their sorrow, Arthur may've lacked formal schooling but his intuitive intelligence was topnotch. He didn't read Lord Acton's book, but he found out just the same that power abhors a vacuum, and he figured out if he created one in the space that Brian occupied, the power would then probably pull *him* in to exercise it—for *himself.* All he had to do was make Brian go into a very deep sleep some night, and immediately take control; then *he* would *have* the power.

"'I doubt Brian G.'d taught or intended to teach Arthur that. Most likely he didn't realize McKeach'd learned it until the instant when he got out of the back seat of his seven-passenger black Caddy Fleetwood in the parking lot behind the old Boston Arena and saw his best pal McKeach coming out of the shadows, firing. There's gratitude for ya, huh?

" 'We're inclined to believe what he was firing was probably his favorite weapon, thirty-caliber M-two selective-fire military carbine fitted with a thirty-round, staggered-row box magazine, modified to about eighteen inches in length by sawing off the stock. We think this because we found nineteen spent shell casings in the immediate area. Medical examiner determined that a total of eleven out of thirty rounds hit Brian G. in his head and thorax. The wounds were instantly fatal. Doctors in the emergency room at BCH dug three rounds out of Brian's driver and the lab techs found four bullets embedded in various parts of the limo. We dunno where the other slug went, but if he could put nineteen pretty much where he wanted them, firing a light-weight and very nervous weapon at full automatic, you'd have to say that McKeach probably deserves his reputation as a marksman.

" 'Brian's driver recovered nicely, but to the surprise of absolutely no one had no idea who could've shot him—and couldn't help us at all to find out who drilled Brian. After the chauffeur got better, McKeach showed his compassionate side by making him the manager of a Brighton liquor store his late employer'd controlled.

" 'Further—we know that shortly afterwards, McKeach teamed up with Nicholas Cistaro, a.k.a. the Frogman, and they conspired with each other and with divers other persons whose names are unfortunately unknown, to do and commit sundry illegal acts, including bankrolling major shipments of illegal drugs and providing safe warehouses for the storage thereof, and——'

"And so on," Naughton said, "far into the night. The problem is we *can't* do it that way, frustrating though it is. We have to go through the grand jury and we have to have witnesses who helped McKeach do bad things, but've now had a change of heart. Usually people undergo such changes because they're very proud of the tans they cultivate at the beach every year, and believe us when we tell them if they don't talk they're never gonna see the sun shine again. They become upset, and want to tell us about what they did with such people as McKeach, and what they saw them do to others.

"So, in order to hook him we've gotta find people who know what he's done because they helped him plan it and then helped him do it, or did it for him, on his orders—and convince them to testify for us. The only way I know of doing that that I ever saw work—even it doesn't, always; some people're too proud to become finks—is to make them more afraid of what we can and will do to them, if they don't talk, than they already are of what McKeach can and will do to them if they do.

"Mighty hard to do, and that's a big advantage for him. Potential witnesses know whatever pain we may inflict on them if they refuse to help us, we won't maim or kill them—or their loved ones. And, with good reason, they're *convinced* that if they do help us, McKeach is not only capable of doing such things but absolutely certain to do them. He will kill them himself or have someone else kill them, to prevent them from harming him if he can or to punish them after they've harmed him. Even if he has to reach out from prison or the grave to do it—both of which they believe he could do without breaking a sweat.

"When people really do think that, there's no way we can make them believe that we can protect them. Where McKeach's concerned there's no such thing as a Witness Protection Program. They believe he *can* and he *will* find them, get at them from wherever he is—wherever they or their loved ones are—and retaliate against them, if they go up against him. That's why we've never had any witnesses, simple as that. His henchmen and his lackeys, disgruntled prat-boys and spiteful ex-girlfriends—they won't *have* that lovely, law-abiding change of heart. No one'll dare help us. Proof's in front of your eyes—he's devoted a mere quarter century or so since he did his last stretch to blatant criminal activities, day after day and night after night, right under our very noses, and we haven't laid a glove on him.

"It's an aura that he has. A lot of people who dislike McKeach—and a lot of people who fear him—he's never done anything to, personally. They've just been hearing stuff about him ever since they were young kids—this all-encompassing *power* that he has, to do evil. The people who repeat these stories without having any idea of whether they're true—they're doing McKeach's work for him.

"And there's a hell of a lot of them. Sometimes it's like they're like Seventh Day Adventists or Jehovah's Witnesses—everywhere you look in Greater Boston, there's another one. If his name comes up when you're talking to someone in the main Registry Office, and Rita Gaspari's within earshot, she'll drop what she's doing—come over and tell you what a savage bastard McKeach is. Her sister married Malachy Gallagher."

"Brian G. was her brother-in-law," Dowd said.

"You got it," Naughton said, nodding. "Brian . . . My father *knew* Brian Gallagher. He had a lot of money that he didn't get by workin' hard, but he wasn't some mystery figure with magical powers that McKeach is now—he wasn't glamorous. People tended to avoid him unless they did business with him, but they weren't afraid of him on general principles—the way they are of McKeach or even the black gangbangers you got today in North Dorchester.

"Brian G. was a criminal, sure; he was outside the law. But at the same time, he stood for order. If you as a private citizen figure that there's bound to be crime, no matter what the cops do—as most people do, and I'm one of them—then what you want is some assurance that if you tolerate it you won't get hurt. And that if you *don't* take part in it, you won't get hurt by the cops. Brian didn't pretend to answer officially for the cops— though on behalf of some I think he could've 'cause I think they worked for him—but on behalf of the outlaws, Brian G. gave that assurance. And his word was good.

"Brian G. got respect as the head hoodlum. In a rough sense of justice you could say he deserved it. He was good at it and knew it. He kept the peace.

"Before Brian, our guys did it the same way we did things across the water, stealing pigs and poaching pheasants from the Protestant landlords. We were all independent contractors— just went out one night and did it. One guy ran the protection rackets—another one smuggled the Irish Sweeps tickets in; set up his own network to sell them. Prohibition? Bunch of guys got fairly rich bringing the booze in on boats. Haulin' it up and down the coast, one bunch the bootleggers who owned the boats and trucks, another group that retailed it. There was no structural continuity to it—all freelancers, strictly short term. They made an alliance to do something; lasted ten years? That was unusual. They respected a guy because he had what they needed to do what they wanted to do, sell what they had to sell, *today.* Thirty years later still fly-by-nighters, sellin' TVs off the backs of trucks when TV was still a novelty, one day, hijacking a load of dry goods in Connecticut the next.

"Brian G. was your solid citizen. He set up and ran a diversi- fied, ongoing business. Knew how a good chief executive hood should act. With dignity. Looked like he was offering pretty much the same goods and services the underworld'd always of- fered—but his philosophy was different. He *unified* the people who delivered the goods and services in Southie—and later on, outside of Southie. The law said nobody could deliver that kind of stuff *anywhere* in or outside of the city, but he did it. He did it by consolidating the common interest in doing business without interference. So when he got through it was impossible for anyone from outside to come in and strong-arm him, and it was impossible for anyone inside to rise up and compete with him.

"Before and right after the war if you wanted to play the numbers, according to my father, you saw Toby Hannigan. He was World War One disabled vet, bad left leg. Ran the newsstand, Toby's Corner, sold the numbers with the papers and cigars and cigarettes on the corner of East Fifth. He probably paid protection to some guy from Dorchester—who didn't really protect Toby very much but came around faithfully for his cut. Toby had no complaint—the upside was he kept most of the profits. The downside was that he had to keep a certain cash reserve on hand—which obviously made him worth holding up. Therefore Toby kept his nineteen eleven Colt forty-five army combat pistol under the counter—any losses came out of him, so he was willing to take risks to prevent them. So there was that element of danger to it, but basically it was entirely *his* business.

"After nineteen fifty, say, if you went to Toby's and you bought a paper, you were still buying it from Toby, the person, but if you bought the number, you understood that you were buying it from Brian. Still the same number; found it in the same place—last three digits of the Treasury balance, back page of the *Record* Seven Races. Mathematically, nine ninety-nine to one against you; the payoff if you hit was six hundred to one.

"That aspect of the business Toby now ran for Brian. Brian's runner picked up the play in the afternoon. Brian's runner brought back any payoffs the same night. Toby had the same interest in the number you bought as he did the bottle Coke you got for a nickel out of the machine; he let the Coca-Cola people put it in and keep it filled: he got a commission. Didn't have to keep the numbers bankroll in the shop anymore—someone hit the number, Brian's runner brought the payoff around. But now no one in his right mind even *thought* about sticking Toby up— that'd be robbing Brian G., which'd amount to signing your death warrant.

"If you hit a run of bad luck bettin' on the ponies with Tommy the Book—lost a little more'n you could pay right off and couldn't borrow it from the credit union—that'd mean you'd have to tell the wife, and she didn't know you bet? You'd go down Butchie Morgan's after work on Monday night and borrow it from Jakie Doyle. You probably asked Jake for two hundred—the hundred you're down with Tom, plus another hundred, planning to get back what you already lost, plus a fat profit from investing on this other horse on Saturday you *know* is a sure thing. This's called 'digging your hole a little deeper.' The second horse turns out to be a dog too, naturally, so on your payday every week after that for forty weeks 'til you got Jakie paid off, you gave him fifteen bucks.

"That didn't hurt too much and it seemed reasonable enough. Five bucks came off the deuce you borrowed. That went back into Jake's bankroll. This was Brian's capital investment in the business, and a very good one, too, as long as there were pigeons like you dumb or desperate enough to pay six bucks to borrow five for a week.

"Ten of your fifteen dollars was the interest, five percent per week of the two-hundred-dollar whole amount, no matter how much you'd already paid back. Jakie put two dollars in his own pocket for his trouble and gave eight bucks to Brian, because the two hundred bucks you got from Jake to pay Tom was Brian's return on his investment with Jake.

"In the event you didn't pay Jake, and Jakie couldn't reason with you, well then, Jakie would tell Brian, and Brian'd send a guy around to see you. He would either make you pay, make you bleed, or make you lame. Sometimes when you couldn't pay he'd make you choose what you did instead. For some reason this did not make it hurt less. Sometime in the late fifties, early sixties, McKeach became that guy. So, after Brian G. got things organized to his satisfaction, it all still looked the same—you still bought the same things from the same people. But the profits went to Brian.

"McKeach's nowhere near as smart as Brian was. He was just cute enough to see that Brian had a weakness. Brian drew the line at certain things, such as shooting a cop or ambushing a prosecutor. Double-crossing your godfather or your rabbi or your friend, unless he did something to you first. Deadly force Brian would use only on someone who gave him no choice. A competitor who wouldn't back off? A friend who decided to go into business for himself on Brian's turf? He became a competitor. And even then, Brian didn't like to do it. He would've looked at you funny, if you'd asked him why he didn't want to scrag anyone but a competitor—and that was how he would've put it—that he didn't want to. Not that he *wouldn't.* 'Well, if I have to,' he would've said. 'If the guy gives me no choice. But it's noisy. Bad for business.' He was smart enough to know if people thought you'd stop at nothing, do anything, they wouldn't be as likely to try something out on you you probably wouldn't like.

"Put that same question to McKeach, you wouldn't *get* an explanation. McKeach's never ruled out any tactic absolutely. Brian thought he could rule by being smart. McKeach's nowhere near as smart, but he spotted something Brian G.'d overlooked. If you would do something to a friend and mentor that your friend'd only do to a mortal enemy, you could take your friend's place. And his money. Ruthless beats smart. That's why we've never gotten McKeach."

The waitress approached with the tray carrying their meals.

Naughton said, "The problem now is that we don't know the new kids, the blacks anna spics, dealing dope. And we still haven't nailed the old gunmen."

6

TIM SEXTON'S HOUSE AT 68 CHICKADEE Circle was a low-slung lima green vinyl-sided six-room ranch house with an attached two-car garage in a development of thirty-eight low-slung six- and eight-room ranches with attached two-car garages built on one-third-acre plots parceled out of what had been the fourteen-acre Peaceful Breeze Dairy pasture overlooking Route 138 in Canton, first offered for sale at $27,500 and $32,500 in 1958. Sexton was nine and his sister Patricia was seven when their parents, Jay and Lorraine, became the first owners.

Trish relinquished it as her home address in 1972 when she graduated from Simmons with a degree in physical therapy and moved to Burlington, Vermont, for a job in the University of Vermont Athletic Department. Tim, having retained it during his two hitches with the First Cavalry Division, Airmobile, in Vietnam, and his six years of restorative surgery, convalescence, occupational therapy and training in VA hospitals to equip him for life as a paraplegic, in 1976 saw no reason to go elsewhere when he was at last discharged at twenty-seven to begin life on his own.

So on the cold grey March afternoon in 1998 Rascob gloomily pulled the old Lincoln into the driveway in front of the garage that had become Tim's broadcast studio and office. It remained the only permanent residential address he had ever had.

"I would've had enough on my mind then anyway, finally going out on my own, without trying to do it somewhere else," a reporter from the *Quincy Patriot Ledger* quoted him as saying in a Veterans Day profile and interview published nine years after he came home. "Dad was 62. He and Mother both wanted early retirement; they could move to Arizona and get started playing golf—while they could still walk the courses. Made a lot of sense for all of us, I took this place off their hands.

"The resettlement lump sum for my disability was supposed to set me up—I could live as much like everybody else as you can when you'll never walk again. Just about enough for a down payment to take this house off their hands, and get it fixed up the way I needed. And it was a place I *knew*, familiar. If you spend as many years as I did, one strange place after another, you get so that word 'home' means an awful lot to you. It gets so just about all you can think about is going back there, *home*, someplace that you know. So that's what I did. They moved to Arizona. He still hasn't broken a hundred and five. Every time she comes back here, Mother says she misses the seasons. So I guess I'm the only one who came out of the deal completely satisfied. But I did—I'm real glad of it. It made a real nice fit.

"Probably had a lot to do with the success I've had in business, too, my coming home like this. Things're a lot easier in life, people recognize your name."

The reporter noted Sexton had been a *Boston Globe* Division Three All Scholastic two years as a running back in football and once in his senior year as a guard in basketball, while his sister had made the Girls' All Scholastic in girls' basketball for three years.

"There's something people want, or need, or simply got to have, they'd rather buy it from someone that they know. Keep the money close to home. And if they know you served your country, well, there were times when I wasn't sure that that'd be a plus, all the protests going on, but as the years've gone by, some of the old wounds've healed, I'd have to say it has been."

The workmen who'd converted the garage had removed the overhead doors and walled in the entries. In the left portal they installed a triple-glazed picture window with a planter underneath; the previous summer's petunias drooped brown and dry over the front edge. Where the right garage portal had been there was a twelve-pane window with a window box below it crowded with brown dead geraniums, and an aluminum combination door beside it. The carpenters finished the job with an improved grade of lima green vinyl that still hadn't faded quite enough to match the original siding around it, and a wheelchair ramp made of marine plywood, now delaminating, that led up to the door from the driveway. Rascob parked beside the custom-stock metallic-blue Dodge Ram Maxivan with flag-crested red, white and blue Massachusetts Disabled Veteran plates. When he crossed between the front of the Lincoln and the studio he could see Tim back to in his wheelchair at his light grey Formica control desk, black padded earphones on over his brownish grey hair gathered with a rubber band into a ponytail, hunching toward the microphone on the boom rising from the panel top.

Inside, the small black speaker cube on the reading table in the reception area broadcast a raspy male voice Rascob didn't recognize. "*Hell* the Indians, 's what I say—bleedin' hearts moanin' and groanin', we stole this country from 'em. Did no such thing. That was four hundred *years* ago, almost. Never mind what happened then—we weren't the ones that did it.

"*Now's* what we should be concerned with, and the crying need in this state now's for better education. And, as we now know, quickest way to fix it's with charter schools. Need more of them, better funding for the ones we've got. And the way to get it's *not* to sit back, twiddle our thumbs; let the Indians start up casinos here, like they got Connecticut and so forth—and keep all the money. It's to do the same's Nevada does—license private-run casinos. Only we do it *right*, here, and really screen the people who apply, so the Mafia stays out. Which you can't do in Nevada because the mob *owns* the place—didn't *exist* before they got there.

"And then really *soak* 'em, everyone comes to gamble. Get the money for ourselves. And *our* needs, for a change. We're the ones who pay for ev'thin'."

Through the double-glazed big window set into the maple-veneer sheet-paneled wall between the reception area and the studio, Rascob could see Sexton in right profile, his right hand at his throat and the microphone aimed at it, the ponytail swishing back and forth across his shoulders as he moved his head. His reddish muttonchop sideburns and goatee looked freshly trimmed. Over the padded door next to the big window a red bulb encased in a cage made of thick grey wire burned over a white sign with red letters: "SILENCE PLEASE—ON AIR."

Tim's wife, Theresa, was at her desk talking on the phone. "Two to four," she said. "Then we cut away for Mutual News, weather forecast, Today in Sports, Market Reports and Outlook, so forth, 'til seven. Then Musical Selections for the Dinner Hour, which we buy all on tape, no local announcing except station breaks. Then we come back on again live with Nashville Sounds, which we do right out of here, eight 'til ten. Then Evening Wrap-up, national anthem, and sign off at ten-thirty. Back onnie air at five-thirty A.M."

She smiled when she looked up at Rascob and he grinned at her, mouthing *Terry,* and pantomiming a kiss. She shook her head, pretending to blush, and fluttered the fingers of her right hand, the long nails painted chrome green. "Well, why don't I just send you a list then, what's available, and you can look it over and make your own decision. If I could just have your address again. I know you've given it to me before and I must have it someplace here, but just to be on the safe side, make sure I get it right...."

Rascob sat down on the molded green plastic-and-chrome chair next to the reading table in front of her desk and watched her write, saying "mmm huh" twice into the phone, wondering again what magic Sexton had used to attract and capture her. She was in her midthirties, too young to have been the high school sweetheart who'd been proud of her man in uniform and pledged eternal love when he went away to fight for his country—and then'd bravely, and stupidly, stayed loyal and devoted when he came back, long afterward, doomed to a diminished life. With her assets she should not have been obliged to settle for a hopeless cripple; her face was ordinary enough, but she was tall, 5′9″ or so, and had an excellent body.

To Rascob the tight jeans and knitted tank tops she wore, and the way she moved, suggested at least a normal sexual appetite. Assuming that her husband satisfied her, and not daring to ask how they managed, each time he came to Canton he imagined her doing the same thing with him that he thought she must do with Tim—naked, straddling his erection and, once coupled, moving up and down on it, flexing and relaxing her leg muscles, her tits bobbing in rhythm. As usual Rascob found the image cause for arousal as well as envy, and had to adjust his position.

The speaker broadcast a different voice, initially disturbing; metallic, distant and echoing. "Well, yeah, the idea *is* appealing. But keep in mind that was the whole argument years ago, behind the state lottery we've got now. Most successful in the country, what we hear is true. Hard to remember now but it was supposed to go to finance public education—solve all of our problems. A bonanza it'd be.

"Well, I guess it has been, if you don't count all the damage, ruined families and heartache that it's caused. Problem gamblers it's created, working men and women who've lost everything they had. The revenue's regularly diverted to just about every other *boondoggle* our crafty politicians've been able to dream up—and our schools're *still* in *crisis*.

"Far as I can see, the only people it's turned out to be a real bonanza *for*'re the ones who run it, run the lottery, and the people who run the ad agencies they hire to promote it. So we might want to think twice, 'fore we did something like that."

"Well, I'd want to think twice about doing that," Theresa said happily into the phone, not seeming to notice that she'd echoed her husband. "We're just a little station. Only five thousand watts, and the people who listen to us don't move around a lot. They stay home all day, have us on in their kitchens. Not the ones you're thinking of, people who commute back and forth to Boston. Our tower's down by Ninety-five, so our broadcast area's Holbrook on the east to Sharon onna west; Avon anna West Side of Brockton to the south. If they tried to listen to us when they're driving into Boston, well, they couldn't do it— they'd lose our signal, soon's they got the other side of the Blue Hills.

"And anyway, people don't think about doing inside painting when they're in their *cars*. They think about doin' that when they're *home*, with all those dingy-greasy painted *walls* in front of them. So with what you've got to offer, I'd think you'd be much better off promoting your Radio Paint Sale during the *first* hour, two to three. That's the time of day I think people who're thinking about *painting*, sprucing up the inside of their *homes*, mean so much to them and all, most money most of them're ever gonna spend on any one thing their whole *lives*, *that's* when they'll be thinkin', kind of paint they ought to get." She listened for a while and then said, "Well, yes, why don't you do that. Think it over, and then call me, and we'll see what we can set up."

She hung up the phone. "Mister Roth," she said, "True Value Store over Cobb's Corner. Calls every week or two, 'ever things get slow. Always the same set of questions. And I give him the same answers, pretty nearly, like I know what I'm talking about. Which I know I do with pret' nearly *all* the people who own stores and stuff that call in here about askin' about doin' ads— sound like I know more about their businesses'n they do. But with most of them I only have to do it *once*—must be Mister Roth doesn't write down what I say. Or else he just gets lonesome."

"Doesn't have Tim's show on in the store?" Rascob said.

"Not so I can hear it when he calls here," she said. "Of course maybe he does—I never go *in* his store. When I need something from the hardware store, I go the Home Depot in Avon. He could have it on out in front or something. Where the people who're shopping can hear it. We always suggest that, and then stress it to new sponsors when we're selling air time. How many of our advertisers tell us they keep us on all day, in their places of business. How much it helps."

She frowned. "I don't know's it actually *does* help that much, though—people actually pay attention to it. I never listen the radio, it's on in someplace where I'm shopping. Besides, if it *is* on when you're already *in* there shopping, and you hear it, how's it do them any good? Doesn't get *you* in there, which I think is what they *want* when they advertise. You're *already* in there, knew what they had to offer, if you hear us in their store—that's why you're there."

The speaker broadcast a male voice loudly praising a Subaru dealership in Sharon. "I hate that ad," she said, and shuddered. "He's the guy that owns the place. Sounds just like that in person, too. Not too many of our advertisers do, but he does. 'The personal touch.' That's what he calls it. Thinks if he hollers enough at you, and laughs all the time, you'll like him and do what he says." She paused and frowned again, then looked at the watch on her left wrist and folded her hands on the blotter. "Tim's almost through," she said. "Off in less'n two minutes."

"You're both doing okay?" Rascob said.

"Oh... yeah," she said. "I guess so. It's... you know how it is. Same-old same-old, one day after another. You think, 'Jeez, I wish something'd happen.' And then something does, to someone you know, like their kid gets diagnosed with multiple sclerosis or something. Then you think, 'Jeez, if that happened to us...' So yeah, I guess we're doin' okay."

She smiled sadly. "Still not makin' any kinda living this thing here though, that's what you're gettin' at," she said. "Not that I'm knockin' it or anything—it's a godsend to him, this thing. His handle on the world; how he makes himself matter. He goes around and gives his talks, school auditoriums, church basements, and he says his life's the support group, Missing Cords Bind Tighter. That makes everybody feel real good, that they're doing good, and when you're facing every day the kind of stuff folks in their position hafta, morale is darn important.

"But what he tells them isn't true. MCBT's important to him, but WCTN—this station's what keeps him alive and sane. Don't know where he'd be, what on earth he'd do without it."

Tim's resonating artificial voice came through the speaker, over the sound of Scott Joplin's "The Entertainer" building in the background. "And that's it for today, boys and girls, here around Tim's Cracker Barrel. Tune in tomorrow... talk about... what's goin' on... what ought to be... *and*... what really... shouldn't. Stay with us right here now for the—Mutual— News—of the Day." In the background the concluding bars of the piano music swelled up and died out.

"But that don't mean it's started bringing in enough to pay

the rent," she said. "What it costs to run it—don't believe it ever will. Wasn't for that check from the VA every month, I don't know what we'd do. Wouldn't party—that's for sure." The speaker went dead. She pursed her lips and twisted the fingers of her left hand with her right, studying them. She shook her head once. "'S why," she said, "'s why I always feel as though I should be glad to see you." She looked up. "Even though I'm really not." The red light went off. She stared at him sadly. "Not that it's anything to do with you," she said. "Just the reason, you know?"

He raised his eyebrows and shrugged.

"Yeah, I know," she said, "any more'n you're really glad to see me. Just means that you hadda come here again. You wouldn't if you didn't hafta." She pushed her chair back from the desk. "You can go in now," she said, getting up. "I'm going in the house, get him something to drink. Can I bring you something? Iced tea or Diet Coke? Lou was over last night but I think we may still have some beer."

"Ah, no, thanks," Rascob said, watching her get up and leave her desk and go into the office behind her, her buttocks working in her jeans. When she had disappeared from sight he stood up and started for the studio. Through the big window he saw Sexton using both hands to remove the headphones, the small black plastic device he used to enable him to speak sticking out of his right hand above his head. He was looking straight at Rascob.

Inside the sound-deadened studio, the padded door on its piston closing silently behind him, Rascob said "Hey, Tim," his greeting sounding oddly muffled to his own ears. He walked over to the control desk as Sexton used his left forearm to push the chair away from it, shifting the prosthesis to his left hand before he extended his right hand to shake.

"Max," he said, now holding the device to his throat as he shook Rascob's hand, his voice electronic and magisterial but also disappearing at once into the white composite-tile walls, "always good to see you—even if I do catch you, ever' time you come in here, lookin' at my wife's perfect ass, thinkin' about fuckin' her again."

"I never fucked your wife," Rascob said, uncomfortable but trying not to show it. Depending on Sexton's mood, that kind of talk could be a bad omen, the run-up to his poisonous routine about making her "available to special friends. And not just men friends, either. If I tell her to go down on another woman, she'll do it, eat her out. She'll give you a blow job, if I tell her to. Or fuck you, doesn't matter. Everybody wonders how I got her, why she stays with me. That's why. For the excitement. She never knows what I'll make her do, she'll have to do next. I've got the power over her, total, absolute, complete power. She has to do what I say—anything.

"I told her that the night we first went with each other. 'The only way I'll let you come with me is if you become my slave. Because the only way you'll ever be happy with a factory reject like me is if you accept me as your master. If you *promise* me you'll always do what I say, anything I tell you. Absolutely anything. Because the minute that you don't, the first time you tell me "No, I'm not gonna do that," that'll mean the spell is broken. What's between us will be gone.' And she agreed to that, accepted it, you know? Became subject to my will. She made me that promise."

Repelled but also fascinated, Rascob had repeated the routine to McKeach. "That's pure bullshit," McKeach said immediately. "Cheap-sick, fuckin' bullshit. We gotta get you laid more often. He can see how horny you are and he's a bored sick puppy. Don't get out much. So what he does's jerk your chain. Fuckin' with your mind. Either something happened to his balls, same time as his legs, so his own dick's useless, or else he's been crippled up so long his fuckin' brain got warped. Prolly gets off talkin' like that, poor sick twisted bastard."

But nonetheless ever since hearing Sexton's claims, Rascob each time he had gone there had found himself simultaneously musing that he could have her for the asking and despising himself for believing it was so.

There was a black tweed swivel chair behind Sexton and Rascob went behind him to pull it out and around in front to face him. He was sitting down as Theresa entered the studio with two tall glasses of iced tea.

"You hear that, honey?" Sexton said, sounding from afar, accepting one of the glasses. "Max's just admitted he studies your National Landmark ever' last time he comes to see us. Thinks about jumpin' your bones."

"Good," she said, resting her buttocks on the desk and sipping the iced tea. "Keep you from takin' me for granted."

"But as gorgeous as your ass is, dear, Max is a busy man," Sexton said. "He don't drive all the way out here just to look at it. Whatcha got on that mind of yours, Max?"

"I hate talking business, rooms with microphones," Rascob said. "Man'd shoot me, he saw this. 'I didn't teach you *nothin*'? Bad enough when you just *think* a place might be miked. Must be *nuts*, talk like you did, they're right in front your eyes.'"

Sexton laughed, making a sweeping gesture with his left hand. The prosthesis didn't look like a box at all. It reminded Rascob of the container-applicator of Kiwi Elite black liquid polish that he used on his dress-up loafers when they became badly scuffed. The top end, about an inch and a half long, was at an oblique angle to the vertical handle, about four inches long. It contained the batteries and the small oval speaker mounted in the bottom end. When Sexton held it away from his throat, as he did when he laughed, his convulsing mirth was soundless except for deep wheezing sounds that made Rascob fear he was choking.

The first time he was present when Sexton did it, Rascob had made a mistake and showed he found the sight unsettling.

Sexton had been gratified and explained more than he meant to. "Like watching a man laugh on TV after you hit the Mute button, ain't it?" he'd said viciously, revealing that it was a tactic he used to prevent the visitor from getting through the encounter without revealing revulsion for afflictions. "'Cept you didn't, and I'm not on TV—I'm right here, in front your eyes. Ain't *normal,* is it? Isn't *natural.* Crippled man should be *satisfied* with that, just to be a helpless cripple—not act like he's gonna up an' *dah* right in front of you, on top of it. But that's what it sounds like, all right—doesn't sound like I'm havin' *fun,* it sounds like I'm gonna *die.*"

Rascob still found the display disturbing now as Sexton held the prosthesis away from his throat and laughed at him for admitting fear that he might be being taped, but he no longer winced. Concealing disappointment, Sexton put the appliance back against his throat. "When the mikes're out where you can see 'em, Max," he said, "you can be sure you're safe."

"So—the stuff. I know the quality's all right, finest money can buy. FDA-approved, bonded-warehouse-certifed, absolutely pure. *Honest* dollars can't buy better, for real human pain. So that can't be the problem. What is it brings you out?"

"Quantity," Rascob said. "Guy who handles for us says he needs more product."

"Jesus Christ," Sexton said, "how's the man think I'm gonna do that?"

"Don't believe he has," Rascob said. "Thought about it, I mean. That's not his style, thinking *how* someone's gonna do something he wants done. Doesn't waste his time on logistics. His style's more just to tell 'em, say, 'This's what I want, and when I want it by.' Then come back when he said he expected it to be there. Only gets mad if it isn't." He paused. "More like that, you know?"

"Because, Jesus Christ," Sexton said, the Lord's name chinking unnoticed into the sound-deadened studio like a small metal tool dropped onto a carpet far away, "the reason why what we've got works so good is because we took the time, make it work that way." He frowned. "And we kept it small, only people that we've known a long time, and we know we can trust. Question is, can we expand it so it still works just as good, and stays just as safe, but brings in a lot more stuff?

"See, the secret's in the paper and the way that we present it," he said. "Most people with bogus prescriptions look like party animals out foragin' for supplies, next block party in their neighborhood, the next rave on Long Island, race week in Laconia—because that is what they are. Mean and dirty, maybe, but if you don't count the STDs, the runny eyes and open sores, bleeding gums and lesions, just as healthy as can be.

"We look like legitimate patients. We are. And the reason we don't set off the alarms, we go in the stores to buy stuff we're gonna sell the Man, 's because we go into them so often anyway, just for what we really *need*. Knowin' the procedures in the places where you're buyin'. Knowin' the kind of forms they use; how many hoops they make you jump through, stop you from doin' what it is we wanna do. That's how you keep 'em from stallin' you around an hour or so, givin' you the hairy eyeball while they wait for the cops to get there.

"This state and Rhode Island, also Connecticut, I think, ten, eleven others—what they did a few years ago is go to this three-part form, all right? The doctor makes it out, say, for Dilaudid. Narcotic analgesic, very popular among people who genuinely need it, really have a lot of pain which ain't gonna go away— 'cept when they finally do themselves.

"Like someone has, say, bone cancer. In the early stages, the doc is gonna gradually go from the two milligrams every six hours, eight migs a day, to four milligrams every four hours, twenty-four migs a day, as the pain gets worse and worse— which is what it always does; it doesn't go away until the reaper comes. So what the doc is essentially doing's pain management, all right? That's all, all the poor bastard *can* do, matter how sorry he may feel for you—nothing he can do'll make you get better. And nowadays the doc's'll do it faster, deal with pain, get to triple doses, 'cause where the thinking used to be you didn't want to get the guy addicted, never mind that he was *dying*, fuckin' *agony*, now it's 'Jesus *Christ*, this guy's in *pain*, if he could he'd shoot himself. So who gives flyin' fuck if he's hooked when they put his best suit on him and and put him in the casket?'

"So, where it used to be that the schedule ruled the patient— 'Don't give him the next dose until the clock says it's time, never mind how bad he hurts, kindah names he's callin' you'—now it's, 'What the hell're we *savin'* the stuff for, if he's hurtin' this bad and we know it'll help him, the pain?' Which, having been here while the change was goin' on, I can tell you as a patient I know which way's the one I like. And most doctors, they will tell you, they like it better this way too.

"So this's now the system, and we know because we're in it. Seventeen of us now, in this group we put together, play the system carefully—we know how to do this, right? That's how we all got to know each other—all of us belong support groups, for the problems we have got.

"Dennis from MCBT in Wakefield gets paper, special watermark and so forth, so that when we take it to the store and they hold it up the light, looks like what they're used to seeing.

"Lou from Southern NE Stoma runs a little print shop out of his basement. He's got all the computer equipment, scanner, state-of-the-art everything down there you could possibly imagine. Once we decide how much we wanna get this time for resale, we go to him for the scrip pads. He makes them up down there. Also the VA insurance cards and the HMO stuff; all the IDs we need.

"So all right, now let's say it is Dilaudid we're after. We're gonna be gettin' it from stores where we haven't been before, naturally—have to branch out our network some 'cause you said we need more product. Whole idea of doin' this the way we do it is to do it 'thout gettin' *caught*. Since the best way to stop a guy from findin' out you're buying for the street's to look like you need it yourself—that's what we're tryin' to make it look like.

"First time the druggist sees me, I look like I'm comin' in for meds I need myself. Which I do, of course, but I'm already gettin' them legitimate, somewheres else, under my own name, where I've been for years now. New druggist doesn't know this, so he's not suspicious—he gives me what the scrip says. The next time I come in'll be when I normally would, a refill, I was taking those meds myself.

"Okay, so here I am now, first-time patient for this store up in East Bumfuck, Vermont. Scrip says my name is Clyde Standish. Pharmacist never saw me before—don't know me from a load of goats. But he's gonna *get* to know me—every month from now on until maybe February, next year, I'm gonna bring in a prescription for a month's supply, thirty days' Dilaudid.

"When the druggist looks at me, see if I look like a Clyde who needs Dilaudid, he's gonna see this guy, a wheelchair, with a thing so he can talk. So he's immediately gonna think, 'Guy's got cancer,' which I did, in my throat, but I don't now. 'Of the bone,' which I do not and never did—reason I'm inna chair is because just like a perfect asshole I fell off a staging we were puttin' up for a USO show, I was in Vietnam, broke my fuckin' back. But this guy doesn't know that. 'And he's got it through and through.'

"As many real sick people as he sees all the time, this guy will not be able tah help himself from feeling sorry for *me*—there I am, a fifty-year-old guy with cancer, hasta use a wheelchair, get around, and then another thing to *talk*? They gotta be tough, look people over very carefully 'fore they give them stuff, because they know there's a market. But at the same time, they don't wanna do what they call 'get hardened' to the human suffering they see all the time. So very few pharmacists'll argue a prescription with a guy who needs a gadget like I got to have to talk with. This druggist isn't gonna be surprised a *bit* when he reads my prescription and sees my doctor, Stephanie Roper, M.D., thinks it's okay if I have the max recommended dose, twenty-four migs every day, seven-twenty migs a month."

"What if he decides to *call* Doctor Roper and make sure there really is a Doctor Roper and she really wrote that prescription?" Rascob said.

"Doctor Roper'll answer and say she did," Sexton said. "When we go out to break in a new drugstore, the doctor's phone number Lou prints on the script pad's for one of our cell phones. Druggist calls it, he gets Terry or someone else workin' with us, and she verifies the scrip. The code on the pad for the doctor's license is the actual number for an actual doctor's federal license to dispense narcotics. It's not Doctor Stephanie Roper's—but druggists never check that far, 'less you do something, practically screams at them 'This paper is a phony.'

"We don't. Which is why, two or three months from now, maybe a little sooner, it won't surprise the druggist that I've now got trained when I come in for a refill and he sees that Doctor Roper's started writing me what the book says is an overdose—*six* migs six times a day—because he'll've seen me looking like I'm getting smaller, shrinking. Which he will, because I'll now be wearin' a shirt that's way too big for me; some of Terry's make-up on, puts big black bags under my eyes. I'll *look* like a man who *needs* ten-eighty milligrams a month. Just so he can maybe sleep.

"Every time I go to see him, right from the beginning, we'll have some conversation. Regular-guy stuff. This time of year, I first go in, some talk about the Red Sox, spring training, how they look. Or Bill Clinton with his dick out alla time. Never this disease that's killing me by inches, how much time have I got left. That I bear it all with fortitude, trust in Jesus—never talk about it. Idea is so he gets to *know* me, poor Clyde Standish, and he gets so he admires my courage, all the suffering I have. I'm dyin', absolutely. And I keep gettin' weaker and paler, paler and thinner, month after month, until by the end of next winter he won't be surprised at all that I stop coming in and my daughter or my son-in-law that I've told him I'm staying with has to come in for my prescriptions every month.

"And then *they'll* stop coming in," Sexton said, his artificial voice rising and eyes shining. "*They* won't come in any more, either, because of course brave old Clyde's time finally came—he either died or else it got so hard for them to take care of him at home he hadda to go inna hospice. Because the way you do this without getting caught is to make it realistic—and then *keep it that way.* What this druggist now assumes must've happened to Clyde is what really happens to cancer patients who need that much painkiller—the pharmacists know the docs're giving it to them because they're dying, and that's why Clyde now has to die. In the natural course of things, dying people *die.* And the pharmacist never suspects a thing.

"It's funny, actually. The hardest part of this racket, hardest thing to do, is kill off this character that works so well. You feel like you've *become* him—you get so *you* think he exists too, actually kinda *like* him. And make the druggist who's been helping him through his sad last days feel bad, *too,* he realizes Clyde is gone. But you *have* to do it. Act's too good to let him live.

"You keep a dying man dying on a fifty percent overdose of Dilaudid for *too* long, more'n two or three months, say; pretty soon the pharmacist is gonna get suspicious. 'This guy's holding on too long. Dilaudid alone should've killed him by now.' Then he *will* start making phone calls, and that's the last thing that you want. The way you can tell you played a string out too long is that nice scruffy-lookin' guy at the counter waitin' for them to mix some pink cough syrup for his poor little kid turns out to be from DEA—and you gotta setta cuffs on.

"It don't matter what you're getting," Sexton said. "If you're scoring Darvon, say, which's nowhere near as strong, your max daily dose's sixty-five migs every four, three-ninety every day. Give them a month's scrip for fifteen thousand migs or keep going back too long and you'll light up the switchboards in every cop house around. The benzoes, *every*body's favorites—Halcion and Valium're both not over sixty migs a day, habit forming as can be. You start presenting at that level, eighteen hundred a month, you run up red flags. Demerol—max nine hundred migs a day. Xanax—absolute max is ten migs a day, five tabs. Not supposed to be a permanent part of your diet. Go over two months and you make the man in Walgreens think your problem's not anxiety or panic—you're just not happy in this world. Paxil you can have up to fifty migs a day; over fifteen hundred a month and you're asking for it.

"What we have to do is figure out how one person can get a lot of more of this stuff than a person who's about as sick as you can get, but not dead yet, or no more'n normally fucked up, 'd ever need to stand the pain or craziness, okay? The opioids like Dilaudid, any of the stuff that does for you what morphine does—not supposed to be for recreation. They're for *pain*, like when the cancer's eating your jaw away, or your spine, like that. Or for real bombed-out craziness, all right—you're so fucked up in your own mind that you'd rather die 'n face another day. They are *not* for having fun with, and the government don't like it, that's what people use 'em for. That's why they're so hard to get, and so expensive when we get 'em, and why this'll take some time."

"But you can do it, though," Rascob said.

Sexton's metallic voice actually sounded happy. "For the right price," he said, "anyone can do almost anything. And will."

7

SHORTLY AFTER 5:00 P.M. THE SAME day, FBI special agent Jack Farrier shut off the Ampex reel-to-reel audio recorder on the Officemaster Rentals grey steel desk he as senior agent in charge of the installation had chosen for himself as one of the four least dreary locations in the squad's temporary quarters. For the foreman of the College Muscle Furniture Movers he had signed the General Services Administration delivery invoices "Ronald Clayton, Int. Div.," satisfying the young guy's curiosity by saying, "Intelligence. IRS. Actually—special audit unit. Local. That's all I'm allowed to say."

The foreman had looked alarmed, then nodded knowingly. "Of course. Tax time coming up next month. Some poor bastard has to get it. Scare the shit out of the rest of us." Farrier had smiled.

The desk was next to the window at the southeast corner of the third-floor short-term rental space of the McClatchy Medical and Professional Building on the westerly side of Route 1 in Norwood. Every hour Farrier had a view of women in spandex leggings passing between their cars in the parking lot and Forever You Fitness on the first floor.

"Not all of them're fat," he told Hinchey (Hinchey had no window). "Some of them're in *very* good shape—come here three times a week to stay that way." Through his shoes he could feel the floor begin to pulse at 5:00 every afternoon, when some forty women started synchronized aerobic step-exercises in the basement.

Taylor at the second window had mildly disagreed, saying Farrier's eyes must be going bad; most of the women he saw going back and forth were heavy. Taylor called the 5:00 P.M. session "bouncing blubber hour."

"You're not crew chief, Taylor," Farrier had replied. "Quitcha looking out the window—keep your mind onna tapes."

By removing his padded black earphones and straining slightly, Farrier could hear the women shouting "*hut-hut, hut-hut, hut-hut*" in time with some throbbing disco music that he couldn't identify. He smiled and put the earphones down on the yellow legal pad next to his ballpoint pen. To the left there was a stack of 25 black-and-white 3M boxes face up, to the right a stack of six face down. He pushed his chair back and stood up, turning toward the window. Rush hour on Route 1; as usual traffic clogged three lanes southbound and three northbound. The lights made two broad skeins, like bunting, white headlights at the top and red brakelights the bottom, in the dark blue winter twilight.

Fifty-one; 6′2″; 189. Farrier had lost most of his black hair; he combed the remainder uselessly over the bald spot. He'd developed four brown liver spots on the back of his right hand. On his left wrist he wore a Tag Heuer diver's matte black watch his first wife had given him at Christmas 1981, when he was assigned to the Buffalo, N.Y. Strike Force, about to go free-diving off Key West in January with three colleagues who played golf and skied. "More active in those days," he'd recall, with some regret. "People there were closer." He wore a pale blue broad-cloth shirt with an eighteen-carat gold collar pin, a blue tie of Italian silk gabardine, and dark grey flannel trousers.

The collar pin had been a no-special-reason gift in 1994 from his second wife, Cheri—she'd been a secretary in the Buffalo field office—when they'd been together two years, about a year before their divorces became final and enabled them to marry. In those days she was still surprising him with vanity presents, and he still came home with flowers.

There were eleven other Officemaster Rental desk-and-chair sets in the room. At the northerly end: three long grey steel tables holding three videotape editing machines, boxes of 3M videotape, and six straight grey metal chairs. Each of the other desks also held an Ampex reel-to-reel recorder and two stacks of 3M audio tapes. Taylor was out with the flu; besides Hinchey there were eight other well-groomed middle-aged men bowed over their work at the other desks—six white, two black, also wearing shirts and ties. Now that they had heard or glimpsed Farrier knocking off, after a short but decent interval they'd begin to shut down their machines.

Hinchey at the desk ahead of Farrier's shut off his Ampex, turned his swivel chair, put his glasses on, clasped his hands over his fly, and said: "I don't *believe* these LCN guys. How much braggin' they do."

Hinchey was completing his first year assigned to the Organized Crime Field Office of the FBI Boston. Farrier as senior man on the squad was his rabbi. Hinchey was forty-six, exactly 6' tall, 170. He'd retained most of his curly blond hair, and was resisting awareness that the hearing loss he had developed in his right ear after being struck on the temple by a foul ball at fourteen in Pony League ball had recently begun to worsen. He wore a white button-down shirt with a dark blue figured necktie and blue wool trousers. Megan, the youngest of his three childen, a sophomore at Colby College in Waterville, Maine, had just celebrated her twentieth birthday and was living off campus with her boyfriend, twenty-two, but Hinchey had logged sixteen years of dedication to the cause of divorced fathers denied adequate access to their children, and still reserved Thursday evenings for meetings of the Natick chapter of Fathers for Justice. He thought his selflessness—"My own childen're grown now, but the courts're still shafting daddies"—made his arguments stronger, and never failed to mention it when he lobbied legislators, represented divorced fathers on bar-association panel discussions, or commented publicly to reporters when another father skipped with his children during visitation.

Farrier laughed. "War stories, Bob," he said. "Somebody recorded us, they'd get the same kind of shit. Put it behind you. Means this time we *hang* the bastards, using their own words. Make America a place where the Mafia's extinct.

"Course it also means we've spent another day we'll never see again sitting on our big fat asses, turning little dials. Marking places where what's on that frigging tape might as well be in mandarin *Chinese,* all the sense it makes to me—fuckin' accents and the TV blarin' all the time. All I'm doing is *assuming* that it's got to be in English, probably with some Sicilian dialect thrown in, just to confuse me—fact is, I don't know. But now for a few hours that won't matter. This part of this day is over."

He bent at the waist and stared at Hinchey. "Here is the meaning of life," he said. He patted the short stack of 3M boxes face down on the right. "Tonight there're two more boxes on this side'n there were this morning. Two more eventful days *and* fun-filled nights in the rich and varied life of *capo* Carlo Rizzo and his evil henchmen, but only *one* day out of mine. While on *this* side"—patting the tall stack with his left hand, each box with a small white sticker on the upper right front corner carry-ing a black notation of the date it was made—"there are actually two *fewer.*

"Few men can measure out their days and accomplishments, however humble, with such hair's-breadth precision. I am a for-tunate fellow. Though because this particular day is only just be-ginning, not one *excessively* blessed."

"Late dinner with the lads for you and Darren, I take it?" Hinchey said. "Little walk on the wilder side tonight with our peerless leader?"

Farrier nodded. "Affirmative," he said. He frowned and shook his head, looking down at the surface of the desk and moving the pen an inch to the right. He looked up. "I still don't know," he said.

"How he's taking it?" Hinchey said.

Farrier nodded. "Yeah," he said. "As my dear mother used to say, back when she was teaching, drew a kid who didn't get it, matter how much help she gave him—'He's willing enough but he's not an apt pupil.' Brother Stoat plays well with others, shares his pail and shovel, doesn't hit or bite, and follows instructions well, but he just doesn't seem to show the consistent steady progress that we like to see. And I suspect, that wife he's got, this guy hurts for money. Never a hopeful sign.

"Now, I realize he's still new at this, whole new different world. Twilight all the time—*everybody* needs some time, get used to being in it. *I* needed time, get used to it, when I first was breaking in, I know guys must've wondered if I'd ever make the grade. I don't care what you were doing, 'fore you started doing this—you weren't ready for it. That's a fuckin' given.

"Where most of us come from; kind of people that we are; want to join the FBI—we tend to be pretty straight-arrow types. Have to be honest with ourselves, with each other, at all times.

See ourselves for what we are. Recognize our limitations, imper-
fections—how they influence our judgment. Law enforcement
implied power—that was what we wanted. Thought we'd handle
power well; kind of people who should have it; that authority
was *meant* for. And how what's happened to us since has to have
affected that kind of person.

"Ordinarily by the time a guy makes it into OC, he will've
had his rougher edges worn down from the other stuff he's
done. Lost his naiveté. You know, ITSP, ISMV, couple years bank-
robbery squad; you've been there yourself, so you've got some
idea, you know? You find out what's going on. What kind of
people do these things, what these guys're like. Because those
other categories, yeah, they're mostly isolated, individual acts,
guys freelancing in a life of crime.

"Well, they're also the kind of things that OC guys do, too,
but they do them *all the time.*

"If you're going to do this work, that concept is key. That's the
central difference with them—the ordinary, boring *dailiness* of
it all. Robbing banks and armored cars, bringing in a tonna
dope, hijacking long-haul trailers? '*Yeah*—what else is new?'
These are not big *events* to them, like they *are* to other people.

"Regular law-abiding, lawn-mowing, fence-painting, snow-
shoveling, kid-raising people—the closest they ever get to that
kind of excitement's when they see it on TV or in a movie. And
even then, unless it's somebody's shaky handheld home video,
shows a cop whaling the shit out of some poor-bastard minority guy, gave him some lip—in which case you can't see that
much—they know it's only actors, make-believe.

"To your basic career hoodlum, sticking up banks and shaking down smugglers, shooting a guy in the head or actually emp-
tying a thirty-round banana clip into him—those're things they
do—not on TV, real life. Normal routine; their *occupations*—just

like restocking cookies and chips in aisle twelve, correcting thirty-two science tests or getting ready for the annual going-back-to-school sale, the kind of things that normal people deal with every day, and every year, their lives.

"Robberies, smuggling; hijacking and fencing; the odd murder now and then, like shooting some guy in the *face*? While he's *looking* at you? And probably *talking* to you, *begging* you please not to *shoot* him? These're just the normal things that the hoodlums're always planning, like we plan and shop for cookouts, New Year's Eve parties. Stealing a getaway car, set of plates somewhere else; making sure you got a gun that can't be traced and a good supply of bullets—this is the way they *live*. But now, when somebody gets *caught*, he'll almost always sell a friend to save his own white ass.

"Stoat doesn't understand this yet. He saw the goddamned movie. But *The Godfather* is history. Don Vito Corleone really *is* dead. Marlon Brando ain't runnin' 'this thing of ours' anymore. Isn't like it used to be, as Stoat still assumes it is; *omerta* rules the day. It doesn't. Just the opposite, in fact. Once OC gets involved now, and we bag one of them, someone's going to snitch. It's practically a footrace to see which rat talks first. The old days of *rispetatto*'re over.

"You got to get to know this type of guys, how they think and how they act, how they're liable to react, any given situation. Because they do think different, and they act different, too, like they're wired another way.

"Darren Stoat has not done that. He had never been OC until he came up here. As the man in charge. He's got no *sense* of things, all right? The confidence that makes you feel like you know how to make decisions—and they won't always be wrong. May not always be *right*, no, but you won't *always* be wrong. How to *act* around these guys. So when you're around them, in each other's company, and you both know who you are, you're not saying things or, you know, *doing* things, that will make them... that they will then look at each other and say, 'Whoa, what the hell is goin' on here? What the fuck is this guy doin', tellin' me is happ'nin' here?'

"Because the minute they start doin' that, your little parlor game is over. When these guys play Monopoly, they play it with real money. They draw the 'Go to Jail' card, they know it's not in fun—they're really going to *jail*. The rules say you can take away from them every single thing they got? By doing what they do? They know if they get careless, give you half a chance to do that, that is what you're gonna do.

"And at the same time they assume that *you* know if they can, they are gonna do exactly what will get them all the stuff they want. Hot babes and the cars, and their own safe houses when the heat's on, down the Florida west coast. The tuna boats and Vegas trips, Kentucky Derby, Super Bowl—everything they want.

"What they want is what counts. They do not do resignation. So if getting what they want when they want it means they'll do *anything* they have to do to get it, up to and including killing people, well okay then, it takes that. And they do it. And then when they get away with it—and we have to face it here, generally they have, or will at least until we get these tapes transcribed and enhanced so the jury doesn't have to be Sicilians to understand them—they do not *quite* laugh right in your face, no; that would be impolite.

"But when they see you on the street, they smile when they say hello. That smile means, 'So far we've got you beat.' And you have to be able to smile right back. 'I know it, but just "so far." Not forever. Don't get cocky yet.'

"Carlo—that bastard, for years he's been smiling at me. You think I'm not gonna smile at him, the day we bring him in? Bet your sweet ass I am.

"You don't go in knowing all that shit, what you are is fuckin' *doomed.* You cannot be friends with these guys. You can *respect* them—hell, you *have to* respect them, if you want to get anywhere. You don't, well, you're finished. They can *smell* disrespect, like dogs smell fear, and once they get a whiff of it on you they won't give you another thing from that day forward. Even on a guy they hate, their own worst enemy that they think is worse than dogshit—if they don't first think you have respect for *them,* they'll be toast before they'll tell you anything that he did or plans to do.

"So, even though you *don't* think that, you don't in fact respect them, you still have to act like you do—convince them that you agree that they're just as important, just as powerful, doing what they do, on their side of the law, as we are on ours.

"But then that is *it.* Mutual respect. That's as far as it can go. You can horse around with them, shoot the shit and have some laughs, but you can't be buddies with them; they can never be your pals.

"That kind of stuff Stoat don't know—where you draw the fuckin' line and how the fuck you draw it. And that's what worries me. At first I didn't understand why he reacts the way he does when you tell him something. Like say you drop a two-oh-nine interview report on him, all right?

"Like this case, all right?" Farrier made a sweeping motion with his left arm to encompass the room. "Make believe none of this's goin' on. Go back eleven months or so in your mind, all right? It's now nineteen ninety-six again, ninety-early-seven, and you aren't you, now, you're me.

"You haven't been in the Boston office that long, never mind this squad. Three years. Two careers ago, in the old days, you didn't have the turnover that you've got today. Guys got on this squad and stayed forever, fifteen years or so. Three years then was yesterday. All right, but times've changed. Fogarty's only gone six-eight months or so, and you have not been here that long, but now you be *da man,* as they say. Fogarty made that clear.

"When he retired he said, 'I do bequeath you all of my right, title and interest in the, ah, what to call it, *collegial* relationship that first Albert A. DeMarco, may his memory be ever green, and then I, with his tutelage, have built up, cultivated, nurtured and developed, with two professional gentlemen of first Al's and then my longtime acquaintance, whose occupations, some would say, border on disreputable. If not felonious.'

"Okay, now I know I got it, but I'm not exactly sure yet what exactly this thing is.

"Then Stoat comes out of nowhere, no experience at all, and gets Fogarty's job. Naturally I'm pissed off; sulk a week or so. But then, 'Well, okay, can live with this. I'm a career guy; too many years in onna pension, kiss it all off now. I can work with any-one. Maybe he's all right.'

"Gradually, I find out he's not.

"I make a routine contact with a low-level guy I've known a while, about a hundred years. Could've been an accident, bumped into him on the street, or maybe he called me—wasn't anything I'd planned. Drops one on me for nothin'. Says some-thing that I know means it might not do me any harm to go and noodge another guy, tomorrow or the next day—see what more pops out.

"So I dictate the two-oh-nine and it goes in the pipe, and a day or so goes by and I do some other things I had on my list to do, but also in the meantime also make damn sure I see this other guy. Really nothing yet, but still, know from my experi-ence, the first guy I talked to—sure, he may be lower echelon, but when he tells me something it's at least warm when you touch it. Not something that'll keep—fact generally it's *hot.* Thing to do is run it down, soon as possible.

"Say the first guy's Abe, which he wasn't, anna guy I went to see because of what Abe laid on me's Bob. Also not his name. By the time Darren's read my two-oh-nine, what Abe said to me—and keep in mind that all of this's still strictly maybes at the point where I did that memo, nothing definite—but now things are taking on a shape. I've talked to Bob, and now as a result of what he gave up to me, first thing I'm gonna do when I get in tomorrow, I'm gonna see what kind of activity there's been lately in shipments of high-fashion women's clothes.

"As long as I been at it, I still get excited. Old war-horse smellin' cordite. Nothing's certain—may be nothing; but it *also* may be something.

"Well, next day, almost quittin' time, turns out it *is* something, *definitely* worth looking into. And so first thing inna morning, gonna take a deeper look.

"This's when I run into Stoat, on the way out that night. He's on his way out too, something with the wife or something—he's in kind of a hurry. But I think this's hot, something that he should know about. I should bring him up to speed, so he's aware of where I'm headed.

"Now, I know he hasn't seen the second two-oh-nine, the interview with Bob. Be better if he had—have less to explain—but I know he hasn't. I just finished dictating it to Ginny. As fantastic as the kid is, she ain't got it typed up yet. Still, he oughta know I got this stuff, be abreast of it, so I do the best I can. Give him a quick fill.

"The first thing's to make sure that he read the one with Abe. Otherwise he's got no context, and he'll never understand. So I ask him, did he get it?

"And he says '*Yep*.' Proud of himself, how efficient he is, which of course he always has been. *Efficient*'s always been his hallmark, every desk he's been assigned, all through his career. Every kind of work he did, before he came up here and he got the squad? The reason wasn't that he knew a thing about the mob; it was that he was *efficient.* Which in every instance, matter what his title was—and I know, because when I found he's gettin' this job, for which he's not qualified, well, I looked the bastard up. Find out what experience he's got that's better for chief, OCS, than workin' OCS.

"Movin' paper's what it was. Movin' fuckin' paper. From the box on left side of the desk, where he found it inna morning, to the box on the right side when the quittin' whistle blew.

"Which of course is not enough—no field experience at all. But in his case it was. Because apparently when it comes to pushin' paper, man, this guy has got no equal. He's the very best on earth. *Except* for the one shuffler who's even *better* at it, and that's the guy above him who decided eighteen years of moving paper's the best training and experience that there is to head up an organized-crime squad in a major center of La Cosa Nostra.

"So, *yep,* Stoat *has* read read my two-oh-nine on Abe. 'It was on my desk this morning, got to it this afternoon. I'll be very interested, see where this thing leads.'

"'*Okay,*' I say, a sigh relief, but I'm not really thinking. 'Now like I said in it, the next thing I was gonna do, I contacted Bob today. Bob's a really plugged-in guy—nothin' major happens 'thout him knowin' least one guy that's involved in it.'

"Doin' a little *sellin',* here, because as you and I both know that Stoat's the kind of guy who's always thinkin', 'Taxpayer dollars bein' spent here. Got to be sure this is *guaranteed* bonus points down at Seat of Government, Best Allocation of Resources.' So I'm givin' him a pitch.

"'And on the basis what Bob told me I have got a good idea I am gonna find tomorrow when I call *another* guy I also know about a hundred years—used to be Manhattan PD, worked the DA's office, let's say his name is Charlie—now with New York insurance office of the central clearing house, and I tell him that

I bet they've had a doozy of a recent major claim in the garment business, right? High-priced women's suits and dresses. And if he hasn't seen it—which he may not've yet because this information's *smokin'*; these national retail chains've got layers and layers and layers 'tween the warehouse and front office; people that he talks to may not have the word themselves that the goods're really gone—he is gonna pretty soon. And get him started checking on it, see what he comes up with.

" 'Because if Charlie tells me what I'm pretty sure he's gonna tell me, we get on the horn tomorrow, I think I know where we find about eight hundred thousand dollars' worth of Calvin Klein, DonnaKaran, Ralph Lauren, and AnnTaylor women's *clothes*. So goddamned hot they're barely outta sweatshops where the kids sewed them together. Not even *tagged* yet, Worcester distribution hub, the chain where they were headin' when the wise guys cut 'em off.'

"Naturally Darren doesn't understand a fuckin' word I'm sayin' to him. This is because he's just told me he didn't understand a fuckin' word in the Abe two-oh-nine. That he just *read*. And he just *told* me that, but I wasn't listening to him. All he's seen's what Abe said. His reaction is that he'll be very interested, see where that's gonna lead. But it's not gonna lead *anywhere*, except to Bob, who might have something, or not. Which is what I said in it, and what I just told him I talked to Bob today. And it did. Exactly what the Abe two-oh-nine told him I was gonna do, and Bob told you exactly what your two-oh-nine predicted he might say.

"You see what I mean. You do your very best to keep Stoat up to speed, something large breaking, and already he's falling behind the curve. By the time he catches up to what Bob said, and what Charlie says, you'll be on your way to Dave. Already thinking about how you're going to approach Eddie. So Stoat's comment is inane, and you are wasting both your time telling him what happened next—he can't understand it. He's got no idea of process. He does not know what things *mean*.

"He's never been *line;* always he's been *staff.* He's a *freak* in his job, least in my OC experience—and by nineties standards I've been at it a long time. He's never been a field officer, out among the troops where the shooting's going on. Always been at head-quarters, thinking what someone he's never met and never will is going to say, they testify before House Ways and Means, Bureau Budget for next year.

"When you were ITSMV, chasing stolen cars in Wichita; I was hunting fugitives in Houston; he was rinsing out the coffee-pots at Quantico, taking CIA courses at McLean. When he came here he didn't blow in from Seattle with a classy record on the fraud squad. He came from *Washington,* for *seasoning,* get some experience in the *field*—the brass's favorite adjutant detached from HQ down to his own first real command, battalion.

"Took me a while to realize this, implications of it all. That first day I did not. That what I'd just said to him meant about as much to him as all that chaff and gibberish on the tapes that I couldn't understand today. Doesn't follow things as they de-velop, way that we do. It's because he's never *seen* things develop. All he's ever seen's the way cases look *after* they've developed. The way the whole fat case file looked, twenty, thirty two-oh-nines, lab tests, and everything. When it was submitted for ap-proval, prosecution.

"Which was long *after* I took what Abe said, and went and talked to Bob. And then took what Bob said and called Charlie in New York. He checked and got back to me and said 'Yeah, the clothes're gone,' and 'This's where they were when they last saw them, when they disappeared.' Who it was that last saw them, and where they were headed next. And who'd known when they're coming in, and so on and so on and so on, far into the night. Which meant I had to talk to Dave, and with what he had to say, I had enough to go to Eddie.

"Because we're *experienced*, and *know*, 'thout even havin' to *think* about it—you *never, ever* ask a guy with any weight for anything important until you already *know*, all right? Until you're absolutely fuckin' *sure* that *he* knows what you're after. And he also knows you know, and it's important enough to you so if he doesn't give it to you, you'll get it from someone else and then maybe jam him up.

"All of this's clear to him—he's also been around. If he doesn't give you what you know it is he's got, then it's no more Mister Nice Guy. He's dead meat with you thereafter and you will break his balls for him the next chance that you get, and *every* chance you get, as long as you two're alive. So Eddie ain't no rookie neither, and he did have what I wanted, just exactly like you figured, and he gave it up to me.

"So *finally*, get through going around and talking to about six other guys, finding out what they could tell you, *then* you had enough to say, 'All right, okay, it's time to see our top-echelon informants.' And tell McKeach and Nick the Frogman what you needed them to get, so that you could then write up the case report for Stoat, and after him the Special Agent in Charge and Assistant U.S. Attorney Marsh, Seat of Government and Department of Justice. And if all of them liked what you had as much as you did—as you knew they *would*, 'cause it was *prime*—Marsh would get your Title Threes from the judge, electronic surveillance warrants, and those orders would get you *this*."

Farrier spread his hands, taking in the room again, the other agents stretching and rising from their chairs, the tape decks and the video-editing machines, the stacks of audiotape boxes, the rows of videotape boxes, the computers and the pads. He smiled. "Although he doesn't know it yet, Carlo Rizzo by the balls. *Carlo* authorized that hijacking. Time to go for him.

"Until that day finally comes, all that Stoat sees is that you've been *boring* him, day after day, week after week, building this bundle of two-oh-nines six or seven inches thick, with holes punched through them, and then binding all of them together with those vicious silver fasteners that'll cut your fingers nastier'n any razor blade you ever saw, because the cut they leave is ragged. The same kind of package that used to come down to Washington when he was there and landed on his desk one morning, with a thud, and maybe made him kind of shudder. But he did his duty—spent that whole day reading it—efficiently, of course, never mind if he knew what it *meant*—and bumped it out again that night.

"That's what he's seen going across his desk here, and gradually accumulating in the secure files when he used his key at night, and then one day I—meaning me—bucked it to him with your memo saying 'Think it's ready,' and he then signed off on it. When we get through all this stuff here someday, if we ever do, what was in all those two-oh-nines and what's on all of both kinds of these tapes—all of it'll get presented to the grand jury, and AUSA Marsh'll get his okays from all the people that he needs and draw up the indictments. And the USA'll check off again and the grand jury'll true-bill it, like all good grand juries do, and the next thing that'll happen'll be that the warrants issue. We'll go out to make arrests—papers and TV that night'll say that what we did, we "fanned out"—and Stoat *still* won't understand. How the hell we did it—what all went into it.

"That's the problem with him, and it always will be. You say 'case' and I hear 'process.' Say that same word to Stoat and what he hears is 'product.' He thinks when we're having dinner with

McKeach and Nick tonight, the purpose is retelling war stories, how we four're getting Carlo. Forgetting we don't got him yet, we're still getting ready to.

"And the one thing that you never do with the guys like them who help you is make it seem like you believe they like what you are doing—just because they help you do it. They don't. The reason they help you do it is because we're doing it to somebody who's competing with them, and therefore they don't like them *more* than they still don't like us.

" 'The enemy of my enemy is my friend'—that's all it is. They help us to do it to Carlo because Carlo's got fire power and he doesn't fuck around, so if we will get it done and take him out it'll be much less dangerous for them and one hell of a lot cheaper than if they do it themselves. And from their own point of view the result is just as good. We're not friends, we're allies, from different sides. All the difference in the world. That's what Stoat doesn't understand."

"You really do not like this guy," Hinchey said thoughtfully.

"You got that right," Farrier said. "The asshole drives me nuts."

"You gonna do something to him?" Hinchey said.

Farrier thought a moment. Then he said, "Maybe after we do Carlo. After that? Who knows?"

8

AT 5:35 IN THE AFTERNOON MCKEACH looked at his watch and decided he was tired of listening to Junius Walters' husky high-pitched voice. "Walterboy"—or "Waterboy," an option if the person saying it knew him well and he was in the kind of mood that made it all right to be funny—was 6'7" and to McKeach looked as though he was still pretty close to his playing weight.

"Two-forty, forty-five, still mostly muscle—must work out," he said to Cistaro two hours later, fifteen minutes late, picking him up in his salt- and sand-streaked metallic blue '86 Pontiac Parisienne Brougham at the Towers at Chestnut Hill. "Hadda work him over some, then go home, shower, change, like you and me're goin' onna double *date* with Farrier and him, the other guy, the funny name."

"Stoat," Cistaro said absently. "Darren Stoat."

"Yeah," McKeach said. "Anyway, that's why. Hadda ask Dorothy drop my clothes inna machine, 'fore the stains set. I dunno about the jacket. Prolly drop that off the cleaners, see what they can do—if they can get blood outta suede."

"The hell happened?" Cistaro said.

"*Ahh,* thing I hadda do this after—shape those fuckin' niggers up. Didn't go so good. Never does, you get involved in one of those things, explaining things to people know already, very well, you're sayin'. Trouble is they also know as soon's they admit it, it'll start to cost 'em money. So quite naturally they're gonna stall you, just as long's they think they can.

"Still pisses me off when they do it, though, play those fuckin' games. Especially this guy—I know he knows better but he did it anyway." McKeach took his right hand off the steering wheel, leaned forward slightly, and patted the right side of his jacket twice. "Hadda hit him—he kinda sprayed around."

"Well," Cistaro said, "he wouldn't go the cops, would he?"

McKeach snorted. He turned the Pontiac right at the light on Hammond Pond Parkway. "Shit, no," he said. "Guy's dumber'n I thought he'd be, but not that dumb, I think. Knows I'd clip him if he did." He laughed. "Knows *now* anyway."

"So, as long's you got it done," Cistaro said, settling back into the seat as McKeach guided the Pontiac out of the S-curve at the bottom of the hill and took the ramp to Route 9 westbound, heading for the townhouse in Framingham. "Way I look at things like that, if you find you got a problem, makin' people understand you, how you get it done don't matter.

"Look at me—same kinda thing. I was prolly late myself, gettin' down to the garage. Day I had, bein' with the guys I hadda be with? Same kinda people, same kinda routine—pretend they don't know what you're talkin' about. All they're doin's wastin' time—they are *gonna* fuckin' *do* it. You are gonna make 'em see that. Except I didn't have to hit nobody—not that I would've minded, but after bein' with those guys, I also hadda have a shower 'fore I feel like goin' out." He laughed.

"Fuckin' Helen? I tell her where I'm goin' and I'm goin' there with you, and as many years's we've been doin' this she *still* does not believe me. Not one single word I'm sayin'. 'Uh *huh,* you and

Arthur're going to have dinner with the FBI. Well, that makes it nice—this's my night to go bowling with the pope and Virgin Mary.' Every time we go to see them, she thinks we're out scoutin' strange."

McKeach laughed. "Last night at the office I thought all you hadda do today was go stick a broomstick all the way up Jinks's monster ass. Not that that's any fun. But where the hell else'd you have to go this after?"

"Ahh," Cistaro said, slumping down in the seat, "it wasn't just this after—nothing any different from any other damned day— one fuckin' thing and get that done and then go see another asshole, one right after the fuckin' other. Before lunch I hadda go and see this airy-fairy faggot on New*berry*-fuckin' street, got the loan for ninety large off the new kid, off of Tony? Barber shop down there on Broad? That's been a good location, 'cept when something like this happens, customer don't understand what he's doin', who he's dealing with. Thinks he got the money from his fuckin' *mother*, something, so no hurry payin' back. Back in February this one happened. Up until three weeks ago? Everything is fine there, absoutely ice cream. But something then apparently goes wrong for this fairy—his soufflées don't rise no more; things begin to turn to shit. So now the guy's three weeks *behind*. Isn't ice cream anymore.

"So I go in, way outta my way, and, this and that, and say to him, 'What's goin' on?' You know? 'What gives?' Like, 'Where's my fuckin' *money*?' And *he* acts like, well, I dunno, like it's a big *surprise* or something, I might be somewhat *concerned*. He's onna phone when I go in, talkin' to some fuckin' broad, and *he's* the one now pissed at *me*—I'm comin' in with no appointment—like I'm *interruptin'* him. Just what am I *doin'* there?

"Well, geez, I mean, what'm *I* supposed to do? He's three weeks late. He owes us thirteen thousand bucks and change, plus the ninety underneath. I'm gonna write it off this week and next, 'til things turn around for *him*? Who the *fuck* are these people, anyway, we're now doin' business with? He thinks I won't break his *knees*, he's such a classy guy? He's some kind of a good *cause*? I wasn't such a gentleman I might get mad at him, you know? Let him have a couple good ones.

"He explains it all to me. Very patient, you know? Like I'm maybe not too bright. Maybe I don't *understand*—he's usin' our dirty old money to bankroll this very hush-hush, very high-class, artsy-craftsy operation—Cyprus, somewhere, maybe Egypt—and then it goes through Switzerland, and then after that New York.

"I'm supposd to be *impressed*. Once I understand what a high-class deal this is, I'll be so *honored* that him being three weeks late'll be perfectly all right. Something I laugh off.

"Right. I know what they're *doing*—some thievin' fuckin' Arabs, Greeks, Iranians, maybe gypsies, *I* dunno—they are robbin' *graves*, all right? Lootin' ancient temples. Indiana fuckin' Jones, all so glamorous.

"I don't buy it. Stealin' from *dead* people—my mind this is not a thing takes balls. Diggin' up their tombs and cemeteries, takin' all their pots and pans, and coins. Statues of their gods, and dogs and cats and so forth, plates and jewelry and stuff their families buried with them three thousand years ago, so they'd go to the promised land." He laughed. "Didn't have Las Vegas then.

"But this guy with our money, up to his elbows in one sick-oh operation, and for us he's got an *attitude*? Ninety that we loaned him was a fuckin' *contribution*? I mean, give me a fuckin' *break*."

Cistaro laughed. "But I go easy on him. I get his attention and explain things, all right? So when I leave there I am pretty sure he now understands. He does—when I go back this affternon, he has got the dough for me and don't give me no further shit. Think it's gonna be okay now.

"Then I go the Terrace, lunch—hafta deal with Albie Bryson. You wanna know something? I don't like that fuckin' guy. Here he is, he's comin' to us, paying us for peace and quiet, Local Eight, all right? Because it's cheaper for him if he pays us five grand and we give Ernie Warner two, one for him and one for Bev, and tell him never mind if some his people go the shows and see along with not too many Local Eight guys there's a lotta scab help, too. Albie's always *whinin'*; that's what I don't like. How he's giving gigs to old-time acts, starvin' without him, and the only thing that keeps it going is cheap towns that underwrite it. And they're always threatenin' him—'Taxpayers're complainin', this's prolly the last year, and...' I get sick of it, you know? Who the fuck's he kiddin' here? He acts like when we make *him* pay, the fuckin' money's comin' outta Little Sisters of the Poor—when you and I both know, without even *askin'*, he's givin' the same line of shit to the towns, and the acts, and a few guys in Local Eight. He's *keepin'* most of it.

"All just a load of shit. He's beatin' every one of us out of diddly spare change, and that's why we let it go. That's the *genius* of the scumbag; how he gets away with it. Same old fuckin' story. Steal a million bucks off one guy and you'll really piss him off—prolly hunt you down and kill you. Steal a buck off every one of a million people? None of 'em'll even notice. We all just stand around, you know? Playin' with ourselves. 'Ah fah Chrissake let it go.' It's like what he's doin' is, he's sneakin' inna back at night and goin' through the trash. Deposit cans and bottles.

"But it *isn't*, when you think about it. He gets finished cheatin' *all* of us, then it all adds up, nice big piece of change for Albie. Albie Bryson's shit and I don't like dealing with him."

"As long as we keep Ernie, we gotta," McKeach said. "Ernie come to us after Brian G. went down." He kept the Pontiac inconspicuously steady at forty-four mph in the right lane, one-and-a-half car lengths behind the car ahead, allowing left-lane traffic to slide by at over fifty. "He asked were we takin' over everything that Brian had, and did we want the local. If we did he'd stay with us. We could've said 'No, go with Carlo and report to Providence,' but we talked, you and me did, and we decided, 'No. Give a piece of steady business to those Ginzo bastards, after which they'll only want something more, another piece of something else, in our territory?' And we decided we'd keep it."

He spoke slowly, in a calm and moderate tone, his voice slightly guttural. "I still think it was the right decision. Every one thing that we've got feeds off all the others, and the others feed off it. So the more things you got going, the stronger I think it makes you—so the more things you can get. Ernie's been good business for us, and he's a loyal bastard. He don't give us any trouble—an' he gives us a lot of leverage into places which without him we'd never get. Not just the movies and the stage shows—also sports and big conventions. Like political campaigns and fundraisers and stuff."

"We never did anything, that political bullshit," Cistaro said.

"No, but if we wanted to," McKeach said. "That's what I am saying. If we ever decided that for some reason, we did. Like if they ever got a national convention—Democratic Convention, Republican Convention, wouldn't make no difference—come to the Fleet Center. Say Ernie for some reason—like, we asked him to—didn't feel right about it, that particular week, and decided, shut it down, or even only put it off a week or so, 'til someone made him feel better. He could probably do it.

"'Ernie,' we would say to him, if we ever did decide that we could make a dollar off it, 'this national convention thing—we'd like it if it didn't happen. All the Local Eight guys get bellyaches or something, and you decided best thing'd be, call it off. At least 'til you all feel a little better.'

"I'd make book on this—Ernie would then say right off, 'My stomach doesn't feel so good. Probably some kind of bug, some germ that's goin' round. I think I'll go lie down. Oh, and I don't want no kinda noise and big excitement goin' on around this town, I'm restin'. Like any of those big-time convention guys're always makin' all the time—none of that shit, right? Just upset my stomach more.

"'All our guys in Local Eight—check on how their stomachs feel. Make sure they ask the other guys that they might know—like the Teamsters, Electricians, Carpenters, the Hotel an' Restaurant Workers—how their bellies feel. You know what I'm trynah tell yez? Just shut downah fuckin' town.'"

McKeach paused for several beats. "If we ever went to Ernie, really needing something done, and it was a thing that he could do, then he wouldn't ask no questions—he would fuckin' get it done. That's the kind of friend to have. So what I say is if we hafta deal with Albie once or twice a year to keep Ernie and the local on our side and backin' us, very handy inna pinch, then that is what we hafta do, and I say that we do it. Deal with Albie, pig he is, and keep our big mouths fuckin' shut."

The Pontiac was quiet for an old car. For a while the only sound inside it was the rushing wind noise generated outside by the protruding rain gutters, glass moldings, and chrome trim parts attached to automobiles manufactured before aerodynamics rounded all exterior surfaces.

Cistaro cleared his throat. "Then after him was Jinks," he said. "He was smellin' around again today, too, I was over Strawson's with him, tryin' to talk business with him, and you think that I can do it? *Nooo;* he's *still* tryin' to find out do I maybe know any more'n he does about how Jerry Mutt went down. How long ago is that now? Gotta be two years, he's chewin' on that bone. Fuckin' *Jinks*—thinks he's so fuckin' *cute*—he doesn't watch his fuckin' ass, pretty soon he'll be able tah talk to *Satchie* about Jerry. Talk to Satchie every day, inna dinin' hall and gym, walkin' the exercise yard." He laughed. "Maybe sign up some college courses, huh? Read *stories* to each other. 'Once upon a time in Boston, there're these two fuckin' assholes who thought they were very smart.' Even wind up the same cellblock." He laughed again.

McKeach did not say anything.

"Anyway, Albie and Jinks—two of them in the same day, on top the *other* asshole that I had tah see this morning—got me thinking, you know? Fuckin' Jerry Mutt again. How we didn't take it far enough, dealing with that bastard—what we should've done was clip 'im. Jinks and Albie, back to back. Didn't have either one of them to worry about before Jerry went away. Now we got 'em both.

"Jinks I'll give you—him we have to put up with, at least for a while. Jinks's major money and if he ever gets it done, what we've got him fronted for, he'll be worth the aggravation. But fuckin' *Albie*—we could hang onto Local Eight without him, I would bet. Ernie'd be glad to lose him, if you offered him the chance. He must know the same thing we do, what a little shit he is. Albie, fuckin' Albie—just another one those rinky-dinks we never should've taken on—not inna million fuckin' *years.* Just another one Jerry's chicken-*shit*, piss-*pot*, dog-*ass* operations that was a big part of the reason why it was 'at you and me and everybody else we know was all in favor, didn't shed a fuckin' *tear*, when the first guy who suggested it—I forget now who it was—said he wouldn't mind a fuckin' bit if fuckin' Jerry made some history."

"It was you," McKeach said. The light was red at the Walnut Street intersecton and he pulled up in the long line of cars in the right lane well east of it. Next to the Pontiac in the left lane in a white Chevrolet Malibu sedan a middle-aged dark-haired woman in the passenger seat was using the visor vanity mirror to apply lipstick. McKeach watched her idly, mimicking her manner of stretching her lips over her teeth without seeming to be aware that he was doing it.

"What was me?" Cistaro said.

"It was you, and you gave him to Farrier," McKeach said absently, now observing the woman intently. Then he collected himself and shifted his gaze to Cistaro. "You're the first guy that said Jerry Mutt should go, and if we didn't want to clip him we should then give his name to someone who could do something about him. I remember it. I dunno what he did that day to piss you off, but that night you had a *hair* across your ass. You said, 'Because he is a shitbum *rat,* and those guys never change. If we don't get rid of him then someday some cop'll *nail* him, 'cause he isn't like we are, you know—he isn't very smart.'"

The car ahead moved forward about two car lengths and stopped again, and McKeach closed the gap. "'And because of that,' you said, 'when he does get nailed he'll panic. Which he will, get nailed, sooner or later, for some nickel-dime thing, and he won't just keep his big mouth shut and do maybe, what, a year? No, he'll think he's one the big boys; if he's nailed the whole world's ended and he has to make a deal. But not just any deal, like where he'd get two or three, *nooo;* Jerry's *delicate,* and that means he can't do time—Jerry has to *walk.* So you know what he'll do—he'll sell us all, one at a time, 'til he gets a deal he likes.'

"You would *not* let go of it. 'Cops aren't stupid, you know—you give 'em half a chance, they take it. Jerry thinks he's smart—he isn't. They're *much* smarter'n he is and they won't give him what he's after until they get all he's got—which if we keep playin' games with him, gettin' tied up in his deals—so he's got loads of shit he can tell them that he knows we did, because he helped us do it—will be every one of us.'

"You *couldn't*'ve forgotten," McKeach said. He slapped the wheel with his left hand. "You can't possibly've forgotten, even this much later on, all the stuff you said. You made a fuckin' *speech*. Maxie triedah argue with you. Said well, gee, he didn't think so, Jerry seemed like a nice guy to him, small-time, maybe, not in our league, but still, an okay guy.

"And you said, 'No-no, he isn't. What he is's a disaster lookin' for a place to happen. And you know what he'll get, tradin' you an' me, and all the rest of us? As many as it takes? Witness Protection. Bank on it—all of us'll be goin' to jail, one by one, and he'll be inna safe house onna Cape somewhere, eatin' steak and havin' beers, he gets through testifyin', puttin' all of us inside. Then a new life in Australia for him, fuckin' fuckin' kangaroos. That's what you'll be worth to him, and as soon as someone offers it, your life outside is *over.*'"

"Well, if I did say that I was right," Cistaro said. "And that's why I gave him to Farrier. Because Jerry did have a lotta scumbag little nickel-dime deals going on, all at the same time, and sooner-later I know he's bound to lose track of them, how one of them was gonna get himself grabbed by some kid Statie two weeks outta the academy. And if it was the Staties got him, or the first fed with a clear shot who wasn't FBI, you and me'd be going too. We wouldn't be protected.

"This's a very nice little arrangement you and me've got, but it's only good as long's we make sure if something happens might affect us, it's Farrier and them in charge of doing it. So that it doesn't."

The light changed and McKeach moved the Pontiac forward, accelerating back up to speed.

"Anyway, it doesn't matter," Cistaro said. "I had stuff I hadda do and I got it done. You find that Junior kid you said you hadda go and see? That who sprayed on you? What is this kid anyway, some kinda fuckin' skunk?"

McKeach chuckled. "Well, I don't think he meant to," he said. "Mess me up, I mean. Things just got so they looked to me they might be gettin' outta hand. And of course you don't want that, so I thought I'd better do something, and I did. That's the long and short of it—I wasn't really prepared. Must be getting old. That's how you tell, they say. Start overlooking small things, then fall down an' break your hip. I *thought* I was ready, but I really wasn't, and so as usual, that kind of situation, I hadda do a thing I didn't think I'd hafta do."

McKEACH AND WALTERS SAT ON TWO wooden packing cases stenciled WHEELERS in faded red paint, face to face across the fourth in the row of a dozen unpainted wooden work tables bolted to the floor opposite the pedestrian entrance about thirty feet from the southerly end of the workbay of the warehouse. Wheelers men had used the tables—eight feet long by three feet wide, the legs and crossbraces made of two-by-fours carriage-bolted together, the tops of eight-ply composition wood—to crate household and office goods for long-distance shipment, leaving them behind in the stillness of the Wheelers bankruptcy like implements of a ritual that had failed. In the late afternoon there was barely enough pale winter sunlight to illuminate the long windows under the eastern eaves twenty feet above the two men at the table. The golden light that picked up trace lanolin in the pores of their skin and made their faces gleam—the right side of Walters' burnished brown, like a polished mahogany surface, the left side of McKeach's glowing russet, burned by wind and sun and whiskey—was the output of the double-mantle Coleman gasoline lantern near the end of the table to Walters' right. Now and then one of his men shifted his position in the shadows, his shoes making soft scraping sounds.

"Junior, you and me," McKeach said, his elbows and forearms in the black suede leather sleeves of his tanker jacket resting on the table, hands dangling out of sight below the edge, "I got to say that I don't like the way things seem to be startin' off between us here, you sayin' to me 'Sure, come over,' like you don't know what's goin' on, or who the hell I am and so forth. And now me comin' here in friendship, set to do a man a favor, and findin' myself in this." He nodded toward the shadows behind and around Walters where he knew at least three other black men clad entirely in black clothes stood as still as possible when he conducted business—knowing far more precisely their positions and postures of uneasiness than he believed that Walters realized. "This, ah, kind of a situation, here."

"*Junius*," Walters said, regret in the lines around his eyes. He kept the alto voice low and pleasant, being gracious, forgiving McKeach while correcting him, as though meaning to soothe him; at the same time he smiled the universal minimal smile, upper lip raised only slightly above the four upper teeth he showed in front. His eyes were dead. "'Junius' to you, Arthur, if we already know each other so well that we're going by first names. 'Junius' is mine. White people do sometimes find it an unusual name, and I don't insist they use it. But if that's what they want, well then, I think, no matter how pec-cu-u-lar it sounds to you, you ought to get it right."

The man in the gloom to Walters' right coughed and led the others murmuring quiet amens and endorsements—the man behind and to his left stirred audibly—then the one in the center sighed further approval. Walters smiled a little more. He used an undertone of teasing. "Now whatchou doin' with them *hands* of yours, you got where I can't see 'em—you *playin'* with yourself there, man? Gettin' *nervous* on me here?" He shook his head. "Tsk-tsk-tsk," doing the fussy aunty on McKeach, "no need for that here—you be the big lion, we jus' the lambs; we *have* to be . . . your *friends*."

McKeach did not change the position of his forearms or his torso. Below the edge of the table he clasped the fingers of his right hand back against the palm. He inserted his little finger into the loop of the leather lanyard he had snugged against the inside of his wrist and began to pull it down. "I'm comfortable," he said. "Maybe if I tell you why I'm here . . . so there won't be no misunderstanding."

He had entered the warehouse by climbing the four wooden steps leading up to the battleship-grey steel door black-stenciled EMPLOYEES ONLY at the back, using his left hand to remove the Ray-Bans and his right to turn the knob and pull the door open, and then, once inside, give the door a yank before releasing it to boom shut behind him. While his eyes adjusted to the dim interior he had pushed the Cubs hat back on his forehead and un-zipped the black suede tanker jacket, moving his shoulders and sucking his belly in, passing his hands around inside his belt, tucking his shirttails deeper into his jeans, palming the sap out of the place where it lived in the hollow at his waistband over his right kidney. It was second nature to him now, after all the years, gathering his fingers together and inserting his hand through the supple nine-inch looped lanyard he had fashioned six years before, cutting the cobbler's-grade oiled cowhide stock from the pattern he had made by slitting the stitching of the one Brian G. had shown him how to make, modifying it to make the lanyard an inch longer.

"More whip," he explained proudly to Cistaro, showing it the day after he made it. He had also added an inch to the pouch, to accommodate more BB shot—another ounce or so, he figured. "More wallop, take some of the doubt out of it." He had never actually weighed the old bludgeon and he hadn't put the new one on a scale either, but he liked it even better—"Better heft— ten ounces or so." He slipped the pouch up under the black knit-ted wristlet of his jacket so that it lay against the underside of his right forearm, the lanyard looped around his wrist against the base of his thumb.

"You been here five weeks now," McKeach said. "Brought in

six truckloads so far you put under the floor here, and while the trucks're still comin' in you took some of it out, cut it and repacked it, and shipped four trucks out again. Two of them were for Detroit. Don't know where the other two went, yet—by tomorrow night I will.

"This's a lot of work you and your guys've gotten done here. While no one bothered you, *at any time,* you were doin' it. You been around enough to know that that's no accident. This place is protected. For that coverage you pay me.

"And since you been around enough to know that, I shouldn't hafta drive out here and tell it to you. I hope I don't also have to tell you that if I know what's come in here, and I know what you've done to it in here, and I know what's then gone out, and where it was headed to, I can stop it comin' in, stop you working on it, and stop it going out—any fuckin' time I want. You must know I can do this.

"You shouldah come to see me *before* you come in. You didn't. You shouldah come to see me since you been here. You didn't. Okay, you're a proud man. Or maybe you're just a foolish one. But I been around a long time and dealt with both kinds; can deal with either one—as I have and as I will. In your case I decide that I will make this special effort, try and make you understand. I will come and see you, as I am doing here, right now, tell you what you already know. Take a good look—here I am.

"The price's twenty to come in here. That's permission. Ten a week to stay. The twenty plus the five you been here, plus the next week in advance. I'm gonna hafta come and see you to collect the rent? All right, then; I will do that. But if you want room service, you pay in advance.

"That's what I'm doing here."

Walters gazed at him for a few moments, his smile gradually widening and his eyes beginning to sparkle. Then he put his hands palms down on the table, arched his back and threw his head back, laughing richly, like a man who's heard wonderful news.

The men in the shadows behind him were beginning their supporting chorus of laughter as McKeach came out of his seated position, clamping his left hand on the table as a fulcrum; using his right hand and forearm to swing the blackjack out in a backhand arc away from his body; rising up on the balls of his feet in the compact semicircular motion that a lefthanded player connecting solidly with a baseball performs, pivoting his body in his followthrough on the swing, only his front hand remaining on the bat.

The pouch full of BBs sailed out at the end of the lanyard in a wider, faster arc from the web at the base of McKeach's right thumb and forefinger, catching Walters on the base of the socket of his right eye and his upper right jaw, the pouch flattening on impact, smashing the temporal, zygomatic and maxilla bones and driving sharp fragments of them into the right eye and sinuses, breaking off four upper right molars into his mouth, open in laughter. The blow knocked two of the broken teeth clear, so that they plinked along the table and skittered onto the floor and the darkness, but Walters aspirated the other two and began at once to choke on the combination of bone, enamel, mucus, saliva and blood, making a wet, roaring, strangling sound of shock, pain, rage and fear, at the same time furiously attempting to rise but unable to get his balance and toppling backward off the packing crate, then crashing onto the floor. While he was reeling, trying to stand, McKeach, moving fast to his own left, with his left hand swept the Coleman lantern off the table onto the floor, so that it broke open and exploded on impact, creating a ball of white light. Walters, still roaring, unable to save himself, fell into the fire.

McKeach, running low to the ground, heard one of Walters' men scream as he reached the door, jerked it open, and went out, slamming it shut behind him—allowing himself to slow down then, approaching the car, grateful for the clean cold air he was gulping into his throat. He unlooped the lanyard of the blackjack from his wrist and stowed it again in his waistband. As he opened the door of the car he heard another small explosion, muffled, in the warehouse behind him, and as he slid onto the seat he nodded, smiling. "Fuckin' *aye*," he said.

"YOU KNOW," MCKEACH SAID, "as many times I do it, I still have to admit, I do still go in thinkin' that I know what's gonna happen when I'm gonna talk to guys that I don't really *know*. And I really *don't*. But I still feel like I do, think if I say something, I know what they'll *do*? You know how you think that?" He snorted. "I don't. I never do. I've actually got no idea.

"Inna first place, guy is black. All four of them're black. I'm tellin' you, my friend, and I've said this time again—I don't give a good shit, anybody wants to say about how we all're brothers, all the same? They're fulla shit. May have good reasons for it, really want it to be true. Well, I'm sorry but it isn't. It *isn't* fuckin' true. Those bastards're wired different. They just do not think the same.

"Most of them, I swear to God, I wonder if they *do* think. But even with the ones that do, you're still not outta the woods. Because when you try to tell 'em something—'You don't do what I tell you, I will break your fuckin' head'—and you think 'Now they have to get it,' you made it so damn plain—they didn't. It's like you're talkin' a foreign language to them. Nothin' that they recognize. They sit there starin' at you like you just got in from Mars, thinkin', 'All those moving pictures on TV and stuff, green men and flying saucers? Those guys got it all wrong. These outer-space guys're mostly the same shape like us, 'cept their dicks're prolly smaller and their skins're kinda pale. Wonder if they're good to eat?'"

Cistaro laughed.

"I tell you, it is true," McKeach said, also laughing. "I went in there, 'kay? I'm in a good mood. 'Gonna cut this kid some slack. He did me a nice favor once—owe him one for that. He didn't *know* he was doin' it, and my guess is he made a lot more for himself off the guys who paid him to do it than I made off of bettin' other guys he would. But he did it, just the same, and therefore for a guy I don't even know, who is one big spade to boot, I got friendly feelings for him."

Walterboy as a sophomore power forward had averaged 23.4 points, 8.6 assists, and 9.3 rebounds per game for the '77–78 University of Kansas basketball team. Ranked nineteenth nationally for nine straight weeks during December, January and February in the UPI Coaches' Poll, "the surprising Jayhawks" made it to the Sweet Sixteen round of the NCAA championships in March of '78 before losing 87–68 to twelve-point underdog East North Carolina. Walterboy limped off the floor with 1:07 left in the first quarter of that game, complaining of a severe right hamstring pull, after scoring five points, one rebound and no assists. He was unable to return to the lineup that night.

"Had the time to follow teams, then," McKeach said, referring to his stay at the Federal Correctional Institution at Fort Leavenworth, "which if you're planning to put money on them's the only smart way you can do it. Pay close enough attention to their games and how they play so you get some kind idea what's liable to happen, they get inna particular kind of situation. And plus which in prison—and this's something naturally that you yourself would not know, you being such a pussy all your life, never took a major chance on nothin'——"

"Never saw a situation return looked good enough to me, is why," Cistaro said laconically. "I look at something and I see a risk involved? What I do then is think, 'Is what I'm gonna get if I take this chance good enough so if it don't turn out right, I won't mind that I got lugged and I'm gonna hafta spend the next eight years my life beatin' my meat, like some fuckin' *kid* who's got so many pimples he can't even get a fuckin' ugly girl to pull his pud for him—'stead of fuckin' like a man who's got some fuckin' self-respect? Because if it isn't I'm not takin the risk.' And so far I haven't seen any scam looked like it would be, and so I never did."

He paused one beat. "Whereas you, I guess, you're so fuckin' money hungry eight years of lopin' your pony doesn't bother you. Or else bein' a mick you think that's okay because it must be what the priests do, but gettin' laid's a mortal sin. Plus which, spent my bulletproof years inna service. Got all the wild-ass young stuff outta my system, so time I got out, I had some sense, got hooked up with Hugo."

"You got a point," McKeach said. "I did some dumb stuff, I's a kid. But you've also had shit luck." He took the Pontiac down the last long hill in Newton into the valley under Route 128, still crowded with heavy traffic, and commenced the long ascent up Route 9 into Wellesley Hills. "Still, can be educational. In prison you hear certain kinda things you're not always gonna hear on the outside. Or at least not as soon.

"So I got to where I thought I had a read on these guys, on this team—Walterboy especially. To the point where I thought I could tell pretty well what he'd do if he got in the kind of situation where he had a choice. Where if he did one thing another thing would happen—his team would win the big one. That being the thing most people who follow the team'd expect in that situation. Because they think they know you, or at least what makes you tick—when they actually do not. Whereas if you *don't* do that thing, the one that they expect, and you do the *opposite*, then as a result the team'll lose. Or at least not beat the spread enough to make the bettors happy."

"Well, of *course*," Cistaro said, chuckling. "Heck, *every*body knows that."

"Okay, you can laugh," McKeach said. "But you keep on for-gettin'—the things that everybody knows, most people in fact *don't* know. And those're the things we *do* know, and make most of our money on.

"So I think, What if what this great player wants to have hap-pen *isn't* what the fans want—huh?

" 'Fuck them, and fuck the fuckin' team,' he thinks. 'What're all them fine white folk doon fo' *my* ass? I'm just a big nigger from Harlem to them. Who's playing this fuckin' game anyway? Who's the talent here?' Get yourself in *that* frame of mind, then you don't give a shit about anybody else—just want to do *your-self* some good."

The dark imitation Gothic spires of the convent school high on Maugus Hill to the left ahead of them made columns of solid darkness against light pollution generated by the gas stations and fire station clustered in the valley of Wellesley Hills beyond it. The building had been converted years before into a Massa-chusetts Bay Community College, and the lights in the windows of the evening-class rooms below the towers burned like camp-fires.

"Keep in mind now, this's twenty years ago. That's a long time. Lotta things've changed since then. Don't seem that long a time, two old guys like us, but to most people and in lots of things it is. Pro sports is one of them. NBA didn't draft kids out of college then, they still had some eligible years left. Even they dropped out first year, never played a game. Which meant they either played the four years or else they sat on their ass 'fore their chance at big dough legit. And that was not as big then either.

Teams gave bonuses back then, sure, but only to the guaranteed top players. Which Walterboy was not. He was good, yeah, no question, but he was no Larry Bird.

"Word that I'm gettin' while I was inside was that for a player, he may not've been that burn-the-world-down *good*, but he was fairly smart—which not all of those guys are. So I figure if he's smart then he knows at least what I know about his pro future— pretty much a tossup. And I also figure, 'He's this smart, he wants money.' Why else do people do things? What the hell else is there? Money more than anything. And if possible, money *today. Now.*

"This is the other thing that the people who bet on his team to win this game themselves want, and therefore think that *he* wants. But the difference is that he can *do* something to make the game come out the way he wants, and they can't. Therefore if I am right about him, he'll know how to find somebody who will give him serious money to do something so the way the game turns out, as far as *he's* concerned, the result will then be *great*—for him. For the people bet on it, it will've come out bad. If I'm right when the time comes, he will do the *different* thing than they all expected, them and the sports books too, and his team will've *lost*—or at least not beat the spread.

"Naturally I didn't know *how* he'd do this, make it happen, but I was pretty sure he would, and so I got down on it. And I make ten grand on ENC over Kansas, taking points."

"That's the kind of bet I would've made," Cistaro said. "Only suckers gamble."

"Exactly," McKeach said. "Now today, he's got three-four of his buddies in there with him. Not all as big as he is but they're not exactly *small*—and anyway I'm not there like I went there to make trouble. So I tell him all of this, everything I just told you. I feel like I know him from before, even though I really don't.

"And then I say to him, all right? Still trying to be nice. 'When

I hear you're in my territory, naturally I think, "This is the same Walterboy that I know of from a long time ago, I think we can do business. This's real good news."

"'So I make it my business to run into you out here and I make the connection, all right? You don't know it but you did me a good thing a long time ago. I'd just as soon do you one now. I mean, it doesn't set me back too much and not too many other people hear about it. So I don't then have them comin' around all the time and asking me, you know, how come I do this for you, this spade from out of town someplace who's not even from around here—and I won't do it for them. This's a good deal I'm offering you here, and all this talk and stuff you're now givin' me about it, I don't expect I'm gonna get that, I first told you what it is. Throws a wrench into my plans.

"'But look, it's gettin' late here and I gotta be someplace. So look, all right? It's ten thousand dollars a week. You had at least a hundred kilos of the white stuff in here for three weeks now, and nobody bothered you. *Reason* that it happened that way is because this is my turf, and even though you didn't ask me when you first come onto it, I find out that you are here, as I always do, you're on it as my guest. You owe me seventy thousand bucks and you're gonna pay it me, now.'

"And you know what he *said* to me, in that woman's voice of his? You know what the fucker *said*? He said—first he laughed at me, all these big white fuckin' teeth shinin' out at me, like he's got a string of pearls in his big black fuckin' *mouth,* puts his head way back and *laughs*—and he actually then says to me, 'Go fuck yourself, white man. I go where I *want* to go, and where I go's *my* turf. *That's* why nothin' happens to me—where I am, I am.'"

"Where the fuck're you, all of this's goin' on?" Cistaro said, anger bubbling in his voice.

"The old Wheelers warehouse," McKeach said. "West Roxbury? You go out by the railroad tracks there, follow them on top the hill? Road bends to the left and you keep on goin', pretty soon you're gonna find yourself comin' out back on Route One. You with me there so far?"

"There'a shopping center there," Cistaro said. "Then a big fuckin' movie theater, whole buncha fuckin' screens, and a couple discount stores and some kind of a big car dealer, sells about a dozen different makes. I forget the name."

"That's the place," McKeach said. "Brick building anna parking must cover three-four acres, dunno how much land they got, a really huge-big parking lot."

"Yah," Cistaro said, "I know the place you mean. Last time I was by there, forget what I was doin', snow was onna ground. Not too much though—most of it'd melted out there onna parking lot. Dead weeds growin' up all over, stickin' up through holes, the pavement. But Wheelers trailers're still out there, way down back there by the tracks. Made them look like they were lonesome, made me feel a little sad—six or eight of them, you know? Bright yellow and red paint they used to use, used to see them everywhere—'THE WHOLE WORLD ROLLS ON WHEELERS.'

"Now you don't see them no more. What happened to that company? Who owns that big plant now?"

"You wanna know something?" McKeach said. "Fact is I don't really know. Some kind of business in the front part. This small sign out front, not sure really, what it says. 'Something something Systems.'

"Like it's one of those computer things nobody else can understand. Bookkeeping for other people, got their own businesses they mostly run all by themseves but they don't wanna keep their books. Basically the same thing as Maxie does for us—keep track of the money, how much we got of it. But Maxie also brings it in, which I don't think they would do—all they do is keep the books.

"I think they rent front space from whoever owns the building now. Who's out back or what they're doin' there? I doubt these people inna front know or even care who that is, what they're doin' in the space or bringin' in and keepin' there.

"Us, the way I first heard about it, whole back the building being absoutely vacant, I was over Marybeth's house havin' dinner one night, maybe three-four years ago. She invited me, said, 'We never see you anymore—you got to stop around more.' Which of course we both know they don't's because if there's any chance at all that Emmett might come along, then she doesn't dare invite me. Because Emmett told Caroline some years ago, and she then told Marybeth, he first made superintendent, he realized she'd still wanta keep in touch with her sister. And that naturally this would mean now and then that they'd also be having dinner, sometimes, one house or the other, with Marybeth and Peter. And that kind of thing would still be all right because he always did like Marybeth, and what with Peter being in what to him always looked something like real law enforcement—Peter's in industrial security, New England district manager, Watchguard Security—him and Peter'd still be all right.

"But as far as *him* still seein' me? Well, he knew Caroline probably would, time to time herself—just by accident. She was over Marybeth's and I happened to drop by to see Peter about something—that would be perfectly okay. But he personally hadda stop doin' it. He just couldn't afford it anymore, him now bein' command level, if word started gettin' out, newspapers or something, he's associatin' with known felons. Such as me. Even though I dunno what kind of big change it could've made made, his goddamned career, him makin' superintendent, him and Caroline her sister and her sister's husband havin' dinner, Peter's house, and Pete's brother dropped by.

"I mean, Marybeth didn't marry *me*, for Christ sake—she married my brother, Peter. And as to what the hell *I* do, or did, no matter if it's right or wrong, Peter never had a fuckin' thing to say or do with it. Don't believe me then ask him. So how do *I* figure into this, Emmett bein' superintendent? Never really understood that." He growled, abruptly, like a dog frustrated chained.

"Anyway, like I say, I'm over there one night havin' dinner, Peter-Marybeth's house—which I did fuckin' *buy* it for them, goddamnit, gave them the fuckin' *money* for. Back when Peter's makin' chump change, workin' an installer, back 'fore he started doin' good. It's not like I got no *right* there, don't *belong* there.

"Anyway, I'm there havin' dinner, catchin' up with my brother, talkin' various things, and at one point I ask him what he's been up to lately. Not that I expect much of an answer— that being the type of question he doesn't ask me very often, either, or expect much of an answer the few times he does. But this time, I dunno, I did, and he says they just took on what to him's a fairly interesting client, kind of a challenge, really—'The old Wheelers Moving Company headquarters building, not that I guess it's that old—built around nineteen-seventy or so.' And do I know where that is, so forth.

"Well as a matter of fact I do know. That's the place me and Jimmy Locatelli got into the night after Jimmy heard the Collier family art collection was bein' temporarily stored there, and the next day we took it. Right out the pike, just before the Charlton cutoff."

"*Sure,*" Cistaro said. "I forgot you guys did that. All the Rembrandts in this collection, biggest one in private hands——"

"Cezannes, actually," McKeach said. "Not quite as valuable as if they'd've been Rembrandts, but still, worth lot of money. All this crime-prevention equipment they had then, pressure plates and infrared rays, all that kind of fancy stuff every dog kennel's got today but nobody had back then—no one could figure out how the hell we did it. And it was simple. We just got on our coveralls, got in the back of the truck while they're loading it with the paintings the day before, up in Peabody. Guys from Wheelers thought we're with the estate; guys from the estate thought we're with Wheelers. Rode in with the paintings that night, in the back of the trailer.

"That night while everybody's focused onna warehouse and the yard, guards and dogs and lights all over the fuckin' place, walkie-talkies all around, biggest worry I had was that Jimmy's fuckin' snorin's gonna wake up one of those monster German shepherds Wheelers used to have around when they had real valuable cargo, and someone'll search the truck. But they didn't.

"And then the next day onna turnpike, me and Jimmy get the gas masks on, light off smoke bombs inna back. Cops behind it in the unmarked cars see the smoke all comin' out, think the load just caught on fire. Radio the fuckin' driver, 'Pull over! Load's on fire.' Guys're drivin' it and all the escorts, *everybody* stops their cars and then comes piling out, this great scene beside the road, everybody runnin' round, shootin' off fire extinguishers and screamin', 'Someone get a fuckin' fire truck!' Drivers from the company pop the doors the sides and back the trailer? An' while all of them're piling in, lookin' to see where the fire is, hopin' they can put it out 'fore it ruins all the art, me and Jimmy light a long fuse on a string of two-inch salutes. And then we come piling out, shooting off our *own* extinguishers. Nobody pays attention to us; nobody even sees us. Jump inna cab, keys in the lock, start 'er up and wait a couple minutes, seems like a couple days, hopin' no one notices engine's started up again—and also that we didn't make the fuckin' fuse too long so someone finds the damned salutes, or steps on it and puts it out before the things go off. It seems like a couple *days.*

"But then, *bang-bang-bang,* start going off, and that sets off this huge stampede, people jumpin' out the fuckin' trailer, now they think it's gonna blow, an' we're watchin' in the rearview mirrors, watch 'em fallin' onna ground, gettin' back so they'll have cover, and I say to Jimmy, '*Hit it!*' and he sticks it into gear.

"By the time they see what the hell's goin' on, figure out what happened to them, we've gone off an exit about two miles away, got the trailer on a culvert, throwin' paintings off the bridge, and down below there we've got Jimmy's little brother Joey and this other guy we had, with a Ford deuce-anna-half on the two-lane underneath. Me and Jimmy, laughin' so hard we can hardly grab the paintings—could just barely hear the sirens catchin' up to us when we tossed some more smoke bombs inna trailer and went slidin' down that slope on our asses, laughing like bastards all the way."

He laughed again with the pleasure of the memory. "That was one great fuckin' day. Kind that makes you think you'll live forever. Nothin's ever gonna stop you now." He snuffled.

"Anyway," he said, "me and Peter like I said, two of us're havin' dinner, and he tells me about the warehouse, how Watchguard just took it on. 'And naturally, of course,' he says, 'as long as it's still vacant we're not gonna keep a man on duty in there day and night, guardin' empty space. We'll have a man swing a patrol car by there, two or three times every day, three or four times every night, regular door-shake detail, and we're on good terms with all the cops, so that's all that it should need. If the cops see there's something wrong, doesn't look quite right to them, they'll of course give us a call before they go bustin' in. And if we find there is something we think they should take a look at, well then, we'd call them.

"'But just the same, we don't want to be bothering them every time kids start hangin' around there weekends. Maybe use the parking lot to fly their model planes, drive their radio-controlled cars. Make ourselves look foolish.

"'So, you get around, you hear things. You get wind there might be someone doing something there that doesn't sound quite right to you, appreciate it if you'd, you know, take a look around the place. See what you can find out. And call me, you know, if something's wrong, something you can't straighten out, and I'll then call the cops.'

"So I been doin' that ever since," McKeach said. "I go there and I see something, then I take a look around. And if the guys I find in there're reasonable people, we can do a little business. 'Til Walterboy, they all have been. Now and then I duke Peter a few bucks, help with the kids' college fund, which he appreciates—fuckin' kids can *buy* Harvard now, if they want. I mean, if a guy's own brother *asks* him, what else would a guy do?"

"Absolutely," Cistaro said, "absolutely. I think it's a beautiful thing."

9

LILLIAN WEYMUSS STOAT—"DO CALL ME Lily," she always said upon introduction; "Ducal Melilly," Cheri Farrier christened her, snickering—lived with her second husband, Darren, in a grey white-trimmed two-story, seven-room, two-and-a-half-bath townhouse at 4 Gaslight Terrace, Number 7, in Framingham. Using about 2.8 percent of the million or so she'd accumulated in her investment portfolio by investing the quarter-million lump-sum settlement she'd received nine years before, pursuant to a prenuptial agreement, when her first husband, Wallace Weymuss, a former Memphis undertaker, divorced her (his fourth wife), she'd provided all of the 20 percent down payment of $27,000.

"Wallace was much older'n I was of course when we married—he was sixty-*one* and I wasn't even *thirty*? But the way he lived and all, he'd stayed all tanned and muscled, very nice flat belly and all his parts still worked real good—well, you never would've known it.

"He'd sold out his family's funeral business a long time before—he was the fifth generation run it? By the time he came along the family owned and ran eleven homes in Tennessee, one across the river, Mississippi, in West Memphis? People used to say that if they didn't lay you out at Weymuss's, you couldn't've been really serious 'bout bein' dead. But then that Service Corporation British thingamabobby there that goes around all over the damn world buyin' up the mortuaries fast as they can find them, they come into Memphis, and the way he sized it up, it was inev-able?

"Wallace is a fine man, but first and foremost—and he will tell you this himself—he's a businessman. She mimicked him effortlessly, with delight entirely free of malice. " 'Specially in the business of grief management? Cain't let your 'motions rule your haid. The business'd been in my family, and a big part of our life, too, for a ver' long time, 'most ninety years. But times change, and so do ways of doin' things, and I had to change with them—that or just get left ahine.'

"So he didn't let his sentiment get in the way of that, of doing what he felt simply had to *be* done. Single-family ownership just could not compete with this big international corporation. So sooner or later they're goin' to own *everybody,* 'cause the ones they couldn't *buy* they'd just run out of business? And the way Wallace looked at it, the one who sold the first in any given town'd get the best price from 'em—simple as that. And that if that was how it was goin' to be, then the one who got the best price in Memphis was goin' to be *him*.

"I learned a lot from Wallace.

"His first wife, her name was Rosalie, she told me that he made it sound like he was doin' it purely for those business reasons. 'All that talk he made—I admit he took me in. "This here's shape of things to come, wave of the future. Training in bereavement psychology, therapy and counseling; the scientific approach to grief; latest techniques getting to closure. And logistics, economies of scale and so forth. In the very near future, during our own lifetimes, I promise you, this's literally going to become the only way to go." Oh, he could go on and on. But the real reason that he did it was so he could spend more time rodeoin'. Wallace does like the ladies, but he may like rodeoin' more.'

"He was married to Rosalie twen'-seven years. I have met her and we talked about it, what it was like being married to Wallace then, when she was, and when I was, seven years later, his fourth wife, and neither one of us could see much difference. I think she's a nice lady—even if she did get most of his money so there wasn't that much left for his later wives like me—'cept for the annual dividends. Which was a lot, I'll grant you that, but nothin' like what she got. I said somethin' like that to her once, when we're havin' cocktails? And she said I was a real smart girl and I had that exactly right. 'I did the same thing with Wallace that he did with the family business.' That was what she said to me. 'When I saw how things were goin', well, I didn't like it, but at least I was the first to cash him out, so I got the best price.'

"I got to know all this before I married him because just like I promised my daddy, I stayed in school during my year as Miss Memphis, traveled back and forth to Knoxville making my appearances during junior year, finished my BS in marketing, graduated with my class. And then my first job was executive assistant to the vice-president of private banking at the Memphis Safety Deposit—Mister Roland Dexter, he's a good friend of my daddy's. My daddy said that if I studied Mister Roland Dexter while I was workin' for him, I would learn a lot about all smart businessmen. 'And one thing you learn is that no businessman who's really smart will mind it in the slightest if he happens to find out that a real good-lookin' woman also's a real sharp-*thinkin'* woman. If he's as smart's he thinks he is, he'll like her even better.'

"And my daddy was right about that, like he was about so many things. That's how I met Wallace. Mister Dexter put me in charge of keepin' track his portfolio, and also let it slip Wallace was *single*? And so then when I first laid eyes on him I was so *impressed*? There he was in his western shirt and leather jacket, real tight jeans and these gorgeous handmade boots? And I said to him, 'My goodness, sir, this's how you look? Reviewin' your portfolio, its extent and all, I don't know, I guess I must've expected a much older man.' He did seem to like that."

At the time of purchasing the townhouse she had wholeheartedly agreed with Darren that the wisest financial course for them was indeed as he suggested—to leave his government pension fund and his IRA undisturbed in the admirable mid-six figures they had reached during his twenty-two years of bachelor frugality and maximum allowable deductions from his FBI pay. That way they would not only avoid severe IRS penalties for early withdrawal but prepare for his late and her early fifties a bountiful thirty-year federal retirement, to cushion nicely their transition into a doubly rewarding second career for him in state law enforcement or the private security sector and for her, as well, continuing her midlife blossoming as a freelance certified private investment counselor.

"Back in Tennessee, most likely, but somewhere in the middle South, for sure—we both still got family there." That downpayment contribution—"as long's the place goes in my name, of course" (as it did), "you're still young and in good shape, but one thing you learn bein' married to a mortician; take the cash and leave the promises for someone else, 'cause anybody's light can go out any time, and often does, they least expect it"—enabled her to think happily of his savings as theirs and of their residence as a desirable small parcel of northeast residential real estate and thus one of her shrewdly diversified investments. She did not conceal that view of things from others.

The first evening when Darren came home from the office and told her he had agreed with Jack, without consulting her, that it was Darren's turn to host a dinner with Nick and Arthur, she said that meant that they'd be six for dinner. She said that that was good because it meant she could make a nice leg of lamb or a beef Wellington, either one of which was just too much for less than six people, and no matter what anybody said, no one really liked to eat leftovers, and no matter how comfortable they might be in life, by which she meant well fixed, she did "just *abominate* waste, like my daddy always taught me, 'never throw good food away.'"

Darren explained to her that in fact Cheri Farrier had not been invited and would not be coming, just as Lily had not been invited to the first two such dinners he'd attended with Nick and Arthur at Jack Farrier's brick townhouse on Adams Street in Quincy. Lily said at once she didn't see what that had to do with it, since she hadn't been able to move north to join him until almost eight months after he was transferred to the Boston office and this organized-crime-squad cloak-and-dagger business that he'd never been mixed up with anything like before, by which time he'd already been to a couple of those funny dinners.

"Of course I hated being separated from Darren, all that distance, but I'd just barely started my MBA program at GW and I didn't want to lose the first-year credits. I knew if I got them I could transfer them up here, so I finished out the year." She confided that to new suburban Boston clients attracted to her in part by her MBA from Babson. To Darren she said, how could she have been invited the two times he'd already gone to Farrier's "for those hush-hush dinners of yours" if they had happened before she'd even come up or gotten settled in, or so much as met Cheri Farrier, and she said she therefore couldn't understand what that had to do with whether Cheri should come to *their* house when *she'd* be cooking one of them there. Or why Cheri wasn't even going to be *invited*, if that was what he was telling her, as apparently it was.

"Dearest," Stoat said, "the reason is because apparently a long time ago when some agent named DeMarco, and Nick and Arthur, started this... oh, I don't know, this *custom*, long-standing *practice*, where they'd get together and have dinner every now and then, to talk about, you know, what's going on in the circles that they move in, have their business interests in, so forth—no one but the handling agent and the Strike Force group supervisor were included.

"It wasn't a custom of excluding *women*; it was a matter of confidentiality; excluding *everyone*, of *either* sex, who wasn't directly involved. So Nick and Arthur could talk freely about their competition, LCN, which's primarily what we're interested in and they hate as much as we do—where our interests coincide. What the local LCN, the La Cosa Nostra people, they seem to've been up to, and it looks like they're probably going to be *doing* during the next two or three months. What they've picked up on the street. What the local hoods're saying."

"But these men, they're real criminals, aren't they?" Lily said. "And you and Jack're FBI, and you're supposed to be *catching* them, and putting them in *jail*—aren't you?"

"Well, of course," Stoat said, "that is and remains our stated mission. And that's basically what we're doing, all the time we're doing this, every time we do it. Finding out what the criminals're doing, what it is that they've been up to, and making plans, arrangements, so that we can either stop them from doing it, catch them in the act, or if they've already done it, the crime has been committed, then how we can set things up to get the evidence that will then enable us to go into a grand jury and charge them—and then bring them into court, and try them and convict them.

"That's what the whole *purpose* is of these dinner meetings. Jack and I get together, meet with them, a given place, we all think it will be safe, we won't be inadvertently giving more away to the enemy than we're getting out of it ourselves. Now, do we *enjoy* ourselves when we sit down and have this kind of dinner? Well, I can't speak for the others—although I suspect that Jack does—but I personally do not. They're not my kind of people, Nick and Arthur—they make me nervous. But it's part of my job, and I have to do it.

"And fortunately for me, the way it's evolved over the years has been so that there isn't any set interval—so that you could go to your desk calendar and say, 'Well, let's see now, next week have we got a meeting scheduled?' And then find it and say, 'Yes, and this time it's at Jack's house. Seven-thirty Wednesday.' It's all very clandestine. We don't keep records. Jack'll say to me, he runs into me in the hall, he'll say to me he thinks it's time again we got together. 'With the lads, you know. Next Tuesday be okay?' *Without* using their names.

"What I'm saying is that this's all on a strictly need-to-know basis, that we even *have* this confidential relationship with them. If someone from the outside asks us if we have it—could be another law-enforcement agency, state police, IRS, DEA, or ATF, doesn't matter who, U.S. Attorney's office—what we do is deny it. 'Nope,' we say, 'it isn't true.' No matter who is asking."

"You lie to them," she said. "To the other cops, and prosecutors."

"Well, they almost never ask," he said. "Law-enforcement people as a breed're quite closed-mouthed. Fact is, I shouldn't even be telling you, but I know you know how to keep secrets, so *you* can get the stock *before* it shoots up, not after. But if someone does ask, you *have* to lie. This's *not* something we want to have everyone—meaning even other agents, in our own field office—*knowing*, all over the place. There'd be a leak. Someone might get killed. And even if they didn't, that'd be the end of it, all the good that it's accomplished. And I *can* tell you this much—it's been a *lot.*

"This case Jack's working on right now, will be for next several weeks—he's got eleven men working under him processing the raw surveillance tapes that're *so* darned important to this all-out anti-LCN effort that we're making here. It'll put the New England Mafia pretty much out of business. This is a major, major case, and it's one Nick and Arthur helped us make. Helped *Jack* make; it started long before I got here. We simply would not've ever been able to've made it without this relationship that Jack inherited some years back from this agent named Fogarty. Who trained Jack before he retired. As *he'd* been trained by DeMarco.

"Jack tells me DeMarco originally developed it twenty-five or thirty years ago purely as his own idea. This sort of association wasn't an established specialty within the bureau, that agents were trained to carry out. But since DeMarco, every agent who's followed him in here has used his formula, developed and nurtured the association over the years, this relationship 'with the lads.' Jack's in the process of training Bob Hinchey, so that when, as and if Jack moves on, say up to SOG, Hinchey'll be ready to step into line.

"These informal dinners have been very significant in the cultivation of the relationship. For years and years the agents've been setting up these occasions to meet and have a meal, the agent in charge of running 'the lads' and whoever the squad leader is; maybe some wine, a few drinks—although I've noticed Arthur never really has that much to drink, no more'n one or two; 'fraid of losing control, I suppose. And, well, just *talk,* man to man, in a calm and relaxed kind of atmosphere, a quiet setting free of pressure.

"Secure. Where you don't have to be wondering all the time

who might just happen to walk in, you know, as they might very well do in a restaurant or a bar—as anyone could; public places, after all. Then you'd never know. Who'd come in, not recognize *you* but recognize *them*, sitting with *you*, and as Jack says, 'Whoosh, all your covers're blown.'

"Because they'd then go and buttonhole someone else and say, 'Who's that with Nick and Arthur?' And the other guy'd recognize *you*, and the two of them'd think, 'Hey, that's kind of funny—what're *they* doing together?' Find it a little strange—FBI guys'd be having dinner with these particular two guys, talking like old pals, like they've known each other a while, and have something in common—as of course we do, but we don't want to *publicize* it.

"And so, having it in our homes this way, we avoid that danger, see? This way we can talk, and that's how come we do it, three-four-five times a year. Or so. One guy or the other's place—just to keep in touch. So we know what's going on."

"But they're still criminals," Lily said.

"Well, yeah, yeah, sure they are," Stoat said. "But when we get together like this, very quietly, sub rosa, they can then feel protected telling us what they've been hearing the LCN's up to. Then we know where we should be watching for."

"But I thought this big case that you're making *is* this Carlo Rizzo," Lily said. "That you've got him now, and all it is now is a matter of time until you bring him in."

"Well, it is," he said. "And the way that we *made* this big case against Rizzo was by Jack some time back taking what Nick and Arthur told him, and following it up, tracking down the leads they gave him, and then putting it down in the affidavits that he made up for the assistant United States attorneys, Warren Marsh and this new girl he's got working with him now, name's Andy Sung, the Chinese tiger, Andrea Sung—very nice young woman, even tougher'n he is. And they then went before the judge and presented them as the basis for warrants under Title Three, U.S. Code, which deals with wiretapping and electronic surveillance, that kind of thing. She's an expert on it. And the judge said those affidavits did the job and gave us the orders to do the surveillance, and we did, and now we're processing what we got from it. And when Jack and his group get that done then we'll give *that* to the AUSAs and they'll play them to the grand jury, and——"

"Oh, I don't care anything about all that stuff," Lily said. "And don't talk to me like I'm a child and you can put me off with all this mumbo jumbo. The point is that you want to have Jack Farrier and two big criminals from the underworld to dinner here in *my house,* and me to get out of the way, and before that I assume you expect me to shop for it, and set the table for it and maybe even cook it——"

"I don't expect you to do any of those things," Stoat interrupted. "And if that's the way you feel about it, I don't want you to. This's my house just as much as it is yours—you may've made the down payment, but I'm the one who pays the mortgage and the heat and lights and everything else, with *my* money that *I* earn, while you go to your investment clubs and have your coffee with the other women investing money that *they* got off of men, one way or the other.

"I wasn't *always* married to you, keep in mind, and I didn't starve to death then either. I've shopped for food hundreds of times, and cooked plenty of meals in my time—served them and cleaned up the joint afterwards, all by myself, before I had you floating through my life and in my home every day like the vision of loveliness you are. And if you want the gospel truth, your chicken cacciatore doesn't hold a candle up to mine, and since what all four of us agree Italian's the kind of food we like to eat, I not only *can,* I'd just as soon—I'd *rather*—cook it myself."

Lily gazed at him thoughtfully. "You're afraid of him," she said.

"Afraid of who?" Stoat said. "Afraid of the lads? No I'm not. Not as long's I'm FBI, I've got my badge and gun. If I *wasn't* FBI, I was only a civilian, and I found out that those two guys were sniffin' round my business, *then* would I be worried or afraid of them? You're damned right I would be. Those guys're dangerous."

"No, not of them," she said. "Jack Farrier—you're afraid of Jack."

"I am not," he said. "Jack reports to me, for Godsake. I don't answer to him."

"On paper, yes," she said. "But we don't live on paper, honey. We live in the real world, and that's where you're afraid of him."

He did not say anything for a few moments. Then he swallowed. "Not really," he said. "It isn't really fear. It's ... look, all right? This slot's my make-or-break assignment. I didn't really want it, myself, that much; I was happy where I was, doing what I was doing. But this assignment was a plum. I personally know three guys in Washington, well, two other guys in Washington and the other one's second desk in Chicago, that were *pantin'* for this job here, absolutely *droolin'* for it. Would've done *anything* to get it. And they weren't the only ones. Jack Farrier wanted it, too. He was already *here,* and then there are at least two other OC guys, one down in Miami and one in Buffalo, that I got leapfrogged over ..."

He let his voice trail off, shook his head and spread his hands. "I told you at the time that Lanny Ellsworth was the one behind it. Lanny in the office of professional ethics and responsibility. My sponsor and good friend. Always has been. Used to be my boss in plans and policy. He's going to be moving up pretty soon. It's wired—to assistant deputy director, which on paper's one of the five third-highest jobs in the whole FBI, a very powerful office, but for *my* money's one of the five *second*-highest. The director's a political appointee. He's a very sensitive one, and if any future president's ever foolish enough to think he can do what Nixon did and appoint another empty suit like Two-day Gray, he'll find out in a hurry the same thing Nixon found out thirty years ago—you can appoint a loser director, if you get your heart set on it and the Senate goes along, but don't screw around with the bureau itself, or mess with career FBI guys— the outfit still means something to us, and we'll protect it, against the world.

"I told you, when you said you didn't want to leave Bethesda, at first I didn't want this job—it was Lanny's idea I should take it. He said, 'When I go up where the air starts getting thin, I want it so that you go up along with me—I want someone I can trust watching my back for me. But unless you've done something besides sit down here and read reports, something in the field that I can point to and say "This shows he's got the street smarts too," someone with another guy in mind for the same job is going to be able to shoot your plane right out of the air.

" 'This thing up in Boston is a year or eighteen months away from becoming a career year for the guy who's running the show when the big balloon goes up. So go up there and be him when it happens—run the circus. You've run lots of other stuff, and when you supervised assessments and evaluations, you showed us you know how to manage.

" 'Contrary to widespread belief, that is all the guy who runs the OC squad needs to know. Not who dumped Kid Twist out the hotel window back in Prohibition days, or that Lucky Luciano's real name was Salvatore Lucaina—no, what he needs to know is the same stuff that the guy in charge of the fraud unit needs to know or the chief of the antiterrorism unit needs to know; which agents're doing real good work, and which one's let his personal life get in the way of his duties, to the point where his buddies' efforts to cover up his problems've impaired the unit's function. And then first what needs to be done to stop it, and then second to have the common balls to do it.

" 'Those qualities I know you've got, so I know you can do this job. Now go up there and do it, and then come back here combat ready. After a year or two in an all-out pissing contest with the Mob, paper tigers in this place'll look to you like little pussycats.'

"So, all right—didn't want to be, but I'm here. The other guys who wanted to be here are not. But on paper they're still more qualified'n I am, and you can bet that they're still watching, waiting for me to slip up—just once. And Jack Farrier—he won't do anything to sabotage the job, just to make me look bad. But anything that he can do to make it so that anyone looking at it down in Washington would know I may've been the man in charge but Jack did all the work? That thing he will do.

"So, no, I'm not afraid of Jack, but I do have to be careful. Not to do anything that he might interpret as my trying to usurp credit for something he actually did. And also not to make any real dumb mistakes that he could use to undermine me at SOG. Get on one of the back channels that these old OC hands all have, every single one of them, and fix it so when this thing breaks, he's the only fair-haired boy.

"If I went up against him now, stood up and challenged him for being cozy with the lads, I'd be questioning what's been under way in the Boston bureau, in the OC squad, for about thirty years. If I said 'This doesn't *feel* right, doesn't *smell* right, doesn't *look* good—maybe we should pull back here,' I'd be bucking a tradition set down by guys who went on to become *legends* in this specialty—just as their work was about ready to bear the precious fruit they cultivated so long and patiently all the years I was doing something else, completely unrelated, down in Washington." He paused two beats. "My FBI career'd be over. I'd be *crucified*."

She said, "Pigs don't bear fruit."

"Oh, cut it out, Lillian," he said. "I don't have a choice here, I have to play the cards I've been dealt. And that's really all's involved here—take my word for it."

She gazed at him for a long time and then she nodded. "Well, okay," she said, "if you say so. But it still looks funny to me."

He gave that some thought. Then he nodded. "Well, I'm sorry to hear that," he said. "But I also have to remind you that if things work out the way that Lanny's got them mapped out, and I do get that promotion to be his deputy, then that would mean I'd go up about four pay grades, plus a lot more in the pension poke, every year thereafter. Just—like—*that.*" He snapped his fingers. "And the way that I recall it, that kind of consideration's always been important to you. Or did I get that wrong?"

She smiled and patted him. "No, you got that right," she said. "You boys have a real nice dinner."

10

STOAT HAD HAD THE TOWNHOUSE to himself since late afternoon when Farrier arrived and rang the door chime—the first
seven notes of "Dixie"—just after 6:45. Having filled the house
with the smell of tomatoes, wine, sage, garlic, and chicken, dou-
bling the cacciatore recipe; turned down the heat under the pot,
leaving it to simmer; and disposed sensibly of the half bottle of
Chianti Classico left over from from the preparation, Stoat had
run out of things to do and appropriately drink alone shortly
after 6:00, and was genuinely glad to see him. Smelling strongly
of wine, he led Farrier to the left from the front entrance into
the entertaining area, making a gesture with his left hand meant
to suggest that Farrier select a place either on the black leather
couch or one of the two black leather club chairs flanking the
coffee table.

But Farrier instead stood still at the couch and looked on, a
smile at his mouth, like an adult watching a child deal with a
new kitten. Stoat snatched up the thick oatmeal-colored china
navy mug of tea steaming atop the copy of *Time* open on the
coffee table, and, muttering "guess we can turn this damned
thing off now," bustled somewhat unsteadily toward the twelve-

inch Hitachi TV set on the rotating base at the wall end of the pass-through counter between the kitchen and the dining area, as though to shut off the ABC Evening News with Peter Jennings. But after veering right into the kitchen and disposing of the tea in the sink, he appeared to have forgotten that intention, and Jennings, with an air of weariness, continued with a report of "yet *another* in the recent series of fatal confrontations between rebellious Palestinians and Israeli troops in Jewish settlements along the West Bank of the Jordan."

"Get you something?" Stoat said in the kitchen, rinsing the mug. "Now that you're finally here I was thinking I might have an actual drink myself."

"Got a beer?" Farrier said, sitting on the couch. He clasped his hands in his lap and the amusement disappeared from his face. "I'd been sort of off it quite a while, last summer sometime. Forgotten how good a beer can taste. And then Cheri had me invite Bob Hinchey over our place Saturday, meet another one of her new girlfriends from the flower shop—I tell her that it isn't gonna happen, but she isn't gonna rest, she gets him married off again. Although I do have to say if any one of the candidates oughta have a chance, this one should—legs that go all the way up and a rack should be insured with Lloyd's of London. Brain about the size of a peach pit, but if a man could block his ears a couple hours, once or twice a week, tell her slowly and distinctly what to do and when to do it, she could be a *memorable* lay. Too bad Bob's still so damn *Catholic.*"

"I didn't know he was one," Stoat said idly, opening the refrigerator and bending from the waist, peering into the lower part of it.

"Oh, yeah," Farrier said. "He doesn't make a big thing out of it or anything, cram it down your throat, but one the reasons— he told me he's been divorced since ninety-one, never remarried or even lived with a woman since he left his wife in *eighty-two*. Sixteen nonfuckin' *years*. I doubt he's even had himself a one-night stand along the way—to do that you at least have to recognize when a woman's coming on to you, wants to get laid and she'd like you to do the decent thing. But I doubt our Robert'd let himself. That'd be... *adultery*. Told me he doesn't understand how Clinton can behave the way he does. 'Not a Catholic, I know, but it's against his religion too.' As though Slick Willie had one."

Stoat, moving articles around in the refrigerator, said "*Damn*."

Understanding Stoat's comment to refer to something other than what he had said about Hinchey, Farrier said, "Anyway, instead of a bottle of cheap red wine, he brought a twelve-pack of Corona. So I had one. And it was really good." He laughed. "'Course then I had three *more*, which's far too *many* you accept Cheri's expert opinion, but that is a real good beer."

"*Ahh*," Stoat said, his voice coming out of the refrigerator, "as a matter of fact, I do have beer." He straightened up. "I got Pete's Wicked Ale and Watney's Red Barrel. I like to try various kinds. Which you want?"

"Gimme Pete's," Farrier said. "Ale, beer, it's all beer to me. And that English stuff—must be fresh, they drink it there. Lukewarm. But the time they get it bottled and they ship it over here? *I* think it's stale."

"Pete's it is," Stoat said, pulling two bottles out of the refrigerator with his left hand and closing the door. He arched his back and rubbed the small of it with his right hand. "You know what I'm gonna get someday?" he said, turning toward the counter opposite the refrigerator. "When I retire and quit moving around, get a real house of my own, my very own damn building, single-family dwelling, no other people living other side my outside walls? Where I can play my CCR and Eagles, BST and Chicago, and my Janis Joplin CDs just as damn *loud* as I like, any *hour* that I like, the rest of my damned *life?*"

"You devil, you," Farrier said. "No. A putting green? Or maybe a real beer tap?"

"A real beer tap, half-keg in a little icebox? They make those now—home beer taps. Expensive, but it might be worth it. But no, not that. What I'm gonna have is a refrigerator where the part I have to see into to find the stuff I'm looking for, like a beer when I want one, is the part I'm looking into when I'm standing *up*. Instead of the part I practically have to get down on my hands and knees to look into it, and the part I *don't* need to look into, except maybe Easter and Hallowe'en, the damn freezer, is the part on the top." He opened the first beer. "You wanna glass?"

"Yeah, you don't mind," Farrier said. "I never did get into this new-vogue thing, drinkin' long neckers outta the bottle. Never appealed to me, somehow. Tried it once—gave me gas."

"You're probably too old for it," Stoat said, putting the two beers and two pilsner glasses on a circular pewter tray and starting toward the living area.

"That's probably it," Farrier said. "That's usually the explanation for most things I don't understand lately."

"Something, anyway," Stoat said, bending again to set the tray on the coffee table in front of Farrier. As he straightened up, Farrier leaned forward, picking up a bottle and a glass and tilting it in order to pour the beer down the side. Stoat backed over to the club chair nearest the door and sat down. He absently watched Farrier pour as though not really seeing, seeming to have become lost in thought.

Farrier put a two-inch head on the beer in the glass and sat back again on the couch. He looked at Stoat. "What're you, you're not having a beer? Or're you saying grace there or something?" he said.

Stoat shook his head once, frowned and collected himself. He leaned forward and took up the other glass and bottle. "No," he said, duplicating Farrier's care in pouring. "No, I was just thinking, is all." He put the empty bottle on the table and sat back.

"Dangerous habit," Farrie said. "I'd have to check the manual, but if I recall correctly it's not generally approved for SAs with less than twelve years' experience, at least nine of which've been in Interstate Flight to Avoid Prosecution—or Transportation Stolen Motor Vehicles, also always a crowd pleaser. About what?"

"About the Frogman, mainly," Stoat said, scowling. He drank about a quarter of his beer. He kept the glass in his hands. He shook his head again. "Lily isn't comfortable, what we do with these guys. Having gunsels in our homes. Says it doesn't look good. Of course she's not your basic FBI wife—she's always had her own career, had it long 'fore she married me, and she came to this later in life'n most the bureau wives I know. Doesn't have the same outlook."

Cheri Farrier mocked Lily Stoat every time her name or her husband's came up. "*Oh,* Ducal Me*lilly,* with all her *degrees?* She's so fuckin' smart, somebody tell me—how come she married that *dork?*" Farrier lived in mixed dread and thrilled anticipation of the night when Cheri after too many vodka tonics at a bureau Christmas, farewell or retirement party, instead of taking off her high-heeled sandals and dancing on the bar, as she still did now and then, or going topless as she had one night in Buffalo—when she was still but resentfully married to her first husband, to wild approval that night and stern reprimands next day—would commence her imitation of "the internationally famous belle of Memphis, *Lily—Weymuss—Stoat.*" He had timed one private performance at more than eight minutes, and found it hilarious, so much so that he knew a more public one before Lily and other bureau people who also knew and disliked her would be devastating.

"Ah, background doesn't matter," Farrier said at once, smoothly. "*All* the wives I've ever known who found out about it, got to know about it—and I mean every single one of them—Helen Fogarty; Don Hulse's wife, Jill, and Bobbi Sherman, Kenny Sherman's wife, when they worked with Fogarty; my wife *Cheri,* for heaven's sake, and she's a bureau brat from the day she was born—*none* of the women married to men who got close enough to this understanding Al developed with the lads, they actually knew about it, *saw* how close it was—*none* of them've ever been comfortable with it. Ever." He paused and thought a moment. "Maybe it's a guy thing; they just *can't* understand it."

"It's not a matter of *understand,*" Stoat said. He drank some more beer, and seemed calmer. He belched silently, inflating his cheeks and then swallowing. "*Understand*'s only the word that they use. And as usual they're not being candid with us. What it is is a matter of *like.* Or *approve.*" He shook his head. "Which they don't." He kept the glass in his hand. "McKeach and the Frogman," he said. "The two of them, coming here—bothers her. And therefore, it bothers me, too—some. The Frogman especially. Bothers me, I mean. I mean, I *know* he's evil, 'cause I know what he does. He *has* to be evil, to do that. But we don't seem to have much *on* him. He doesn't *have* a record, to speak of. Some juvenile stuff. Sealed. Service record, navy—medals—actually looks very good. Fine." He shook his head again, frowning. "But otherwise—*nope,* can't find out that much about him. How do we know he's for real?"

Farrier laughed. "Okay," he said, "one thing at a time. First thing, about the wives—I'll buy that. May have something there—it's not that they don't understand it—it's that they don't approve. But this thing—well, bear with me here, now; I'll get back to the Frogman."

"Okay," Stoat said. He finished his beer.

"'Disapproval,' okay," Farrier said, "probably part of it. But there's another reason all the women always get uneasy when they get around this LCN stuff. It's not because they think it's violent. It's because—and I don't think they even know this, or realize they know it if they actually do? It's because the OC squads remind them of the clubhouses we had in the woods, when we were kids. The best thing they had about them was the signs—'NO GIRLS ALLOWED.' Always had those signs—in big red letters.

"Which they never would've seen if we hadn't shown them to them, let them know they were excluded. The treehouses and the forts we used to have, you know? I assume you Rebs had them too."

Stoat laughed. "Oh yeah," he said. "*Ours* had Confederate flags." He frowned and studied the empty glass, the residual foam brownish on the sides.

"Right," Farrier said. "Well, the mob still has them. Grown-up, adult, dangerous men have all the rituals and stuff, the voodoo initiations with the holy cards and finger pricking, and the taking of solemn oaths? You look at this objectively and you have got to think that basically it's *silly*—it is *really*—*silly*—*shit*.

"If you brought a smart woman into one of those super-secret, mystic-shrine, *omerta* ceremonies, all right? Unless you had her bound and gagged, she would bust out *laughin'*. 'What the *hell* is goin' on here? Have you guys all gone *nuts*? What time's the tooth fairy arrive? Are we goin' trick-or-treatin'?'

"Because *organizationally*, before they get to what they do and why they do it, that's what the Mafia is, what it amounts to—a big fuckin' treehouse, the exact same kind of thing. The boys're a lot older, and bigger, more brutal, but otherwise it's the Secret Blue Knights and the Shady Lane Outlaws and that stuff. It's a wonder they don't have softball leagues." He paused but Stoat did not laugh. Farrier picked up his glass and drank about a quarter of it. He set the glass down again and contemplated it. "You know, that's really not bad beer at all."

"It really isn't," Stoat said, appearing to rouse himself. He considered his empty glass, turning it in his left hand. "You know," he said, thoughtfully, "I think I might have another one." He stood up with it in his hand, looking at Farrier. "You?"

Farrier shook his head, laughing. "No, no," he said, nodding to his glass. "I still got some of mine left. But you go right ahead."

"Well, I will, then," Stoat said. He bent and put his glass on the coffee table and turned away. "You keep talking, though," he said. "I can still hear you. This's all stuff I should know."

Farrier shook his head and smirked at Stoat's back as he disappeared into the kitchen. "Oh, I dunno," he said. "It's all ancient history, going back to the Crusades, Sicilians getting together and arming themselves to fight off marauding Christian knights returning from the Holy Land. You've done all right without it, so far. We work in the modern day."

Stoat returned to the entertainment area with two more bottles of Pete's Wicked Ale. He put one down on the table and poured the other into his glass. "For when you're ready," he said, nodding toward the second bottle. "Save me a trip." He sat down, heavily.

"Thanks," Farrier said. "Anyway, the only real differences between the LCN and other big-boys' social clubs like the Lions, Elks and Moose're the outlawry and the violence. LCN *exists* to break the law. And in addition to being a *violent* fraternity, it's also a union. Used to run—still *tries* to run—a closed shop. The guys who belong to it got their invites to join because the guys who already belonged to it and did bad things for a living spotted *them* doing bad things and said, 'Hey, this kid's got *promise*. We don't need him competing with us. Let's ask him to join.'

"In the old days if he didn't join they killed him. Or if it turned out he really *was* as good—meaning as *bad*—as they thought, or were afraid he was, then he killed off *them* to take over the club."

Stoat drank some of his beer. He had begun to look contented.

Farrier, observing Stoat drink, picked up his beer and drank a long pull. "This's the basic difference that makes women nervous when their husbands hang around with Mafia.

"Generally, FBI womenfolk all tend to be fairly clean-cut, like their husbands—in most cases even more so. My first wife, Linda, all right? I met Linda when I was a junior at Saint Louis U, majoring in English, and among many other BOMC things that I was doing, I was taking ROTC—and doing very well at it. I was expecting to become cadet colonel in my senior year, and then when I got out, in nineteen sixty-nine, I was going to be commissioned, and then go to Vietnam.

"Now, I was *different* than the kids that everyone remembers, the late sixties, seventies, using drugs and getting laid, demonstrating 'gainst the war. This did not bother me—I *wanted* to be different. I was probably going to be assigned to JAG—in those days the army was so glad to see a college boy who actually wanted to go, he generally got what he wanted. That'd look good on my law-school applications when I got out three years later. And if something happened, so I didn't get JAG, then I had a lock on Intelligence. For law school, almost as good.

"So, when I met Linda, Linda Slattery, in October, junior year, her freshman mixer at Fontbonne College—where well-to-do Catholic couples from Missouri send their comely daughters to take courses in education and music and browse Saint Louis U for husbands—my future through the next seven years was pretty much *set*, all mapped out. Senior year, my army hitch, and then three years of law school—I *knew* where I was going.

"Knocking Linda up was therefore *not* on my agenda. *Getting* knocked up was not on Linda's; she wanted her degree. Purely a case of raging hormones, temptation—no condoms, of course; good Catholics didn't carry such items—and opportunity. One warm weekend at her parents' house, spent the day out by the pool, Linda in her white bikini, spilling out of it. In the evening we're alone—old folks seeing *Showboat* at the Light Opera. *Off* with Linda's white silk panties; *in* with my stiff dick, and in a jiffy, there we were, prospective parents ourselves, having to get married.

"Both of us were absolutely *flattened.* This was a *disaster.* She was going to have to drop out of college, and Linda's a smart girl. Children were for later. She wanted her education and a shot at a career, and she'd wanted me to have the one I'd planned on, too—what'd looked like a bright-line armed service, then legal career, made to order for a shot at politics. Which we'd already talked about, politics as a career. Now all those dreams were in shambles.

"So we did what you do—the best we could. We'd get married, which'd take care of the family-disgrace matter—hard to believe now how all bent out of shape people got about that then, unmarried women getting pregnant, but they did.

"Being an expectant father I was now exempt from the draft, but unlike most horny guys caught in the tender trap, I had a contractual service obligation—I'd taken all that lovely ROTC pay, and now I'd gone and done something that made it look as though I wasn't going to keep my promise to serve. So my father and Linda's father pulled all strings they could locate, and somehow they cut a deal so that I could work it off if I got accepted by the FBI. Which I did, no trouble.

"It was like *morning.* Everything was *golden* again. This was *great.* Farriers and Slatteries—all of us were patriotic—we *all* thought it was great. I could do the right thing by this lovely young woman that I'd ravished, who'd loved every blissful minute of it, and still serve my country, too? Redemption during *this* life—it was wonderful.

"Point of it is, if any young FBI couple should've been able to weather the stresses that come with the job, you would've thought it'd be us. But by the time I got to Buffalo, our marriage was in trouble. I'd already started spending more time on my career when I was still in Houston than I had on the two of us—and by then our *three* kids. And then once I got to Buffalo I just about disappeared.

"See, being brand new there, no one on the street knew me. I was a natural for the Strike Force, hanging out the strange joints and keeping the weird hours, up to no good with strange people. Working under cover, you lead a whole new different life. And you really have to *lead* it, act like a real hood yourself. And furthermore, you'd better make it *convincing*—wise guys get really pissed off when they catch on one of their big pals is an undercover cop.

"We were so damned *young*, compared to you and Lily. Besides growing up in University City and going to college, all that Linda'd ever done in her whole life was be Mrs. John H. Farrier and the mother of his children, married to the FBI. She *defined* herself that way, but *now* all of a sudden there she was, all by herself, East Aurora, New York. We had a nice place; it's a nice enough town, and she did have the kids—but *I* wasn't there.

"I *couldn't* be, being Franny 'Soot' Barillo thirty miles away, just blew into Buffalo from LA with a whole load of connections in the movie business. Soot called it 'the industry'—you could *tell* he'd been around. I could do that shit then, be Soot Barillo—I'd been Soot in high school, I was playing ball, lots of black hair I still had, and so when somebody said 'Soot' I quite naturally looked around.

"Anyway, the upshot was I discovered I had a positive knack for it. I *loved* being someone else, especially a gangster. Gangsters live large; act like they don't give a shit, even though there's always some cop watching them. *I* didn't have even *that* concern.

"So I was having a great time for *my*self, but with me out of character like that, Linda didn't know who she was anymore. Didn't know how to behave around *me* anymore, what little time we did get to spend with each other. And I had my share of trouble remembering how to act when I was with her. Made me kind of sympathize with actors, what they must have to go through, becoming different people every time they go to work." He leaned forward, picked up his glass, and drained it. He refilled it from the second bottle.

Stoat drank thoughtfully.

"Made me very self-conscious," Farrier said. "I couldn't let go of it, just be with my wife. All the time I was calculating, same way I did on the job—'Now, how does Soot Barillo act if he's suddenly around this nice, white, boring lady, who bleaches her own hair at home, wears shorts from Sears disguised as skirts? This nice young mom who takes such good care of her three kids while her boring workaholic husband's far away?'

"It was like I was *seducing* her, when I slept with her. Doing two mean things at once. Fucking around with this nice housewife while her nice straight guy was out of town, and at the same time cheating on my *girlfriend*—which I had, by the way, after three weeks in the part. Told myself I had to—Soot was just that kind of guy.

"Of course I had a wife somewhere. Everybody's got one. Soot's wife's name was Irene. We got married way back in our early twenties, hardly remember it now. She's a good broad, cosmetologist, works in television, does make-up at CBS. We live in West Hollywood, nice little two-bedroom stucco, jacaranda the front yard and a whole damn bunch of jasmine, two blocks up from Beverly, one in from Sequoia. But Soot didn't see her much, you know? 'Always onna road these days.'

"Okay, you talk the talk and walk the walk, you better live the life. Soot in any town he went to, gonna be there a while, he would get himself a girlfriend, okay? Nothing *serious*, but hey, you know how it is, the guy's in *Buffalo*, for Chrissake—everyone knows how cold it gets there inna winter. It's even cold there inna *summer*. Besides, Denise's nineteen, *fresh*, with a *very* nice chest, ass; this chick is a *cookie*. And of course a pushover for a guy who's with the *movies*. *She* is Sootie's *type*, all right? It all fits together nice—if I corrupt union guys for the FBI, must be okay if I fuck Denise for my country as well. Part of the schtick.

"So now, this Linda chick—like what gives with this, all right? What's he doin' with this older broad? Soot's type she's not at all." He drank again and set the glass down on the table.

"When I was in the clubs and bars, the back rooms, all right? Everything's fine. When I did get home, long weekend I'm supposedly back in LA, 'taking care of a few things,' but I'm actually in East Aurora, *nothing* was right. Linda and the kids were just not Soot's type of shit at all—and neither was Soot theirs. I could've told them that, they asked me—Soot wasn't a bad guy at all; he was fun to be around—but he was not a family man.

"So after a while, lookin' back at it now, your basic unbiased observer, the fact that Jack's job meant that Jack and Linda couldn't spend *much* time together—that wasn't the real problem anymore. The problem was that they had *any* time with each other anymore. It was such hard fuckin' *work*.

"For the life of them both she could not seem to get it through her head that the rule was I was not supposed to tell her or anybody what I did when I was gone, where I went and who was with me. She was always after me. And when I did give in to her, allow myself to open up with her and *tell* her a little bit, not mentioning Denise, of course—it didn't make her happy. All I could do was hope to Christ I didn't talk in my sleep. Or *do* something, I'm screwing Linda, old times' sake—not that I ever minded screwing, and besides, she did *expect* it—that I'd learned in bed with Denise.

"Well, it sounded to her like I was getting so I actually *liked* these cheap hoods, and thugs, and gangsters—which I did; they're *funny* bastards, not always on purpose—and was getting more and more *like* them, the more time I spent with them. She could not understand that this was what I was *supposed* to be doing, putting my whole heart and soul into it. Not being her darling faithful husband, which of course I could assume she knew I still was, and always would be, but as a loyal, hard-working and *talented* special agent of the FBI.

"So that pretty much did it. We ended up getting divorced. We took the no-fault route, but she could've named either the Mob or the bureau co-respondent.

"Now *your* wife," Farrier said. "What she's got going for her, Lily—though of course she doesn't know this, and there's no way you can tell her, least that *I* would recommend—is that even with the Frogman and McKeach in your own house and eating dinner, you are nowhere *near* as exposed, nowhere *near* as closely tied up to the mob as I was, my days and nights, 'round the clock in Buffalo, being Soot Barillo. And therefore you're nowhere near as close to even *risking* being compromised— much less *killed*, as I would've been they found me out—as I was then. And I came through it, no stain on me—being Soot, in the life."

Stoat nodded, looking gloomy.

"Now, you said Frogman," Farrier said. "Frogman especially bothers you, having him here in your house. You and Lily too?"

Stoat nodded, and drank some beer.

"Aw right," Farrier said. He drank some beer. He set the glass down and folded his hands. He nodded and belched silently. "This's the story, the Frogman. Why no matter what you do, you can't find out much about him. Now don't leave the room, go to the bathroom, sneak out for a smoke, if you still do that—this's a very short story. Which shows you how smart the guy is.

"Nick Cistaro's father was a stonecutter. He worked for all the cemetery-marker guys, the harps who made the gravestones out of good old Quincy granite. There used to be a flock of them around here, like one on every corner, but that was when I guess the only way they had to cart the stones around to the grave-yards in various places was by horses pulling wagons. And they couldn't go that far. So the companies that made the markers hadda be near the railroads, to bring the new stone in, and then not too far from the graveyards, where the finished markers went. Nowadays they got the trucks, big heavy trucks and cranes for lifting them on and off with, so distance isn't a problem. But people still die—still hafta get buried, so there's still a lotta monument companies around. Just not as many.

"When Nick was a boy, the Corrigans and Carrigans, Mulli-gans and Moriartys, they all called Guillermo Cistaro when they had a new name needed cutting, and he'd write them in his book with a little stubby pencil, and every week he'd make his rounds.

"This week he went to the places where they sold the new headstones, putting on the names of people were the first deaths in their families since they came into this country. Then the next week and week after, he'd go to the cemeteries, cutting new names into old stones, an' the dates that went with them, under the old names that he probably'd cut into the stone years ago, when the stone was new.

"Now, you ask yourself, how can such a nice, hard-working, steady man have for a son a man like Nick, a gangster through and through? I have the answer for you. Guillermo never made much money. Nick wanted to make money. Lots and lots of money.

"He told me that himself, one night. We're in the Friendly Ice Cream there, Washington Street in Brighton, it's about seven-thirty and we met there for a sandwich. This isn't that long after Fogarty retired. But we've known each other, Nick and I, a good year or two by then, so it's not one of those jerk-off sessions when you spend most of your time sparring with each other, you know? Wasting everybody's time. I'm the third FBI guy he's had now for a contact, and we're all pretty much the same—I am not that different. And after Buffalo and then workin' with Fogarty here, it's not like I still think a wise guy's got hooves and a long tail, keeps a pitchfork in his car. We've both now long since reached the point where we can both relax and have a cheeseburger without shittin' our pants.

"And he said something, not important, I forget now what it was, exactly, but the gist of it was that he'd passed this cemetery that day, two of them actually, both sides of the road.

"'There I was,' he says to me, 'I'm just comin' in from bein' down on Route One in Norwood there, all mornin', where I hadda see a guy, comin' back LaGrange Street, West Roxbury, all right? Two cemeteries—Saint Joseph on the left and Mount Benedict on the right.

"'I start thinkin'—all the days, and there was a lot of them, winter, summer, didn't matter, that my father spent out here, kneelin' onna buncha rags, sittin' on his wooden toolbox. Rain comin' down on him, year round, snow fallin' on him inna winter, wearin' gloves with no fingers in 'em so that he can hold the chisel—this was how he made his living.

"'Well, I take care of my family. I take care of Assunta. I take care of our Regina. I take care her little sister, Angela, with the bright eyes, and I take care of her brother, Giacomo, and his little brother, Nicolo, him with the sad eyes, my father always said I was too serious, boy should have some fun, but Nicolo, with the sad eyes, and we have a happy life.

"'Never heard the man complain. "Did he ever have a day like I am having now?" I think? "Where everybody's after him, he can't get nothin' done?" No, I doubt it very much.'

"'Well, sure,' I say to him," Farrier said. "'Probably he didn't. But you got a complicated life, and unless I am mistaken, you went and you made it for yourself. Did he drive out to those graveyards in a big black BMW sedan, climate control for heat on cold days, cool on hot days, for what'd cost an honest citizen ninety thousand dollars? Did he have to juggle time he spent with a stylish girlfriend and the time he spent with Assunta, so neither one of them felt neglected? And balance the money he spent on the two of them, neither one had her feelin's hurt?'

"'Well, no, he didn't,' Cistaro says to me, 'but that's the whole point of it, see? Why *I* did it. Why I can do those things. As hard's my father worked, every fuckin' day his life—get up inna morning, have some breakfast, coffee, always coffee, lots of coffee; make himself some sandwiches, big black Thermos full, more coffee; go to work with his toolbox, on the trolley, least when I was a kid; got his first Ford pick-up third or fourth hand, naturally. He was so proud. I remember that—I was eight. So then after that he drove, least made it a little better—though the truck cost money, too, it was always breakin' down. Come home at night, exhausted, beat to shit; have some dinner, go to bed, rest up for another day—he never got nowhere.

"'Watched him do it, day after day, I was growing up. Never makin' any progress, never gettin' anywhere, and I thought, "I dunno what I'm going to do, don't know where I'm going to do it, but one thing I do know, I grow up, I'm gonna make a lot of money."

"'And everything I did since I was twelve years old or so, I did to keep that promise to myself. May've changed my mind a lot of things, seen some people come and go, but the one thing stayed the same, and is never gonna change—no matter what I do, I will make a lot of money. Always have more than I need, and then even more behind that.

"'Now I figure,' he tells me," Farrier said, "'I sit down and I think about it, and the one thing that occurs to me right off when I start thinkin', is, "Okay, if I'm gonna make the kind of money that I need, kind that I have got in mind, which is a lot of fuckin' money, there's no doubt that I'm gonna hafta do some things that aren't gonna always be strictly by the book. I mean, I'm not gonna be a doctor; never gonna run a bank. No one's comin' up to me some fine day when the sun's out, and sayin' to me, 'Well, don't *you* look like a good smart kid—bet your momma's proud of you. Here's a couple good-sized oil wells, see what you can do with them.' I'm gonna have to know how to take care of myself and then I'm gonna need somebody who can show me what to do."'

"The thing that people never seem to realize about these guys," Farrier said, "is that the ones who really make a mark for themselves in the underworld, start from scratch, and rise up through the ranks until they get to the very top, or damn close to it, and then *stay* there, *and* stay *alive,* until the day that they retire, is that the *ways* they do it, strategy and tactics, 're very similar to the ways that ambitious honest young guys make their marks in the legit business world. Or in the government. Gain position, they're still young, any way they have to do it. Build on it as they get older. Make alliances and break them, and surround themselves with friends. I don't think the Harvard B School has a Mafia professorship, and I doubt anyone who's qualified'd be interested in an offer—couldn't take the cut in pay, much less pay taxes on his earnings. But in the abstract there's no reason why the chair could not exist; there's sure enough case histories, lots of problems still to solve as these guys change with the times.

"First of all, Nick finished high school and did not wait for the draft. 'You stayed in school because back then the diploma was your ticket to a good assignment.' As I also knew, of course. 'Then you enlisted, before they drafted you—got to pick your branch the service, the speciality you had in mind. So I did that.'

"What he did was navy, UDT—underwater demolition team. Became an expert in explosives. Also in commando tactics, sneaking in and creeping up on people, killing silently or making lots of noise and taking people by surprise so that by the time their friends reacted, he'd done what he came to do and gone away again. He was very good at it. Won himself two bronze stars and a fistful of citations. 'Not an easy thing to do—medals *meant* something in those days—when the point of what you're doing is to do it secretly, so that nobody finds out.' Told me that himself. 'That's why I'm the Frogman, just in case you think I'm just a piece of shit who doesn't love his country.'

"The second thing he did was make the decision he would never touch a thing that didn't feel right to him. 'I can't tell you how it is that I know when something doesn't. It may look perfectly okay to anybody else, but to me not a thing to do. But I know, I always know. I can't tell you how many times I said No, and shied away from something that looked prime. Sometimes I've been wrong, and missed out on a lot of money. But that's always been all right with me. My rule's always been that if I dropped out on four sure things, and everyone went in on them made a whole shitload of money, and I also passed on one cakewalk where it then turned out that everyone who went in went to jail, I was smarter'n all the guys went in on the other four.

"'You, you're still new in this town,' Nickie said to me. 'You been here what? A year or two. In this town that's like you just blew in yesterday. You been *here* a little while, five or ten years, say, like Al DeMarco was, and you find out what's goin' on, you will meet a lot of guys who'll tell you all kinds of things about me. I done this and I done that; I done the other thing. Sayin' that I killed guys, even, put them in the hospital? Well, let me tell you what to do, somebody tells you that. You say to them, "Now is that so? He sounds like a real bad bastard. How come I run him through the files, I don't find nothin' on him? J. Edgar's record and the Frogman's are identical. One of those guys at least is smart. You don't think—both of them?"'

"And then he looked at me and smiled," Farrier said. He drank some of his beer and Stoat, now morose, drained his second glass.

"So, all right, that's all he told me. Now the question is, what's he done? That we know about, at least, even though we can't prove it?

"When he came out of the service, he joined up with Hugo Botto. Hugo Bottalico of the South End, North Dorchester and Roxbury, parts of Rozzie and JP—before the blacks moved in."

Stoat shrugged. "Means nothing to me," he said.

"Didn't to me, either," Farrier said. "Fogarty filled me in."

The door chimes played "Dixie" again.

11

"I'm still learning here, of course," Stoat said, addressing McKeach as he reached over Farrier's right shoulder, first placing his knife and fork securely on his plate amid the chicken bones and tomato sauce, then lifting it deftly off the beige woven-reed place mat and placing it onto the pass-through counter next to McKeach's. "Seems like I should be up to speed by now, I know, been up here two years in May, but you guys and your competition committed a lot of history around here before I came on the scene."

He moved behind Cistaro and cleared his place, putting the knife and fork in his left hand and taking the plate in his right, bridging it across McKeach's and Farrier's plates. Then he put Cistaro's utensils with his own on his plate and, turning, lifted it onto the counter next to the two empty bottles of Chianti Classico Riserva.

"You know, you're pretty good at that," Cistaro said, talking to Stoat's back, tilting his chair and grinning mischievously at McKeach and Farrier. Farrier, lifting his glass, raised his right eyebrow. McKeach showed watchful disapproval.

"At what?" Stoat said, in the kitchen now, sponging the plates and loading them into the dishwasher, turning on the coffee maker.

"Waitin' table," Cistaro said. "Looked good with the wine too, openin' an' pourin' that. Like you knew what you're doin'—very smooth an' *professional.* Anything ever goes wrong with your day job, too much crime on your shift or something, you could fall back on the restaurant business. Be glad to call Marv Scotti, put a good word in for yah."

"Who's Marv Scotti?" Stoat said. "Never heard of him. See, there's another one I don't know—you know who he is, Jack? Is he anyone I should've?"

"*Sure,*" Farrier said, looking at Cistaro as he elongated the word, surprised amusement on his face. "I know who he is. Been here as long as I have, get to know most of the players. But I wouldn't say *you* should—be more concerned, you *had.* Wonder maybe you'd been waitin' 'til after I go home nights; goin' out by yourself without supervision, havin' me along—hangin' out with the wrong type of guys."

"*Hey,*" Cistaro said, "what kind to talk is that, now, 'wrong typah guys'? Marv Scotti's an upfront guy, perfectly respectable businessman."

"Okay," Farrier said, "we'll have it both ways—Marvy Marv's a respectable businessman, just the kind that only comes out at night. Places he runs're perfect for lunch after seein' your parole officer; go for drinks and dinner after an exhaustin' day takin' the Fifth before the grand jury."

"Well, nights're when he *works,*" Cistaro said. "That's when his clubs're open."

"'*Clubs,*'" Farrier said.

"Yeah, *clubs,*" Cistaro said. "He must own at least a dozen bars and restaurants. They got entertainment? *I* would call them *clubs.*

"Pretty fancy places, too, Darren—get in lotsa the big tippers. Getcha night shift, one of those joints, all the moves that you've got, you'd do all right. Might do even *better*, in fact, you forgot about payin' taxes onna tips, 'n you do workin' now for Uncle Sam."

"Got too much mouth on you sometimes, Nick," McKeach said, his eyes narrow and dead.

"Take it easy, Arthur," Cistaro said, showing irritation. "I'm just havin' some fun here."

"Jeez, Nick, *that* many?" Farrier said, eyebrows raised and amusement on his face. "He's got a *dozen* joints? I didn't realize Marvy Marv had access to that much capital—you and he'd gotten that close."

"Uh *huh*," McKeach said; he nodded once, his eyes glowing anger.

"Well, you know," Cistaro said. "Where he gets his money— that of course I wouldn't know. But I get around, you know? And he's the type of guy that also gets around—so I see him now and then. Tells me about various problems he's been havin', some guy he thinks maybe I can help him out with. But who backs him? I dunno. That I do not ask him, and I therefore couldn't tell you."

"*Course* you could," Farrier said. "And now I know too. You been *keepin'* things from me, Nick. I knew he had a piece, of course, the usual ten- or fifteen-point slice the owners give their managers, the guys who run the places. So they'll be on the owners' side and won't let the rest of the help steal 'em blind. In maybe one or two—in the Terrace out on Soldier Field, Beacon Tap in Brookline sure, he probably had a bigger interest. But those aren't what I'd call your fancy *joints*, exactly—and I had no *idea*, a *dozen*? You must really trust the guy. How long've you and Marv been runnin'?"

"*Hey,*" Cistaro said, "quit bustin' my chops, all right, willya? I'm just trynah give my friend Darren here a hint, you know? Some the contacts that we got, things we could do for him, day ever came he could use a little help."

"I could use some of that," Stoat said, putting mugs on the pass-through counter. "That's why, Jack, what I was asking you there, history of what happened here, ten and twenty years ago. Made things the way they are now."

He opened the refrigerator, talking into it. "The definite sense that I've been getting here is that this area's atypical, if it's LCN activity that you're talking about. I don't find the patterns I'd been told to expect. In other cities the mob's been well established and entrenched since the twenties, Prohibition at the latest—it's more or less a monolith, monopoly arrangement."

He paused and closed the refrigerator but remained facing the counter next to it. He shook his head. "Oh, yeah," he said, recalling his train of thought. "Didn't used to have it here, any great extent, at least. Mob came in quite recently, big-time anyway, after the Korean War."

"Well, it is atypical," Farrier said, gazing at Stoat's narrow back and shaking his head slightly. "That's what I've been telling you, ever since you first came up here—we started getting you embarked on this whole thing here." He looked at Cistaro and smiled.

Stoat, looking troubled, turned away from the counter next to the refrigerator and put a small pewter pitcher on the pass-through counter. Next to it he put a small pewter bowl with a small spoon in it, and placed four teaspoons between those pieces and the four mugs. He began pouring coffee into the mugs.

"Well, what you said about it so far, you've got it about right," Cistaro said. "The basic thing you *had* here, used to have here, there really wasn't any well-established Mafia. Like in other cities like, say, New York. When we were all growing up. I'm not saying that you didn't have your basic Mafia organization here, because you did. But it was small, the LCN—not that people called it that. They called it anything it was 'the Mafia.' Or 'the Mob.' Most people called it 'the Mob.' But no, back then it wasn't something everybody knew was *here*—like a *bank*, or the *church* or something. That you just didn't have. Things were much more fluid." He nodded and said it again. "Fluid."

"'Fluid,'" Farrier said, grinning at Cistaro now.

"Well, *yeah*," Cistaro said. "Take in my case for example. First got back here from the service, got discharged in fifty-four, October of that year. There wasn't any bunch running things around here that you would've called 'the Mob.' Except in the North End—there just *wasn't*. Oh, the organization was here, but it was small—a small beachhead.

"New York, you had the Five Families." He shuddered. "There you *really* had it—they ruled the *world*, and I mean *everything*."

McKeach stirred unhappily in his chair, moving his shoulders in the blue flannel shirt, hunching forward over the table, scuffing his fingernails on his place mat, frowning and working his mouth.

"You don't agree, Arthur," Farrier said. Stoat came around from the kitchen and put the creamer and sugar bowl at the center of the table.

"No, no, I don't," McKeach said, "but it's not because... it just don't make any *sense* to talk like that, bullshit kind of stuff." He shook his head again.

Stoat put a mug of coffee at each place and sat down at the end of the table at the pass-through counter. "You," McKeach said, squinting at him. "Someone like you comes in from down south, way out of town, and you're here a year or two, and you see you're not gettin' a grip on a thing. And you think, 'Well, now, why don't I know everything there is to know, how all these people here who lived their lives here'—and there've been a *lot* of us, over the course of the years. 'Everything they did since World War Two' is what you're asking, stretch of time I'm talking. Over fifty years. That's a lot of stuff to know.

"By now a lot of the players I knew're dead. And you? You *can't*, just by coming in here, find out everything they did. All you see now's the results." He paused and thought a moment. "I'm not coming at this right. It's very complicated.

"Look," he said to Stoat, "begin with you, all right? The reason I am sitting here, where I'm sitting now, and the reason you are sitting there, where you are now, and he"—looking at Farrier and indicating him with his right hand—"is where he is, and my friend Nick"—indicating him—"is where *he* is, and we're all here together"—using his right hand to make a circling motion—"having a meal an' talking? Just like ordinary people?

"The reason's Al DeMarco. One man—Al DeMarco. This was all his idea, and I don't think he even knew, at the time he's having it, just what the hell it was. What it would turn into. What it all would mean. So if you think you don't understand it, coming in now like you're doing, well, maybe none of us do, either, really know what's goin' on.

"Al. The first time I went away Al was already here, here with you guys, FBI. But he was new then. I knew him but not really that *much*. And he was just a kid. We were *all* kids then. Al and me and Nickie, although I'm not sure I knew Nickie yet. I don't know if Al did, if they knew each other. He might've."

"This would've been when, now?" Cistaro said.

"Fifty-three," McKeach said, looking solemn. "Went away in fifty-three. I was gone 'til sixty-two." He opened his blue eyes very wide, as though taking in a vista otherwise too vast to comprehend. "Over forty years ago, all of this got started. *Everyone* was just a kid." He shook his head wonderingly. "Jesus, forty years it's going on. Al's been gone now, what, the last eighteen? Me and Nick're the only ones still around, 've been involved since the beginning, an' we're old men now. Like Ted Williams, something. And it's still going strong." He pursed his lips. "It's really something, isn't it? When you think about it?" he said. He seemed not to expect an answer. He looked at Cistaro. "Anyway," he said, "you know DeMarco then? 'Cause I know he was around then, I come back from Leavenworth."

"No," Cistaro said. "I don't think so. Didn't know DeMarco then. Would've been right after when I got back from Korea. I was in San Diego one year, little *less*'n one year, ten-eleven months. Thought I might stay out there. Nice and warm. But what was I gonna do there? Didn't know nobody—all the guys I knew there I knew from the service. Pretty soon, they all went home. So that's what I did, after a while—need to have your friends around.

"Still livin' off my service pay then, what I saved up in the navy and I got from playing cards. So when I get back I didn't do anything, almost a year. Because basically I didn't hafta, had the time to learn ropes. How things'd changed, I was away. Didn't know where anybody fitted into anything. Who the players even were. An' that included Al DeMarco."

"Yeah," McKeach said. He considered that for a while. He nodded. "Anyway," he said, looking at Stoat again, "DeMarco was, and is, the key to all of this. And now I don't know where he is. I don't even know he's still *alive*." He looked at Farrier. "Al DeMarco still alive?"

"You know, I don't know," Farrier said. He looked at Stoat. "You got any idea, Darren, Al's still among us?"

Stoat feigned exasperation. "Now how the hell would *I* know?" he said. "Everybody up here's always talking, 'Al De-Marco, Al DeMarco.' I never kept track. All I know, I know his name. That's it—didn't even hear *that,* until I got up *here.* Since then I heard a lot of things. But all of them since I got here. Before that," he said, shaking his head, "I knew *nothin',* the guy. I ran into him on the street now, he could *bite* me—I wouldn't know who he is." He looked resentful.

"Well, I didn't know," Farrier said. "You were down in Washington, did a lot of stuff in personnel and so forth. So I thought, you know, it could be, might've run across him someplace, processed papers, current status, so forth."

"No," Stoat said vehemently, shaking his head, "take my word—it never happened."

"*Oh-kay,*" Farrier said elaborately, "we have now got *that* established." To McKeach he said, "All *I* know is he's retired—retired for what I guess'd have to be at least the second time. I got that from Fogarty, few weeks after I came in here. He was goin' down to Florida for some big dinner in Al's honor. One of the racetracks on the west coast, don't know now which one it was. He'd been their head, security, and done quite a job for them, so now that he was retiring, I think this's what Fogarty said; was turning seventy-five and this time he was gonna *do* it, really hang it up for good. So they're givin' him a time.

"Way I got it from Fogarty, this'd *not* been one ah those window-dressing cases where they hire a retired FBI guy to buff up the public image—who cares if he still can feed and dress himself? This was one bad situation. The DA was all over them for runnin' boat races—you could find out Tuesday before which horse's gonna win the fourth on Wednesday, you knew the right people. *All* that shit—dopin' horses, fixin' the trick bets, you know? The doubles, the perfectas, the trifectas, the exotics? All kinds of bad things. Licenses in jeopardy, stewards onna take, horsemen makin' statements sayin' they were pulling out. Had a lotta people worried; the track was a big part of the economy there.

"Well, DeMarco went in, and gradually after that the boys found out the rules'd changed. It took him a *hell* of a long time, but he finally got it cleaned up. And before he got it straightened out at least one guy, fairly well-known name, too, related to a senator—Entwhistle, I think it was—disappeared for several months; they thought he'd skipped to Brazil. But then he turned up; he'd been murdered. Found him in the trunk of a car at Miami Airport, and this'd been a guy with *clout.* So, had to've been a professional job. Al did not have an easy job there. I know it took him a while."

McKeach and Cistaro gazed attentively at Farrier. They did not react or look at each other.

"Ah, anyway," Farrier said, shaking his head as though to clear it, "I do know DeMarco's retired, and if Fogarty knew him half as well's he thought he did, he's most likely playing golf."

McKeach thought, nodding. The others waited. "*Golf,*" he said at last, drawing it out. "Fuckin' waste of time *that* is." He drank some coffee, black. Farrier used sugar and cream and pushed the containers toward Cistaro.

"Anyway," McKeach said, "the first fall I took, it was basically what it usually is, some wise young punk goes to jail—being stupid. What I did, I believed if you went in on a thing with Bernie Gallagher, you didn't have to worry. He was Brian G.'s brother, and therefore if he got his tail caught in the crack—because *he* fucked up on some *other* little piss-ant job that you weren't even in on—being Brian's brother he would *never* then just turn around and save his own miserable ass by givin' *you* up on the first job, the one you did with him—while leavin' *him*self completely out of it."

He shook his head. "You *knew* he would never do that, so much you never even *thought* about it, that he might." He drank some coffee and then set the mug down, clasping his hands around it. "And he did," he said.

"Oh, nice," Farrier said.

"Yeah, very nice," McKeach said. "The only reason that I didn't have somebody clip him then, right off the bat, was because when Brian found out what his asshole brother'd done, he made a special trip himself up to Billerica where they had me, and gave me his solemn word; he told me if I'd suck it up, and didn't pay off brother Bernie, like I had a perfect right to, then when I got out, well, he'd make it up to me, give me something really good—and take care my family, I was away.

"This was important to me. By then my father was really sick. After he retired, booze got him. Nothin' else to do. Down at Butchie Morgan's every morning by eleven—mother wouldn't have the stuff in the house, what it was doin' to him, and I didn't blame her. But at that point the reason, what was doin' it didn't matter. Peter was only fourteen. He couldn't do anything for them without droppin' out of school, which I knew from doin' it was not a good idea. If I was goin' away they needed someone lookin' out for them. Brian G. said he would do that? *Banks* took Brian's word. I said, 'I'll take the fall.'

"What Bernie G.'d put me in on was this big armored-car job in Methuen back in nineteen fifty-one, Daisy Arnold and them guys? Killed a Brinks guard. Got the chair, but it took two years to catch 'em? I wasn't on the job itself; wasn't anywhere *near* the place the day it happened—didn't even know about it until *after* it'd happened. All I did was, only connection at all that I had with it, was me and Bernie, I was doin' him the favor—we stole four cars they used when they were planning it, following the truck around and seein' where it went. But that guard dying, and then Daisy and them makin' it to Canada? Never should've come back, never inna million years—should've known what's gonna happen, they did. Once you run, you keep on runnin' 'til you *know* the heat is gone."

He scowled. "But anyway, before that, when the cops finely

got 'em? If the cops knew who you were, and what you looked like, before, and you were even in the *state* the day they did it, you were radioactive. Didn't even hafta ask; you just knew it—someone hadda hard-on for you, liked you real good for it. I was in the state and the cops knew who I was, and I knew who it was that did it because I did some of the stuff for them, but I didn't know where they were and if I had've known, well, still, I wouldn't've told the cops.

"So the cops naturally knew this, and they ran me, and I didn't. I got fifteen and did eight, old bastard Judge Ford, for doin' a favor for Bernie. That made me Kitty House's trophy; he was PD Boston. He's the one made Bernie flip and Bernie gave him me. Kitty gave me to the feds.

"Kitty wasn't a bad guy. I actually got so I kind of liked him. Used to see him now and then after I got out. He would come around, have a little chat with me. By then I think he felt bad for me, just a fresh kid I was then—gettin' all that time for what I did? Which was really nothing, you came right down to it, once they had Daisy and them, guys who really *did* it. If they *didn't* have 'em? Sure—'Make the little bastard sweat, and if he doesn't tell us hit him with the *big* hammer.' But by the time I go to trial, they've got Daisy and them. An' I still got *fifteen?* Just for stealin' a few cars? It was way too much.

"Kitty was just tryin' to be sure of no hard feelings. Just doing his job—I understood that. But once Bernie tipped me in and the wheels began to turn, what he could do about it? There was nothing he could do. So I *liked* him, all right? I had nothin' against him. But I never got too close with him, you know? Because of that very thing—what can this guy, you know, do for me? Not just *to* me; *for* me. And, no reflection on him, he just couldn't.

"Now with Al and Fogarty and you guys, one fed right after another—you *can* do things, and that's why we're all here. It ain't *love*, why we're doin' this, any of us; what we're doin' here, this is *business*. Boston PD? Kitty House could do things *to* me, put me in jail, but otherwise he couldn't do nothin' *for* me.

"Emmett Naughton? Same thing, couple years later. Also triedah get next to me. He makes detective, comes around. Naturally, he'd do this. I knew Emmett a long time, from the town. We're growing up, he's one of the guys—always see him around. His father was a good shit. He was with the Edison there. He'd help a guy out, had some bad luck, so his lights at least didn't get shut off. Emmett's the same kind of guy. Him and my brother, Peter—married sisters. I could've helped Em, I would've. Question never came up.

"I *have* thrown a few things his kid's way. Todd. While he's waitin' his name to come up, get onna cops. He keeps my cars, couple my friends' cars, runnin'. Also keeps his mouth shut. So I pay him more'n it's all worth. A very nice family, the Naughtons.

"So when Emmett approached me, back then—this's *before* he's married—I'm friendly, but I never do anythin' for him. I don't think he really expected me to. It was like he was playin' it safe. Like he could've thought, 'Hey, someday someone might come around and ask me, "You must know McKeach. You come from the same neighborhood, grow up about the same time? How come you never triedah talk to him?"' And he would then be able to say, 'Well, I did, back in—' whenever it was, years ago, now. 'But it never went anywhere.' See, to me he was like Kitty— a very nice guy, but he couldn't do nothin' for me. He just didn't have the resources.

"Anyway," McKeach said, "I am still in Billerica. I been tried, convicted, sentenced, and I'm waitin' transportation to the joint where I'm gonna do my time. All I'm doing's the only thing I can do—stayin' outta trouble. I got all this time to do, which I still say wasn't right, at least I wanna get out when I am supposed to, all the good time I can get.

"Al DeMarco comes to see me. He was also still pretty new here then, travelin' around town, checkin' things out, strikin' up a few acquaintances, few guys he might like to know. And I knew he'd been one of the FBI guys, the Methuen armored-car case. But when he came to see me, I had Brian's promise in my pocket. Too late for Al to do anything for me. So the day Al showed up I wasn't inna market for any new friends who're cops.

"And anyway, as even *you* prolly know, Darren, when you're in prison, you do *not* want people who're in there with you gettin' the impression you're real cozy with the cops, any kind of cops at all—and that included you guys, FBI, in *spades*. I know guys wound up with shanks in their backs, got that kinda reputation, havin' the wrong kind of friends. So all Al got the day he came to see me—*obviously* FBI, 'always make a good impression,' new suit, clean white shirt, dark blue tie, fresh haircut, shoes shined and everything—no one in jail lookin' at him would've thought he's Groucho Marx."

McKeach did not smile, but Farrier did. "But as good as he looked, all he got for himself that day was an inside look at the prison. I don't think he liked it that much, but at least he could get his gun back and walk out.

"So I do the time and get out, and sure enough, no flies on Brian G. Just like he said, Brian G.'s got something beautiful, nice and safe, lined up for me—collecting rent the bookies. In those days before they had the Lottery and the legal number, and also made it so all you guys could bug the bookies legal, those guys made very good, steady money. And even though I'd done some awful dumb things, back when I was young, I was not a stupid kid. So I know collecting bookie rents is something that if I don't screw it up, I can do the rest my life, make a damned good living, and never meet another cop who's on official business.

"But I'm still *young,* then. I don't have *sense* enough, be satisfied with that, this nice quiet living that I'm making, more money'n I can spend. Not that I ever went in that much for livin' high and so forth, but I *am* ambitious and I'm runnin' late."

He smiled tightly. "And after I've made money, I like to keep my money—see if I can make some more. I've always been the type of guy who no matter what he's had goin' on's always liked to have a little something *else,* you know? A little something of my own, goin' on the side."

His expression was calm, his tone the patient monotone, varied by occasional emphasis, that an earnest instructor would use addressing interested novices. "Now like I said, Brian G. was a good guy. He didn't mind guys thinkin' this way." He glanced around the table much as such a teacher would, making sure of comprehension. Cistaro was amused. Farrier was alert. Stoat's eyes were bleary; his mouth was partly open.

"Darren, *hey,*" McKeach said, reaching out with his left hand to shake Stoat's right forearm. "You still *with* me now, on this? You're the one, asked me explain—don't want you *sleepin'* on me here."

Stoat shook his head a little and opened his eyes fully. He moistened his lips. "No, no," he said, "wide awake. Don't you worry 'bout that."

"Well, all *right,* then," McKeach said, drawing his hand back. He picked up his teaspoon and toyed with it, fixing his gaze on the table, studying memory. "Brian G. was unusual. A lotta guys, the LCN guys, for example, they had a tradition. Old dagos called it 'wetting the beaks.' Younger guys—'Havin' a taste.' And they *didn't* mean, 'Let's you and me go have a drink.'

"The deal was that when you made a lot of money, more money'n you needed, and you wanted it to go to work—well, you know, you put it on the street. So it was makin' more for you without you thinkin' about it. And you could then concentrate on doin' what you'd been doin' before, to make it all inna first place—so that you made even more. Well, fine by them if you did that, but you hadda do it with *them*. You wanted to make money off the money *you'd* made workin' for them? You had to let them make money off it too.

"That was their rule, no exceptions. LCN guys always hadda get a piece of your investments. 'It's just a little piece,' they'd tell you, 'just the normal five percent. Not a very high price, the protection that we give.'

"Which it wasn't, a high price, for an *outside* guy doin' business with them. But *you* were the protection, the guy who went around to outside guys, if they either didn't pay for workin' their piece of the territory or butted in on some other guy's protected turf. Your boss called you in and he told you about this, either him not gettin' paid or guys not followin' the rules, and so then"—without altering his calm expression and even tone—"you went to them and said, 'Hey, you want your ears cut off, an' have me stick 'em in your mouth? And then I cut your dick off and use it to then ram 'em down your throat? That what you want, *asshole*?'"

Stoat's eyes were very wide now; his lower lip was slack.

"Which of course you probably couldn't actually do, because when you cut the dick off, it probably wouldn't *be* hard. Most likely be soft, you been talking to the owner like that." He chuckled. "Fact you probably would've hadda feel around in his pants for it, all shrunken up 'n' hiding, you decided, cut it off. But the point is that *you* doin' this, *you* were the protection, the insurance—it was *you*."

Stoat gaped. Farrier stirred uneasily in his chair. McKeach looked up at him inquiringly. "No, nothing," Farrier said, fluttering the fingers of his right hand. "Go right ahead, what you're saying."

McKeach nodded and looked down again at the spoon. Farrier caught Stoat's horrified eyes, and with his own gaze and a slight movement of his head warned him to alter his expression. Stoat shook himself again and resettled in his chair.

"Anna *reason* that it worked," McKeach said, "was because people knew that if some guy pissed the boss off, he would tell you to go around and see him and do something like that to him—*and* that you would *do* it. The people he did business with *knew* this.

"That was the kind of thing I did, when I worked for Brian G. And since I've been working for myself, for me, when I hadda. So the people Brian G. did business with generally did what they were supposed to do, and the people I do business with, the same kind of thing. For me. So as a result Brian didn't hafta *say* it very often, and I didn't have to *do* it—very often." He smiled. "Things change, but not too much."

Farrier managed a small smile. Stoat, plainly alarmed, glanced at Cistaro. Cistaro shrugged and smiled. "*What?*" McKeach said, looking at Stoat. "You didn't *know* this? That's the way it works. That's the way it's always worked. You're me and you are in the kind of business that we do, some guy owes you major money, say a couple hundred grand, or the same amount in something else that he was bringin' in for you, and then the first thing that you know, the silly bastard goes and tries to fuck you over. What the fuck you gonna do? Gonna go to court and *sue* him?"

McKeach's laugh was short and harsh. "No, you can't do that. He *knows* you can't do that. So, you would go and see him. Or you would send a guy like me or Nick to see him, and one of us, whichever one, would say something like that to him, about his fuckin' ears and so on. Meaning every word. And then you would say, 'Now you tell me, this's what you want me to do?' And then they generally paid."

Now McKeach smiled. "Of course when they didn't, when they made you make a point—it happens now and then, some-one hasta try you out. Well, then, as much as you might not wantah, you hadda do something. Cut off *one* ear, maybe, like I heard somebody did with that asshole high-roller broker who lived down there in Cohasset—what the hell was his name there? McGillavray? Couldn't seem to see his way clear, pay that one-thirty-seven marker he built up when the stock market kept on not doin' what he thought it was gonna do? Said he didn't have the money. Too bad, but hey, maybe sometimes it's the truth—the guy really can't pay.

"Well, you hate to see it when that happens, but you have to make him see that if he doesn't *pay*, he's gonna get *hurt*. Some people don't believe you when you tell them that. They think when someone gets hurt, it was an accident. A car crash; they tripped and fell down a flight of stairs. Not: someone else hurt them on *purpose*. So when some guy tries to give you some shit instead of money—'I know I oughta pay, and if I had the dough I would; I just don't have any now'—you have to make him *see*.

"So, do that to him. Let him walk around with that a while, go to work with one ear missin'. Explain it to everybody—'I was shaving, see? Use an old-fashioned straightedge razor, have to strop it every day. Genuine Rolls—my wife bought it in London for me, gave it to me Christmas. Really a beautiful thing, but you got to be careful with it. I wasn't. My hand slips. And as you see, I cut myself a little. It's nothin' really serious. Doc says in a month or two it'll grow back, good as new.'" McKeach paused, again, inviting laughter.

Stoat looked stricken. Neither Farrier, avoiding his eyes, nor Cistaro, keeping his eyes on McKeach, said anything.

"Right," McKeach said, shaking his head. "Jesus, I don't know." He laughed. "Okay," he said, "let's say it didn't actually happen quite the way I told it. I don't think he really did that—went to work with a bandage on his head an' tried to explain it. That was a *fantasy* I had there, benefit of all you guys. Like the old TV show? *Fantasy Island*? Midget inna black tuxedo'd come runnin' to the big tall handsome guy, white suit—'Da prane, boss, da prane'? I was just sayin' how it prolly would've been, if he *had* gone to the office. That make you feel better?"

None of the others said anything. McKeach looked defiant. "Look, even havin' to stay home, *asshole found the money to pay us.* Even found some *more* money, someone built him a new ear. But the word still got around, no doubt about it. The week after *that,* in this town, quite a long time after that, *everybody* paid on time. *Nobody* was late." He smiled. "And that's why that kind of thing hasta happen sometimes—'cause it *works. Reminds* people—makes 'em *believe* again."

Farrier snickered and gave Stoat a stern look. Stoat forced a chuckle. Cistaro looked at each of them and nodded, then looked back at McKeach, and with his face expressionless slowly, almost imperceptibly, shook his head once. He said, "That should do it, Arthur."

"Yeah," McKeach said, clearing his throat. "Well, anyway, the point is that anything you did, you went with them, the LCN, you always hadda do it so you stayed dependent on them. So they knew every dime you made, how you made it, and who off of, and could see if it looked like you might be building up a war chest of your own—might have some plans in mind. So they could then head you off. And that was what I didn't like, them ever getting bigger in this town.

"Brian G. couldn't see that—the LCN guys were a threat. Because he wasn't like that. But I saw if they got a foothold, they'd take Brian out. Make us all work by their rules. Brian had the attitude that if you were hooked up with him, then that meant you

were with *him*. Just like if you were hooked up, then he was with
you. And he was not gonna assume you must be cookin' something up against him if in addition to the things that the two of
you had goin', that you had with him, you also had a few things
goin' belonged strictly to you. Like he had a few things goin' that
belonged strictly to him.

"I myself personally back around the time when all the
trouble first began around here, you had people gettin' shot and
goin' down—everybody wonderin' the hell was goin' on—I
had quite a bit of money by then onna street. Plus which I was
still makin' more, myself, still workin' for Brian, doing what I'd
always done. So I had something to lose.

"I was not the only one. Before the shooting started, guys all
over town're doing good. Everybody makin' money, and nobody
gettin' hurt? You had Hugo Botto, Hugo Bottalico; he had his
business runnin' good, his part of town. You guys'll have to ask
Nick about how that was, if that's what you want to know, and
I'll stop talkin' while he tells you. Because he was with Hugo
then about the same way that I was with Brian G."

McKeach paused, an expression of inquiry on his face. Farrier and Stoat looked at Cistaro. Cistaro shook his head and said
"No" in a soft, clogged voice, then cleared his throat and said
firmly to McKeach, "No, no, you're doing fine. You were much
higher up with Brian'n I was with Hugo anyhow, know much
more about it. How it went, up at that level."

"Yeah," McKeach said, gazing at him and frowning. "Well,
keep that in mind here now, my friend, all of this's your idea.
Tellin' everything."

"Darren's ever gonna help us," Cistaro said, "he's gotta know
this shit."

"Yeah," McKeach said, "right." He turned to Stoat. "The basic
thing you had was Hugo Botto and Nick here, and a couple
other guys—they had Somerville and north of Boston. Malden,

Medford, Everett. East of Route One, along the beach—Lynn, Revere, Saugus, and the North End—mostly LCN.

"Botto's organization was a little bigger'n ours, by which I don't mean that he had all that many more *guys in it,* but it was so spread *out,* a lot more ground to cover, and so he hadda have more'n just the one guy, like Brian G. had me, workin' under him—to watch over all the other guys he had workin' under him. And Nick was one of his. But except for size, Hugo and Nick and two more guys operated Hugo's business in the parts of town he had just about the same as Brian G. and me did in the part of town we had, and *there wasn't any trouble.*

"Before the shooting started, only problem me and Brian G. had was the one you always had; it never went away. One or two guys, maybe more, but never more'n three or four, you thought were workin' for you, with you; they would get together and decide they could run it all much better, and keep all of what came in, if they split off and took the part of your turf you had them working in.

"Say, the financial district—sports bookin', loan-sharkin', some fencin'—hot jewelry for the hotshots' girlfriends. Rich territory. Now it's gonna be *theirs*—no cut for you. And they can make it even richer, doin' things you wouldn't let them do— like getting on the import end of bringing coke and grass in, dealin' in that shit. Which we never have allowed—still don't to this day.

"So I don't mean that the shootings came as a surprise. Sometimes it has to happen. But when guys started disappearing, and we didn't know the reason, or where the hell they went—few days later one of them'd turn up with a couple in the head—that was when we started to worry.

"Not always, now; sometimes when someone disappeared— guys would do that all the time, get to fucking someone else's broad, or someone else's wife, then hear the guy involved found out? And he wasn't happy, he'd been asking around for them, sit down and have a chat. Guys in that position often would decide the best thing to do was get out of town a while. So that could be a reason why a guy would disappear.

"Or maybe someone they knew dropped outta sight, and it'd go around he might've made some kind of a deal with cops, and he knew a lot of things that would make some people *nervous*— so *he* would disappear. Like guys do now when the talk onna street is the reason why you haven't seen someone a while was because he took Witness Protection. They didn't call it a 'program' back then, but the cops could do the same kind of thing." He looked sad.

"But back when I'm now talking about, with Brian and Hugo still in charge, when the guys started turning up dead, one by one? After the first one or two then you knew this wasn't some pissin' contest over a bum check that got outta hand, a beef about a loan that went south, or a fight two guys're havin' about a woman. This's now gonna be war."

He looked worried. "The first three or four guys—no one much cared about them. If they were dead then they were dead, and that's too bad, hard on their families, but the fuck, who's gonna miss 'em? Must've pissed somebody off. Can't go to war about fights over women and fights over money and somebody called someone out from a barroom—those things've had nothin' at all to do with business.

"But then the big guys get involved in private fights, one of *them* floats in onna tide? Reason don't matter—if he's big then his guys're involved, they don't have no choice. It's then a matter of honor. And besides, if the guys who *aren't* dead, if they expect to keep what they've got, well then, they'd *better* get involved too. Show some respect for their guy who is dead, and retaliate, right? Because otherwise the guys who did *him*'ll come around and do *them,* take over his whole territory. So—never mind *why* he got dead, he is *dead*—revenge is their duty to him, and themselves, to show they're still men, who don't stand for that shit to happen.

"So, I forget the order now, things happened in. I think two or three guys'd gone down, but only a couple, and no one knows what's going on. And then someone took out Brian G. A clear setup job, 'hind the old Boston Arena. Obviously someone'd called him on the quiet, 'Okay, let's have a meet, see what we do about this.' *Really* hush-hush—he didn't tell me about it, no one but Danny, kid he had drive him. Who also got hit, of course, but not fatal—he got better, I gave him a job. And where was I at the time? I was out gettin' laid—which I would've put off and gone with him, not that I would've liked the sound of it; would've tried to talk him out of it first. But he didn't tell *me* about it. Anyway, that took care of any doubt anyone may've had—if Brian was dead, it was war.

"After that things started happening fast. Rocco Monti went down two nights after Brian. Brother Bernie, heir apparent, all right? *He* thinks, little shit: alone with the cops he's a fist fullah butter, but now with, he thinks, Brian's guys behind him, now he's just fulla courage. Doesn't *dare* come to me, ask me do something for him, obvious reason. So he hired the guys that did Rocco, and naturally one of them, Sean McGary, shot off his mouth—so he's the next one to go.

"Then Bernie hires Mickey to work full time for us, Mickey Hunter, and that was one *mammoth* mistake—Mickey *loved* to shoot people; he'd shoot *anyone.* And then he'd tell anyone who'd listen all about it. Or anything else that he did. With Mickey, nothing he did ever was finished 'til he told a lot of people. So it got around fast he now had steady work, and someone said 'No, we can't take this,' and went and took Mickey out.

"Word about *that* got around, and pretty soon the rumor was, 'The talent's from Federal Hill—Providence.' Which of course meant the Mafia.

"Everyone *believed* it. It felt so right, they wanted to. Explained so many things—guys going down for no reason anybody knew—could their *friends* be doing this? No one wanted to believe *that*. So, the *Mafia*—of course.

"It's right about now that Al shows up again. This's when he makes his pitch. That's another thing he had—he had timing. He not only confirms the Mafia rumor, and gives me the obvious reason, I already thought of myself—he tells me what's gonna come *next*—and this's what gets my attention.

"Smarten up, kiddo—they're already here. Groundwork was laid months ago. Now all they're doing's expanding. You guys started shooting each other last year? They decided, 'Boston can be had.' So they put in what amounted to a new outpost or two, tested you out for a while. And sure enough, you showed 'em you're ready for the plucking—so busy clippin' each other, you didn't even notice them. They'd thought Boston was *ripe*, and it was. Pretty soon, you won't have the manpower to fight them.

" 'They think they can come in here now and set up an office, take over what you guys've built up. What Brian G. had and what Hugo has got, but won't have now for much longer—he'll be the next one into the trunk; only question now's which night and which Caddy. And then after Hugo they'll take out the Frogman—the same time they come after you. If you two guys don't do them the favor, which they think you might, of killing each other off first.

" 'And you know they're right about that. You're watching Cistaro now. He's watching you, and both of you're planning ways to get rid of the other one.

" 'Then no matter how many of your guys're still left, they'll be outnumbered—nothing to worry about. So what my fellow

Italians'll do then is what they always do, every place that they go in—buy up the local PD. Given what cops make, this's easy. And cheap. They're very astute about that.' I'll never forget him sayin' that. 'Very astute about that.'

"Al was a very intelligent guy, which was another thing. Keep in mind now, I am getting close to thirty. Got more sense'n I had than the first time I met him, I'm inna can. I listened the guy. You know how I know how intelligent he was? I can tell you how, very easy—he knew enough to treat me like I also was, a very intelligent guy. Not like I was an *educated* guy—which *he* was, went to Saint John's in New York, think he said—because I wasn't, and he knew it and I knew he knew it. So if he'd've pretended he thought that I was educated, I would've known right off he was a phony. But an *intelligent* one? Different thing—you don't have to have an education to be an intelligent man.

"Now, tell you the truth, I'm not really sure that was true, least in those days. Or that Al really thought it was, either. All I really knew, you came right down to it, was how to do things that if you didn't get caught would make you a lot of money. And if you *did* get caught would probably get you a fair amount of time—and then how to do the time. But even if he didn't think it, he was smart enough to act like he did, and since this was something that I naturally *wanted* to think about myself—everybody does, that they are intelligent—pretty soon he had *me* believin' it, too.

"Even got me readin' books. Al was a great one for reading—he was always talkin' about books, some book he'd just read, and enjoyed. So *I* hadda, too, to keep up. Understand what he's sayin' to me. Found out I could do that, no trouble—just never'd done it before. I got so I really enjoyed it. Which of course made me think, 'He is right—I am an intelligent guy.' Al DeMarco's one very smart man.

"'It's always the first thing they do,' he told me—now he's

back to tellin' me about the Mafia. 'And you should listen to me now; these're my people now we're talkin' about, even if I don't think much of the way they act and I'll do anything I can to stop them—I still know how they think. The first thing they do when they come into a new place is corrupt the police, and after that it's just a matter of time 'til they own the town.

"'After they buy the cops, then if *you* book a bet or shylock a loan, it's still against the law that the cops've never enforced, but now you are gonna get grabbed. Guarantee it—that's part of the deal they make. But if *they* do it, that's okay, and a cop standing next to them when they loan a guy five for six Friday won't see a thing going on. So unless you've now got as much clout with the cops as they will when they get up to speed, you'll be doomed the day they open up.

"'Newton's first law. The conservation of energy. A body in motion tends to stay in motion. A body at rest stays at rest. When the Mafia comes into a place or a community where they haven't been, they don't have an established organization, it's not because they think the people who live there don't want what they have to sell—it's because they know the market's there, and now that something's happened, they think they can take it.

"'They don't infiltrate convents and Cub Scouts, altar and rosary guilds—no money in those outfits for them. But they know they can make money in Boston running gambling, lending money, fencing hot goods, and financing people who hijack trucks and rob banks and so forth, because *you* people've been doing those things for years, and making boatloads of money. So all they have to do is two things—get rid of you, then take over your markets and expand them.

"'So, assuming you don't want this to happen, I think this's what you should do. First—unless I'm wrong now and you're not the boss and Bernie G.'s now in charge, you should sit down with Hugo and Nick, or maybe just Nick, pretty soon and see if you can't get together. Split up the town like it was before and stop shootin' guns at each other.

"'And the second thing is, you should talk to me. Nick should also talk to me. I'm a straight guy. What I want is your information. Just in the course of doing what you've been doing for a good many years, and Brian was doing before you and someone did long before him, *you*'re now going to be finding out a lot of stuff I want to know. Because you're going to be competing with LCN, what amounts to the same block of business. And the Frogman and Hugo—same thing.

"'Your answer is, "What do I get? What's in it for me, I should do this?" And my answer to you is this, I'm an ambitious guy. I want to do my job well, because that's where the big money is. I'm assigned here, but I work for my boss, the Seat of Government, and J. Edgar's butt is in Washington.

"'SOG has discovered the mob. For years SOG's been harping on communist spies, stealing secrets about atom bombs— that's what the Congress was worried about, so that's where the big budgets were. The way your ambitious FBI man made a big name for himself was digging out Russian agents. Then Bobby Kennedy landed on Hoffa, and his brother made Bobby AG, and now all of a sudden that's where the action is—same place it's been for at least forty years, starting when they said "No more booze." But now it's okay to know that.

"'You make me look good by filling me in so I know where to look when the Mafia's got something good? *I* will look good down in Washington when the Boston Field Office makes major mob cases. In exchange for which I'll look out for *you,* and cover for you when I can.'"

Stoat inhaled deeply and then exhaled most of it, not realizing he was following the instructions he had learned for preparing to shoot in close-range combat-firing of small arms. He was pleased to hear his voice sound as he wished it to, pleasant but nonetheless firm. "What, exactly, did that mean?" he said.

McKeach snorted. "You know," he said, "that's almost the same thing I said, when he said that—'And just what the hell does *that* mean?'

"And he looked at me, and he smiled, and he said, 'Well, it doesn't cover murder, won't ever go *that* far—that much I am perfectly sure of. You do anyone, and you mess it up? If you get caught you're on your own. Not that I'm suggesting you'd do such a thing, but if you do and get caught, for my purposes you are gone.

" 'Obviously what I'm telling you is that I don't expect you to stop running the businesses we both know you're running, against state and federal law, because if you did then you wouldn't be competing with LCN anymore, and not only would you have nothing to gain from talking to me—you'd have nothing to talk about.

" 'So, this much at least—as long as you're talking to me, if you get snarled up in some federal matter, I'll do what I can to get you out of it. Or if I can't do that, I'll get word to you. So that then when the indictments come out, you can arrange to be . . . out of town. And insofar as I have any clout with the state cops, the same thing with anything state—do the best that I can to protect you from getting indicted, or at least let you know when it's coming.

" 'Beyond that, I don't know what it covers. But it's still early yet. I'm making this up here as I go along. So far as I know, no one's done this before. If they did, they sure didn't tell me, and there's nothing in the manual—I don't have a set of directions. So I've got no more idea'n you have what comes next. What you'll want me to do; what I'll want you to do; what we'll be *able* to do, you and me and the Frogman; or where it'll all go from here? Short answer is—I dunno. And that's probably as specific as I'm ever gonna get.'"

He paused. "I dunno, though," he said, "Nick maybe did, sometime when I wasn't with them. You ever ask him, Frogman? He tell you something he didn't tell me, exactly what he could do?"

"Nope," Cistaro said. "Nope—I didn't ask him. And nope— he didn't tell me. After Hugo went down was the first I saw of him. He told me the deal that he had with you, which was basically what you'd already told me. I said that sounded all right, as far as it went, but I asked him, 'How far does that go?' And he said to me what you just said—he wouldn't know until we'd tried it out. So I went along on that basis, and like you say, it seemed to go okay. I didn't ask him again."

"Long time ago," McKeach said. "Al got his commendations, think he said they were—you law guys're big on that shit—and they got him transferred, just like he wanted. Sent him to the promised land, where they play golf all year 'round. 'I always did like happy endings,' he said, the last time we had dinner like this, him and Fogarty and us. What'd I say that was, eighteen years ago? I forget. Quite a while. I thought same as he did, everything'd gone good—I never did ask him again."

"Because you...you didn't have to," Stoat said, somewhat bleary. "By then you knew and he knew what was involved, without talking about it... and all of you... made out just fine."

"Well, so've you guys," McKeach said, his eyes narrowing again. "You guys've got Carlo and all of his cowboys right by the short 'n' curlies. Whole bagful of scalps for your personnel files. You ain't done bad out of this either."

"We realize that," Farrier said soothingly. "All Darren's saying, as I understand him, is still being new here he has some concern that we all know about where we stand. For the future.

Now that it looks like old Carlo's group's going. I think that's all that's concerning him now."

"That what's on your mind?" McKeach said to Stoat, his voice hard and flat.

"What is?" Stoat said. "I don't understand your question."

McKeach glared. "My question's simple. I wanna know if what he just said, what Jack just said to me there, is about all that you got on your mind here."

"Well, I don't know," Stoat said. He belched softly, pouching his cheeks and putting his chin down against the base of his neck. Then he lifted it again. "The way that I feel . . . what you've told me, tonight . . . is that you haven't told me a lot. That tells me just where you think we stand now. With Carlo's group now on the skids. I think what you've said leaves me and Jack—well, maybe not Jack—but leaves me . . . pretty much in the dark. And I'm . . . well, getting uneasy about this."

Farrier, Cistaro and McKeach frankly studied him for a while, saying nothing. After he had rotated his gaze onto each of them twice without getting reassurance, he put his hands on the table, pushed his chair back, stood unsteadily, and said, "Gennelmen . . . ah meeting's adjourned."

12

CONVINCED OF SPRING'S ARRIVAL by the breezy cloudless afternoon bringing the first seventy-degree sunshine of the year, on the fourth Wednesday in April, Rascob in the old grey Town Car turned right off Old Colony Boulevard onto B Street in South Boston and immediately swung right again, into the off-street loading zone behind the two-story store on the corner. The building was whitewashed, its window and door frames painted emerald green. On the northerly wall under the four long narrow windows a foot below the top, three rows of bright green block letters eighteen inches high, decorated with a cluster of six bright green shamrocks, identified it in the top row as FLYNN'S SPA; in the second as offering Beer & Wine * SUPERETTE * Fresh Fish & Choice Meats Daily; and in the third offering Lottery, Newspapers, Cigarettes, Gov't Checks Cashed, Money Orders, Fax.

Rascob drove the Town Car all the way into the narrow space remaining at the southeast corner of the chain-link fence enclosing the loading area, easing it carefully tight against the fence next to the shiny bronze '96 Lincoln Mark VIII coupé John Sweeney had backed into the space nearest the building. He jammed the transmission into Park, shut off the ignition, reached around into the back seat and working by feel pulled a large black nylon zippered duffel bag out from under his trench-coat, then slid across the seat and, being careful not to ding Sweeney's car, squeezed out through the passenger door.

The Naughton kid, his black hair cropped against his skull, his face and arms deeply tanned from his Patriots' Day package weekend—four days and three nights in the Cayman Islands—showing off his muscles with a tight white tee shirt and belt-less jeans riding low on his pelvis, using both hands slammed out onto the cement loading dock through the double-hinged wooden doors with the curved steel dolly bumpers on the bot-tom, letting them bang back and forth behind him. He came to the edge of the platform and leaned his left shoulder against the four-by-eight steel upright supporting the corner of the corru-gated steel roof and siding closest to the street, shaking one cig-arette out of a pack of Winstons in his right hand and snapping a flame up from a neon-blue disposable lighter with his left thumb. When Rascob had fully emerged from his car, Naughton shouted, "Max, my *man,*" exhaling a billow of smoke and grin-ning, his teeth gleaming.

"Well, Jesus, Captain Marvel, ain't *you* pretty now," Rascob said. "You'd've been that dark ten years ago, you would've gone to Southie High—judge would've bused you over here, all the other jigaboos."

Naughton's grin widened. "Max," he said, "you're gettin' in deep shit, drivin' that shitbox. Good King John says you embar-rass his fine *ride,* parkin' that old beater beside it every day. When you gonna give in, admit it, you gotta get a new car?"

"When you get your start date, the academy," Rascob said, opening the trunk of the Town Car. It was nearly filled with small brown paper bags. "Soon's I know you can get along 'thout the dough I'm always givin' you to fix it." He put the duffel bag into the trunk and began stuffing the paper bags into it.

"Well, Max," Naughton's kid said, "get ready to *shop* 'til you *drop*. I'm in the class startin' May."

Rascob stopped his activity. Exaggerating his motions, he straightened up and turned to face the loading dock, leaving the paper bags and duffel in the open trunk. A gull overhead, flying north toward the Fort Point Channel, shrieked loudly. "*Son* of a *bitch*," Rascob said, feigning amazement, "so *that's* why you got the deep tan. And the very next week you get in. Made the minority quota work *for* you. You're smarter'n I thought you were."

Then he grinned. "Hey, though, congratulations." He started toward the loading dock, extending his right hand, Naughton's kid crouching and extending his right hand to meet him, but then Rascob stopped, held up his left forefinger, wheeled around, and slammed the trunk lid shut.

"Yeah, you'd *better*," Naughton's kid said. "Wouldn't wanna go leavin' *that* open, someone come along an' help themselves, the work."

Rascob still grinning turned again and this time made it to the dock. "Yeah, but pity the guy who tried it," he said. "He'd be one dead fuckin' man." He shook hands with Naughton's kid, clapping him on the right elbow with his left hand. "But son of a bitch," he said again, this time with undisguised pleasure, "that really is great news, Todd, just the *greatest* damned news. Your dad and mother must be very proud." He laughed. "*Shit*," he said, "old man must be *insufferable*, takin' *this* news to headquarters. Pity the people have to work with Emmett this week."

The Naughton kid's smile faded a little. He frowned and shook his head once. "Well, I don't know about that," he said. "I don't think I'd be too sure."

"Well, Jesus Christ, *why?*" Rascob said.

Naughton shook his head again. "Dunno," he said. "I told him night before last, got home from over Hagan's, get cleaned up 'fore I went out—the department envelope's waiting. So I opened it and made sure it said what I thought it did, and then I waited, he got home, before he went to work. And I showed it to him, told him.

"He said, you know, 'congratulations,' but he didn't look that happy. 'Hope you enjoy the job as much as I have. And at least try to treat it as well.' But he wasn't keen on it. Heart wasn't really in it."

"Really?" Rascob said. "The cop's cop's not happy, his son wants to be a cop? Doesn't make sense. What's his problem? Afraid you'll get hurt or somethin'? Shouldn't be; he never did, and old Emmett never ducked nothin'. He should have faith in his genes."

Naughton shook his head once more. "He's jumpy," he said. He frowned. Careful to avoid splinters, he put his right hand knuckles down on the rough wooden floor of the loading platform and pivoted on it to jump down onto the ground in front of Rascob. "We know each other, right, Max?" he said. "I know I feel like that, at least."

"Well, geez, so do I," Rascob said. "Eight or ten years, isn't it, you started pumpin' gas at Hagan's? Anything I can do?"

Naughton hiked up his jeans. "I dunno," he said. "Gimme some advice, I guess."

"Fire away," Rascob said.

"My mother, 'Lady Caroline,' my father calls her that. He says we may all be peasants but she's always been a true aristocrat. Her attitude's always been . . . I dunno. She's never put any pressure on us, what we'd be when we grew up. Never said much about it. Since Eileen and Ed and I've been old enough, seems like, say what we'd like to be, from her it always was that we should be whatever *we* wanted. Cowboys, firemen, pitchers for the Red Sox—'anything but priests or nuns.' Which surprised people now and then, they didn't know her, but she meant it.

'It's an unnatural way to live. That's why there's so many disgraces.'"

He folded his arms and leaned back against the dock. "I don't think any of us, growing up, ever once said we'd like to be a cop," he said. "And Dad never said, even once, to consider it. 'How about becoming a cop?' But he never said we shouldn't, either, touted us against it, like 'too dangerous'—'too hard on the family.' Which of course we all knew that part anyway, growin' up with him a cop. But he just never promoted the idea.

"Didn't occur to *me,* I might wanna be a cop. Until one night last November, I don't know why, everything just *got* to me. I'm still in college, second year at U Mass Boston, transferred over my Northeastern credits, year before. Not that there were that many—if I hadn't *dropped* out, I would've *flunked* out."

He creased his forehead. "That night it just dawns on me. I know exactly what I'm doin'. Hadda face it—just spinnin' my wheels. Either I just wasn't cut *out* for college or I wasn't ready for it. Either way, didn't matter. I was doin' a shitty job of it.

"So I figured if I told him that, then for sure he'd go along with what I was gonna tell him I therefore hadda do next—stop doing it. Because that was one thing that he'd *always* harped on to us—'if you're gonna do a thing—I don't care what the hell it is, mow a lawn or build a bridge—*do the damned thing right.* Never do a thing so that later when you look at it, you can't be proud of it.'

"Wasn't tellin' him I'm stupid. We both knew I wasn't—I just hated school, is all. There I am, I'm twenny-one, already two years behind when I should be graduatin'. Still livin' at home, pickin' up a few bucks fixin' cars at Hagan's Getty, workin' three nights a week over Watchguard Security—Peter put me onna switchboard, dog-watch weekend relief, and usually I get a couple more nights, sometimes more, doin' the patrol rounds for some regular, called sick or something. Plus what I get for fillin' in here, takin' deliveries 'round inna truck, old people and shut-ins, Sweeney's too cheap to hire full-time help. Like I do everywhere I work, generally makin' myself useful doin' things for people, need someone to help out.

"So, I'm makin' a few bucks here and there, you know? Nothin' steady—which I could have if I wanted, all I hafta do is ask; Peter'd hire me in a minute, told me he would, many times, this's 'thout me askin' him, go on permanent at Watchguard. But you know, I don't say this, but what I think when he says it? 'Right. Who the fuck wants that? Drivin' around all night inna snow and rain, gettin' outta the car and shakin' doors at factories, shinin' flashlights inna windows, spendin' my life doin' *that*? *Ahhh,* I do not fuckin' think so.' Although that *is* how Peter started out, I mean; his first job with them was checkin' doors, seein' if they're locked secure, all that kind of boring shit, and I do hafta say that it's done all right by him. But still, I mean, that was also *okay* for him then—it isn't okay for me. Now. I got better things to do. This I know.

"The trouble is," Naughton said, "or at least the trouble *was,* then, it was that it was beginnin' to look to me as though I *didn't* know—I couldn't tell you exactly what they *were,* you know? Those better things I had to do. Looked to me as though I was mostly goin' nowhere, fast. Gettin' older, gettin' *heavy*—which I was then, back last fall, packin' weight on like a *bastard*; beer'd started gettin' to me; hadn't started workin' out—and still I got no more idea what the *hell* I'm *doin'* 'n I did when I was *twelve.*"

He shook his head and smiled ruefully. "Wasn't all that easy," he said, "admittin' that stuff to myself. I always been the type of kid when I was growin' up, if I tried ah play some sport and found out I was no good? An' no matter what I did, how long I played or practiced I was never gonna be? Like hockey—found out I was a shit hockey player and stopped playin' it. And now this particular light last November, I finally see it—this college thing of mine's beginning to look like the first thing in my life I ever did where I been at it long enough to see that not only am I no good at it, can't play this game at all—I don't really want to. I just don't give a shit.

Rascob pursed his lips and frowned. He shook his head. "Not really, no, I don't," he said. "I don't follow you at all."

"Oh," Naughton said. He looked worried. "Aw right then, maybe *this's* what I'm sayin'—this college thing of mine was beginning to look like the first thing in my life that I ever did where I'd been at it long enough to see not only am I no good at this, can't even *play* the game—I don't really *want* to, I don't *give* a shit.

"This's all *new* to me. It *was* like it was a *game* I was in, all right? But I'm playin' by myself. Maybe playin' *with* myself." He laughed. "But that night I could see, which I could not see before, that if I lost it, as I knew I was going to, it was gonna finish me.

"I am serious about this. If what I decided to do that night last November was try to tough it out as usual, keep on going just the same, until the fuckin' game was over, sooner or later, maybe when I'm thirty, I would get a fuckin' piece of paper— and what would that paper say? To me it would say that I'm some kind of Energizer fuckin' Bunny, lots more like me inna store; I kept on going 'til I got it. And why did I do that? Because that's what I fuckin' *do*—I keep on fuckin' *going*. Even though there's no *point* in it; got no *idea* of where I'm *goin'*, anything at all, except that when I get there I know very fuckin' well ain't gonna mean one fuckin' thing.

"In other words," Naughton said, "for the rest of my life I am gonna be an asshole. With a college degree." He rearranged his features, scowling again, and reflected on what he'd said. He inhaled deeply and exhaled. "Well, I didn't wanna be that," he said. He nodded, and snuffled. "Yeah," he said, with satisfaction, "I think that covers it. I think that's what I mean."

Rascob nodded, pursing his lips. "Well, okay," he said. "So now if I follow you, that's the night that you decided to become a cop."

"Well, yeah," Naughton said. "I mean—kind of. I didn't have that exactly in *mind*. I didn't have *anything* exactly in mind. All I knew was that I hadda stop goin' to college, pretendin' I'm doin' something meant something. And that I hadda have something I could actually do, and *want* to do, you know? Not something where I'm gonna get up every mornin' the rest of my fuckin' *life*, sayin' 'What am I gonna do today? Oh yeah, I forgot. The same thing I did yesterday. I really do wish I was dead.'

"So," he said, "I tell this to my father, right? I go downstairs and there he is, it's Sunday night; he's got the night off, and he's watchin' football. Last game of the day, West Coast. Cowboys at Chargers, I think—I'm not really sure. He's really into it. 'Football's what I do now'—he will tell you that—'now I've gotten older.' Meaning all he *does* is sit on his *ass* and *watch* young guys play ball—which he does *not* want you to mention.

"He used to play a lot of golf, a fair amount at least. I wouldn't say he was a *fanatic*, exactly—he didn't have those orange balls so he could play on snow when it got good and crusted over. But as soon as the ground thawed, and the wind dried out the turf in March, the early part of April, so you could hit an iron shot 'thout tearing up a foot of sod and they'd then let you *on* the course, he wasn't going to sit around and wait for them to get the cups and flags put in; he'd be *out* there. His hours were so crazy he had trouble finding partners who weren't on the force, and for some reason the guys on it he liked well enough to play with always seemed to be on different shifts. At least that was what he said—myself, I think from other things he said it was more he didn't want to get too close to guys either under him then or might be over him someday. 'Do *not* want to hafta miss an easy putt, or ruin my career.'

"So he played in pickup foursomes but for his regular competition he more or less relied on us. I don't mean Mom—Mom does not like golf, and Lady Caroline is not the kind of woman who's been known to change her mind about things. So it was us. Ed played a lot with him before he went off to Notre Dame, and even Eileen now and then, too, although she gave the game up early—she said she wasn't good enough to make it worthwhile staying with it. Same thing as me and hockey. Dad said it meant she didn't like it well enough to *concentrate*, and learn to play.

"But me, I used to play with him a lot. When I was in high school, summer vacation, I'd go a round with him two-three times a week. We both got to be pretty good, real competition for each other—which's how you *get* good. I had distance on him—I was young, and playin' sports—*flexible*, you know? But the short irons and the greens—he had the finesse. It got to be a ho-hum thing when we broke a hundred; at least one of us'd do it once or twice a week.

"My junior and senior years we had this sort of a campaign we were on; how many different public courses we could play. In addition to George Wright and Franklin Field, and Putterham Meadows. Wollaston and Ponkapoag, Sandy Burr and South Shore, D.W. Field in Brockton; I think we only got to about six or eight, mainly because there were a couple of them we liked so much we kept going back to them. Ponkapoag, they got two there; number one course was our favorite. Very pretty set of links. But crowded? Jesus, lemme tell you, it was *crowded*. Otherwise I think we would've gone there all the time.

"But that's the kind of thing I mean—it didn't used to be just watchin' football was all he thought about. But then he ran out of kids. I was the last one in line and the same thing happened to me that's happened to him and Ed. I got tied up with school. And then workin' crazy hours myself, all kinds of different places, and after a while, you know, just makin' the arrangements took up all our time—it just got too hard to do. So we don't do it anymore.

"As a result, football's what he does now, and fall's now his favorite season—the exhibition games do nothin' for him, but regular season through the Super Bowl, you know? The TV set belongs to him—*get out of his way.* All the seniority he's got, he can have any days off he wants, and so he naturally takes Sundays and Mondays. Three games on Sunday, and"—he shouted—*"Monday Night Football."*

"'Your mother gets the Saturdays, Saturday nights I do things with her.' Which she then always points out they spend doin' things he likes just as much as she does—take in a movie, have dinner with friends—the usual boring things guys their age always do, and they actually look *forward* to it. So I don't know what difference it makes, who wants to do it, since both of them do, but whatever—means something to them? Fine by me. This's the way that they think.

"'Sunday nights I say oughta be what *I* want to do. What I want to do's watch ball games. I'm not selfish about this. I'm always glad to have her join me, any old time that she wants, but being a nice guy, I don't insist.'"

"Does he bet?" Racob said.

"Hell, no," the Naughton kid said. "He doesn't bet on *anything,* way too straight for that. Ask him and he'll tell you, 'Bettin' is illegal.' But he's fanatic, just the same. He's said a lot of times if they had football all year 'round, he'd probably invest in a satellite dish—thirteen games every weekend.

"Now I like watchin' games myself—hey, who doesn't? This's America, right? Hafta watch the games. Have a little *pizza,* drink a little *beer,* shoot the shit with the guys. Sure, it's great. But, *thirteen*? Jesus, be over my limit. Maybe even over his. But I don't know why he doesn't get one anyway. He prolly *would* watch thirteen, if he could, flippin' back and forth like mad, and he can *afford* ah fuckin' thing—makes a hundred K a year, he gets through, overtime and all. But anyway—he's really into it. If the Patriots're playin' that night I decide, college, everything, I think I would've waited for some other time to tell him. But they're not, and besides, this's *important*, an important decision I'm makin' here, I'm gonna tell him about now—more important'n Chargers-'n'-Cowboys. So I interrupt him. And I tell him.

"'I'm gonna finish the semester,' this's what I say to him, ''cause I've gone this far I might as well get what I can out of it. Take the credits so at least I'll have 'em, have that much, so if someday my thinking changes, I decide I'm goin' *back*, I won't be goin' *all* the way back to Square One. I can pick up where I left off. But that's it. I'm gonna take the finals and then I'm gettin' out.' But not to expect too much, you know? Because if I was doin' good at all, I would not be doin' this, and gettin' out.

"And naturally, well, of course he's disappointed. He didn't get his own degree 'til after he'd been a cop a while. Nineteen seventy-three. He'd always wanted college but his parents, they were finely gettin' their own house, that's what they'd been savin' up for, an' so even with the Edison, when he got out of high school, the money wasn't there. So for him it was the same thing it'd been for *his* father—first the service and then when he got out, get married, have a family. That's what everybody did, everyone respectable that didn't go to jail. And what's he gonna do, support a wife and family? Get onna cops, no choice. Easy.

"So the degree—to him it really meant something—a lot. Went to school nights over BC under this federal law they passed after they decided that the county'd be better if the cops're educated. So that cops would get degrees. Something like the GI Bill. The government would pay for it, and then if they did go to school, they would then get more pay.

"'And I'm very glad they did that,' he said. 'It's meant better money for your mother and me, our ability to do things for the three of you, and a lot of other things besides, some of them in-tangible—it's good to have that degree. Gives you confidence. Makes you more a finished man. But all the same I also know that's not the way to do it, you're juggling your job and your family with the books. It's not the same experience as if you went full time, concentrated on the books, what it is you're learning. You *can't* get as much out of it, no matter how you try.

"'But still,' he says, after I told him, 'if you don't wanna do it now, then you don't, and that's all that there is to it. What do you think you want to do? Go in the service? Maybe go to school that way?'

"'And I said No, and then I told him. 'No, I want to be a cop.'"

"Well, what did he say?" Rascob said. "Made you think he didn't like the idea."

"He said," Naughton said—"well, keep in mind by now it's pretty late, second one of his nights off, and since it's Sunday dinner they had daiquiris before, and then the glass of wine with it, and . . . not sayin' he's *wasted*, now, but then after that he's had a couple Lowenbraus or so while he's sittin' there, watchin' the game. So maybe, when he's hearin' this, he's not exactly at his *best*, all right?

"At first he just sort of gives me this look, like maybe I'd lost my mind. Then he gives me a regular *speech*. Said, 'I hope you don't think you can be a Boston cop, an' at the same time do the things you do now, with the people you're doing them with. Using the marijuana; pickin' up the extra money doin' God-knows-kinds ah stuff for kind ah people *you* know you shouldn't even know, much less hang around with them, doin' things you shouldn't do—and don't think 'cause I keep quiet, I don't know you do them. Not and be a Boston cop.

"'You sure you realize what's involved here? What it is you're plannin' to do? Comin' into *my* department, it'll be known you're my *son*? You'll have more people watchin' you'n David Letterman. You gonna be able to take that? And survive?

"'You come in as a recruit, you make forty-one and change. But that's before they take out *taxes,* all those other little items that you've never had to get used to yet, workin' off the books an' gettin' cash under the table.

"'And the cop pay doesn't get that much better fast, either, case you might be thinkin' that. Full salary after three years, least under the current contract, that's only fifty-two or so; you'll be lucky if you see seven hundred bucks a week by the time you cash the check.

"'You sure you can get by on that? Or is it your thinkin' maybe that you're gonna live with *us* 'til the day comes *you* retire, cut your overhead that way? Like you're doin' us a *favor.* "I'll be right here, Dad, take care of you, you and Mom start gettin' simple"—that what you're gonna tell us we'll be gettin' outta this, while you're moochin' room and board?'"

Rascob laughed. "My father said the same thing. I was thinking about maybe getting a master's in tax. 'Not moving back here, I hope.'"

Naughton, also laughing, said, "I think old Emmett had it all prepared, what to say if this came up. 'Oh, I can hear it now,' he says. '"I'll mow the lawn and shovel snow, put out the barrels every Wednesday and put up the lights at Christmas. Every Sunday I'll take you and Mom to church, help you up the icy steps. And all you'll have to do is feed me, keep me warm, at no cost at all to me—oh, and also overlook it when your beer's all disappeared—like you've *been* doin' all my life. Never notice I'm here." Is that what we're gonna hear? 'Cause if we are, I hafta tell you—I don't think that's such a hot idea, you free loadin' your whole life away. We're not gonna go for it.'

"So I tell him, 'No, that is not the way I'm thinkin'. I'm gonna get myself a place in JP, nice two bedroom condo, I can have a friend stay over, I get lucky over Doyle's, 'thout those fishy looks from you. Figure I'll be workin' nights—nice mornings I can play golf over Franklin Park or maybe shoot out to George Wright, still be a nice easy shot—hey, maybe get you out again, play eighteen there once a week.'"

"Didn't faze him," Naughton said. "Didn't even break his stride.

"'Yeah, well, you may say that you will do that, and I know you probably mean it. But you haven't done it yet, and so you don't know if you can. I've got a proud record; I've spent *years* buildin' it. I will *not* have you pissin' on it. Even though you are my son, and I'm proud of you, I don't want you comin' onto the force with me if you're gonna embarrass me, not in any god-damned *way*. And if you think you're gonna keep on doin' stuff onna QT for Uncle Arthur, as you like to call'm—which he is, I know; you don't hafta remind me—but McKeach is who he is; hangin' out with punks and all the junior-grade apprentice hoods that kiss his ass night after night, tell him what a great man he is down at Flynn's over on B Street—then that's *exactly* what you'll do. You'll endanger my good name.'"

"That what *you* think I am, Todd?" Rascob said. "An ass-kissing apprentice hood? Never thought of myself in those terms."

"You don't exactly fit, do you?" Naughton said. "I suppose Dad'd say you do, though—you work for McKeach; that's enough."

"Pretty neat, isn't it?" Rascob said. "Government puts me in jail, and then when I come out, takes away the only way I have to make an honest living. And then when I go to work for the only kind of guy who'll hire me, cops say I'm now a hood. Talk about Catch Twenty-two."

"Oh, don't take it so hard, Max," Naughton said. "My old man wasn't talking about *you*—he was just hugely *pissed off.* 'Think you can kiss those doper friends of yours good-bye? And get by without the money you're gettin' from the hoodlums, doin' things you don't want me or any other cop to know about? Tall order, son, mighty tall order.' "

"You use *dope*?" Rascob said. "You're kiddin' me. Heroin kills people. I thought only niggers're dumb enough for that shit."

Naughton laughed incredulously. "Max," he said, "you shittin' me? *No,* I don't do *that* shit. 'Dope' 's what Dad calls anything that isn't good old booze. Sure I do a little weed. What's a little spliff with friends? Nothin' heavy, none of that shit, but *weed*? Everybody does."

Rascob shook his head. "I'm gettin' old," he said.

A man slightly bent at the waist backed out through the swinging doors behind him, dragging a large dark green plastic tub with black wheels over the steel threshold out onto the loading dock. He wore jeans, heavy black lug-soled work boots, a long white bloodstained lab coat and a dark grey scally cap. A large tan-and-white cat lithely extending and narrowing itself trotted swiftly though the doors alongside the tub, jumping on top as the man pulled it through and the doors slammed behind it. The cat sat down, fixing its gaze on the man in the cap, and balancing itself regally rode on the tub the rest of the way out to front of the dock at the dumpster. There it craned its neck and peered down over the edge of the tub at Rascob and Naughton.

"Mouser," Rascob said absently, ignoring the man in the scally cap and using the same respectful tone to greet the cat he would have used to acknowledge another person. The cat registered him and shifted its gaze back to the man in the grey cap and long white coat. It licked its chops.

The man straightened up and put his fists on his waist. "Goddamn you, I told you No," he said to the cat. The cat cocked its head to the right, raised its right paw and waggled it at the top of the tub, as though explaining something. The man laughed. He turned and faced Rascob. The front of the grey cap was blood-stained. "Max, can you *beat* that?" he said. "This *fuckin'* cat. There's meat in this—beef scraps, I been makin' up roasts—and he wants them; he thinks they're *his.* We keep him for the same thing we kept his mother, Rosie, sixteen years for, to keep the mice out of the place and catch the ones that come in, don't know the policy here. And she did an excellent job. But *he's* too fine for it. His taste runs more to *steak,* and fresh cod.

"*No,*" he said, disgustedly, looking back at the cat. "'Mouser' my ass. We got mouse shit under the bakery shelves. We got mouse-shitty droppings inna backrooms. Anywhere you wanna go, anytime you wanna do it, make an effort, move some shelves and really take a look, you'll find mouse shit inna store. From which *I'd* conclude at least that we've got some *mice,* probably quite a few of them. Board of Health'll think so, too, next time they inspect us, and they'll shut us *down*—unless first we get the rat-'n'-bug guy, cost us three-four hundred bucks, shut the place down for the day, keep everybody out, Stop and Shop gets all our business, so that he can gas the bastards. And then after he gets through, come back the middle of the night, tear the god-damned place apart, cleanin' up the mouse shit. Which is a big pain in the ass, and why we keep a cat around—so that we won't have to do it.

"This would be you, Official Cat. But you don't do your job. Far be it from *you,* go runnin' after *mice.* 'At's beneath your *dignity.*"

"You don't hafta take this, Mouser," Naughton said. "You can report him for upsettin' you, insultin' your feline gender diversity. You happen to be a cat that doesn't like huntin' and then eatin' mice. Most boy cats don't. And for this he's threatenin' to discriminate against you."

"And *you* can stay outta this," the man in the grey cap said. "You don't understand what's involved here. A *principle*. This's exactly how welfare families get started. Feed one shiftless breedin' bastard, pretty soon none of 'em work. Lookit what his momma did—hooked up with some fly-by-nighter, hadda raise her kid by herself. 'S why we had this one gelded. Put a stop, this foolishness."

"*Right,*" Rascob said, "and *that's* probably the reason Mouser isn't following his family profession—you had his balls cut off. You expect him to do cat work for you, after you did that to him? Stopped him from acting like a self-respecting tomcat? Would you work for a man who had that done to you? He thinks you owe him a living now—I think the cat is right. Whadda you think, Todd?"

"Absolutely," Naughton said. "Give the cat some meat, Doran."

"Uh *huh,*" Doran said, nodding, but turning and bending to lift the lid on the tub, causing the cat to jump off at once, turning acrobatically in midair so that it landed next to Doran's right foot, sitting down immediately and rising up on its haunches, fluttering its front paws at him. "Here we got the cop-to-be, promotin' free loadin'—I'm surprised you're not tellin' me to get him a cruller an' coffee." He opened the tub and reached in, sorting through it for a moment before bringing out a handful of red-and-white flesh trimmings that he held up for a moment, tantalizing the cat into beseeching him further by meowing and rising off its haunches, climbing partway up his right leg.

"And," Doran said, glancing slyly at Rascob, "also the man who keeps the books, always very sensitive about the balls and what their purpose is, and even more so lately, huh?" He raised his eyebrows and tilted his head as he dropped the scraps onto the platform and the cat pounced on them, using its front paws to gather them expertly into a neater pile, then settling down on its stomach to eat, growling huskily in its pleasure as it chewed the flesh.

"Isn't that so, Max?" Doran said. "New life in the old boy lately?" Rascob's face reddened deeply. He did not say anything. "Or did I hear that wrong, Todd?" Doran said to Naughton, laughing. "I thought someone or other said best news Max had in *years* was Sweeney givin' his poor lonesome sister a job here, she finely kicked her husband out—first she'd seen of him this year."

"You know, Doran," Naughton said, "the big problem the department's gonna have, day we find you inna harbor with a couple in your head, is where to find a place that's big enough to round up all the suspects. Foxboro Stadium, I think, unless by then the Pats've finally built a new one."

"I don't have time, this happy horseshit," Rascob said, turning back toward the car. "I got to get the work in."

"Max," Naughton said after him, causing him to turn around. "You do know who the friends were, who my father meant, don't you?"

Rascob frowned.

"Those bad friends he said I'd have to give up, 'long with weed, if I got on the force," Naughton said.

Rascob grinned. "I could make a wild guess," he said. "Look at the bright side—you probably won't have that much trouble givin' up the weed."

13

NARROW BLOCKS OF PALE ORANGE setting sun remained near the front of the smoke-stained acoustic tile ceiling of the big office at the front of the second floor of Flynn's Spa when Rascob in his red-striped shirt-sleeves, his narrow dark blue tie pulled down from his collar and his dark grey suit jacket draped over the back of the orange plastic chair, finished toting up the work. The big office was rectangular, about thirty by twenty; he sat at the center of the eight-foot plastic laminated banquet table that occupied the middle. Overhead, translucent ceiling panels concealed tubular flourescent bulbs that hissed and crackled, flickering every so often.

Over the years he had learned to ignore that distraction and all the others disturbing concentration in the big office. In the winter the room was always chilly, despite the excessive dry heat intermittently blown out by the two-burner Universal gas stove in the northeast corner, a squat four-foot brown steel cube on six-inch legs. It whooshed softly every five or six minutes; its thermostat, fastened too near it on the northerly wall six feet away, fired up the propane burner behind the heatproof glass door when the temperature in that corner had dropped below 75 degrees—the low 60s elsewhere in the room—sighing off again when the thermostat had risen back to 75. In the summer the 14,000-BTU Fedders air-conditioning unit mounted in the front wall under the windows groaned mightily to maintain the office temperature below 80. When summer came again Rascob would shift to short-sleeved shirts, leave his tie and coat at home and ignore the heat and noise as he ignored the terms of winter.

McKeach and four other unskilled workmen had built the room in two days after Brian G. acquired the spa from John Flynn as a favor, enabling Flynn to retire to Florida.

McKeach resented disparaging remarks about his carpentry. "Brian G. bought this place, wasn't 'cause he wanted it. John'd had a heart attack. Doctor said next one'd kill him. He needed to retire and this business was all he had, keep a roof over his head. All Brian said he was doing was 'making it so John and Bridey could enjoy the fruits of their hard work.' He had in mind to sell it.

"I thought we should keep it. That's why I did the work. We needed someplace private. Get something better? We move. The stove came from some rooming house on K Street, guy's con-vertin' to apartments. Saw it sittin' on the sidewalk same night he put it out. Air conditioner fell off a truck one night, old Jor-dan Marsh warehouse over Squantum—thirty, forty fell off that night, Bobby Gleason and his brothers workin' there, temporary loading-dock hands? They found 'em. Brought one here. 'Fore that all we did was sweat our balls off up here, April 'til Novem-ber. I tell you it was fuckin' *awful*, underneath that flat black roof, bakin' inna sun all day. All you could do to even come up here, got to be July and August. Hadda go right back downstairs, outside, sit down onna loadin' dock, needed to talk about a thing. And this was not a good idea. Didn't know who was around, staties tryin' out their new *toys*, aimin' parabolic mikes your way.

"Of course it's bargain basement—nothin' I went out and *shopped* for, 'cept the studs and that crap, Grossman's.

"And that's the story of this place. Nobody ever planned it. It never was supposed to last, not long range anyway. Put that air conditioner through the wall there? That was damn hard work, but by then you could see it's worth it, that much work; place was workin' well for us.

"People left us alone here—*people* meanin' *cops*. Say you get inna habit—and Brian used to do this, even though I told him 'No, this's not a good idea,' didn't always listen to me—where you're meetin' with the guys at night in the back room of some guy's bar. Isn't somethin' that you planned, just like this place wasn't planned; you just sorta fell into it. Night after night you're meetin' with the guys, and it's always *inna same barroom*. And I don't care which one it is, Butchie Morgan's like Brian G. did, or me when I'm first gettin' started, goin' over The Curragh.

"You do this, night after night, always goin' the same place, you are liable—hell, you're *gonna*—you're gonna run into a lotta *cops*. Cops enjoy a glass of beer—and this don't mean, and I'm not sayin', they're a buncha drunks. Lot of them can handle it—they're the ones you gotta watch. They're off duty, goofin' off, like to have a few with the boys. Just like everyone else. Not bad guys to hang around with.

"So you go in and there they are, you both got a right to be there, and, well, that's the way it is. What you are doin' is, you're hanging out with people who're supposed to put your ass in jail.

"'Ah, calm down,' Brian would say. 'This's Butchie Morgan's. We own Butchie Morgan's, anna cops come in there know it.'

"'It is, though, Brian,' I would say—'it really is a problem. Someday those cops'll get us. An' that is what it is. You go in, there they are—it's all perfectly normal. You get used to each other. Stop even thinkin' about it. Well, I don't care, they are.

Because off duty, on the clock—that doesn't mean shit to the cops if that is how they get to know you, who you hang around with, what it looks like you're up to, all right? They see you, get to know you, well, they also get so they know where they can not only find you, but also all the guys you run with, they might have a bug to spare, listen in your conversation. And for you this is not good. You *gave* them the PC.'" He sighed. "Brian wouldn't listen.

"What you have got to do if you want things to stay good is start thinkin' like the cops do. When the cops are off duty, after dinner they don't say to their dear wife, 'Hon, I think I might swing 'round Flynn's *Spa* a couple hours, see how the cabbages're doin', izza *water*cress all right.' That isn't how they think. No normal person does. *So,* when we started comin' here to get together, talk about some things, we didn't always find a bunch of cops standin' around. Didn't drop around Flynn's Spa, they got off work, lookin', have some beers. And even after they knew this's where we come to talk, well, what good did that then do them, huh? Nothin'. They wanna overhear us here, first they've gotta getta warrant, get an order from a judge, and this's not, I'm glad to say, an all-that-easy thing to do. In America."

Here he would pause. "And if some cop should *get* a warrant, and install a bug this place, the very most he'd have it would be one week, the outside. I'd find it, pull it right out by the *roots*—that is guarafuckinteed."

McKeach would not explain the basis for his assurance. "That don't matter," he would say. "The point is after that much time'd gone by, after we first came here, and we'd felt no cryin' need to find another place, and Brian G. was dead, the chances then were we weren't going to, and so then we settled in." Then McKeach would pause again.

"And when you think about it, you know, there *are* some advantages to havin' walls that you can hear through, when you're on the second floor and conductin' private business. Gives a man a little warning, someone comes into his building, got no proper business there."

At the southeasterly end of the passageway outside the office there was a chain-flushed toilet with an overhead tank, also enclosed by thin paneling. Now it flushed loudly and a man belched nearby noisily enough to be heard over it. Rascob shook his head and snorted. There were eight other molded orange chairs grouped haphazardly around the office and he grimaced every time as coming in he grabbed the handiest to the door and pulled it to the table to commence the work. Each time he reminded himself that the chair provided no support, so that he must sit up straight with shoulders back, and it did not matter; once engaged he gradually bent forward over the table, hunching his shoulders, so that when he finished his back was once more killing him. He heard the toilet door close down the passageway. The deep affronted tone of a diesel tractor's horn bawled on the boulevard outside, drawing sharp cries of objection from two or three automobile horns. He put his hands on his lumbar region and arched it, taking a deep breath and moaning.

He heard someone passing in the corridor hesitate near the office door and place a hand on the knob, perhaps considering violation of the iron rule that although after Sweeney unlocked the door in the morning it remained so all day until relocked by the last person leaving at night, each person entering or leaving the big office during the day closed the door behind him, and except by invitation it was only to be opened by a person with a key—Rascob, Sweeney, the Frogman or McKeach. So Rascob at once laughed and said, loudly enough to carry through the hollow wooden door: "Nothing serious, I'll live." The man outside—perhaps Doran; he had no business in the office—said, "Had me worried for a minute." Rascob heard him walk away. He shook his head and rubbed the back of his neck.

The paper bags from the trunk now lay crumpled in the grey metal wastebasket next to his left leg. There had been twenty-two of them, for the fourth time one less than McKeach had told him to expect. Taking them one by one from the black duffel bag, now empty under the table next to his right leg, he had emptied the contents onto the table and tallied them on the printing calculator he kept in the top right-hand drawer of the grey steel desk under the windows. The desktop was taken up with a black telephone, a pop-up phone-number indexer, a five-inch Gran Prix black-and-white personal TV, and Sweeney's account book, a large black looseleaf notebook open on column-ruled pages captioned APRIL PRODUCE, APRIL BAKED. Rascob had tried the armless wooden castered chair behind it; it was more uncomfortable than the orange plastic chairs.

He had coded the entries as usual by location, using letter designations based upon an alphabet beginning that month with the letter *T*. McKeach, initiating Rascob: "Brian G. said, all any code can do's *delay* the cops. No code, even a tough one, is ever gonna stop them from figurin' out what you're doin', from your records of it, if you give 'em enough time. Our code isn't very tough. Cops ever get their hands on it, they'll crack it—half an hour.

"But it *can't* be very tough if you're gonna use it *and* also be able change it. Your people've gotta know it, and use it—without *thinkin'* more about it than they are about the business that they're doin' in it. You make it too tough, an' what happens *then*, they don't *use* it—so then what the hell good's it to you? Might as well not have it at all.

"At least with a simple one like this, you got somethin'. Yeah, cops'd figure it out, but they'd hafta hit the joint just right, on a make-up day, and grab the work before you had a chance to add it up, and *mix* it up, and flash the bags and tape.

" 'Doin' that would take great *timing*,' Brian said. 'Which very few cops I ever heard of had.

" 'Not to mention—half an hour's quite a lot of time, you know what to do with it. Someone who wasn't busted but who knew the raid'd happened could make one shitload of phone calls, half an hour, to other guys who'd like to know. Give them time to clean up *their* joints, 'fore cops came to visit them.' "

Adams Canteen Catering in the Randolph Industrial Park had been Rascob's fourth stop of the day. In the office at the back of the freight terminal that Jackie Adams leased for his garage and shop, Rascob had marked each of the five bags Jackie gave him with a *W*. In the office above the spa he had written the same letter next to each of the five sub-subtotals he had reached on the calculator, leading to the *W* subtotal for the Adams Canteen Catering location of $11,930, 430 twenty-dollar bills and 333 ten-dollar bills.

As with the contents of the other bags, he had used wide beige rubber bands to collect four hundred of the twenties into eight stacks of fifty, putting the remaining thirty bills aside for combination with twenties from other locations. He had banded three hundred of the ten-dollar bills in three stacks and reserved the remaining thirty-three for banding with tens from other locations.

When he had emptied and tallied all of the bags, there were four complete rows of fifty greyish-green thousand-dollar stacks and an incomplete row of nine stacks on the table in front of him. He had piled loose bills amounting to $375 to his right on the side. He folded those into a thick wad and put it into his left front pants pocket.

He tore the tape along the serrated edge at the top of the calculator and folded it four times. Then he pushed his chair back from the table and bent over, rolling the dark blue silk sock on his left calf down below his shin bone, wrapping the tape tightly around his ankle and then rolling the sock back up over it. He humped the chair back up to the table and deleted all of the entries he had stored in the memory of the calculator. Then he reached down and unplugged it from the black extension cord leading to the wall outlet behind him, flipping the cord back to rest against the mopboard. He stood up, gathered the cord around the calculator and replaced it in the top right-hand drawer of the desk.

Returning to the orange chair, he stooped and picked up the grey wastebasket and put it on the table. Then he reached down again, picking up the gaping duffel. He put it at the center of the table and went around to the other side. Using both hands and forearms he gathered the stacks of currency together and dumped them into the duffel bag. He zipped it closed.

Picking the wastebasket up with his left hand, he carried it to the brown stove and set it down on the floor in front of the silent stove. A two-foot iron poker with a wooden handle lay on the floor under it. He went to the wall thermostat and turned the lower pointer on the dial clockwise to 90. As he turned back to the wastebasket, the stove grunted and ignited. He opened the door to the combustion chamber as the gas jet filled it with flames. He took three or four of the lettered paper bags from the wastebasket and drew the poker out from under the stove. He put the bags at the opening of the stove and used the poker to shove them into the flames. They burned brightly and quickly. He kept adding bags until the wastebasket was empty. Then with the stove door open he stood erect and went back to the thermostat, resetting it to 75. The stove subsided, sighing. In front of it again, he crouched and peered in, satisfying himself that no legible fragments remained. Then he replaced the poker beneath the stove and shut the door.

He went back to the table and shrugged into his suit jacket.

Then he nudged the orange chair that he had used back among the others along the southerly wall. He picked up the duffel bag with both hands. He stood holding it and looked around, nodding when he was satisfied that no one surmising what he had been doing in the big office would be able to confirm and prove it from anything that he would leave behind.

"That's the secret, Maxie," McKeach had told him after he had met and sized him up in the old Pilothouse beside the Fort Point Channel. "You decide to work for me, for us, you got to forget your strongest instincts. You're a certified public accountant, trained to keep neat and permanent records. Clear enough so people who had nothin' to do with keepin' 'em can take a look and know right off all they need to know about the business you worked for.

"Our business, that's last thing we want anyone else to be able to do. What we want you to do is make the record *right,* but also make it *temporary.* So as soon's we read it and we got it in our heads, where we keep the real records, the one you made *disappears.*" He studied Rascob as though appraising him as bodily collateral for a large loan. "And at the same time we do that, you have to make the record that *you* kept in *your* head while you made the written one also disappear." He smiled. "Think you can do that?"

"Hey," Rascob said, three weeks out of jail, living in one seedy room, bath down the hall, in the old railroad Hotel Diplomat across the street from South Station. "I'm runnin' outta money. Guy I met inside down at Plymouth, knew my situation, said he never met you but from what he heard about you I should get in touch with you. Tell you I really need a job.

"There's only one thing I can do. The law says I can't do it. That means I got sentenced twice, once to do the fuckin' time, and then to starve to death.

"Well, I did the first one. I'm not gonna do the second. If it's against the law for me to do honest work, I'll do *dishonest* work, and if the law can hang me for that, well, they gotta catch me first."

"And if they do," McKeach said softly, "are you sure you'll be *willin'* to hang? You already told me how you hated jail. You sure you can face goin' back, most the rest your life? 'Cause that'd not be your only choice, you know, cops catch you workin' for me. They'll do that—they're gonna ask you, just like I am askin' now—'You wanna *hang*? Do *twenny years*? Or wouldja rather go into the Program—help us hang McKeach, then we'll disappear you, send you to New Zealand, someplace green.' Still think you'd be willin' to hang?"

Rascob licked his lips and coughed, but his voice sounded strong to him. "Arthur," he said, "how the hell do I know? Of course I am gonna say Yes—I need the damn job. But 'til I'm in the position that you just described, which I hope to God I never am, I don't know what I'd do."

McKeach nodded. Then he reached across the table with his right hand and clapped Rascob on the left shoulder. "You're an honest man, Max, I'll say that for you. Nobody knows in advance what he'd do—stand-up guys have the guts to admit it. Myself, I would bet if they get you by the balls again you'd trade your mother to get loose. But like I said, no one knows." He paused three beats. "You do understand, though, if you get caught, and fold on me, then no matter where they send you or how long it may take me, I will find you and I'll kill you."

Rascob nodded. He moistened his lips again. "I thought that's what you might say."

At the door Rascob took both handles of the duffel bag in his left hand and used his right to open it. To the left and right in front of him there was an unfinished passageway four boards wide created by the rear wall of the big office and the row of two-by-four studs on the other side. Sweeney in a Columbus

Day weekend frenzy of unskilled carpentry years before had nailed them to the joists open on the other side beyond them. The space was chiefly lighted by two naked bulbs hanging in silver metal shop-light fixtures suspended from a cross rafter under the flat roof, wired in the same circuit as the fixture in the toilet operated from the single switch at the foot of the open staircase at the end of the passageway to Rascob's left. Pink Fiberglas foam insulation lay between the joists. In the center of the rear wall, eighteen feet away, was a single twelve-pane window, the glass filthy.

The plan that had existed only in Sweeney's head had called for the studio apartment in the space. In it the window was to have been replaced with a copper-clad bay window flanked by two casement windows, "which you could then crank them open in the spring and summer, for ventilation, see?"

John Sweeney was a tall, heavy man whose brown hair had receded early, leaving him a sharp prow of it at the front that drew attention to his long sharp nose and bright dark eyes. For his fortieth birthday, in 1976, he had cultivated and then kept sharply groomed a Van Dyke beard that filled in dark red.

"Looks like a crow, don't he?" Cistaro would say at meetings in the big office, in the mood to get at someone. "Just like a fuckin' two-hundred-an'-fifty-pound crow, lookin' for some smaller bird's nest, he can go an' rob the eggs. Or some poor bastard's little garden, trynah grow himself some plum tomatoes he can have fresh pasta sauce, Big Boys for his salad. Crow'll go there and stab alla tomatoes with that big fuckin' beak of his, suck out a little of the meat, leave 'em rottin' onna vine. Ruin 'em for everybody else.

"Same thing, some high-roller tries to stiff him. Jawn doan hafta tellah guy he'll send *McKeach* around to see him—just gives him that killer-crow look; stiff'll turn the little wife out onna street by sundown, suckin' cocks for double sawbucks to pay off Jawn." Then Cistaro would laugh. "Jawn's *own* wife's got him scared to death—poor fierce old crow is pussy-whipped, but he's hell on guys don't pay."

Straddling the two joists in front of the window and illustrating with his hands, Sweeney had enthused about his plan. "Anna big window in the middle here'd give you all the light you'd need in the main room here, where you'd have your dinette, and your couch and your TV, of course, see? And then up there next to where the john is now, all you'd have to do is put your sink in, and disposal, and just tap inna main plumbing tree, already there—got your water and your waste pipe and your drain right there; wouldn't hafta put a new one in. And you would use the same toilet where it already is, cut a new door in this side of it, or if that bothered people, going to the john in what would then be this apartment, well, then just put in another one on this side of the cubicle that's already there, and a Y-joint in the waste pipe, take care of that. And then install one of those Fiberglas stall showers that they've got all ready made now, and then you would be all set, ready for whatever happened. And this's *not* a big project—'nother week or so, you'll see, it'll all be finished. Nice. Always have a place to stay."

To this McKeach had said, "No."

"Whaddaya mean, 'No'?" Sweeney had said. "I know this's zoned commercial but I already checked the city and they say there's no reason at all the owner of a business like a spa or say, a drugstore, can't put a bed in if he wants, and a place to take a shower and so he can cook a meal. Hell, we've already got the microwave an' little fridge anna coffee urn on downstairs inna backroom there, day and night, Chrissakes, gets more attention from the help 'n the whole rest the store does—what the hell's problem?"

"The problem is you ain't the owner and I am and I don't want you livin' here," McKeach said.

"It's my name's on the deed," Sweeney said.

"Yes, it is," McKeach said, "and it's also on the liquor license, and that's *why* it went on the deed instead of mine and Brian G.'s. So the name on the deed and therefore the license application wouldn't spit out a criminal record when the License Board plugged it in. And that's the *only* reason—and you should keep that in mind, unless you maybe now decided what you now want is your name comin' *off* the deed, which I can do, just as fast I put it on—in which case it might get chiseled on a headstone."

"Well, I wouldn't be *livin'* here," Sweeney said. "I'd just be *stayin'* here a while—just until I can get things straightened out again with Kay."

"Which'll be never, and you know it," McKeach said, grinning. "Just like it was with Annie, and just like it'll be when you finally figure out you can't stay married to Kay if you're gonna keep fuckin' *Ginny*, any more'n you could stay married to *Annie*, you first started fuckin' Kay. You're worse'n Elizabeth Taylor— you think anything you had your dick in more'n twice, it then hasta marry *you* and you hafta marry *it*, or God'll punish you. It's a wonder you didn't hafta divorce your right hand when you started fuckin' Annie and decided, marry her.

"You know what your problem is? I'll tell you what it is. Your problem is your dream's to be fucking two women the same time, but be *damned* if you can figure out how the hell to do it. When I told you and I told you but you just don't seem to get it, that the only way to do it is the first thing that you do is, you completely stop worrying about what either one of them thinks. Never *mind* what they are thinking. You remember how it was, way back when I was with Traci, and then I started seein' Dorothy and Traci just went *bullshit?*"

He paused. Wonder and then amusement passed across his face. "Jesus Christ," he said, "I just said that and it hit me—that was *thirty* years ago. Nineteen sixty-six I think it was, that we broke up. So it's *over* thirty years now, since I was with Traci? Shit. I really must be gettin' old." He shook his head.

"Traci died, didn't she?" Sweeney said.

"Oh, yeah, years ago," McKeach said. "Kids hadda move back in with their father, poor little bastards they were, everyone was sayin' then, havin' to go back and live with him, their no-good father, and the only reason they could even do that was it so happened when she got it, Dennis'd just gotten out from whichever place that he'd been in, dryin' out that time, and 'How long's that gonna last, you think?' That's what people're sayin'. And he then surprised the world, got those kids and said 'Aw right, you'll live with me, then,' and he went and got his job back, working for Gillette. Raised those kids, took care of them? So far's I ever heard at least no one ever saw him take a drink again. Really an amazing thing."

"Yeah," Sweeney said, "but Traci there, didn't she get *shot?*"

"Oh, yeah," McKeach said, "she got shot. But that wasn't anything, you know, had anything to do with *her*—she was just there, with Richie Dugan, when his turn came to get it. Which most people were surprised it hadn't happened to him sooner, fuckin' renegade he was, sell his mother for a buck. It was him that they were after, whoever it was that shot Traci. Naturally when they got him, since she was there, it hadda be two-for-one day—shoot 'em both. Richie, he'd been gettin' to the point where he was makin' people nervous. Very friendly with De-Marco, Al DeMarco, FBI. Very friendly guy, DeMarco. They say he didn't hafta *take* the candy from the baby—he could talk the kid into givin' it to him. And you know how Richie was—didn't take a DeMarco, talk him into doin' somethin'. Word was he was gonna tell DeMarco who did the Kingston armored car—made some fairly hard guys nervous.

"Traci had to've heard it, he had people lookin' for him. Should've known what's gonna happen, she happens to be standin' next to him, they find him. Didn't take 'em long. Hampton Beach. Which *anyone*, I mean, *I* could've told you, that's where he'd go if someone told him, 'Now just go lie low someplace, all right? Not long, a week or two, while we work it out with Washington.' So what if it was wintertime, the merry-go-round was shut down and everything was boarded up except a couple clam stands? Wouldn't make no difference, Richie—Richie just loved Hampton Beach. It was his favorite place to be. And so that was where he went, an' Traci-little-bitch went with him.

"Those were hard guys, involved in that, that armored-car thing. They did something, like clip a guy, they weren't the type of guys who leave loose ends around you know? Fix one problem, make another one? Leave an eyewitness? Uh-uh. You're there they find the guy they want? You must've wanted to *come* with him; you're *goin'* with him, too. Those guys were serious."

He sighed. "But that was Traci, all the way. Liked the bright lights, and the *danger*—I think she got off on it. She was that way I first knew her, she's still livin' then with Danny and there's nothin' wrong with him, but you knew, she kept it up, there was probably gonna be. I even told her that myself—and this's when she was with *me*—that it was really killin' Danny; an' she oughta cut it out. But there was no holdin' Traci. She's stayin' out at night on him, bein' seen with guys like me and Brian? Well, what'm I supposed to do? Leave her standin' in the street, place shuts down at two A.M.? Or take her home and fuck her brains out like she's clearly got in mind? So I did it, I admit it. And loved every minute of it. But you just *knew* something'd happen, and then sure enough, it did."

He paused and smiled. "She was one good-lookin' babe, though, big blue eyes and all that hair? You did have to give her that. Not the brightest bulb in town, no, but lookin' like that, you tell me, how bright did she needah be? As long as she's still young. Why she ever married Danny and then had those two kids with him, that's one thing I never knew.

"But anyway," he said, "that was before, long before we got together. And then I started goin' out with Dorothy, a few times, and Traci heard about it somewhere, by then she's livin' with me, and did she ever get pissed *off*. She said I hadda cut it out. Well, I just told her, I said, 'Traci, this's something you decide now, what it is you wanna do here. If you want to stay with me, then that is what you should do. And when I'm here with you, I'm with you. And when I'm not, I'm not. And you leave me the fuck alone. An' if you don't want to do that, well then, I don't think you should.'

"And I was takin' a chance there, and it's not like I don't know this—although the time if you'd asked me what I thought was gonna happen, I would've said, 'Well, my thought is she won't do it. She ain't got the balls to go.' But either way I couldn't let it happen, let no woman run my life. That's one thing you cannot do.

"I will say she did cross me up, though, little bitch—it turned out that she did have 'em. She did have the balls to leave.

"But hey, okay, she made her mind up, that was how she wanted it—okay, that was still all right with me. Then that's how it's gonna be. But anyway, beside the point, John, far as you are now concerned. Point for you is if Kay now knows you're fucking Ginny and as a result she's not happy; or if the other one isn't happy, Ginny, knowing that you still fuck Kay; *any* of that happy horseshit—just never mind it, all right?"

Sweeney looked puzzled. McKeach sighed. "I'm making this too complicated," he said.

"The way you do it is, you fuck the one that you wake up with, and then you go out for the day and do your regular work.

And then when that day's over and it's time now to relax, you then go fuck the other one. And then either go back to the first one, that you fucked in the morning, so you spend the night with her again anna next day's the same as the one before, or you stay that night with the second one—anna next day it's then the same thing, but reversed. And you never tell the one you're leavin' in the morning, don't matter which one it is, if you're coming back that night. She asks you, you say 'Dunno.' Period.

"And that is how you do it, if you get it *up* enough so that you *can* do it—which I would think that most guys can, get their rocks off twice a day. They would think that was about right, specially with two different broads; you'd have some variety.

"And that, incidentally, is one thing you've got goin' for you, this's what you're doing here—fucking two women every day—they don't think we *can*. All the stuff they read in all the fuckin' magazines and see on television, gettin' laid and so forth, fifty different ways to do it—it's always about how of course they can come off six or seven times a night without even breathin' hard. But all we can do it is once. Or maybe, when we're still young studs, *maybe* twice in the same day, if we could sneak a nap in. So it will generally be quite a while that you can fuck two women before either one of them'll really believe it. Even if the evidence is in front of her face. Because she doesn't think you can. She thinks if you're pullin' down her bloomers, she must be your only one. But you still have to face it—sooner or later one of them'll find out, and then if the other one don't know, well, it's just a matter of time—she's gonna.

"And then what? Well, if either one of them don't like it, then, well, you make your decision and you let one of them go, tell her to just beat it. 'I'm tiredah yah noise—take a hike.' And you keep the other one—who then thinks she won. While you start keeping your eyes open for a new one for the place you now got open. The key's not to let it get complicated.

"Not that *I* care how you do it, just so you don't get to thinking you're comin' in here an' livin' over my store. I'm not gonna have some half-crazy woman that you're fuckin' while you're fuckin' someone else come in here some night after dark, hollerin' and screamin', maybe wavin' a gun around—gonna reduce competition, shootin' up the joint and drawin' cops. This's where I have my business, and the kind of business *I* do, where I *do* my business matters. Anything else that goes on in here comes way second after that."

Shifting the duffel to his left hand in order to pull the door closed with his right, Rascob then used both hands to lug it in front of him down the passageway until he had passed the northeasterly corner of the big office. Then, steering the duffel around to his left and counting his steps on the wide planks he could not see underfoot, he carefully followed the bag into the gloom of the space between the studs supporting the interior wall of the big office and the bearing studs of the outside wall of the spa. The dirt accumulated on the inside of the narrow windows under the eaves made the thin remaining light of late afternoon in April into the pale twilight of evening.

When he had counted six paces, he stopped and used his left hand to grope in the gloom at shoulder level, once more—again to his mild surprise and relief—finding the seventh stud in from the passageway, then locating by touch the rocker switch for the single-bulb shop light suspended overhead. He pressed the switch and the bulb came on.

Up against the studs of the outside wall facing B Street there was a faded red steel floor-model Coca-Cola cooler. Three feet high, four feet deep and six feet long, with a top that was hinged at the middle and equipped with a handle at each end, it had been designed in the fifties for use by the Coca-Cola Bottling Co. to ice down as many as two dozen twenty-four-bottle cases of Coca-Cola—576 six-ounce bottles—for free good-will distribution at public gatherings at which Coke was the only beverage served. The front carried raised white block letters that read DRINK and larger white letters in flourished script reading COCA-COLA.

John Flynn had obtained it and three others for a Fourth of July celebration on Broadway in 1953, after Ike had stopped the fighting in Korea, and had so arranged matters that when the Coca-Cola people came to retrieve the coolers on the morning of the fifth one had disappeared. Thereafter each year on St. Patrick's Day and other public celebrations he used it to chill beer served from the loading dock to loyal customers and friends who knew about the informal gathering behind the Spa, three blocks west of the parade route on Broadway.

Rascob set the duffel down on the planking and used both hands to open the top of the machine and lift it off, resting it against the left end of the cooler. Then he lifted the duffel onto the left-hand corner of the cooler and rested it there.

The cooler was about a quarter full of currency. The contents of the duffel would bring the total it contained to slightly over $631,000. He had finished stacking the currency from the duffel in the cooler and was replacing the cover when he heard the first footfall on the wooden staircase below. He sighed as he spun, reaching out and pressing the rocker switch that shut off the light overhead. He took a deep breath and held it.

The person approaching began to hurry up the stairs, extending his left arm to hasten his ascent by pulling on the railing, making it shake audibly. Then a second person followed the first.

"Max," McKeach said, first in line, reaching the top of the stairs, "I assume it's you in there, just had the light on with the money. If it's not, you'll wish you were Max, me and Nick get through with you." Rascob exhaled and turned the light on.

"Well," McKeach said, extending his arms and putting his hands on the studs making the opening into the passageway as

Cistaro sidled past behind him, "did my man Junius's man, the Bishop, have the money at Wheelers today?"

"No," Rascob said. "Bishop, he say to me that *Junius* say for him to say to me, that the people at the *hospital* there, where they still be treatin' him for all those *burns* he get that day he meet *the man, McKeach*? Before he realize who he *is*? Well, don't they go and they change Junius's day for therapy *again*, they just at him day and night, and he just purely hasn't had the *tahm* to go and get together that large sum of *money* that he knows you been expectin' fo' this week an' las', countin' on him there to have, but if I will come by tomorrow, he will have it fo' me then. If I tell him I will do that, or that *the man himself, McKeach*, will do that, just come by tomorrow mornin', then he will most definitely have that money there and waitin' for me then." He paused and snickered. "That be what the Bishop said."

McKeach displayed the small smile. "I see," he said, "I see."

14

"YOU'RE FROM DOWN AROUND THERE, RIGHT?" Dowd said
on the way to Canton. He was the passenger in Trooper Henry
Ferrigno's unmarked cruiser, a white Chevrolet Impala. They
were southbound in heavy traffic on Blue Hill Avenue in Matta-
pan, the twilight darkening into evening at 6:20. Coming up on
Morton Street, Ferrigno expertly avoided a white Cadillac Sedan
DeVille double-parked with its engine running in the travel
lane; as they passed he nodded toward it, saying, "One warm afternoon and summer's here, I guess." Dowd followed his gaze to
the young black man in the right rear seat exchanging currency
for the small parcel held out by the older, very tall and long-
armed black man with beaded dreadlocks in a red tee shirt
crouching beside it. Dowd shook his head and said, "Nah,
drugs're a trade for all seasons. Kidding ourselves, we think
we're ever gonna stop it."

Ferrigno said, "Mmh."

"Nice if we could, but we can't," Dowd said. "It's an evil way
to make a royal living. Way better'n an honest job onna garbage
truck. Well, do the best we can. You ever *heard* this radio guy?
Heard him or heard *of* him?"

"Actually, I have," Ferrigno said. "Both. My mother used to tune him in on the kitchen radio every afternoon, she got home from the Town Clerk's Office. Strange dude, very strange dude."

"Know his signal off hand?" Dowd said, reaching toward the standard broadcast radio in the dash.

"Oh, never forget it," Ferrigno said. "'Ninety-eight-point-eight, FM—five *thousand* boomin' watts.' Guy's a little warped but he does have a sense of humor. You'll be wasting your time now, though, this side of Big Blue Hill. My mother could just barely get him where we lived, in Holbrook. Only Randolph 'tween him and us. His transmitter's down in Sharon someplace, 'on some dirt we sort of mounded up there—pretty *big* pile of dirt, though; biggest mound of dirt around.' Wait 'til we get on the other side of Big Blue; then see if you can get him.

"Back then I didn't understand it, the appeal he had for her. But hell, I was still a *kid*. Well, I was in college, eighty-six or seven; didn't *think* I'm still a kid then, nineteen years old, twenty—I knew everything. Used to say to her, 'For Gossake, Ma, this guy's not to be believed.'

"Not that I was completely off—he's a pretty lame excuse for a talk-show host. I mean *literally*—he's a *talking machine*. Had his larynx out. Got this mechanical thing that he uses to talk, and the *sounds* he makes with it? Jesus. He gets in too close the mike, sounds like someone callin' *moose*.

"He was right for her agenda," he said. Bringing the Impala to a stop in the left lane at the traffic light at Morton Street, he took both hands off the wheel and looked at Dowd. "It wasn't how good a talk-show host he was. It was him being in a wheelchair, and what put him there. Another victim of a careless, thankless country."

"Vietnam," Dowd said.

"You got it," Ferrigno said. "To this day she believes that if we'd only gone in a little harder; stayed a little longer; gone all out and *tried* a little more; not let the protestors make so much noise; stood behind our presidents the way we always did before that—right? She bought into the whole scenario of betrayal. Somebody, I dunno—was it Goldwater said it, when Jane Fonda went over there? 'Hope and comfort to the enemy'—that's what Hanoi Hannah meant to the Cong.

"Everyone's to blame. 'Both parties,' she'll say, when she really gets going. 'Republicans and Democrats, got us so involved there. His Highness JFK—in a very big way. He thought it was a grand idea. Adventure. They *all* did. *Sure* this was what we should do. They all lied.'

"That is what she *thought*, and that is what she *thinks*, to this very day, and no matter what anybody says to her, she will *not be* talked out of it. She *believes* this, and she always *will* believe it. Because my father got killed there, 'and nobody cares, the way they do about the ones who died in World War Two, and World War One. Even in the Civil War, people still care about them— the Revolution. But not the men who died in Vietnam.'"

"Such a loss has to mean something," Dowd said.

"Well, exactly," Ferrigno said. The light changed and he put his hands back on the wheel, moving the Impala forward. "This guy Sexton was in Vietnam, First Cav, just like my father was, only not at the same time. He was there long after Dad 'got sent home to me in a bag'—actually a metal box but she always says 'a bag.'"

"Well, she obviously loved him," Dowd said. "We got him killed, his country did, and while some of us were doing that to him, a good many of the rest of us're acting like we're ashamed of guys like him. Or, 'they were suckers.' Understandable, she's bitter."

"Oh, I know," Ferrigno said. "All I'm saying is, she's not a stupid woman, but she listens every day to this stupid show, this loud-mouth small-town blowhard. It's not what he *says*, about abortion, or drunk drivers, gun control or prayer in the schools—it's the Vietnam connection.

"The way she heard about him, the *Ledger* did a story when he came home, he wasn't quitting even though he couldn't walk. 'Look at him, the sacrifice he made for his country. And he won't let it get him down. Say what you like about him—I admire him.'

"My grandfather," Ferrigno said. "Always bought his tires from John Natale. He didn't even *like* Natale. Said he was a lyin' ratta-bass. Sullivan's in Rockland always had a better price. So why'd he buy from the lying rat bastard? Surprised you hadda ask. 'He's an Italo, is why. Keep the money in the neighbohood, the fam'ly. Always buy from your own.'

"Sexton and my father's neighborhood was Vietnam. What was Dad's is hers. I don't think she knows how Sexton lost the use of his legs—neither do I. I assume she thinks combat. As you naturally would. But she doesn't know if he ever saw combat. And I doubt she thinks having to spend your life in a wheelchair's *quite* as big a sacrifice as giving it *up*, completely, stepping on a mine and getting blown to kingdom come. Doesn't matter—he was an American soldier and it happened in Vietnam.

"Therefore she may not *necessarily* believe what he says, but she will listen to it, give it a fair hearing. As far as I know, every day." He laughed. "They're old friends. Been together over twenty years."

"So this's going to come as a big shock to her," Dowd said. "We arrest this guy and charge him with dealing drugs."

"Absolutely," Ferrigno said. "Gonna take me at least a week or two to live it down. But from what Jameson says this cancer patient told him, we're not gonna have much choice."

"Well, no, but we don't want to be too hasty here," Dowd said as the Impala approached River Street at the intersection with the Cummins Highway, the traffic barely moving now. "The way

I understand it, we've got the cancer patient all nice and se-
cluded, right?"

"*On ice,*" Ferrigno said. "On ice. Did just like you told me. He
told Jameson, the drugstore, he can't afford a lawyer, and———"

"But this's *after* he signed the waiver, and talked to us, right?"
Dowd said. "We don't want him doing any soul-searching, hiring some shyster and giving Sexton the heads up on the phone
'fore we get to Canton."

"Not gonna happen," Ferrigno said. "Jameson's with the cancer patient. Bobby says he *owns* him. 'Looks like he's ironclad—
caves in like meringue.' The thing he sent up to you, what'd he
tell you about him?"

"Not a hell of a lot," Dowd said. "His call came in, full ah
bells and whistles, I'm in one of those *delightful* meetings with
the colonel. About the Mullahy case and are we makin' any
progress on it yet."

"I'll bite—are we?" Ferrigno said.

"No," Dowd said. "Jody Aragon keeps thinkin' he might be
gettin' someplace with some kid he used to know from the Do-
minican, apparently now up here with the Latin Kings. In
Lawrence. And since they're of course competin' in the drug
business with the black posse guys who did Mullahy, Jody's
tellin' the *Latino* thug he should give us the *black* thugs. But so
far he's not buying.

"Colonel was displeased. Does not like bein' interrupted
when he's cuttin' you a new asshole—he assumes you had the
call set up 'fore you came in for the procedure. So I told Jameson
to take it all down, what he's gotten from the guy on the details
of the business, and fax it to me, so I can read it at my leisure like
a proper Christian gent. So that when I talk to Sexton I'll sound
like I was hiding in his closet every time he had a meeting for the
past six months. And leave the personal background on this
cancer-ridden monkey 'til we both've got more time.

"And that is what he did. Dictated me a four-page fax on the Sexton operation which I read before you came, and I dunno if I now know *everything* that Sexton ever did, but I can sure *sound* like I do. Bobby may talk like his first language's Polish, but he knows how to debrief a subject, and when he's got the wind up him he can make that voice-recognition gadget of his *sing*." He sniffled. "But nothing personal about the subject, no. I told him there was no time."

"He gave it to me," Ferrigno said. "Guy's name is Louis Sargent. Lives in South Dartmouth. Name onna scrip he gives the druggist at the CVS in Mansfield's Andrew Chamberlain. Says he lives at Forty-seven Lincoln Street, just over the line in Norton. There is such an address. Street directory says people who live there're named Harriman, but he's ready with the casual chitchat, an explanation for his showing up at this CVS with this paper—Harriman's his married daughter, Joan. He's staying with her and her husband up here for a while, seeing specialists in Boston. Finding out if they've got some miracle cure the folks down in New Jersey haven't heard about yet. Maybe can do something for him Trenton doctors overlooked. Also resting, trying to regain his strength. Says he's got bone cancer. Needs the Dilaudid for the pain.

"Dose's *on the money*. As a matter of fact it's the dose he's actually taking, and getting, under his own name, in South Dartmouth—his own legit prescription. This second helping that he's after—Wheelchair Timmy's gonna sell it and they're both gonna make some dough—is also for sixteen milligrams a day, four-eighty for thirty days, right in the mid-range of acceptable and therefore normal dosages. In street terms? Two-hundred-and-forty-two-mig caps, sell 'em for anywhere from two bucks apiece to six, eight—depending on availability of other shit, how desperate people are.

"But the pharmacist don't *know* this, that Lou is gonna resell it, turn his twenty-buck investment into that kind of profit. Or that he's got three other druggists in three other towns working on prescriptions for the same stuff, under three other names, just as well historied, so that he stands to scam this week close to a thousand pills, and gross about a thousand bucks, for blowin' smoke at druggists. He may be sick but he can do this; isn't heavy liftin'.

"It should've worked. Everything this druggist sees, and the other druggists see, says this guy is okay. You had some experience with people on painkillers, this's about where you'd expect a guy to be who's got what he's says he's got, still getting around. He's documented. Complete ID as Chamberlain, driver's license from New Jersey, address there in Ewing Township, just outside of Trenton, credit cards—whole schmear. Same for the other three guys he says he is.

"All fake. No such person, no such address; the accounts exist but not under that name. But very *good* fake. To begin with, not only does the scrip look all right, *he* looks all right—meaning he looks very *sick*. To any pharmacist, assistant, used to dealing with sick people, his appearance's normal—meaning, he looks awful.

"He should've *sailed* through. Why doesn't this Mister Chamberlain's?

"Simple—bad luck."

"Criminals also have bad days," Dowd said. He chuckled. "Funny, but they never think of that possibility. Almost never occurs to a street thug that the next well-dressed chap he picks to mug may not only have a fancy watch but also a nasty disposition and a thirty-eight. Or to the stickup artist that the guy in the line beside him at the bank may not only be a regular customer but an armed off-duty cop."

Ferrigno laughed. "Exactly," he said. "It so happens that this druggist'd filled four prescriptions for that stuff in the previous thirty-six hours. Exhausted his supply. He'd already called the distributor and ordered up another batch, but it's going to be a couple hours, before it comes in. So he has his assistant ask Mister Chamberlain to come back, four-fifteen, four-thirty. Chamberlain says fine, he'll do that. But there's a lull around three. Our pharmacist's maybe bored. He thinks, 'What the hell'—he's had quite a demand for this stuff; it *is* a controlled substance; they're *always* getting the nagging newsletters. 'There's an illegal market out there; people're always dreamin' up new scams to get it'; he's got the time—so why not? He makes the call."

The traffic lights showed red at the three-way intersection of Blue Hill Avenue, Cummins Highway and River Street several cars ahead of them. Ferrigno stopped the Impala in the left lane eight cars up, next to a black BMW 740IL with chrome eyebrows on the wheelwells double-parked second from the rear in a line of four cars in front of a Bank of Boston branch with a long line at its sidewalk ATM. The freshly coiffed black woman behind the wheel of the BMW regarded Dowd politely, mouthed "Officer" and smiled. Dowd nodded and smiled back.

"Once he does that, it's all over. Investigator with a good database takes about eight minutes to find *out* it's a fake. Okay. Chamberlain comes back at four-fifteen; serious trouble is waiting. Jameson. He has the pharmacist and his assistant identify our friend as the guy who brought in the fake prescription. Tells him he's under arrest on suspicion of conspiracy to traffic in narcotics, and that's just for openers. Puts the cuffs on him."

The light changed and Ferrigno took the Impala onto the divided boulevard where Blue Hill Avenue becomes Blue Hills Parkway in Milton. The traffic separated into four streams. A few cars took the right onto the Truman Highway. Most continued on to Route 138 southbound, the signage designating it for

Canton and Route 128. Some took the left on Route 28 heading east toward East Milton center. Ferrigno took the Impala out of the pack alone straight ahead. Over the rounded hills to the south the darkness was complete.

"Bobby tells him he's going to take him down to the Mansfield police station and put him in a cell there 'til he can get in touch with us. Tell us that he's got him, so that we can then talk to someone from the DA's office. Find out where the DA wants him taken, how any times it's okay to hit him with a rubber hose. But he should not plan on getting home today in time to catch the end of 'Oprah.' And it is at this point that our silver-tongued con man comes unglued."

"I love it," Dowd said with satisfaction, "the gifted amateur. First-time criminal genius. Everything's going *so* good, 'all the cops're such *jerks,* no idea what's going on,' and then suddenly it comes to a screeching *halt.* He discovers that as sleepy as he thought we were, his brilliant little caper *did* get our attention, and we've got him by the *balls.*"

"Lou Sargent," Ferrigno said, taking the Impala out of the streetlighted neighborhood into the deep darkness of the Blue Hills Reservation on Unquity Road, "is fifty-eight years old." Now Dowd could see a few scattered stars over the black hillsides. "Nine years ago, his life came apart. 'Until then I was never in trouble. 'Til then I was doing okay.'

" 'That's what they all say,' Jameson says. He tells me, 'It's like I hauled off and belted him. I thought he's gonna cry. He tells me "No, I really was." And from what he told me I guess I would've thought that, too. He's forty-nine. He's divorced from his first wife but that was fourteen years ago, and after that they got along fine. "Sometimes I kind of wondered why we got divorced." Finished raising the four kids they'd had together. "They tell you to always worry about that, what you've done to the kids, but *they* seem to've turned out fine, too—least so far."

"'He's now with his second wife, married her four years before—this's still nine years ago now, he isn't fifty yet—and the *wheels* start to fall off. One day he goes to work, "very nice day. Sunny. I remember. World looked pretty good."

"'I can see why it would,' Jameson tells me. 'He's been with this outfit years, Acadia-Johnson, Industrial Underwriters, Taunton Industrial Park. What they do's reinsure companies for unfamiliar projects, jobs that're bigger or just very different than they're used to bidding, risks that might not be covered by their regular insurance.

"'Like if a major road-construction company gets a contract to rebuild a shipyard. Now they're dealing with the ocean. Not just blizzards—*tides,* and currents. Whadda they know about this? "Better go get some more bonding insurance—we fuck up, we don't hafta pay."

"'The way he tells it, this's not a crowded field. Only two or three companies this side of the Mississippi do what they do—and only three or four the other side. Apparently peculiar geographical and population conditions have so much to do with determining risk that there're practical limits to how much territory any one outfit can know well enough to cover.

"'He's one of his company's top risk analysts, knows his job and does it well—and since that happens to be the kind of people that the company can't do its job without, function in the field it serves, he feels pretty secure. But this particular morning he finds out he isn't. They tell him when he gets in that he can turn around, go home. Company's been sold to its major competitor. All it's going to be's a name now, a division. In other words, a shell, and he no longer has a job. And because the field's so small to begin with, obviously the reason the competitor did this, bought the one he worked for, was to eliminate it, and then economize on overhead. Make high-priced people like him redundant, and get rid of them—their salaries, benefits and pensions.

"'Naturally, he's devastated. Almost fifty and here he's going to have to try to find another job, where he can use skills that he developed for the very *specialized* job that now no longer exists. Where does he begin? He doesn't know.

"'He has to get focused. He'll deal with the practical side of things, like nailing down his COBRA rights, the continuation of benefits law that protects people thrown out of work from losing their life- and health-insurance coverage. And a friend who went through something similar when *his* firm bit the dust tells him that given his age and situation—looking for another job— he should take advantage of this great health plan he's only going to have for another six months, go in and get himself a thorough work-up. So then when he's out actively looking for a job, he'll be able to say, "Look, not only am I *unbelievably* highly qualified and so forth, but I just had a complete checkup. My health is perfect."

"'Because hiring people're not supposed to take health into the question. There's a federal law against it, Americans with Disabilities Act. But they do do it; they're just very cagey. They don't say it. They say only, "What's this guy done?" They mean, "How old is he?" And if he's over thirty, "How's his health been? Not interested in hiring somebody's going to come in here, set new records for sick days."

"So, Jameson says," Ferrigno said, the Impala ascending the rise at the Hillside Street intersection, "he takes the advice." Ferrigno turned west. "'He goes to the doctor, and the doctor gets that look on his face nobody wants to see. Asks him if he's lost any *weight* recently. And Sargent says he has—he was actually kind of glad, first noticed it was happening. Been meaning to drop a few pounds; he'd been getting kind of heavy. And the doctor says how many, and what did he do to lose them; anything special, like cut out the sweets, or the beer. And Sargent says no, nothing actually; hadn't given up anything—that was what made it so nice, to have those fifteen or sixteen pounds just melt away. And the doctor says how long ago was that, and Sargent says he isn't really sure, six-eight months ago, and the doctor looks like he smells cat piss and tells him he wants him in the hospital, "not next week; tomorrow," and have a bunch of tests. Which he does, and they find out what caused the weight loss. Not a nice surprise at all. And now it's in his bones.'"

Ferrigno with the Paddock Stables on the left and the base of Great Blue Hill on the right reached over with his right hand and turned on the radio. A male voice came on saying, "RKO Talk Radio, six-eighty on your dial, and this is Howie Carr. Stay with us now as we——"

"I'll do it," Dowd said, leaning over. "Ninety-eight-point-eight, you said?"

"Right, FM," Ferrigno said, both hands back on the wheel now as they passed the parking lot at Houghton's Pond and the lights from the restaurants and filling stations clustered near the Route 138 cloverleaf with Route 128 washed out the stars. "Ninety-eight-point-eight, FM. You'll probably have trouble. There's at least three other stations fairly close to it. Sometimes atmospherics sort of billiard them around. But I promise you, it's there. As the guy said to his bride, 'Yeah, I know it's little, dear, but think of it as your lollipop—there'll be hope for both of us.'"

Dowd chuckled. A woman's high and breathy voice said, "So, do you have any idea what that could possibly've been that was making all that *noise*? And what we could do about it? To get rid of it, I mean?"

A different kind of voice that sounded as though it might have been produced by another radio inside the car radio began by making a metallic panting noise, then segued into words uttered in something resembling the sound of a normal male voice. "As a matter of fact, I think I do," it said.

"You got it," Ferrigno said. "That's him." Dowd sat back.

"In fact," the synthetic voice said, "I think I know *exactly* what it is you hear sometimes in your pear tree at night. As though there's something fighting in it. There is."

"*Nooo*," she said, mild indignation mixed with disbelief. "*Fighting* in it? *Birds* don't fight."

"Oh, yes, they do," the artificial voice said. "Jays bully other birds all the time. Crows steal the eggs from other birds' nests, and the other birds don't like it. When the crows attack, the other birds make lots of noise—if you really listen you can *hear* how frantic they are. To call their friends to come, gang up, and fight the crows.

"But it's pretty early for that. What I think you've got's *raccoons*. Big bushy fat raccoons with burglar's masks and paws with claws that look like fingers—and they use them like that, too."

"*Nooo*," the woman said.

"Oh, *yes*," the metallic voice said. "And of course you also have the birds. And the noise that you describe to me, sounds almost like a woman sobbing, '*cryin' mad*,' you said? Do it again for us, will you?"

"If I can," the woman said dubiously. "Ah, *huh*-oo, *huh*-oo, huh-*oo*? Like that."

Dowd and Ferrigno laughed.

"Very good," Sexton said. "My guess in that case, they sound like that, would be that these're definitely owls."

"Really? Are you sure?" the woman said. "Because we've never seen any, and we've lived here a long time now, seventeen years. And both my husband and I garden. Got this just huge compost heap—it's *gorgeous*. So we're both outdoors a lot. He grows his vegetables behind the garage, lettuce and tomatoes, and zucchini squash, of course—*have* to grow zucchinis. And the eggplants, which we both love. Some herbs we have in salads. Flowers, as the kiddos say, 'are my bag.' I do just love my flowers. Already had the crocuses and daffodils. Glads and then the day lilies. I just——"

"Yes," the mechanical voice said, "but we're talking the birds and raccoons here, and we do want to move along. Coming up on seven here. Owls're nocturnal. You're diurnal in your garden, out there in the dayime. Owls're out at night. In this case, probably little screech owls, probably rufous—meaning red, that's all, fancy birders' term.

"And the reason that they're fighting with the raccoons? Well, my guess is, well, raccoons're very *territorial,* all right? Don't know if you realize that, but let me assure you, they *are.* Stake out their territories and they make themselves a *nest,* a *home* there and that's where they'll spend all their adult lives, all right? If we let them. If they can get themselves enough to eat, which with all the people livin' all around them now, the suburbs expandin' like you've had all around here since right after World War Two, out into what used to be the forests and so forth, well, all the food we throw away, they don't have much trouble. They're just very good *adapters, like* to eat our garbage, and so, if they can get whatever the raccoon version of cable is, no one bothers them? They'll stay there 'til they die.

"But now this time of year, it being spring and all, the young raccoons born last year're now out lookin' for new homes. Their loving parents've kicked them out. We do it in September, send ours off to college, say to them, 'Go on now, *git,* gonna turn your bedroom into an *entertainment* center, monster TV, everything. Be sure and write us now and then, not just when you want money, tell us how it's goin'.'"

The woman snickered and Sexton laughed again, making the metallic panting sound like an engine under load, short on oil and laboring. "But raccoons do it in the springtime, you dig? Kick the young 'uns out, and what those young ones now're doin' 's checkin' out new pads.

"And what they like especially's a good old hollow tree. Which I will bet that pear in your yard's got at least one part trunk that's dead, gone hollow, and what you've been hearing is a disagreement between a young raccoon who's looked it over, likes it and decided he'll take it, start a family there—or maybe it's a she-raccoon, I dunno which raccoon gender does the homesteading—'cept there's this one catch; it's already occupied. And that's what makes the hoots and flapping. The owls already live there. They're saying, 'Not so darned fast here.' They aren't gonna be evicted—standing up for their rights as the rightful residents."

"Well, what do I *do*, then?" the woman's voice said.

"Ma'am," the mechanical voice said, "I don't think there's much you *can* do. Odds favor the raccoon. That raccoon is going to win. And if you should get rid of him, have him trapped and relocated—cost you at least fifty, sixty bucks, maybe more, have somebody come in and do it—or perhaps have someone shoot him, you're not a gun-control freak and don't mind a little violence, then pretty soon some night after that when you're in your yard, you'll hear another war beginning. Your tree's a choice dwelling place, and if you don't have one raccoon, well then, you'll have another. Only thing that you can do, if you don't want raccoons, I think, is have that tree cut down."

"I——" she said.

"And only thing that *I* can do right now for *anybody* listenin' is say, 'So long for now, folks, here around Tim's Cracker Barrel.'" The piano refrain of "The Entertainer" began in the background. "But leave your radio tuned here with us now, if you will, please. Music for the Dinner Hour, coming right up, featuring tonight the Boston Pops. And then later on at eight, your favorite Nashville Sounds. This's Tim, at CTN, your friendly neighbor here in Canton—do call in again real soon, tomorrow if you can, just love to hear from you, and we'll do it all again."

The ragtime piano music came up louder and became the foreground sound.

Dowd reached over and shut off the radio. "Shit," he said, sitting back. "I hate it when they do that."

"Who?" Ferrigno said. "Do what?" The light changed to green at the brightly lighted intersection ahead of them as they passed the A-frame church set back from the road on the left, and he turned south onto Route 138.

"This Sexton guy," Dowd said. "He doesn't know it but he just went and humanized himself. Just like you and me. Cheerful enough guy, got that Darth Vader echo voice you get with a cheap speaker phone, but still, cheerful enough. Probably about twenty-eight percent bullshit, 'bout the same's the rest of us. If either one of us knew anything at all about screech owls and raccoons, hollow trees, we'd probably be bustin' our guts laughing now, all the *shit* he's just handed that poor woman about what's goin' on in her backyard pear tree. Surprised he didn't tell her she's got a partridge in it; her true love sent it to her, Christmas's early this year. And she swallowed it, like honey on toast. But she doesn't know shit about owls, or any other critters he says're involved there—any more than we do, or anybody else does, got a job to do and kids to raise and a wife or a husband at home to keep happy; doesn't have *time* to study raccoons, read up on what lives in pear trees.

"And along with one other thing, he *knows* this—that's his secret. Same as every other con man, scam artist, politician, ballplayer—you go ahead and name it, *any* occupation. If you seem confident; if you can make it *sound* like you know what you're talkin' about—and it's not something everyone has to know, just to get along in this world—you can tell people almost anything. Most of them'll believe you."

"What's the 'one other thing'?" Ferrigno said, the Impala

crossing over Route 128, the traffic thinning out on the interstate below.

"He knows how to make it sound plausible," Dowd said. "Even
though *he* knows it's probably bullshit—in this case with the
owls, a wild guess, it *might* be true—he doesn't laugh while he's
slingin' it. You have to keep a straight face—that's mandatory."

"So why's this bother you?" Ferrigno said. Route 128 was well
behind them now; the Impala was descending into the hollow at
Cobb's Corner.

"It bothers me because the good arrest is a work of art. You
do it right and you can change a two-bit crook into a major law-
enforcement asset, in the twinkling of an eye."

"*Riiight,*" Ferrigno said.

"So I exaggerate," Dowd said. "But hear me out. You need to
go into the arrest in the right frame of mind. The point of view
you as a cop want to have when you go to grab a guy is controlled but righteous anger. You're a policeman. Guardian of the
law. A professional law-enforcement person, employed by society at disgracefully low wages to exert the authority to discour-
age individuals from flouting the rules. Making it possible for
all of us to live together in peace, harmony—and, if possible,
prosperity.

"Now, being realistic, you can't expect every criminal you
grab is going to be the Boston Strangler. Or the guy OJ's looking
for, mostly on the golf course—the guy who really killed Nicole
Brown Simpson and her friend Ron Goldman. A murdering genius that hanging's too good for, go in hoping he'll resist, so you
can *shoot* him. Several times. But depending on what he's done,
the very least the suspect should be's a pain in the *ass*. One cut
below a damn *nuisance.*"

He brooded. "Every self-respecting criminal has a moral obligation to present himself at all times as at least a miserable

prick. So a cop can get some pleasure outta roustin' his miserable ass. Time enough after he's been arrested and his lawyer's talked to him, start look hangdog and fakin' remorse. Practicing the rehabilitated look. This dodge of acting like a basically nice guy *before* you're arrested; this's unfair to police."

"Sexton isn't meeting his responsibilities," Ferrigno said.

"He's *scorning* them," Dowd said. "On the score of that performance. The effect it had on me."

The light was green at Cobb's Corner and Ferrigno going through it let up on the accelerator, allowing the steep grade where Route 138 as Washington Street becomes the Turnpike to slow its progress beyond the front lawn of the Ponkapoag Golf Club. Near the crest of the hill he signaled a right turn and took the Impala into the development on Peaceful Hills Drive. "Well, maybe you could get yourself worked up about *that*," Ferrigno said. "Get yourself psyched on the scorn—so you can be happy to arrest him."

Two low-slung eight-room ranch houses facing Turnpike flanked the entrance to Peaceful Hills, illuminated by the streetlights on the main road and two more close together near the front of the development. The house on the left was cocoa-brown with a grey roof and bright turquoise trim; the drapes in the front picture window were open on a table lamp with a cocoa-brown shade. The shrubbery along the foundation had overgrown the window sills. There was a white Plymouth Voyager minivan in the driveway; a two-wheeled trailer with two shrouded Sno-Cats was parked next to it under the only tree on the shallow lot, a budding maple.

"If we were still a ways away," Dowd said, "then, maybe. But not now—we're here. Won't have time enough to come at it from that angle. Oh, I'll arrest him anyway. After all, it is my job. But unless he acts up some, gives us at least a little guff, I won't get any *enjoyment* out of it."

15

THE HOUSE ACROSS THE STREET was dusty rose with a grey roof and white trim. The garage doors were down. There were ten birdhouses, five red and five white, with silver stars on blue roofs, in the maple tree next to the garage; the low shrubs along the front of the house were bagged in burlap. The drapes were drawn in the front picture window so that only a sliver of light showed at the center. The streetlights on Turnpike were very bright sodium arcs; those in Peaceful Hills were incandescents spaced two or three hundred yards apart, so that the entire neighborhood appeared to be in hiding and only the picture window treatments—drapes closed or drapes open—distinguished the houses from one another in the dark.

Ferrigno seemed to make the Impala sneak among them, taking the first left off Peaceful Hills onto Mockingbird Lane and at the end of it the left into Chickadee Circle without pausing to read street signs. There were three low-slung six-room ranch houses on each side of the approach to the circular turnaround and two more at the circle. There was a streetlight on the left at the edge of the circle. The house positioned in the quarter-to-the-hour quadrant was pale grey with a grey roof and maroon shutters. The one in the quarter-after quadrant was lima green with a grey roof and dark green trim.

"The one onna right, pea-soup color," Ferrigno said. The drapes were drawn partway in the front picture window. A lamp with a maroon shade and a base of a rearing grey stallion made of grey-silver plastic was centered in it on a table. The metallic blue Dodge Ram Maxivan in the driveway blocked the view from the street of the garage that Sexton had converted to his studio and office. There was a light on in the room behind the reception area, visible through the door next to the studio. The outside light was on, illuminating the brass 68 numerals over the big black mailbox, and the ramp leading up to the door. Ferrigno stopped the Impala behind the van, blocking it in the driveway. He shut off the ignition.

Dowd chuckled. "Okay," he said, "if he tries to make a break for it, he finds his wheels blocked, just like any other bad actor. But're you sure you're allowed to do this? Don't you have to give handicapped suspects an escape route, take their disability into account?"

"That's what I'm doing," Ferrigno said. "In the Marathon the wheelchair guys always come barrel-assing down Heartbreak Hill into Brookline *miles* ahead of the runners. I'm givin' him at least an even shot here. I figure, I have got his van blocked; if he decides to bolt, he'll see this; and come wailin' out the door and down that ramp like he was *launched.* That'll give him a big lead; he'll be halfway to the main road 'fore I get the key back in the ignition. I don't care what anybody says—that's a sporting chance, as much any felon, able-bodied or not, oughta get."

Dowd laughed and got out of the car. He opened the right rear door and lifted a black leather zippered three-ring portfolio off the back seat. He closed the door and turned toward the house. It was just after 7:10. He was first at the door with the portfolio in his left hand and his badge case ready in his right,

Ferrigno slightly behind him on the ramp to his left, when Theresa Sexton—in grey suede boots with two-inch stacked heels that made her 5'11", teased reddish-blond big hair that made her seem even taller, tight white jeans and a tight yellow deeply scoop-necked short-sleeved jersey over an extreme push-up bra—answered the doorbell. She had a pilsner glass in her left hand; her long fingernails were painted gold. She took a swallow of beer as she opened the inside door with her right hand, smiling invitingly, merry, her eyes sparkling and wide, the brows lifted, her lips parted in "Yes?"

Dowd held up the badge and she frowned, half opening her mouth, freshly lipsticked dark pink, as she stared at it through the glass of the storm door. Blinking, she began to shake her head, either to indicate confusion and try to clear it, or to indicate No, when Dowd, having stowed the badge case in his left inside jacket pocket, opened the storm door with his right hand and stepped up onto the threshold, moving her back and explaining, "State Police, Mrs. Sexton. We'd like to come in."

She retreated, stepping backward toward the front of her desk in the reception area, somewhat off balance, using her right hand to grope behind her for the front of the desk. The speakers played a Boston Pops recording of "Moonlight Serenade," lush with trombones, saxophones and muted trumpets, from a medley of Glenn Miller Band favorites. "I don't..." she said.

"We need to talk to your husband, Mrs. Sexton," Dowd said, moving forward relentlessly, crowding her back toward the desk, slapping the portfolio down on it, making room enough for Ferrigno to enter behind him, look through the window into the studio and satisfy himself that it was unoccupied, then push past Theresa and the desk, going directly to the right of the doorway leading to what had been the breezeway before the garage conversion and was now the entryway to the kitchen, drawing his dark grey Glock 9mm service pistol from the holster where it rode butt canted forward at the top of his right hip.

Dowd continued to close in on her, his voice gentle and soothing but also as insistent as his forward motion. "Since his truck's there in the drive, probably doesn't go too far without it, we assume he must be home. Out there in the kitchen, is he?" Calculating that she would not want or try to flee, he had her effectually cornered now between the front of the desk, the green molded plastic chair in front of it and the door. He stood close to her, filling her field of vision, so that to see clearly what Ferrigno was doing she would have had to turn her head to the right, taking her eyes off Dowd, making it so that she would fear doing it would make her seem furtive and guilt-conscious, and therefore wouldn't do it.

She leaned back as far away from him as she could, using her right hand now to steady herself against the desk, backing around; calves pressed against the green chair, she held the beer glass aloft in her left hand, nearly at eye level, trying not to spill it, the posture thrusting her breasts out and upward toward Dowd like offerings, her chin down against the top of her chest above them. Her breathing was shallow and rapid, making the breasts heave; her nostrils flared and her mouth was now completely open, her eyes very wide. "Could you call him for us, please? Tell him we're here? And we need to talk to him? Ask him a few questions? We don't want to alarm him. Startle him, you know?"

She shook her head wildly, chewing now on her lower lip, and Ferrigno, moving diagonally from right to left, sprang lightly and almost soundlessly through the doorway, landing combat-crouched on the balls of his feet, facing to the right of the door, his forearms and two-handed grip on the Glock now in the kitchen area beyond the frame of the door. Theresa turned her head to the right just as Ferrigno's coattails disappeared into the kitchen. "*Tim,*" she said, crying her husband's name.

Dowd put his left hand on her right forearm. "Now Mrs. Sexton," he said reproachfully, "there's nothing to be upset about here. We're here simply because we need to talk to your husband. I've already told you we're police. We're with the Special Investigations Bureau of the Massachusetts State Police. Now this's important."

In the kitchen Ferrigno called authoritatively, "Mister Sexton. State Police. Need to talk to you. I'll come to you. Just stay where you are. Say something so I can tell where you are."

"I'm Lieutenant Jim Dowd," Dowd said, stepping back half a pace from her, "and my partner's Trooper Henry Ferrigno. We're assigned to the detective division. We work in plain clothes. That's why we're not in uniform. And we've made an arrest today down in Mansfield, this afternoon, and as a result of that we have a man in custody whom another officer's talked to, and as a result of what this man told this other officer, we now have to talk to your husband." He locked her eyes with his. "I have to emphasize," he said, "this's all very important.

"Are there any guns in the house?"

She stared at Dowd, her eyes wild. "*Nooo,*" she said, "*you can't shoot him.*"

Dowd took her firmly by her right forearm and used his right hand to capture her left forearm so that he could bring down her left hand with the pilsner glass. That caused her to concentrate on not spilling the beer as he exerted gentle force on her arms, enough to maneuver her into sitting down on the green plastic chair. She took a deep breath and let it out slowly. Releasing her right forearm, he used his left hand to put her right hand in her lap and then to take the glass out of her left hand and put it in the center of the blotter on her desk. There was a chunk of lime at the bottom of the glass. He used his right hand to place her left hand in her lap. He stepped back again, this time a full pace, cocking his head and regarding her as a careful house painter might look for brush marks or drips on a panel just completed. Elsewhere in the house Ferrigno called out "Mister Sexton?" at intervals; they could hear him opening and closing doors.

"Well, he's not in a *closet,* you know," she said with dull resentment, hearing the clacking sound Ferrigno made opening and closing a wooden folding door. She looked up into Dowd's face, her eyes now flat and dull, her dark pink mouth pouched sullen. "He can't get the chair into tight spaces."

"Well, you see, Mrs. Sexton," Dowd said pleasantly, as though informing a child that ice cream would not be served 'til later, "we don't know the layout of this house the way you and Mister Sexton do, which doors're for closets. So we have to assume every door's a door into a room—or a space big enough for your husband to get into some way and hide in, since he doesn't seem to want to come out and talk to us."

"He's not *hiding,*" she said, both grim and disdainful. "He's not *afraid* of you. He doesn't even know you're *here.* He's out inna *back,* inna screenhouse. Can't hear you guys in here, hollerin' at him."

"Kind of chilly still, for the screenhouse, isn't it?" Dowd said, edging toward the kitchen entry.

"'S where the grill is," she said. "He's got his jacket on. That's where we keep the gas grill, all right? His father got the first screenhouse for summer, he could grill meat for his dinner 'thout the mosquitoes eatin' him. Then he had the bright idea if he put in a cement floor inna thing out there, second winter after, then he'd be able, grill his meat year 'round. Can't use a charcoal or a gas grill in your own house—suffocate. Inna fresh air inna screenhouse, you can."

Dowd studied her, his mouth working. "No kidding," he said.

"Oh yeah," she said, not looking up, "I'm not kiddin'. His father did it so that inna winter when the ground got all wet, then even if it snowed or rained, he could go out there and charcoal-grill what they had for dinner. Golf's only one reason he retired Arizona, and I don't think it was the main one—out there he can grill year 'round, never need a jacket. Loves the taste of charcoaled meat. But tryin' to keep smoke away here, he built the screenhouse too far from the house. I mean, he walked normal, everything, and he would try to hurry. But it's too far, and he always had the same trouble Tim does inna wheelchair—even withah landing strip that he had put in. Had like a sidewalk paved out to there. Goes like a bat outta hell on it. *Zoo-oom.*" She made a planing, swooping motion with her hand. "When it snows he has a kid come shovel it. So he has a lot of fun, but it don't change anything. Meat's all cold after it's ready, time he can get it back inside here onna the table. Hafta put it under the broiler innie oven. Heat it up."

At the entry Dowd glanced back at her to make sure she wasn't moving. Seeing she was sitting head down with her shoulders slumped, dispirited, in the green plastic chair, he stuck his head into the passage and shouted: "Henry, can you read me? She says he's out in the back. Got a screenhouse out there and he's cookin' meat in it."

"Filet *mignon*," she said resentfully, looking up, as Ferrigno called back "*Yo*," from some point farther in the house.

Dowd looked back at her, pursing his lips, still shouting at Ferrigno. "I *said*—*she* says he's out inna screenhouse. Inna yard inna back. Charcoalin' *meat*. Take a look out, see 'f he's there."

"Aw right," Ferrigno yelled. "Yeah, there's a light out there." Dowd heard a door open and bang shut.

"'*Grillin*' meat,' I said," she said, looking up, regaining spirit as Dowd watched. Now she was deciding that his interest should make her feel better. "His father—strictly charcoal." She straightened up, moving her shoulders back and forth. "Timmy— strictly propane. Says ah charcoal lighter, all it is is kerosene, makes too much *smoke*; gets in his stoma there, an' *chokes* him." She reached across her chest with her right hand, using her thumb and forefinger to pluck at her left bra strap under the left sleeve of the yellow jersey, hiking it up and resetting it on her shoulder. Then she did the same thing with the right strap, using her left thumb and forefinger. She wiggled and bounced on the chair and inhaled. She moistened the dark pink lips with the tip of her tongue. "Plus gives the meat an oily taste. Can't hack it." She sat back in the chair now and nodded, satisfied that she was displaying herself properly.

"I see," Dowd said.

"Uh huh," she said. She regarded the pilsner glass on the desk thoughtfully. "Tonight, see, we're celebrating." On the speaker the Boston Pops segued into "In the Mood." She sniffled. "Lou and Joie're comin' back up here again tonight. To help us celebrate."

"This would be Lou ... *Sargent*?" Dowd said.

"Yeah," she said, "and his wife, Joie? Coming up here from South Dartmouth, soon as she gets out of work. Lou don't have a job. Right now. I thought you're them—they must've got here early. See, they were there *with* us, *saw* it—Rocky's, down in Stoughton? Last Sunday afternoon." She smiled. That's why the filet mignons." She paused expectantly, inviting a reply. Dowd kept his face expressionless and said nothing. "You know?" she said, helpfully.

"Well," Dowd said, "I was trying to think. What it'd be that you'd be celebrating. But I couldn't. Not first day of spring— that was last month. Not income tax day—that was a week ago."

"*Income* tax day?" she said. "Who in *hell*'d celebrate *income tax* day?"

"Well," Dowd said, "never personally had the good luck to've been one myself, I wouldn't know this from experience, but I would think that people finding out that they're getting big refunds on their taxes, they might think that was a pretty good reason to celebrate."

"Oh, *yeah*," she said, frowning, gnawing again on her lower lip. "I never thought of that." She nodded. "I guess that could happen." She glanced again at the pilsner glass; the foamy white head on the golden beer had subsided. She licked her lips. She said, "Say, uh," nodding toward the beer, "'d it be all right if I was, you know, to drink some of that now? While you're still here, I mean?"

Unable to stop himself, Dowd grinned at her. "Well now," he said, "that's an interesting question. Let's consider it.

"This's *your* house, right?" he said.

She nodded, bright-eyed now.

"And that there is *your* beer, right?" he said.

She nodded again. "*Corona*," she said proudly.

"Which you've aleady had some of, right?" he said.

She blushed.

"In fact," he said, "being something of a student of this sort of thing, having had a few beers myself, I would guess that maybe this one might be your ... *second*?" She shook her head a little. "*No?*" he said. "Then this would be your ... *third* ... tonight?"

She nodded happily.

"But you're over twenty-*one*," he said, "so you are *legal.*" She nodded. "And you're not *driving,* I can see." She shook her head. "And you're not *disturbing* anybody," he said. She shook her head emphatically, grinning at their game. "Certainly not ... the *peace,*" he said. He winked. She lifted her eyebrows and beamed. "We do know that, at least," he said. She put her head back and giggled.

Dowd nodded, smiling. "Then I think it's okay," he said. "Go ahead and have some beer."

She was reaching across her body with her left hand for the glass when the door somewhere in the house behind them opened and then banged shut again. She remembered Ferrigno had also come in, and gone out, and the fun vanished from her face. She frowned and started to get up.

"Back in with him, Loot," Ferrigno yelled. "Out here in the dinette." There were squeaking, banging and thrashing sounds. "*No,*" Ferrigno said. "You're not goin' in there. They'll be comin' right out here. Don't give me no fuckin' *shit* now—I'll take your fuckin' *mignons* and put 'em downah damn *disposal.* You just get over there behind that *table,* and you *lock* those fuckin' wheels, and you stay fuckin' *put.*"

Theresa, making a soft cry that was not a word, came out of the chair, putting out her hands to fend off Dowd, but he stood aside to his left and turned his back to the kitchen entry, extending his right arm like a crossing gate, so that she ran into it and stopped. "Slow down now," he said, keeping his voice soothing. "Take it easy. Let's try to keep in mind here what your situation is. Your husband's in the kitchen and he's in police custody."

She stared at Dowd, her eyes wild. "Under arrest, ma'am, yes, he is," Dowd said, taking her by the forearms again as she raised her hands, now fists, to beat his chest. "Charged with conspiracy to possess and distribute narcotics, one charge out of many that we could bring. Have to choose from, you might say." She tried to wrench out of his grip and could not. "But for the moment he's right here and you are going to see him, as I assume you had in mind here when you raised your fists at me."

She exhaled heavily, and disgustedly. "I'm a state police officer, ma'am," he said. "I'm a *cop,* I guess I have to remind you. We've maybe been having a little too much harmless *fun* out here, you and me, than I should've been allowing, but don't let it mislead you. We ain't pals, you and me, and it's still a criminal offense to try to hit me." She looked calculating. "Or try to kick me, or knee me—*anywhere, in any part of my body.* You got that? You do that, and forget about flirtin', I'll *hurt* you. You're thinkin' 'bout doing somethin' like that, *don't.* Understand?" She took a deep breath and nodded.

"Now, if you tell me you can behave yourself now, we'll go out and see your husband. Or if you don't I'll have you cuffed to a radiator so fast it'll make your head spin." She scowled. "Oh-*kay,*" he said, "we'll try it again." Using her forearms he turned her around and sat her down on the green plastic chair again, hard.

"Now, damnitall Mrs. Sexton," he said, "calm yourself down, all right, willya? Don't make me arrest you for chickenshit stuff, A and B onna a cop? *Poof,* that's *nothin'.* Lug teenage drunks for that alla time, every Saturday night. Whereas *you,* you got an excellent chance to be *different.* Right now, unless you make nice with the law, you got a very good chance of makin' the big time. Because unless we start hearin' something we haven't heard here yet, me and Henry, like how much you both wanna help us, we're gonna run you and your *dee*voted husband for some very— grown-up—offenses, such as major-league drug trafficking. Get you folks some *serious* time. Start with fifteen years apiece and then double it—at least, and that's just gettin' started.

"You'll be *famous,* both of you—big-time desperadoes, inna headlines day or two. Course he'll be close to eighty, next time you two get your jollies, and they won't let you dress like that, ma'am, where you're gonna go—other ladies'd go *mad.* But fame does have its price." He smiled. "So's that what you'd rather do?"

Her eyes were wider now than before, and her mouth formed a dark pink oval. "*Timmy!*" she yelled. "Don't *say anything.* Don't you say one word these guys." Then she sat back, hunching her shoulders into the defensive posture, and stared at Dowd. "And I'm not gonna, either," she said, her face and eyes filled with hope that Dowd would allow her to carry out her defiance.

He nodded slowly. "Much better," he said. "Now, would you like to take a moment, catch your breath and collect your thoughts here, or are you okay enough now so that we can go out into what I gather is the kitchen, join your husband and Trooper Ferrigno, and I'll formally advise you both of your rights."

She shook her head. "No," she said, "I mean, I'm all right." She stood up, rubbing her hands down the legs of her jeans as though smoothing a skirt around herself, humming softly and taking a very deep breath, apparently just wanting oxygen. Then at the end of the chorus, she smiled to herself and sang in an undertone, "But you just can't kill the beast."

DOWD SAW THAT THEY WERE a team. Under the expressionless steady gaze Ferrigno maintained on them, standing with his arms folded behind Sexton under the speaker and the grey plastic cuckoo clock mounted over the back door, they communicated as much by exchanging glances as by speaking words. The light in the kitchen and dinette, overcrowded by the four of them, came from two multicolored stained-glass Coca-Cola ceiling fixtures; it had a warm and cozy reddish glow. The speaker at low volume played the Boston Pops version of the Glenn Miller arrangement of "St. Louis Blues March."

Dowd, standing between the refrigerator and the beat-up maple table, feeling as though he was intruding, read the Sextons their rights. While he was doing it Theresa removed a long rolled-up paper tube, secured by an elastic band, from the center of the table and put it on top of the refrigerator. Tim in his wheelchair efficiently collected the three place settings closest to him, stacking the plates at the opposite place in front of Dowd and putting the napkins and the cutlery on top of the stack. Theresa took it from the table and put it on the counter between the stove and sink. "You understand these rights as I have read them to you?" Dowd said.

They conferred by glance and concurred by nodding, she now standing at the table to Dowd's left, hesitating until Tim had rummaged in his lap and found his prosthesis, so that they could say "Yes" together. She sat down opposite her husband in the chair nearest Dowd.

Dowd separated two copies of the advice-of-rights form from the stack he had taken from his portfolio. He filled out the names and location sections at the top and put one in front of Tim and the other in front of Theresa, handing her his ballpoint. Ferrigno stepped up behind Tim and handed his ballpoint over Sexton's right shoulder. The Sextons exchanged glances again before looking down at their forms and signing. "Thank you," Dowd said, taking back the forms and recovering his pen; Sexton held Ferrigno's back over his right shoulder and Ferrigno took it.

"I think I'll just sit down now, myself," Dowd said, bending over the table to date, noting the time—7:41 P.M.—and initialing the executed forms before inserting them and the blanks into different compartments of the portfolio. Taking out a tape recorder and a spiral notebook, zipping the portfolio closed and putting it on the counter, he made his way around behind Theresa and pulled out the chair in front of the kitchen window. He sat down, putting the notebook and the tape recorder in the center of the table, then crossed his right leg over his left knee and rested his right hand on his right knee.

Fixing his gaze on Tim he said pleasantly, "So, Mister Sexton, you've gotten yourself and your dear wife as well into a huge lake of shit. What've you got to say for yourself?"

"I dunno what you're talking about," Sexton said, his blue eyes glowering, his left hand at his throat with the prosthesis. "All Terry and I're doing tonight is we're celebrating with our friends Lou and Joie." He used his right hand to gesture at the tape recorder. "That thing on?"

"Nope," Dowd said, "and as you can see, I'm not writing in the notebook. Like to get to know my subjects first, a little, 'fore I trample on their rights. Your wife mentioned you're doing that, having some kind of a little party tonight, your friends Lou and Joie. And using the five-star menu, too, filet mignon and Corona. That's nice. Whatcha celebrating?"

Sexton studied his wife as though to make sure she was all right. Unaware what she had done, he too now tried to show defiance that would reassure her he was not afraid of Dowd and controlled the situation. He managed chiefly to communicate uncertainty, confusion and timidity. "I do know I don't have to talk to you, if I don't wanna, you know," he said.

"I should hope so," Dowd said. "Every mother's son who ever saw a TV cop show knows that, and if you maybe missed it, I just got through reminding you."

Sexton blinked. He looked at his wife for a cue, being as new to their situation as she was. Since it alarmed her to see this, she didn't have one. She showed the alarm by moving in her chair. That rattled him more, and he licked his lips.

"Mister Sexton," Dowd said, pouncing, "look, I know you're nervous. You and your wife here, both. And you should be— you're both in very serious trouble here. And the fact that you're completely new to it—trying to pretend otherwise, act like you're hardened criminals—this isn't making it any easier for you, either."

Sexton squirmed in his chair.

Dowd ignored his movements. "Trooper Ferrigno and I know all this, and so we'd like to—and *we're* trying, ourselves, honest—to make it a little easier for you."

Sexton looked incredulous. "Oh, don't think so?" Dowd said. He smiled. "That shows I'm right. The usual way to go in to make

an arrest in a case involving charges as serious as the ones involved in this case is to come in with at least eight officers, in
SWAT gear. Surround the house, and instead of ringing the bell
and waiting for someone to come answer it, *open* the door, knock
the door down with a ram and come in over it, guns drawn."

Sexton looked thoughtful. "Sure," Dowd said, "what you're
thinking now is right. The fact we didn't do that oughta tell you
something. Oughta tell you that we think there might be a way
for you and your wife to make things a little easier on yourselves.
But the only way you're ever gonna find that out is if you two
can first stop acting like you think you're starring in some third-
rate gangster movie. So that we can start *talking* to each other—
like four more-or-less reasonable adults looking at a great big
problem two of them've got. And the other two're just as anxious as they are to help them get out of. See if maybe if they
work together there's a way get it *solved,* in such a way that it
won't leave the two who've got the problem in a situation where
their lives're utterly, completely, and permanently ruined."

He paused, turned his head and looked at Theresa. "And Mrs.
Sexton," he said, hardening his voice and fixing his gaze on her
until she lowered her eyes, "I hope you understand this, too.
That based on what we know already, right now you are in this
mess just as deep as he is, and if he's looking at spending the
next thirty years to life in a maximum security prison such as
Cedar Junction, as he most certainly is, what you've got in front
of you is a very long time in MCI Framingham. Where we send
female offenders in this Commonwealth—and we're talking
years here, many of 'em."

Dowd swung his gaze back on her husband and was pleased
to see that Tim was now as troubled as he was frightened. "Mister Sexton, I'm sure you don't want that to happen, any more
than she does," he said. "I realize you've been through a lot as a
result of your military service, and that she must be not only one

252 *At End of Day*

good-*lookin'* lady, as any man can plainly see, but also a damned brave lady. To've signed up with you as she has, and helped you make what looks to me at least like a pretty damned good life— out of what has to've been a pretty damned depressing start."

He hesitated, letting it sink in. "And whatever promises you may've made to her," he said, "I know you were a soldier. Not the kind of kid who ran and hid, and found a way out of the draft. You didn't bullshit her. You told her there'd be days—and might be nights as well; don't know you get those flashbacks way some Viet vets claim they do—when she'd find it very tough, married to a damaged man."

As Dowd had intended, Sexton looked miserable. "But as tough as I know you were, being the fair man you are, as straightforward as you must've been—when you told her things with you might sometimes get to be awful, awful hard—and as tough as I'm sure she was, when she told you she was sure that she could do it—*you* never in your life told *her,* and neither one of you imagined, that if she tied herself to you, she'd wind up doing *time.*"

He heard Theresa suck her breath in. He ignored her and continued to talk to her husband. "You haven't got a record, but you've been as good as locked up, confined to one military hospital after another for as long as you were, no way to get out on your own. Technically you've never done time, but if you go away on this you won't find the experience all that unfamiliar. A whole lot *longer,* sure, but you'll recognize it." He leaned in closer so that his chin was over Sexton's right thigh, and he tapped him with his forefinger on the right knee as he spoke.

"*She* will." He gestured with his right thumb back over his shoulder toward Theresa. "You know 'cause you're a man, and all men've heard, what happens to young good-lookin' guys when they get to prison. You of course got nothing to worry about in that respect now, given how old you are and the fact you're all beaten-up. Unless of course you *wanna* have something to think about, in which case you'll be on your own—and good luck to you; I'm sure you'll find companions without any trouble at all.

"*But*, so'll she," Dowd said. "Whether she wants 'em or not." He sat up and turned in his chair and looked at her appraisingly. He sighed and shook his head. "Which both of you might wanna think about some," he said, turning back to Sexton. "Think about what a couple-three of those two-twenty, two-forty black bull dykes they've got in there, look like NFL linebackers, wouldn't love to try on that fresh white Danish pastry." He glanced back at Theresa; she looked dark and resentful, but she slumped.

"Anyway," Dowd said, sitting up straight again and folding his arms across his stomach, "that's about where we are now. And it wasn't so terribly bad now, was it? Getting to know each other just a little better, where we stand and so forth." He smiled. "*And*, now that it's over with, I do believe I had a question pending. What were you celebrating tonight? Anything to do with that poster?" He used his gaze and eyebrows to indicate the tube on top of the refrigerator.

The little doors above noon on the dial of the cuckoo clock snapped open over Ferrigno's head, making him start, look upwards and laugh. A little red bird emerged slowly, halfway, and cuckooed seven times. Ferrigno and Dowd frowned and looked at their watches. It was 7:51. They both looked at Theresa. The little red bird retreated slowly and the doors closed over it. "It's broken," Theresa said. "It's been broken forever. I keep asking him…"

Her husband fitted his prosthesis against his throat. "And I keep telling you," he said, weary and annoyed, "that I *can't*. Nobody can. It's a cheap cuckoo clock I got in the PX in Quang Gang Bang or someplace—someplace I don't even remember.

Probably cost a buck thirty-nine, made in Taiwan, and I was half in the bag. Dunno why I bought it. If I'd known I was doin' it, I wouldn't've brought it home, but of course I didn't pack my stuff—I was inna hospital. Someone else did all that for me. My father put it up for me when I got home. Did it to surprise me one day, I was at the VA Brockton, getting therapy. Didn't know how to tell him I didn't *want* it put up, ask him to take it down— *I* wanted it thrown away. And when he was gone, I couldn't reach it, take it down. Still can't. Bothers you? You can reach it— you take it down. Either throw it away or *you* try to fix it yourself." He paused, looking disgusted. "But for *Chrissakes* stop *talking* about it."

The speaker played "Little Brown Jug." Theresa Sexton stared at her husband for a long time, her eyes vacant, as though trying to remember where she'd seen him before. At last Dowd cleared his throat. The sound brought her out of her reverie. "No," she said, turning to look at Dowd, "it doesn't matter. I'll show it to you." She pushed back from the table and stood up. Her husband made a sound but she disregarded him and reached up, pulling the tube off the top of the refrigerator and putting it down on the table, taking the elastic off and unrolling it. It was a three-by-five-foot color poster. Standing next to her husband's left side and bending over the table she reached into his lap and lifted up his right hand. She put it down on the poster saying, "You hold the top." He looked resigned and left his hand there.

She straightened up and unrolled the poster, walking back to where she had been sitting, and leaned over the table so that she could hold the bottom down with her left hand in front of Dowd. He found that looking down her neckline he could see the tops of her nipples, dark brown circles among small freckles. Looking up at him she said, "No, at the poster," and along with his gaze he shifted position to his right on the chair, placing his right hand on the edge of the poster precisely at the top of her black panty and looked down it.

It was a harshly lighted three-quarter-angle frontal torso shot, with excellent sharpness. She stood with her arms akimbo, proudly. In addition to the panty she was wore a thin grey cropped tee shirt. She had been drenched, so that her hair streamed down around her gleaming face, shining grin and flashing eyes, and the tee shirt plastered to her showed the shape of her right breast and the fullness of both of them in detail, the nipples standing out in full arousal.

"*Mercy,*" Dowd said admiringly. Without looking up, he said to Ferrigno, "You see this all right, Henry?"

"Oh, yeah," Ferrigno said uncomfortably, attempting to sound listless, shifting his position at the door behind Sexton in his wheelchair, "I can see all right."

"Well, but upside *down,*" Dowd said practically, without looking up, shaking his head. "And you're lookin' over *him* there. What you have to do is come around this side the table. Look at 'em right side up. I mean—these're really something. Gorgeous."

He looked up inquiringly, as though innocently meaning to seek Ferrigno's gaze, but quite deliberately locked eyes with Sexton in his chair and held his gaze. There was savage helpless anger in Sexton's eyes. "I take it, Mrs. Sexton," Dowd said blandly, without looking at her, taunting her husband with his gaze and tone and the faint smirk at the corners of his mouth, "this was some kind of contest? Wet Tee Shirt Night or something? That they had at this place where you'd gone, with your husband and your friends, and you entered it, and *won*? And that's what you're celebrating tonight? When we interrupted?"

"Well, *yeah,*" she said. "But I mean, is it okay now to roll it up now? I mean, you guys seen enough now?"

"Oh yeah, sure," Dowd said, smiling now on the left side of his face. "We've seen all we need to see. You can roll it back up now." He lifted his hand off the poster and returned to his former position in his chair.

Keeping his furious eyes on Dowd, Sexton lifted his hand immediately and fast off the top of the poster, holding it straight up, palm open and flat, fingers and thumb rigid, the fascist salute. Dowd widened his smile and flicked two fingers of his own right hand to receive it. The poster rolled up toward the center as she took away her left hand, so that the bottom and the top met in two rolls in the middle. She began rerolling it from the bottom to the top.

"At first I didn't want to," she said. "You know, when we first got there to Rocky's and we saw the sign and all—to *expose* myself like that. All those people there. But then we had a few beers, and Lou, you know, started saying, 'Jesus Christ, 're you guys *nuts*? What the hell's the difference, huh? Everybody in here can already *see* what you got, best pair inna house—no woman here can beat 'em. You're turning down a hundred *bucks*, you can have for the *taking*?' And Joie, you know, said the same—'It's not like they can't *tell*, you know, lookin' at you, way you come in.' And 'All you'd be really doin's givin' them a little better *look*—it's not like you exactly *hide* 'em.' And like I say, we'd *had* some drinks, and then me and Tim, we sort of just looked at each other, like, you know—'a hundred *bucks*?' And so we said all right.

"But I said they hadda use the hose, just hold it over my head and soak me down like that. I wasn't gonna let 'em, you know, do like some girls let 'em do, and I did some other times myself, me and Tim first got together—come out with the tee shirt dry and an' let them spray me onna stage like that they got there, with the seltzer bottles. Those things 're *strong*, like *powerful*, and guys try to *hurt* you with 'em, aim 'em at your crotch and all, so that it *stings*. And they hadda let me change inna the tee shirt out in back. And the extra hundred bucks you get if you then take the tee shirt off and dry yourself off on the stage there, so you're just there in your *panties*? In *front* of everybody? No *way* I was doing that." She finished rerolling the poster, put it back on the refrigerator, and returned to her seat at the table.

"Yeah," Dowd said, having held her husband's gaze while she told her story, "well, glad we got that straightened out." He cleared his throat and looked around, meeting all eyes. "Now," he said, "a report from *our* part of the forest.

"As you may or may not've gathered," he said, "the friend you expected to join you for dinner tonight, Mister Louis Sargent, has been unavoidably detained. By us. On a felony charge of conspiring and attempting to possess and distribute a Chapter Ninety-four-*C*, Section Thirty-*two*, Class *A*, controlled substance, an opium derivative, to wit—hydromorphine, to wit— Dilaudid, with intent to traffic therein. Which is punishable by a term of ten years in the state *prison*. To be served."

Theresa's mouth kept opening and gaping, and each time she noticed it she closed it, working to receive and process what Dowd was saying and reminding him of a finning goldfish hanging in a glass bowl of warm standing water.

"Having had a chance to think about his predicament and come to terms with what would certainly happen to him if he failed to make friends for himself with the mammon of righteousness, in this instance represented by our Trooper Jameson, Mister Sargent shrewdly elected, as we like to say, to come coco with us.

"And I'm *very* pleased to report that when your pal Lou searches his soul and makes his decision to throw in his lot with the law, he don't mess around. He barfs his guts up. He has given us the whole nine yards, a whole *gang* of information about the operation you two have got running here, and at this point I would like to say—and I can *afford* to do this, make these generous remarks, since we've got you two so cold we could use you to flash-freeze *fish sticks*—I am truly impressed with everything I know about it. The *ingenuity,* the sheer *brilliance* of it, using genuinely sick people to pyramid prescriptions of medications that they actually *need?*" He shook his head and raised his eyebrows. "Well, what can I say, huh? Genius, the work of a mastermind.

"And the *magnitude* of it all—sixteen conscientious people"—Sexton swallowed hard, involuntarily; Dowd pretended not to notice—"out there laboring for you, out there beaverin' diligently around this great commonwealth of ours, bringin' in the pure? One hundred percent FDA pharmaceutical grade *pure?* Breathtaking's what it is; that's the only word for it—*absolutely, breathtaking.*

"So," Dowd said, "knowing as you now do how much, as an expert, so to speak, I have to admire your setup, you'll understand how much it saddens me to say what I have to say now. It's over. You're finished. Toast. We've got Lou in the slammer, and we've got other cars out other places even as I speak, rounding up your other henchmen, rolling your ring up like a rug. We know from Dennis and the paper with the watermark, and before we leave tonight—taking you along, of course——" He paused a beat; Theresa blinked, and bit her lip. "Yes, if we hafta we're gonna take you in—if *you* make it necessary." He paused another beat. "We will've called in enough PC for a search crew to get a warrant for this place that'll be bulletproof—if it's ever tested."

Now Sexton blinked. Dowd saw him do it. "Right," he said, "you just thought of it: 'How come they didn't get the warrant?' *Before* we came to call?" He sighed. "Well, much as I do hate to speak unkindly of my fellow man," he said, shaking his head, "the sad fact of the matter is sometimes he can't be trusted. And even sadder to relate, some of those times have been when my fellow man or woman was the clerk of court. Read an affidavit to support a search warrant; and then, *after* the warrant issued, but *before* it could be executed, went and called the subject of it—so by the time the cops got there the drugs and cash and guns'n' stuff were all *gone*. And quite often the *suspects* were, too."

He smiled. "So, we live and learn. While our colleagues are getting the warrants, if we decide that they're *needed,* Trooper Ferrigno and I'll be sitting right here with you. Helping you to curb what I'm sure're your very strong natural urges *right now* to be running all over the place here, picking up and destroying what I'm even surer must be *lots and lots* of physical evidence— of this very considerable drug-dealing network Mister Sargent tells us you've been running out of this tidy little ranch house for almost three years now. Flushing it down the toilet. Burning it in the fireplace. Wishing to *God* that you'd bought yourselves one of those document shredders'll chew up the *world,* they're al- ways sellin' at Staples. Maybe two weeks ago." He sighed and smiled, sympathetically. "But that's human nature, isn't it now? The fact of the matter 's—you didn't."

Still smiling, he leaned toward Sexton again. "And when I say that network's considerable, Mister Sexton," he said, "as we both know very well, I understate the matter. Mister Sargent had five scrips in play when we grabbed him today. That's ten years times five, in case you're keeping score at home, since you get ten for each offense. And if that's not impressive enough, just *think* what those scrips represented, as of course I'm sure you have. *A thousand hits* of Dilaudid, Lou was getting for you."

Dowd sat back, the smile gone. Sexton watched him as a bird watches a cat. "That was more than double what he *had* been doing, for the past year or so, but even so, *that'd* been pretty im- pressive. The *four hundred hits* a month he'd been bringing in before, combined with about the same amount of goodies you were gettin' from each one of the other fifteen guys 'n' gals you had out there goofin' druggists for you? Of course it wasn't all Dilaudid, so the number of hits varied; but still, roughly comparable amounts of the other kinds of stuff? Sixteen times four hundred? Sixty-four hundred caps 'n' tabs 'n' pills a *month*, before this recent escalation? Times twelve times *a year*? Must've left *lots* of evidence here. Have to be records of that kind of commerce.

"And my *God*, where you were *headed*. You sure are ambitious critters. In the past year you've turned about seventy-seven thousand doses of legitimate painkillers, and mood elevators, and God only knows what all, into underground illegal *pops*, and... well now, we *know* you weren't keeping the stuff for your*selves*. You haven't got dough enough, pay all your accomplices. You haven't been taking the stuff yourselves—you had've you'd both be dead now. And you haven't been dealin' the stuff outta here, 'cause we would've known—your neighbors would've complained. So you *hadda* be sellin' it, someone.

"So now whoever you're selling to wasn't *satisfied*, anymore? He was so hungry *double* wouldn't be enough; you were going to two-and-a-half? Aiming for *two hundred thousand* joy pills? Good Christ, Mister Sexton, Mrs. Sexton, who the *hell* were you two *supplying*? Have you ever thought about that? The Chinese CIA, for Chrissake? Someone who wants to take over the *country*? Without using bombs? By putting us all under first?" He paused two or three beats, then said softly and mockingly: "Do you start to suspect what we want from you?" Smiling again he said, almost whispering now: "We wanna know who it *is*."

He ran the tip of his tongue back and forth against the inside of his lower lip on the tops of his lower front teeth. He could keep his gaze on Sexton and still see Theresa to his right in his field of vision. She seemed to be suffering extreme cold. Her shoulders were shaking; her arms and hands were trembling; she was chewing on her lips and tremors washed across her face.

Sexton's face was immobile; his eyes stared, bulging slightly. The prosthesis in his left hand rested in his lap. He was breathing rapidly. Dowd could see his chest expanding and contracting, hear the air rushing in and out through the hole in his throat.

"Mister Sexton," Dowd said, leaning in again, "let me outline for you the fix that you're in. You won't find it a pretty sight. Even a moderately aggressive assistant district attorney at the very least will make each one of those sixteen deliveries your mules have been bringing to you each month into a separate overt act, when he gets you indicted for your conspiracy. And then he'll have you indicted again on each one of them, as a separate substantive offense. A separate *felony* count. Seventeen times ten?

"He will have as many of those counts as it turns out we can cast for him in cement. We don't know yet how many we'll have, but both of us know—a great many. Almost eight hundred just for the past year. Have you got any idea what a judge's going to do to you—to *both* of you, Mister Sexton—when you get found guilty on *that?*

"Eight hundred times ten. Eight thousand years? That's ridiculous. No human being could do that. Let's be reasonable here. Try ten on the first one and ten on the second and ten on the one after that. Each of those on and after, and then after those first three, the next seven-ninety-seven terms also on and after, but concurrently, with each other. Forty years. No parole. Does that sound like *life* to you yet? Does to me."

The speaker played softly "Take the A Train." Sexton's eyes roved. He said nothing. Theresa made whimpering sounds.

"You got *one way*, avoid that," Dowd said, holding his position, keeping his voice low and soothing. "You got one way you can save your wife and yourself from spending the rest of your lives in jail. And I don't want to hear about how they'll kill you if you give them up—we both know that that doesn't count.

You've been where people got killed for nothing. You saw it every day. You know there're worse things'n just getting killed, and you've got something that if you lose her'll be far worse'n getting yourself killed." He made his voice hard, and louder. "*Haven't* you, Tim? *Who were you selling the stuff to?*"

Sexton shook his head, blinking, coughing strangely, silently. "One way, Tim," Dowd said, his voice low. "Otherwise you go, my friend—and your lady also goes."

Still shaking his head, the ponytail bobbing, his face now decomposing to cry, Sexton with his eyes now down raised the prosthesis to his stoma and urged words out through it. "I can't," he said.

"You have to," Dowd said.

"No," Sexton said, his eyes still down, the tears coming now down his cheeks, "I would. I know what you want. And if I could, I would. For her. I can't. I can't wear no wire. With this. She'll have to be here. No one else can be, but she has to be. She's always here when he comes. If she isn't, he will know. Will know something's wrong. And if she is and I'm wired, then they'll know. Right off. And then they'll kill us both."

"God *damn* you," Dowd roared, coming out of the chair. "Quit your goddamned faking. We'll take care of the acoustics, shithead. We know what we can do and we know what you can do and you'd better do it, you lying piece of shit. You give me the name, you bastard. Who's your pick-up-pay-off guy, and when does he come?"

Sexton was licking his lips, sobbing gusts of air and raising the prosthesis, his eyes wild and rolling, when Theresa moaned, "Thursdays. Used to be on Tuesdays. Now he comes here on Thursdays. Rascob. We sell it to Max Rascob." In the right corner of his vision Dowd could see her put her head down and cover her face with her hands, her gilded nails in her reddish-blond hair, and begin to sob wrackingly.

Keeping his gaze on Sexton, now slumped and motionless, Dowd sat back in the chair. Nodding, he first curled his lips and shook his head at Sexton. Then he looked up to Ferrigno. "*Maxie*," he said, gently, "*Maxie*," and when he smiled again, Ferrigno bowed to him.

16

WHEN MCKEACH IN THE SHINY OLD blue Bonneville Brougham came down West Broadway soon after midnight, the white curtains in windows of the second- and third-floor apartments above the storefronts to the left were still, lighted from the street, the rooms behind them dark. He saw only one man walking on the sidewalk, big and thick in the body, his face red and weathered under a grey scally cap, wearing a bulky olive-drab field jacket and blue jeans; he proceeded slowly and carefully, his hands in his jacket pockets and his shoulders hunched, intent on his balance and the placement of his booted feet. Farther down the lights were still golden in the windows of Armhein's Restaurant on the easterly corner of the intersection of West Broadway and A Street. Two men stood talking in the sheltered doorway cut into the corner of the building, their faces shadowed by the bills of their dark-blue Red Sox B-logo baseball caps; the one on the right took his right hand from his jacket pocket and saluted McKeach's Pontiac with a couple of fingers, and the one on the left used three fingers of his left hand. McKeach lifted his left hand from the wheel, languidly returning a two-fingered wave, and turned right off Broadway onto B Street, disobeying the one-way arrow on the corner.

He drove down B in the middle—Cistaro's maroon Expedition was parked at the left curb next to a No Parking sign—to the driveway behind Flynn's Spa facing Old Colony and turned left into it. His headlights caught the silvered reflectors in the headlights of Rascob's old grey Town Car—the Naughton kid was impassive but alert behind the wheel; he nodded recognition—and the red reflector lenses in the taillights of Cistaro's black BMW. McKeach backed out again and parked the Pontiac at the curb behind Cistaro's Expedition.

He got out into the clear darkness that seemed colder after the warm day and as always took a moment to scan the area. Cistaro made fun of his habit. "Arthur—I bet when Arthur gets the soap all rinsed off inna morning, you know, inna shower? Gets through playin' with himself and makin' sure that he's still got at least as many fingers as he had the night before, he came home and went to bed; that before he slides the glass door open first he takes a look around. What is it that you call it, Arthur? 'Just doin' a little recon'?

"I bet when Arthur's bein' born, you know, he had everybody wonderin', doctors, nurses, everyone—'what the hell is goin' on here? The hell is it with this kid? Had his poor mother here in labor goin' on three *days* now—when the hell's he comin' *out*?' And all it was was Arthur bein' Arthur, just the same as he is now—takin' a look around first. Seein' if there's any *cops* inna delivery room."

McKeach stared for a long time at the darkened windows and the porches rigged with clotheslines at the rear of the A Street triple-decker, ivory with white trim, that backed up on the vacant lot across from the spa on B Street, his eyes accustomed to the scant light from the streetlights, watching for motion at the flowered curtains, the glint of light reflected from a telephoto lens or the anodized barrel of a long-range microphone, the brief orange flare of a cigarette lighter. Nothing. Nothing like the old days, when the bastards smoked, and gave themselves away.

He nodded and walked into the loading area behind the store, nodded to Todd Naughton, and climbed the two cement steps up onto the loading dock. Then he stopped, turned around and went down again, walking over to the Town Car, making a cranking motion with his right hand. Naughton turned the ignition key to the accessory position and powered the driver's window down. "Uncle Arthur," he said, and he grinned.

McKeach, grinning broadly, bent over, resting his left hand on the roof of the car and extending his right through the window. Naughton raised his right hand between his chest and the wheel. They shook hands awkwardly. "Understand you're going to be leaving us soon," McKeach said.

"So they tell me," Naughton said. "Say it's a whole new different way of life."

"Is that a fact?" McKeach said. "Think you can stand it?"

Naughton widened his grin. "Ah, Uncle Arthur," he said. "What can I tellya? Never forget old friends and family. Never forget where you came from. That's the way I was brought up."

McKeach nodded and squeezed Naughton's hand. "Attaboy, Todd," he said, releasing the hand and squeezing his left shoulder before straightening up. "Always've felt safer, havin' you around. Gonna miss you, not seein' you here."

"Oh, I'll still be around," Naughton said. "I'm joinin' the force, not the convent."

McKeach laughed. "Yeah," he said, stepping away, "I know that. Just make sure, you know, keep in touch, okay?"

"You know it," Naughton said, and they both nodded.

McKeach turned away toward the loading dock. Then he hesitated, seeming to recollect something, and turned back to the old grey car. He leaned down at the window again, resting his left forearm again on the roof of the car. "Just for an example," he said, "why we're gonna miss you. I'm not sure yet but I will be when I come out—could you be available for me for something I might hafta do pretty early tomorrow morning? Only drivin' me somewhere, droppin' me off an' then pickin' me up again. You be available, maybe?"

"Sure," Naughton said. "Just tell me what time and where—I can be there."

McKeach nodded again, made a fist of his left hand and rapped the first knuckles on the roof of the car. "Okay, good," he said. "About five, I think. Be through by six-thirty. I'll pick you up, drop you off at the same place. All you have to do's say where."

"White Hen Pantry, all-night store, parkways rotary," Naughton said. "I'll pick up a couple ah coffees."

"Okay," McKeach said, "large black for me. I give you the thumbs-up when I come out, I see you there. If I don't, forget about it."

"Deal," Naughton said.

McKeach went up the steps and onto the loading dock in a hurry, bringing a double-A flashlight from his pocket and lighting his way through the creaking double door closest to the steps into the shadows and the stairs inside, the light bulb in the passageway at the rear of the upper floor no help in the dark on the rough wooden staircase. The boards creaked softly as he ascended, hearing the rushing sound of the gas stove and the low murmur of several voices in the big office above. As he reached the door he heard Cistaro laugh and say, "Maxie, whatchou saying that for, you're not sure that's the reason. Arguing with Rico like that? Of *course* it's the reason. It's so fuckin' *obvious*, everybody knows it—has to be. No, Rico's got you pegged."

McKeach opened the door and went in. Cistaro sat presiding behind the desk under the high windows at the front of the room. He had tilted back in the wooden desk chair and had his legs crossed at the ankles on top of the desk. He had the little TV set facing him and tuned to "The Late Show with David Letterman." "Turn it up, Nick," McKeach said, his voice tired; he shut the door.

"Why? It's loud enough," Cistaro said. "Isn't like I *give* a flyin' fuck about the show or anything. All it is's Clinton jokes, new ways to say 'blow job' without saying 'blow' or 'job.' Got our own sex story right here."

Rico and Rascob sat facing each other across the eight-foot table, Rico laughing and Rascob looking embarrassed but pleased. McKeach pulled an orange chair from the row against the wall and dragged it over to the table, sitting down at the end facing Cistaro. "Because halfway up the stairs I could hear you guys, is why," he said. "I could also hear the stove. But I could not hear the TV. Not supposed to be that way, you over the TV anna stove. S'posed to be the *other* way: TV drownin' *you* out."

"I thought you swept the place today," Cistaro said. "I thought after we meet with Sweeney, got things straightened out with him, you wanted me and Rico out, you're gonna sweep the place. That's why we left you here."

"And that's what I did," McKeach said. "Voltage checks on alla phone lines we got comin' in building—all the current draws're normal. Nothing in the TV set, so that when we turn it on we're talkin' to the FBI or state police. Nothin' in the thermostat. Checked all of the baseboard outlets, ceilin' fixtures, all that shit—nothin' funny inside them. So, none of the power sources'd been spliced, I checked them out. Seven-thirty, when I left."

"So?" Cistaro said. "So, what're we worried, then? Everything's okay."

"Not what I said," McKeach said. "You weren't listening. What I said was that everything *was* okay when I left at seven-thirty. It's now after midnight. I don't know if anything's happened since then. I don't know who was over Congress Street, the phone company at eight, got a court order with 'em lets 'em tie into our lines *here,* onna mainframe over *there.* And I don't know if someone sneaked in here after I left, which they've been known to do, wired a full-time bug into the baseboard, they can now hear us scratch our balls. All I act on's what I know. What you're acting on I don't. Turn up the Korean TV. Make some other kind of cheap noise."

Cistaro turned up the volume on the set. Letterman was bantering with a female movie star and his bandleader, Paul Schaefer. Cistaro raised his voice to drown out their conversation and the laughter it provoked. "You're sayin' that you think they couldah *sneaked* in here, since you left at seven-thirty?" he said, his eyes wide and disbelieving. "Arthur, I do really hate to say this, but I now think you're losin' it. You been takin' your meds lately? You're not actin' like a well man. What is it that they call? 'Paranoia,' is it?"

McKeach's eyes stayed flat; his face lost even the expression of weariness. His voice got colder with contempt. "Paranoia's what the guys in Maximum tell each other guys still on the outside must have. Explains how come they didn't get sucked into the same asshole deals the guys in jail went to jail for. Why it is that they're still free. 'Something's wrong with them. Can't be the reason's that they're smarter'n we are. Must be *crazy's* how they did it.'"

He paused one beat. "Now," he said, "lemme just remind you guys—we operate together. One of you gets in the shit, chances are you'll have *me* inna shit. I do not want that. If it happens I'll do something to the guy that I think did it to me. Won't care if he meant to or not. It may take me a long time but I promise you, before I die, I'll kill him.

"I don't care who it is. This applies to everybody, guys I never met and guys I've known for a long time, been friends with, and

I worked with, and I like." He stopped, squinting a little, and studied each of them, his lips slightly parted, his tongue working at the upper right-hand corner on his lip as though exploring for chancres. "So, any questions?"

None of them said anything. "Good," he said. "So, even 'f you think I'm crazy, you can still see how it might be a good idea to humor me. I've been in. I was in for a long time. Didn't like it. I'm not goin' in again." He paused for a long moment, looking at each of them in turn. Cistaro snorted but then snuffled, covering it; then he shook his head a little, averting his eyes. No one said anything.

"Okay," McKeach said "it's late. I'm tired. Can we now talk business here? What're you all celebratin', all that hootin' an' hollerin' I heard comin' up the stairs? Lemme in on it—I'm interested. Somethin' must've turned out good; we made a lot of money—how much did I make?" He looked at Rascob.

Rascob shifted in his chair. "Ah, no," he said, "it's nothin' like that. They're just dumpin' all over me. Givin' me a bunchah shit, I'm with Jessica."

Cistaro feigned surprise. "*Nooo*, Max," he said, "we're your *friends*. Not shittin' on you—we're *congratulatin*' you."

"*Yeah*," Rico said, "that's what we're doin'. Sayin' how you're lots more *fun* now, not complainin' alla time. Don't look like someone just ran over your dog alla time. Must be now you're well-*adjusted*, you know? *Much* nicer tah be around." He laughed. "Just tonight when I come over, I was talkin' Toddy, downstairs. How he got in the academy, he's gonna be a fuckin' *cop*. And I says to him, says, 'Jesus, Toddy, tellin' you, all this new shit goin' on? Can't get used to it. World is changin' on me here. I don't know what's goin' on. Now pretty soon I see you, you'll be wearin' the blue suit—I'll probably cross the street, avoid you. And son-a-bitch, *gotta* be at least three weeks now, I ask Rascob how it's goin', how he's doin' and he ain't got one complaint.

Now all he says is, "*Fine,* how's it with you?" you ask him. You can tell he means it, too.'

"And Toddy says, 'You know, you're right. I didn't think of it myself, you just mention it to me, but Max's a much better guy now. More fun to have around. Regular Mister Congeniality. Always glad to see you now, pass the time of day, got a friendly word to say. Gotta tellya, he's a changed man these days. I didn't know him before, swear to God, I wouldn't know him now.'" Cistaro was laughing. Rascob looked sheepish.

"'Tellin' you,' Toddy says," Rico said, "'regular pussy's a wonderful thing, what it can do for a man.'"

"And Todd also says," Cistaro said, "says now that you're gettin' some from Sweeney's sister, not only how glad we are for *you,* but how glad *Sweeney* is, for *himself,*" Cistaro said. "Sweeney is fuckin' ecstatic. You calmed down Jessica for him."

"I heard that too," Rico said. "How Sweeney's darlin' sister's been such a handful for him. Not a bad-lookin' woman, Jessie, but what a temper on her. Although what Sweeney says, that fuckin' *husband* she had, *geez,* he gave her plenty, bitch about, good-for-nothin' pieceah shit. But now she finely gets rid of him, and then you get her so she can't get the smile off her face? Sweeney thinks he died and went to heaven. Says he's gonna hafta make a novena, thanks to Saint Jude, put an ad in the paper, all his impossible prayers've been answered." He paused a beat and beamed at Rascob. "Maybe you should too, Maxie. Or whatever you Jewish guys do. Just like JFK said, right? 'Any day I don't get laid, always makes my back ache.'"

"I thought it was his head ached," McKeach said.

Rico shrugged. "Headache, backache, schmackache—what's the difference? Important thing is how you feel, and we all know Max feels better. And we know *why* Maxie feels better. *We* should all take Jessica out to dinner sometime. Thank her, all she's done for us, doin' what she does for you."

"Okay," McKeach said, contemplating Rascob, "so I didn't make no money. But knowin' that was all it was, you guys raisin' hell about up here? Maxie gettin' laid? That makes me feel better. Anyone *did* bug this place since I left at seven-thirty, all he's gotten so far's a lotta shuckin'-jivin' *shit*. Got him pullin' his hair out by now, got him *screamin'* at his wire team. 'You're tellin' me this's McKeach anna Frogman? South Boston hard guys? Heavy hitters? You must've gotten lost, gone to Roxbury, got me a nigger insurance agency.'" He snorted.

"So Nick," he said, "you now had enough of that lockerroom shit? Wanna talk to me now about business? That fuckin' Crawford guy—he makes me nervous. Told you last week he'd stay current now—tonight he show up like he said?"

"Showed up at his place just like he said, and he had it, just like he said," Cistaro said. "Half. Forty-nine five in American money. Had the boyfriend with him again too."

"And he's still not some undercover cop, a wire taped to his chest, just pretendin' he sucks Crawfie's cock?" McKeach said. "You're still satisfied with that?"

"Arthur," Cistaro said, "take it from me—Blair's not a cop. He's the maitre d', Yellow Brick Road. Think he might own a piece of it too. Me and Rico swung by there fag night, last Sunday. We didn't stay, just went in for a drink, take a look around. Stay very long, I'm afraid Rico here'd see something he liked, fall in love and get lucky—I'd hafta drive myself home." He smirked.

Rico chuckled and shook his head once. "Don't understand those guys," he said.

"I dunno if Blair saw us," Cistaro said. "But we saw him, right where he's supposed to be. And he *belonged* there, too—tellin' people their tables weren't ready yet; would they like to relax in the lounge. *Livin' large*, in his *element*—smooth as silk panties. If he did see us, maybe he's bein' polite—now thinks we're also queer, but waitin' for *us* to tell *him*." He smiled. "I don't think the question'll come up. That's a place that I decided I'm not goin' there for dinner."

"Probably have a long wait for a table," McKeach said.

"Yeah," Cistaro said. "No, it's just, somehow I don't think I'd fit in. I don't think he thinks I would either."

"And he's *right* about that, I hope," McKeach said.

"Oh, yeah," Cistaro said. He laughed but his eyes were not involved. "He's got that right." He paused three beats and stared at McKeach. McKeach held his gaze. Rico and Rascob tried to find other objects to look at on the table and over each other's shoulders.

Cistaro shook his head and said: "Anyway, one thing *is* sure—he's deeply in love with his Crawfie. He's the husband; Crawfie's the wife. Should see them together—cute as *bunny* slippers. He's an older guy, very protective, got ten or twelve years on Crawfie, this wavy-gravy dark grey hair—which he's lost quite a lot of, the front. Crawfie can give him a toupee for Christmas, he's got any dough left. Dash of boogie blood, I think, Creole or somethin'—he's about the same color as regular coffee. Not that he isn't a good-lookin' guy; just looks kind of oily to me. I was queer I wouldn't go for him."

"You'd want someone more along the lines of Liberace, probably," McKeach said.

"Rich, right," Cistaro said. "If I'm gonna be takin' it up the ass all the time, I'd want a shitload of money."

"Yeah," McKeach said. "Well, then, you'd better hope that you're right about Blair not bein' a cop—they don't give you big money in prison."

"You'd know about that, too, wouldn't you," Cistaro said.

"All I need to," McKeach said. "Never wanted to try it, myself. Two or three old guys still out there inna world chew their food with federal bridgework they had put in in Leavenworth. Fell down very hard, several times, inna shower. May not remember these days where they put their car keys, glasses, who they are or where they been, but every meal they remember that McKeach's nay meant *fuckin' nay*. Not fuckin' *interested*."

"Me either," Cistaro. "I can't figure those guys. Crawfie *adores* Blair, and he worships his little blond Crawfie. No secret that they're together, you know? Winkin' an' noddin'—pattin' each other onnie ass. *Disgusting*." He laughed uncertainly, then frowned. "I don't even like to see it. Makes me uncomfortable."

"Yeah," McKeach said, "well, then, don't fuckin' look at 'em. As long as he's not a *cop*. He is and he'll put us both somewhere we don't wanna be. Then you'll find out what uncomfortable is. Point is, you got the money."

"Yeah," Cistaro said. "I counted it in front of them. Crawfie looked very sad. Blair was furious—at him as much as me, I think. But then he looked on the bright side and he pulled himself together. Now it's almost over with, they're almost out of it. Tonight, and then if everything goes right, the buyer likes the rarities, next week Crawfie gives me the rest. So getting the money today and then meeting me with it, that was an unpleasant thing, but after next week it'll be just them again, so him an' Blair're making an evening of it.

" 'We're on our way to the client's place for dinner. The two doctors Reynolds? Ken and Christine? From Physicians and Surgeons Clinic in Sudbury? See how she's lighted their treasures, probably just ruined my whole arrangement. But first, here we are with the *money*.' Blair was like a Little League dad, still annoyed that he got into this mess, but still, *very* proud of his Crawfie."

"So on ninety this faggot's now paid us ninety-nine five, is that right?" McKeach said.

"Right," Cistaro said. "He comes through with the rest of it next Wednesday night, it'll then be one forty-nine. Blair said again, he thinks we're being '*very unfair.* No *wonder* there's laws against this.' Then he sniffed at me.

"Don't *like* bein' sniffed at," Cistaro said, laughing. "But I behave, I keep calm. I said, 'Sweetie, I don't give a rat's ass what the law's against, or what you may think. Meet me with the rest of the money next week. And the vig of course, too—twenty-seven fifty.'"

McKeach nodded and leaned forward, resting his forearms on the table, his eyes narrow. "Okay," he said. "Then I think maybe, all the grief and the abuse those two've given us, doing this service for them, they should maybe get some trouble back. Rich people they deal with, very selfish, and mean. Disturbing dead men's *bones,* desecrating holy ground, and for *what*? To make their *living* rooms look nice? I think they should be ashamed of themselves. No wonder there's all kinds of laws against it. Federal especially." He paused, staring at Cistaro. "We ought to think about that."

Cistaro stared back, saying nothing, and nodded.

"Now," McKeach said, "two more things to deal with, and then I think we can go home.

"Item one. Max, a big pickup tomorrow, the Box's house over in Canton."

"This's right," Rascob said. "Talked to the Box's wife right after lunch. She says everything's moonlight and roses. They already had calls from eleven their people, so there're then only five more to report. Said they're all telling her things've been goin' great, no problems with more prescriptions—'just hadda go visit a lotta new stores, but everything went like a charm.' So, took him a month to expand like we wanted, like Jackie said, 'Get me the volume.' But give the Box credit, he's good. He knows what he's doing, and no one can rush him, and result is he gets the job done."

McKeach pursed the left side of his mouth. "Well, so far, anyway. We don't have the stuff in hand yet. How much're we payin' him this load?"

"A buck anna quarter a pop," Rascob said.

"Regardless of what the pop is," McKeach said, "a buck anna quarter a pop."

"Regardless of what kinda stuff," Rascob said. "Me and Timmy agreed we'd go that way. The benzos Jackie says're what they ask for, the guys buy off his trucks. But if they're not available, anything else, and the price's what the driver says it is. So, figure we simplify the whole thing—we pay the Box a buck anna quarter, instead the buck that we used to, because of the extra effort and risk that him and his people've taken on increasing the volume for us. Our end goin' in's twenny grand. Jackie, same reason, now pays one seven five. Comin' out we now take in thirty-five, one eighty profit a year, same number Jackie projects. Like he says—'I was doin' all right sellin' food, coffee and smokes. For gravy, this's good money.' Said his drivers'll love it. They're the ones been beggin' for more stuff, see the market every day, know they'll do even better. He sells to them now at two twenny-five, and they get whatever they can—sky's the limit for them."

"Yeah, but that's all right, they take the big risk," McKeach said. "One stray cop, his eyes open, buttin' in onna line to get coffee? Sees a sale goin' down? Guys drivin' the trucks and sellin' the stuff—those guys could have their lives ruined. They *should* get as much as they can." He displayed the small smile. "As long's they dunno *who* we are, of course, where Jackie is gettin' the goodies."

"They don't," Rascob said, imitating the smile. "And Jackie dunno where we're gettin' 'em, either. I think we got this one airtight."

McKeach nodded. He looked at Cistaro. "This's good, I think, Nick, way it's gone so far. But anything involvin' drugs, got to be supercareful. Not just the cops got a hard-on for drugs— every tailgater in town. I think with this shipment—Maxie taking twenty out to pay the Box, the pills; he then hasta transport them Jackie; he makes the delivery; on his way back here he's got thirty-five large?

"That's four chances for someone to hit him. And this's not like our usual thing, where only the people he sees know how much's involved, an' they're people we known a long time. Like on Tuesdays, example, he picks up the bags—everyone he sees knows what he's doin', there's lotsa cash in his trunk. So some wise guy tailgates him, we'll know who it is and the bastard is dead by nightfall. Our protection there is that knowledge. Everyone knows who we are, what we're doin', sure, but *we* know who everyone is.

"This new operation—makes me uneasy. Too many people— we dunno who they all are. Well, we know their names—names they're usin', at least—but that's not like who they *are*, where they *live*. Whether they're *dependable*.

"Like the Box and his wife—so far they're all right, but we dunno how long that lasts. From what Maxie tells me, they sound kind of *strange*, some kinky shit goin' on there—this crippled kid's pimpin' his wife. I'm like you with the fairies on that kind of shit—I don't care what they do as long as I'm left out of it—but now I know they do this kind of shit, can I be sure what they'll do next? So there's that, then, 'n' the new-people mix."

He cleared his throat and looked back at Cistaro. "So anyway, what I am thinkin' is this—if we're expandin' now, goin' big time, gettin' into distributin' here, maybe we oughta step up our security. You got any thoughts on that for me?"

"I dunno," Cistaro said. "The downside of it is, the more guys you show doin' somethin', the more dough you make people think you've got involved. How long we been doin' this with Jackie, two or three years? Jackie asked us if we could supply him the junk along with the gambling and loans?"

McKeach nodded.

"Okay," Cistaro said, "two or three years and everything's gone along good. People're now used to it, Max comes around. 'Oh, he's just this guy comes to see Jackie on Tuesdays, stays a while, goes away and then comes back. Can't be much—nothin' get excited about there.'

"But now all of a sudden he changes the day. Used to be Tuesdays, now he comes on Thursday, and he's got someone else *ridin'* with him. This hasta mean there's more money involved. You're talkin' precautions—the one thing while you're takin' 'em you don't wanna do is get *other* people's attention.

"Because once you start them thinkin', 'Must be lotsa dough there,' then the next thing they think is, 'This might be worth knockin' off.' Like you say, this would not be connected people, people we know, pull some of *that* shit—not on us. Not unless they had terminal cancer, not long to live anyway. This'd be *assholes,* young guys fulla beans, think they've got the weight, and any time they want they can come *in* an' take *over* from us.

"Now, any guys did try that, sure, we'd find out who it was. And we'd clip them and put them to sleep. But things wouldn't then go back to normal. Doing that would take *time,* and it'd make *noise,* and therefore stir up the cops. Which's always a pain in the ass. So, sure, there's no question, we can protect ourselves, but do we really want all this shit?

"Myself, what I think is the answer is No, but I dunno how sure I am of that. So, little compromise here—how about we do something like this? Rico rides shotgun for Max tomorrow, but in my Expedition, not *with* him. Soon's Max turns in here, Rico drops him. Sort of an armed escort, right?"

McKeach nodded. "I like it," he said. He looked first to Rico, then Rascob. "You two guys work it out. Walkie-talkies or something, some code that sounds harmless so you can keep in touch but means nothin', someone with a scanner."

He considered. "What bothers me here, I think what it is, it's the whole damn operation itself. We know the product but not sellin' it. Always before, when drugs're involved, mostly always we've just been financin'. Like this kid Charlie Ford—got that *major* thing, him, the big million six that's a big chunk of what we get outta Jinksie's last Arabian car deal? Well, I see Ford today, and I'm glad to say, and you'll be glad to hear, that thing's lookin' *very* damned good. More and more I like the way this kid's looking. He's now got his base, bought this house south of here, and it's funny, don't wanna say where? And he's kind of worried he's tellin' me *that*. 'It's not like I don't trust you, I just don't wanna say.'

"I say, 'Course you don't trust me. Don't trust anybody. Fewer people that know stuff the better. You doan needah worry 'bout that. You *did* wanna tell me, then *I* would worry. So you, you don't worry, it's fine.' Next month or so, I think, that investment pays off—he's now projectin' a three-five return for us, maybe a little bit more.

"So anyway, back to the first of the year, I'd say we are lookin' quite good. Back then we take the nine hundred grand we'd built up the Coke cooler, doin' our regular business, since the last time, in August, we bought real estate, the three brownstones on Marlborough Street, and we put it out there with Jinksie. There we double it plus—one million nine.

"One-point-six of that now we've got with the Ford kid. Pretty soon, he tells me, we double-plus again." McKeach laughed. "We're gonna need some more real estate pretty soon, I think. We do know the financing end.

"And the storage end, too, we know that." He paused, frowning. "Not that it always works right." He pointed his left index finger at Rascob. "That damn jigaboo, Junie Walters. You went there again today, Max?" Rascob nodded. "And he wasn't there again, right?"

Rascob nodded. "I went there again and he wasn't there. His gofer, there, Bishop, all dressed in black?"

"They *all* dress black," McKeach said with scorn. "Think they're all nigger Zorros or somethin'. Want you to think they're that Fruit of Islam shit—once you see 'em you run for your life."

"Yeah," Rascob said, "well, this one is Bishop. I recognize him from last week. And the week before *that*———"

"An' the week before *that*," McKeach said. "Lemme think, now, just how long's it been?" Then he nodded. "*And* also the week before *that* one." He paused. "Did he give you the rent, the ten a week? No, of course not, the son of a bitch. He laughed in your face's what he did."

Rascob shrugged. "What he did, gave me nothin' but *shit*. Different shit from the shit that he gave me last week, but still shit all the same—doesn't matter. 'The Man says to tell you he'll see you next week. Or somethin'. Today he is *in therapy*.'"

"Right," McKeach said. "Seventy *grand* he's now behind. And he's still got the stuff comin' in, goin' out. Or so my observers tell me." He looked to Cistaro. "You see any need to discuss this? What needs to be done about this?

"Keep in mind now, I put this pieceah black shit inna hospital once, first time I got this kindah shit. Thought after I did it that'd be enough. Establish we're serious. From what I understand, and my source isn't perfect, I did a pretty good job. Junius had quite a time for himself. The burns that he got, he went into the lantern—apparently they weren't that bad. Not life-threatening's what I am told. Some crocodile skin onna back of his neck—and his shoulder, too, what I'm told. His shirt caught on fire and it melted. Melted his skin along with it. But it should heal up all right, few minor scars. Nothin' to worry about. He's takin' long fast walks now, get back in shape. Every morning, Jamaica Pond there? He's got a big condo up in the Jamaica Estates there, walks around the whole pond every morning, at sunrise. Dorothy's friend she worked with, she was at the Faulkner Hospital? Sees him out there, she goes out, way to work.

"The right eye? That is different. Dorothy says her Mass General friend hears at Mass Eye and Ear that he's still got the patch over it—'Most probably have it for life.' Okay, he can do shirt ads.

"They also hadda wire his jaw shut. Last she got he was livin' on mush—from the blender, you know? Raw cheeseburgers, drink through a straw. I hadda do that onna number of people, generally worked pretty good—but I *still* dunno if they put pickles and fries in. Hafta have Dorothy have her friend ask." He paused a beat for the laugh and it came.

"Up 'til now I taught someone a lesson like that, it's always worked pretty good." He shook his head. "This time around, doesn't seem like it did." He sighed. "Maybe I'm gettin' old." He looked at Cistaro again. "But anyway, old or not, this's one I think I should handle myself. You got any objection to that?"

Slowly and deliberately Cistaro shook his head. He presented the small smile.

"Okay," McKeach said, and he nodded. "Important," he said. "They have to know, I don't forget these things." Then he cleared his throat.

"*Now,*" McKeach said, "last pieceah business. This morning—Max of course knows some of this—I get this call, and it's from Jenny Frolio. Been years since I talked to her. She's surprised I still know her voice. But what she's got to say to me is that

Dominic's sick and been taken to Quincy Hospital. Hasn't been feelin' good, past two-three days, and then this morning around five A.M., which is when he usually gets up and comes upstairs, he doesn't. See, she doesn't say this but what I assume is that since they had the second-floor addition put on there, she's been sleepin' the bedroom upstairs and he's still been sleepin' down. In other words, not in the same bed, you follow me. Although from some the other things she said I think he was still comin' after her from time to time, get his ashes hauled. How often naturally I do *not* know, but I gather enough to suit her.

"So anyway, she gets the coffee goin' and goes downstairs to check him out. 'After all,' she says to me, 'the man *is* eighty-six, and I don't care how strong he's always tellin' me he is, showin' me his muscles like he thinks I'm still sixteen again; still all I think about, he looks in a bathing suit—he's *not* a young man anymore. So it's quite natural he might have somethin' wrong with him, and therefore, get my robe on, go down and check on him.

"'He *looks* all right, he's awake, lyin' there, but he still hasn't got up yet. So naturally I say to him—because this isn't like him, lie around in bed like this after he's woken up. Usually as soon's he's awake, he's onna floor doin' his situps, eighteen situps every mornin'. And please don't ask me "How come eighteen?", "Why isn't it fifteen or twenty?" I dunno the answer that either; I don't think he does himself. Just, eighteen is what he does, and been doin', many years. But this morning he isn't. So I say, "Why?" to him and he says to me, got this funny look on his face, "I dunno. I don't feel good. My stomach doesn't feel good, like I ate something, you know? And my *chest* here, it feels kind of funny."

"'So I say, "All right then, I'm callin' Doctor Farmer." He's this young doctor that they got now over at the hospital that took over a few years ago, Doctor Melia retired. I like him all right but not Dominic, he doesn't. Not that there's anythin' wrong with him. There's nothing wrong with him at all; just Dominic doesn't like change. But it isn't that, he doesn't like him. It's he just says, "No, don't call Doctor Farmer, get the *ambulance*. Ambulance quick."

"'And so then, well, I know that there's really something wrong, and that's what I better do, but before I can do it, even leave the room, he gets this look across his face, and *groans*, like this: "*Ahhhhh,*" you know, very loud, and then his whole body sort of *comes up* inna bed, and his eyes—go completely wide open. And then he starts to sort of *relax*, you know? Like air goin' out a balloon. And that's when I know that I don't think it's gonna matter too much how long it takes the ambulance, to get here. This's it for Dominic. My Dominic ain't gonna make it.'

"And she was right—he didn't," McKeach said. "I guess he was still technically alive when the EMTs got to him, said a couple things to them but it was hard to understand him. The left-hand side his face, and the whole left side his body, I guess, that was all kind of paralyzed. But then he had another one when they had him on the stretcher goin' out the ambulance, and sometime after that probably while he's inna truck. Anyway, when he got the hospital they tried a few more times revive him with the paddles on his chest, but nothin' they did seemed to do it. So Dominic is finely dead."

"I assume you'll be goin' the funeral?" Cistaro said. "I know you and him're never *that* close, but you did know the guy a long time."

"Over forty years," McKeach said. "But that don't mean I'll go his funeral. He was one of the guys I inherited from Brian. I don't even think *them* two were that close. Dominic didn't look all that cut up to me, I saw him after Brian G. went down. Far's I could tell, all that interested him was who he paid now that

Brian's dead, and I said, 'You'll be now payin' me, my guy, the same guy. The same guy you been paying for Brian.' And that was okay with him. Forget now who it was, but two guys before you, Max, the guy before Nino Giunta. 'He now works for me. So from your end it all works the same.'

"And he then said to me, 'If someone interfered with me, at any time, I always knew I could call Brian.' His protection, you see, that was what concerned him. His insurance he was payin' for.

"And I said to him, 'Well, that's what I been sayin'. Someone gives you some shit, you give me a call, and I promise you, he won't give you no shit after that. Like I just told you, we're all gonna miss Brian, but I am a guy Brian sent if you called, so from your end it'll all work the same.' And he was happy—that's all there was to it.

"And besides," McKeach said, "I couldn't go the funeral if I wanted, let the FBI take pictures of me and everybody else there, have 'em inna paper—'Local hoods all seen at funeral'—'cause the funeral is all over. Almost over, anyway. She was having that taken care of this afternoon.

"I said to her '*What?*' when she said that to me, I asked her when the wake's gonna be, make Max go by for me, pay my respects. 'Funeral's this afternoon? What is this, Dominic's Jewish? Gotta bury him by sunset, something?'

"She said No. Seems this's just how he wanted it, both of them did. '"No church for me when I'm dead," he used to say to me, every time someone he knew died and he hadda go to the funeral. "Because otherwise the family and people think I'm mad at him, I don't like him or something. So I go. The only time I go to church is when there is somebody dead there that I like, and then I go. And it's not even for them—they are dead, don't know I'm there. Got no idea I came. It's for the family, all right? That I don't know, don't know me. Doesn't make no sense. I don't go to no church while I am alive. I don't want no-body takin' me to no church when I'm dead."

"'So I do what he told me,' she said. 'Called the undertaker when they come out from the room at the hospital where they've got him and they tell me he is dead. Tell him like Dom told me to, he already made arrangements—"My husband's dead. Please come and get him. Take him away, a wooden box, no embalming, anything, and have him cremated. When they cool off put his ashes in something, bring them to me at my house."' Then she said what she's gonna do is 'like he told me—take him across the street tomorrow night and sprinkle him on the tide going out, "and that is all you'll need to do—that'll take care of it." So that is what I'm gonna do,' is what she told me," McKeach said, laughing. "I imagine she will."

"Jesus H. Christ," Rascob said, "never laid eyes on the woman, but she must be as tough as he was. That'd be one tough broad indeed."

"Oh, she is," McKeach said. "Jenny's got some wildcat in her. One hot number, she was young. Probably still is. But why am I talkin' you about her? You're gonna find out, get to know her for yourself."

"She's gonna run the book now?" Cistaro said, before Rascob could. "Make the loans and everything?"

"That's what it sounded like to me," McKeach said. "Also gonna run the store. Last thing that she said to me was have Max stop by the Beachside tomorrow and she'll have the bags there for you. 'Then we work out how us two're gonna handle it now on. Dominic liked to go the store at three, stay to close it up. Way I always liked to do it back when I was working there, I liked to open in the morning, make sure everything was all right, and then if I felt like it, you know, maybe I go home for dinner, Dominic don't need me there. But in those days, I was young.

Been a long time, I been there. So we'll see what I like to do now, I been back there for a while.' "

"I didn't know she ever worked at the store," Rascob said.

"Oh, sure she did," McKeach said. "That's how the two of them met. Dominic hired her while she's still in high school to keep the books for him—strictly against the law, of course, minor inna liquor store, even in those days, but she kept out of sight in back. She was smart and her family was poor; she worked hard. *And* she was a good-lookin' kid, nice setta tits on her. She knew this, of course, that she was built like a brick shithouse; plus she had what in those days some people called 'pep,' by which I think they meant 'sexy.' Now here's this mature guy, he's a success; sure, he's also twenny-five years or so older'n she is, but he's got some money, knows how to behave; he obviously likes her, and compared to those clumsy high-school boys? Wow. So pretty soon nature takes its course, and they make the trade, standard deal. He gets her pants off; she gets him to marry her."

"Never had any kids," Cistaro said.

"Not's far as I know," McKeach said. "Dunno whose decision that might've been. What I do know is that when Nino came on the scene———"

"This'd be Nino Giunta," Rascob said.

"Nino Giunta, correct," McKeach said. "Nino, a big, funny, good-lookin' guy, knew how to make a girl laugh, only four or five years younger'n Jenny. A year or two before you took over the route, dunno what brought her name up, I said something to Nino about how's my old girlfriend Jenny. Not that she ever was that, but when I was goin' there, for Brian G., I'd always looked forward to seein' her, she was a pistol. Nino said he knew just what I meant, he liked her too, but he didn't see her no more. Said he hadn't seen her in almost a year; one day it'd dawned on him, all of a sudden, he hasn't seen her a while. 'She's not workin' the store anymore.'

"So I said to Nino, not thinkin' about it, 'What is she, knocked up or somethin'?' Because after all, this's gotta be, what—twenny years ago then? She's around forty? Wasn't too far-fetched—could've been that."

Now McKeach smiled. "So like I said, I said that to Nino, 'Got herself knocked up, did she?' And I see that Nino don't wanna answer that. In fact Nino wants nothin' to *do* with this subject— wants to talk about somethin' else, *anything* else, except Mrs. Dominic Frolio. So, okay, he won't talk about her, but I've gotta *needle* him, just a little—otherwise he thinks I've gone soft.

"'Well, didn't you at least *ask*?' I say to Nino. 'She might not be pregnant. She could be sick. Dom'd be hurt if he thought I didn't care, knew his wife was sick and I didn't call. Nino says No, he didn't ask, he'd ask the next time he was there. But I know he wouldn't, he had no intention, and I never asked him again.

"No, I always figured the reason she stopped workin' was because her husband, some reason or other, decided he didn't want her around the place, guys like Nino comin' in. By then our friend Dom was around sixty-five, slowin' down some, but his young wife was still goin' strong. Could be some trouble there, he wasn't careful—if there hadn't been trouble already. But if she didn't see them and they didn't see her, then maybe bad things wouldn't happen. At least that's how I looked at it.

"Then a year or two after that, Nino got grabbed. Furthermore, Nino got grabbed down in *Quincy, Fore River,* Dominic Frolio's old stompin' grounds—where he knew every cop onna force. And even *more* furthermore, Nino got grabbed for possession of heroin, and the big time too, this was—half a kilo.

"Now this, well, I didn't know. Wasn't sure. Nino always was headstrong, and I did know him to moonlight a little with blow, even though I told him a lot of times not to, takin' chances he didn't need to. But he thought he was a swinger, and the swingers used coke, and so that's what he'd do, he'd snort coke.

Never anything else, and like most people who use coke, if he had some he'd sell you a little. But never the half-kilo range. And I never knew him to use heroin, much less to deal any that shit. So ever since then I always sort of wondered, 'Was Nino set up? And if he was, who might've done that?'" McKeach laughed. "Always did have a suspicious mind. And—liked to speak well of the dead."

After the conference McKeach lingered for a few private words with Cistaro. Cistaro agreed Farrier and Stoat would appreciate being tipped off about Crawford's enterprise, after he'd repaid his loan. "But not too soon," Cistaro said. "Queers might figure something out. Make the feds hold off a couple months or so." McKeach agreed.

When he reached the steps outside, Naughton had gotten out of Rascob's car and the two of them were talking about the Celtics. McKeach paused at the foot of the steps and cleared his throat. They fell silent and looked his way. "Nice night, guys," McKeach said.

"Very nice night," Rascob said, "but I got a big day tomorrow—should be using it for sleeping." He turned toward his car, and as Naughton moved aside, McKeach gave him the thumbs-up sign. By then in the driver's seat, Rascob saw the signal, and saw Naughton's nod as well. Rascob looked down at the ignition and turned the key.

17

As the darkness began to give way to the edge of a pale reddish dawn at the tops of the black woods to the southeast, McKeach in the blue Bonneville Brougham came southbound off the West Roxbury Parkway into the rotary and turned off at the second right, pulling up the slope of the floodlighted parking lot at the entrance of the brightly lit White Hen Pantry twenty-four-hour store at 4:58 A.M. Todd Naughton in a dark-blue satin New England Patriots windbreaker and blue jeans came out of the store immediately into the predawn chill, carrying a white paper bag with a drawing of a chicken on it, yanking the right front door open and sliding onto the seat, pulling the door shut as McKeach turned down the slope and accelerated out of it onto the VFW Parkway eastbound.

Officer Andrew Ramona, his Boston Police Department silver-and-blue Ford cruiser parked in the next space, sat in the passenger seat of Officer Owen Hennigan's BPD K-9 Unit cruiser with his cardboard cup of coffee in his left hand and his right arm hanging out the window. He did that so as to enjoy his Marlboro with his coffee without altering the atmosphere inside the cruiser. Hennigan's one-hundred-and-fourteen-pound black-and-tan German shepherd, Good Herman, lying watchfully in the rear seat behind the black steel grille, disliked tobacco smoke. He ignored its lingering aroma on smokers' breath and clothing. He seemed not to notice it at home with Janet Hennigan, who smoked, and disregarded smokers on the street when he was being exercised, toileted or working, but in the cruiser he reacted to it violently, barking and thrashing heavily enough to shake the vehicle anytime he smelled it in the passenger compartment.

Ramona, pulling his head back in the window after exhaling a deep drag, nodded to indicate McKeach's Pontiac as it left the parking lot, said—"Wuddun 'at the ever-popular Arthur McKeon?"

Hennigan behind the wheel sipped coffee through the hole in the plastic lid and nodded. "That's who it was all right—him*self,* the *McKeach.*"

"In a helluva hurry there, too," Ramona said. "Didn't even have time to notice us, give a friendly wave. Kind of rude of him, I think. Think it's because who he's meeting? Didn't want us to notice him, doin' that?"

"Doin' what?" Hennigan said, drinking coffee.

"Pickin' up Naughton, the super's kid," Ramona said. "Didn't want us see him doin' that?"

"Who?" Hennigan said.

"McKeach, damnit," Ramona said. "Pickin' up Naughton's kid. Terry... Teddy... something like that. Toby."

"If you're talkin' about Superintendent Naughton's youngest son," Hennigan said, "his name's Todd. Followin' at last in his daddy's footsteps—just got into the next class, the academy."

"Then what's he doin' with McKeach?" Ramona said.

"Who?" Hennigan said.

"Todd Naughton, *who,*" Ramona said. "What's the matter with you, Owen? You know who I'm talkin'. Todd Naughton just got inna car with McKeach and off they went, like a jailbreak inna movies—roarin' off. What's he's doin', doin' *that,* he's gonna be a policeman?"

"Arthur McKeon's his uncle," Hennigan said.

"McKeach is the super's *brother?*" Ramona said. "What're you tellin' me, Owen? Super's mother had two different *husbands?*"

Hennigan sighed. "No, Andrew," he said, "I'm not tellin' you that. Arthur McKeon has a brother named *Peter* McKeon. Runs a private security company. Night watchmen, gatekeepers and guards. Watchguard Security. Fairly good service, too, everything I've heard. Keep an eye on your stuff and if someone tries to steal it, they call the real cops and get outta the way. Can't ask for much more'n that, for several hundred bucks a month plus a good-sized tip at Christmas.

"Peter McKeon's wife's name's Marybeth. I dunno now what her maiden name was, but she has a sister, Caroline. Caroline's married to Emmett Naughton—so she is Todd Naughton's mother. Marybeth is his aunt and Peter's his uncle by marriage, and I guess that makes Arthur one too. Or so everyone seems to think. I myself? Do not *give* a *shit.*"

"Well, then," Ramona said, forgetting the backseat occupant and bringing the Marlboro in for a last drag, exhaling it billowing through his nose. The shepherd was on his feet at once, barking furiously and springing repeatedly against the steel grille, causing the front seat to judder and lurch.

"Jesus *Christ,* Andrew," Hennigan said, putting his coffee on the dash, then grabbing the wheel and using it for leverage to turn around in the seat, "now look what you did. Get *down,* Herman, damn dog you, get *down.*" The dog looked at him reproachfully. "*No,*" Hennigan said, "now goddamn you, *sit. Down.*" The dog backed off and sat down again, looking pleased with himself, still expecting a reward, and Hennigan said, "Yeah, that's better there, settle down." He turned to Ramona. "And as for you, Andrew, get rid of that friggin' *butt,* for Christ sake, 'fore Good Herman kills us both here."

Ramona lifted his right hand outside the cruiser and used his right thumb and middle finger to snap the filtered stub in a high arc out over the parking lot. "Oh-*kay*," Hennigan said, subsiding behind the wheel and taking his coffee cup off the dashboard, "now we also got *that* put behind us. You got any other problems now? Or can we now finish our coffees and maybe then go back to work?"

"Well, I'd still like to know what the Naughton kid's doing ridin' off with McKeach," Ramona said. He drained his coffee.

"Andrew," Hennigan said, "like I been tryin' to make you see, but you didn't seem to get it, here is some free advice now, with the warts still on it—if you ever expect to get a promotion you oughta learn now is what Naughton's kid does with his Uncle Arthur's a subject to stay away from. It's not police business—it's family."

AT FAULKNER HOSPITAL MCKEACH turned left off Centre Street and drove up the hill into the parking lot behind the hospital, choosing a space off to the left, turning down the volume on the radio as the announcer said "... some were taking as an indication that the Fed might soon raise interest..." He and Naughton got out of the car as soon as he had it in Park. Naughton came around the front of the Brougham and slid in behind the wheel.

McKeach in his black tanker jacket over a grey sweatshirt and jeans went around the back and got into the right rear seat. He unzipped the jacket but did not remove it; he pulled an army multicolored camouflage field jacket up from the left footwell and put it on over the tanker jacket. Then he pulled a black wool watch cap out of the footwell and put that on. There was a medium-sized dark green nylon duffel bag with black webbing straps and reinforced handles on the seat. He unzipped it and felt around in it until he located a small square bottle of Esteé Lauder water-soluble taupe make-up base, a packet of premoistened Kleenex and a sandwich-size Ziploc plastic freezer bag.

Naughton leaned toward the right front footwell where he'd put the White Hen bag between his feet. "Wancher coffee back there with you?" he said.

"No," McKeach said, "coffee after. Don't wanna hafta take a leak, I got this thing goin' on." He opened the Kleenex and put it on top of the bag. He opened the bottle. Holding the cap between the little finger and ring finger of his right hand, he poured a quantity of the make-up into the palm of his left hand. He put the open bottle and cap down on the floor of the footwell. Splaying his right forefinger away from the others he dabbed his right middle and ring fingers into the make-up base and applied it to his forehead, cheeks, nose and ears. Then he used some of the Kleenex to remove the make-up from his hands. He put the soiled Kleenex into the plastic bag. He reached down into the footwell and brought up the make-up bottle and cap. He capped the bottle and put it in the freezer bag. He put that in the footwell.

He groped in the bag again until he found a pair of unlined grey leather work gloves. The forefinger of the right one had been cut off halfway down. He drew the gloves on, rolling back the cuff of the one on his left hand so that he could see his Seiko quartz watch. It read 5:19. He leaned forward over the back of the front seat. Naughton without being asked adjusted the rearview mirror so that McKeach could see his face, now reddish brown, reflected in it. He nodded and slid back on the seat. He clasped his gloved hands together.

"Okay," he said, "now what you do is take a left outta here on Centre Street and go down the rotary, the Arborway. And you take the Arborway and you go all the way up it 'til you get the turnaround, Jamaica Pond. And you *take* the left the turnaround, and then right after you come outta it you take a right, this'd be your first right after it, and that is Parkman Drive, all right? Goes allah way around the pond on the other side there, the Jamaicaway, and comes out on Perkins Street. And there you take a right, all right? A right on Perkins, and you drive down it nice an' slow. Very pretty 'long there now, really startin' look like spring, grass's comin' up, cherry trees just bloomed along there couple weeks ago, rain washed 'em all away—allah ducks 'n' geese're back onna pond again, ready for another summer, though I guess a lot of them've got so they never leave now, go south for the winter. Winters must be gettin' warmer, like they say—or else the ducks're gettin' tougher. Still seems funny, though.

"Anyway, when we get where I wanna be, which I have got it all picked out, I'll tell you 'Stop,' and you do that an' let me out, and I'll go down there inna trees, all right? You with me now so far here?"

Naughton nodded. "Okay then," McKeach said. "Now you wait there for a minute, maybe, after I go down there, and you really keep your eyes peeled—still with me now on this?" Naughton nodded. McKeach patted his right shoulder. "Good. And when I get where I'm goin', things go the way I want, I'll get myself all squnched down in there where the banks've all eroded out, and just situate myself in there. And then when I have done that, then what I am gonna do is, I have got my little flashlight with me and I'm gonna blink it once. And so you'll be watchin' for that. Just once, and first ask you if you seen it and then if you say that you did, may ask you if before you saw it you knew where I was."

"I don't..." Naughton said. "How'm I gonna...?"

"Right," McKeach said. "How you gonna hear me when I'm askin' you—that it? Exactly right. Well, now, if you look right under there." He came forward on the edge of the rear seat now with his right arm over the back cushion of the front seat, pointing the ungloved index finger down toward the front of the seat. "If you put your hand down there and feel around under the driver's seat there, behind where your feet are, there's a walkie-talkie that I put there. Take it out, all right? And hold it up."

Naughton did as he was told, holding up a black Apelco three-watt VHF radio.

"Okay," McKeach said, "and, now you do know how to use it, am I right?"

"Sure, push-to-talk here," Naughton said, pressing the button on the left side. "Turn it on up on the top here." He turned the first knob on the top of the radio and it hissed loudly. "And then you got the squelch here"—Naughton turned the inner knob so that the hiss first disappeared entirely and then came up low and steady—"and that means you're ready, someone calls. And then when you wanna answer, push here to talk."

"Okay, good," McKeach said. "Channel nineteen's what we're goin' to be usin'. You know how to do that, get the channel that you want?"

Naughton pressed the selector button on the right side of the unit and the channel numbers scrolled up in the liquid crystal window.

"Good," McKeach said, "very good. Now don't turn it off. Leave it on until I'm back here inna car with you. Now, after you seen the light, you mark the place where you seen it come from, so that when I call you again on the walkie-talkie an' tell you, 'Come back for me,' you can come right back to that spot sure as if you're a racin' pigeon and it was your home loft I just showed you with my little flashlight, all right? And then what you do then is, you drive away, like you're just passin' through, this's the way you go to work. Happened see the ducks 'n' geese, they got your attention; all so calm and peaceful there, Jamaica Pond at sunup, you pulled over for a minute, take it in, but now you got to be on your way and so there, off you go."

"Where'm I supposed to go?" Naughton said.

"Well," McKeach said, "far enough away so the people that I'm meetin' here don't see the car. I don't think they got a look at it the last time, we had this little meeting where I hadda do a couple things I don't think they liked, but maybe they did, so why take any chances? Now the people sell these things claim the range's three miles. But I dunno. I'd rather you played it safe and just follow Perkins out to the Jamaicaway, all right? On the other side the pond. And take a right there and then just follow the Jamaicaway all the way back down the Arborway rotary again, and get on Parkman Drive again. Find yourself a place to park out of sight, much as you can, and then call me. Let me know you're there in position, and I'll get right back to you, and if that works all right, then leave the set on and wait there for my call. Then if it doesn't, try another spot and try the radio again. All right?"

Naughton shrugged. "Sure," he said. "You're payin' me two hundred bucks drive your car around Jamaica Pond a couple times, I think you oughta get what you want."

McKeach slapped him on the right shoulder. "Attaboy," he said, "really gonna miss you, you go to cop school, you know. But it's your life, I guess. Should do what you want with it." He sat back. "Let's head out."

Naughton heard the right rear door open as he brought the car to a stop in the sixth parallel parking space from the NO PARKING sign on Perkins Street, but McKeach with the duffel bag was out of the backseat and quartering down the short grassy slope above the paved sidewalk rimming the pond so quickly and quietly that Naughton had to look into the backseat to make sure he had latched the door shut.

About thirty feet in front and below the front of the car there was a bench made of brown wooden planks fitted into cement uprights beside the paved walkway. On the surface of the pond there was a layer of gauzy grey mist about four feet deep, and still. It lay over the land too, ground fog; a hundred yards or so ahead the mist hid the dark roots of trees exposed by the erosion of the slope between the sidewalk and the beige gravel shoreline. Many dun-colored ducks and grey Canada geese with white necks slept along the water's edge with their heads beneath their wings.

The Apelco hissed on the seat beside him. Watching Mc-Keach scuttle diagonally down the incline behind the bench and cross the pavement, heading toward the water, into the treeline, Naughton yawned and settled back in the driver's seat. He turned up the volume on the car radio slightly. "In other scores around the league," the announcer said, "Miami Heat ninety, New Jersey Nets eighty-one; and, in what some were regarding as previews of the upcoming playoffs . . ."

Yawning again Naughton looked out through the windshield again; dawn was well into the sky now, the rose-tinted light high and strong enough behind the treeline on the Jamaicaway to illuminate the ground and outline the roofs of the buildings along the boulevard. The sky was cloudless. It was going to be a fine clear morning. He looked back at the pond. McKeach had disappeared. Naughton's jaw snapped shut.

For a long moment he was alarmed. He took a deep breath and calmed himself and waited. ". . . Los Angeles Lakers one-oh-three, Utah Jazz ninety-nine, despite twenty-eight points, ten assists and fourteen rebounds from Karl Malone." The flashlight winked once from among a group of four gnarled trees about forty yards away. Greatly relieved, Naughton picked up the walkie-talkie. "See the light an' mark the spot, four trees," he said in a low voice. Then he realized he hadn't depressed the push-to-talk button; as the light winked again he depressed the button and repeated the signal.

"Aces," McKeach replied. "See yah." He watched the Brougham pass above his nest and nodded. He turned down the hissing walkie-talkie and put it on the crotch of the trees. Then he set to work. He had made himself as small as possible in the pocket the roots created, four trunks emerging from the single large gnarled ball in one of the cavities eroded from the base of the grassy incline. He had seated himself on a black vinyl air pillow and braced his back against one of the trees. Now he raised his knees and dug his heels into the gravel so the root ball enclosed all of his lower body but his left leg below the knee. Two of the trees, their crusty greyish-brown trunks about a foot around, their lower branches thick and close to the ground, framed his view of the sidewalk to the west while at the same time concealing his upper body and head. He leaned his right shoulder against the third tree, beside him. He murmured, "Solid."

He unzipped the duffel bag and took out of it his .30 caliber M2 selective-fire Winchester U.S. military carbine. The brown wooden stock was dull, nicked and scratched by years and use; he had deliberately dulled the exterior blued metal barrel with matte grey paint, but the lands and grooves of the bore gleamed silver and smelled of fresh Hoppe's No. 9 powder and lead solvent and the action smelled of Gunslick lubricant. He set the selector on the receiver to semiautomatic fire, one round for each trigger squeeze. "I was young, I'd use full auto—what a sensah *power. Blam-blam, blam-blam, blam.* But in those days could control it—now the muzzle climbs on me and I'm all over the place." In the trees around the pond, birds unseen began to sing with sexual urgency in the chill but brightening morning.

McKeach fitted the standard fifteen-round magazine clip into the housing ahead of the trigger guard and pulled back the handle of the operating slide on the right, chambering the first round and then pushing the handle forward to lock. When it snicked he murmured, "There." The sun was visible now, the top edge of the orange ball coming up to the southeast of the apartment and hospital towers east of the Jamaicaway, and traffic along it was beginning to pick up; the occasional auto horn sounded.

From the duffel bag he removed a pale green plastic two-liter Sprite bottle he had emptied and rinsed clean and a six-inch looped strip of two-inch silver duct tape. Holding the carbine upright with the stock between his knees he fitted the mouth of the Sprite bottle over the muzzle and eased it back over the ramp sight about three inches down on the barrel. Then he unstuck the ends of the duct tape and taped the neck of the bottle tightly against the barrel. "Poor man's silencer. Could I get a real silencer? Sure, could get one easy. But get caught with a silencer and it's the same as a machine gun—automatic life, no arguing. Get caught with a tonic bottle? They don't arrest you for that, 'less you throw it onna street."

McKeach lifted the duffel bag onto the junction of the two trees framing his vantage and plumped it until he was satisfied it made a soft but solid rest. He rested the front of the stock on the duffel bag so that the pale green Sprite bottle hung clear of the other side of the dark green duffel bag under the dull green foliage. Peering through the rear leaf sight over where he knew the front ramp to be inside the bottle he zeroed the muzzle on a point about three feet above the level of the bench seat at the edge of the walkway thirty feet away. Then he swung the muzzle over to the left so that when he squinted down the barrel again it was pointed at about the place where the midthorax of a man a good deal taller than average and walking briskly would be as he passed the bench. His watch read 5:42.

He picked up the walkie-talkie and made sure he had not turned it off, fiddling with the squelch control until the hiss, barely audible a foot away, reassured him. He put the walkie-talkie back on the duffel bag and with the carbine resting on his knee and the bag sat back against the tree. Then, knowing he had done well what he had to do to make arrangements for the work he'd come to do, McKeach was content, and settled down within himself to wait for the others to appear.

Naughton slowly insinuated the right front wheel of the Pontiac over the sloping curb of Parkman Drive, steering under the overhanging tree limbs so that when he was finished the car lay all but hidden on the blind side of the curve where the drive northbound straightens out along the southwesterly side of Jamaica Pond. The limbs of the trees that had lifted over the hood and windshield and then dragged across the roof and trunk now drooped behind the bumper and the registration plate. He shifted into Park and picked up the walkie-talkie. He depressed the push-to-talk button. "Checking position," he said.

McKeach picked up the walkie-talkie and depressed push-to-talk. "Aces," he said, "sit tight now."

At 5:54 McKeach heard the shuffling-scraping sounds of at least two heavy individuals walking fast on asphalt pavement in deep-treaded footgear, and the chuffing sounds they made as they breathed rapidly and deeply for maximum aerobic effort. Somewhere far off behind the trees at McKeach's right shoulder an ambulance sirened its approach to one of the hospitals on Brookline Avenue and he ignored it absolutely, concentrating on the sounds of his work approaching.

Now he was seeing the forms of the walkers large and black-clothed indistinctly, hooded there-and-then-not-there-and-then-there-again among the overhanging branches, maybe twenty yards away, and with his left forefinger he pushed the safety button at the front of the trigger guard on the M2 all the way through to the right. Another siren picked up to the north-west on Route 9, commuters were getting hurt. He ignored that one as well; he focused on the walkers huffing, breath so heavy with vapor that he could see it now and then in little white puffs before he could see their faces clearly, now coming up around the walkway curve and walking fast up to the bench and when the eyepatched outside one was in mid-stride, left HeavyHanded hand and foot down, right HeavyHanded hand and right foot coming forward, McKeach having taken a deep breath released part of it and squeezed the trigger once and then again. The first explosion muffled down into the soft semblance of a chest cough before the bullet tore through the base of the Sprite bot-tle and the second round followed right after it, somewhat louder, both of them drilling the eyepatched man outside very nicely at mid-chest, close in to the sternum, lifting him off his feet in mid-stride up into the air backward, McKeach muttering, "knock him right flat on his *ass*," and then short-arcing the Sprite-bottled muzzle over as the man on the inside floundered to stop, gaping at his flailing partner, puffing "unh unh unh, wha'," stunned, knowing-and-yet-not-knowing what was taking place; shot him twice too, each round now louder than the one before it, the same places, "just right of the heart," taking *him* back off his feet, and then swung the muzzle back again and zeroed in again on the eyepatched outside man slapped down twisted on the pavement at an angle that displayed the right side of his hooded head to McKeach at good advantage. Shot him twice more right there, in that head, the bottom of the Sprite bottle now blown out wide open and the report of each shot now as loud and shocking as the motorcycle backfires Boston each spring learns again to disregard; "That should do it, shouldn't it, two more inna fuckin' *head*." And then the last step: he swung the muzzle back again as the second hooded man struggled idiotically against the bullets in him to sit up, regain his balance and attend, and shot him twice more in the face, turning it at once to meat—"You be wantin' *fries* with *thet*?"

Then without looking further at the men he had shot down, McKeach, sniffling, annoyed, his nose running a little, "time for *this* shit," sleeved it: reset the carbine on safety; tore the blown-out bottle off the barrel—"got to remember to resight it"—stuffed it in the duffel; gathered up six spent cartridges—two had popped out into the tree roots but without panicking he found them, "nothing like experience"; dumped them all into the bag; then picked up the walkie-talkie, hitting push-to-talk and saying into it, "Time for coffee, babycakes."

Back came Naughton's reply fast: "Gotcha, Aces. On the *way*."

18

SOME FIVE HOURS LATER, shortly after 11:00 A.M. on the fourth Thursday in April, Hinchey at the rented grey metal desk in front of Farrier's put down his ballpoint pen and shut off his black Ampex reel-to-reel tape recorder. He took a swallow of coffee from the Dunkin' Donuts travel mug on his desk. Then he removed his black earphones and turned the onionskin transcript he had been verifying face down on his desk. He revolved his castered swivel chair so that he faced Jack Farrier at the identical desk behind him.

Farrier, wearing black earphones, sat head bowed over the mid-section of a volume of transcript assembled with gold cotter pins and covered with clear plastic, using a retracted Parker Jotter ballpoint to follow rapidly down the wide right margin of the triple-spaced pages the text of the taped conversation he was playing on his Ampex recorder. A white mug of tawny coffee steamed between the recorder and the stack of eleven boxed tapes on its left.

That morning eight other middle-aged men in dress shirts and ties occupied other Officemaster Rentals desks—two chairs were vacant—in the rented office on the third floor of the McClatchy Medical and Professional Building on Route 1 in Norwood. Each of the men had a pair of black earphones connected to a black Ampex recorder on his desk, along with a stack of transcripts and a stack of boxed audiotapes, and was dealing with them in more or less the same fashion as Hinchey and Farrier.

Spring with a second consecutive warm day was becoming serious around Boston and the sunlight through the window beside Farrier's desk in the southeast corner of the office caused him to yawn and fight off dozing. It reflected at the same time blindingly off the clear plastic cover of the top volume of the eleven transcripts stacked on the desk to his right, and glared on the white paper in front of him. He squinted and blinked behind his black-framed glasses. During those few moments Hinchey looked on, delaying interruption; Farrier, trying not to fall asleep, without lifting his gaze from the page irritably shook his head twice and rubbed his forehead with his right hand once, each time as the reels continued to turn, then having to catch himself hurriedly and turn a page, unaware of Hinchey's scrutiny.

Outside, traffic on both sides of Route 1 was light but the driver of a southbound American Medical Response ambulance traveling unimpeded in the passing lane at about the normal speed of 45 miles an hour used his emergency lights and blipped his whooping French-police, horn-and-siren combination to freeze crossing traffic at the intersection just north of the Mc-Clatchy Building so that he could run the red light showing in his direction. The noise was abrupt and shrill enough to penetrate Farrier's concentration. Without looking up he poised his left hand over the switch panel on the recorder; when the pen in his right hand reached the foot of the page he was reading he pushed the pause button on the recorder. Then he flipped the transcript face down and picked up the coffee mug, bringing it to his mouth for a deep draft. Dropping the pen he pushed back with his feet from the desk, using his right hand to lift off the earphones and put them on the desk. He shook his head, blinking several times, and said *"Ahhhhh,"* before focusing on Hinchey. "You, ah, *rang?*" he said, yawning and putting the mug down down before stretching both arms straight up above his head.

"Got something I think you'd better hear," Hinchey said, concern showing on his face.

"Ahh-awp," Farrier said, closing his mouth quickly and jerking his thumb toward the stacks of boxed audiotapes next to the Ampex on his desk, then making a sweeping gesture to comprehend the stacked transcripts as well. "Already goin' deaf 'n' blind, stuff on my *own* desk I got in front of me to get through, and you want me to listen to *yours?* Gimme a fuckin' *break,* willya? Don't make me do everything for you."

"It's not that ... I already done this once," Hinchey said. "I just——"

"Look," Farrier said, "if you're now findin' you really can't understand what the hell they're sayin', I know I said 'deadline, unbreakable deadline, no exceptions for no one'; that anything that you wanted enhancement on, it hadda go in by a certain date. And I also know that date's gone by. Went by two weeks ago, almost three. But I already bent that rule, three tapes for Taylor and four for MacIntyre, decided they now didn't think the tapes they had matched the transcripts, and as much of a pain in the ass as it is gettin' those prima donna 'oh-we're-so-overworked' technicians down in Maryland, wherever the hell they are, ramped up again, I'd a damn sight rather get *them* pissed off *now* 'n have a jury down the line a year from now, these cases ever do get tried, sayin' to the judge and prosecutor, '*Hey,* these tapes aren't sayin' what these transcripts say they say—these guys aren't *guilty.*'

"No, that we definitely do not want. So if you got one you now find you're not sure you know what's on it, I'll bend the rule again to help *you* out. But you should've——"

"Jack," Hinchey said, "this tape's *been* enhanced. It's as clear as gin. No trouble at all understanding what the guys on it're sayin'—none at all. That isn't what's botherin' me."

"Well then what the hell is it?" Farrier said. "Not sure who they are? It's *dated*, for Christ sake—cross-check and find out who the hell was in there that day, that night, when the tape was made. Except the fire escape, only one door goin' inna the place; get the logs out and check who went through it and didn't come out, had to've been in there while the tape was being made. Gotta be one of those people talkin' on it. And if that doesn't do it then look at the stinkin' video—that'll *show* you who went inside that night. Cross-check it again that way."

He snorted. "Have some confidence in yourself, Bobby, willya? You know what you're doin'. You're no flamin' rookie; you're an experienced agent. If you think it's this and you don't think it's that, then the chances are that it *is this*. Don't ask me to double-check you—I got gangs of work of my own. Figure out for yourself what it means."

"Jack," Hinchey said, "this one wasn't all that garbled to begin with, that it really needed the enhancement. You want the truth, I think I probably could've told you who it was and pretty much what they're saying before I packed it up to be sent down. More a case of didn't *wanna* know 'n didn't. Anyway, now I do know for sure who it is, who's talking. I know what they're say-ing. Know what they *mean*, too—no doubt at all. So why do I want you to hear it? Because I dunno what to do with it. Well, I do know, but I also know if I do it, you'll come right out of your *tree* at me."

He paused to let Farrier reply, but Farrier sat silently gazing at him. Then he swallowed and frowned and brought his chair back up to his desk, picking up his earphones with his right hand and unplugging them from the recorder with his left. He held the plug out toward Hinchey. "Hike your Ampex over this way, toward me here, this side of your desk, see if the cord'll reach, willyah?"

The cord was long enough to allow Farrier to audit the tape from his own chair, using the auxiliary jack on Hinchey's Ampex. Hinchey, watching the footage counter, said "Three-forty-nine. Gotta run her back here little over two hundred feet. One-thirty-seven's about where it begins. What you hafta hear." He pushed the rewind button. He put on the headset again, leaving his left ear uncovered. Farrier left his right ear uncovered. "You say we know who's in there," Farrier said.

"Right," Hinchey said. "This's one of the earliest usable ones, twenty-fourth of September. We've now been in there seven weeks, this's toward the end of the seventh, a Thursday night. You remember back in August, all the trouble that we'd had, interference—couldn't figure out where it was coming from?"

"I was on vacation, August," Farrier said. "Lucas was still here then, running things in my place."

"Well, there was a lot of heavy static," Hinchey said. "Turned out it was the exhaust fan inna bakery next door that was makin' it."

"Oh, yeah," Farrier said. "Viviano, something."

"Right," Hinchey said. "Finally figured it out. Had to be the baker hadn't oiled his exhaust fan. So one night Viviano broke there and did it for him, changed the frequency just enough so the static disappeared."

"And when Lucas found out he was *pissed*," Farrier said. "Oh, yeah—he got pissed off *again*, he's tellin' *me* about it. Found out Carl not only didn't get permission 'fore he did it, also stole six cannolies, his way out."

"Right," Hinchey said. "Pissed off that he just went ahead and did it, on his own without permission; more pissed off when he finds out, the cannolies, and then even *more* pissed off when he asks how come he did it. 'Well,' says Carl, like this all makes perfectly good sense, 'they make really good cannolies. So, if we find out the fan *wasn't* what was doin' it; oilin' it *didn't* fix the interference, then that way, me comin' back at least with the cannolies, trip wouldn't be a total loss.'"

"Right," Farrier said, chuckling. "Lucas told me it's three days before he could even speak to Carl, and then... 'member how high his voice'd get when he got excited? Just tellin' me about it, he's *screamin'*. '"You fuckin' *idiot*," I said.' How he asked him, what if the bakery people comin' in there in the morning, what if they'd noticed the cannolies're missing from the day-olds tray?

"'Not sayin' these're Nobel Prize winners, runnin' ah fuckin' *bakery,* but they weren't gonna think somebody's *cat* got in and ate 'em—they'd've been smart enough to figure out someone broke in. And since nobody breaks in a bakery just to steal cannolies, and they got to know who's next door, wouldn't've taken them very long to figure out *why* someone must've broken in, and it wasn't for cannolies. And then mention it to nice Mister Rizzo next door, next time he comes in for coffee. And he would've had the place swept and found our installations, and that would've fuckin' *creased* it. Put the whole fuckin' *mission* inna fuckin' *toilet,* and God only knows how much hard work, how many people, right inna crapper along with it. Never get even *near* Carlo Rizzo's operation again—maybe even get somebody *killed,* Carlo and them ever found out who gave us probable cause, and for *what?* A half-dozen stale *sweet rolls?* You *asshole.*'"

"Right," Hinchey said, laughing. "You'd've been there. It was even better. Viviano listens to his whole tirade, and then when it looks like he's finally finished tells him obviously they *didn't* notice the cannolies missin', and if the fan interference comes back so he hasta go in again, re-oil the fan, this time he's gettin' a *pie.*"

Watching the footage meter, Hinchey said, "I thought Lucas was gonna *shit,* have a *heart* attack or something, he's so mad. Never seen a man so mad. Ah, there we are." He shut off the rewind. "Okay," he said, "one-thirty-seven. Right about here's where it starts. You'll recognize Carlo's best official *capo* voice of course, all low 'n' growly, and Tommy Cavicchi's. And Bacciochi's, plus Tullio; he's the Medford cop who dropped in now and then, see if Mister Rizzo needed him do anything. Strictly off duty, of course. Some cops an' firemen moonlight paintin' houses, puttin' decks in? Heavy liftin'? Tullio don't think so. He'd rather do his moonlightin' for the Mob, get information from the Registry computer or the Criminal Information one at Public Safety. Little dirt on anybody Mister Rizzo didn't like. He's the one with the giggle, does all the laughin', little piece of shit. And of course, our pal Cistaro's voice which you'll recognize, hearin' it so many times."

"Tell you what, you cue me," Farrier said. "Just pause it when you hear it comin' up to something that you think is real important, tell me who's talkin' next."

"Right," Hinchey said, "and I will do that. But Cistaro—it's him especially, I think you got to listen to. Some of what he's got to say here... I dunno, Jack, like I say, what we do about this. Not really that sure where it could take us—an' pretty sure, it comes to that, we don't really wanna go there. But then maybe we've got no choice."

Farrier sighed. "Well," he said, "no help for it now. Let's find out what we're dealin' with. Let the games begin."

Hinchey pushed the play button.

"Yeah, but what I always wonder, what I never understood, you know?" Hinchey mouthed, "Carlo." Farrier nodded. *"An' this's goin' back a long time now I'm talkin', maybe twenty, thirty years. Before there even is a capo here, an' the man you hafta see, and talk to... if you are a made guy now, and there's something you want to do, well, it's still Nunzio, all right? Still him you hafta go to."*

"Nunzio Dinapola," Farrier said, musing. Hinchey hit the pause button. "This's how it used to be—players changed; game stayed the same. What I am to Carlo, Al DeMarco was to Nunzio. Except Al didn't have Title Three or the Racketeer Influenced and Corrupt Organizations Act to hang Nunzio with, like we do to hang Carlo. Changed the whole game, that one rule. We nail Carlo, my guess is he'll turn out to be like the last dinosaur or something. Last of the red-hot Ginzos. Last whale, only no one to protect him. I'm the last Captain Ahab." He smirked. "Almost makes me feel sentimental—brings a tear to my eye." He motioned to restart the tape.

"*All that time ago,*" the voice on it said, "*Nunzio, he is still a sotto cápo, but he is the man in charge of the family's interests in this town, and he wanted you, you know, to become one of us, and join him, and you would not do this.*" Someone coughed. "*You would never join him. Us. You know what he said of you? No? 'The Cistaro boy,' he'd say, 'Guillermo's boy, Cistaro, he's a fine young man. Nicolo. He should be with us, Carlo, you and me, you know? In this thing of ours we have. You see him from time to time. You are close to him in age. Say something to him. He would listen, maybe, to you. Make him understand, you know, how this is important—the Family is important. Not just we are important to him, but that he is important to us, too. So that we are united and it is in this way we draw strength from one another. We are a smaller number here, not the same as Providence, where men of our heritage are many more than all the others, than the Irish, the police. So, even more important here, we unite with one another, stand against those who are against us, make them see that we are strong and take care of one another. You should tell him this, Carlo—you can make him understand.'*

"*He was sure of this, and I could not.*"

Cistaro's recorded voice was firm, assured. Hinchey mouthed the name; Farrier nodded.

"*Well, but he knew the reason. Should've known it anyway. I told it you enough times, you were doing like he said, after me again to join. Christ, there was a while there, Gallaghers and Rocky, Rocco, goin' at it left an' right, I was just back from the service, 'tween Girolamo and his people, an' you and Nunzio, you're...* *both your organizations're after me at once? Jesus, it was awful. Had me feelin' like I must've been turned into, Christ I dunno what, Marilyn Monroe or something. 'Oooh, hee hee, I must be pretty—everybody wants me.'"*

He laughed. *"Maybe that's what I should've done. Told you an' Nunzio, and Rocky Girolamo, 'All right, first one gives me a fur coat anna white Caddy convert, red leather seats, sets me up a nice apartment, his will be the organization I will join.' Become a sweet boy, a* castrato, *have a nice life for myself."*

"Carlo next," Hinchey mouthed. Someone on the tape belched loudly. Farrier nodded. *"Jesus Christ, Tommy, 'chou got any manners? Makin' awful noise like that. Sound just like a fuckin' pig. What if our good friend here, Nick, what if he's got a wire on, huh? Workin' for the FBI, and then when they hear you do that, what they gonna think of us, huh? 'Huh, some kind of bigshot Mafia wise guys these are, makin' noises like they're pigs. Some kind of animals.'"* There was general laughter on the tape.

"Cavicchi," Hinchey mouthed.

"Well, I can't help it, can I? Fuckin' Bacciochi always puts too much oil and peppers, garlic, in that stuff, inna sauce, when it's his turn to make it. Doesn't bother you guys, I guess, but me, I got a sens'tive stomach. That's the way it affects me. So what'm I supposed to do? Sit here watchin' you guys eat, an' I'm not havin' any? Fuck that fuckin' shit, I say, if that's what you guys want. No, just don't use so much, the peppers anna garlic—you'll see then I'll be all right."

Hinchey mouthed "Carlo next again."

"Ah, we shouldn't blame you, Tommy. 'It's all his father's fault. Look what he married.' That's what Nunzio always said, someone like our Tommy here, disappointed him. 'See what happens? Didn't

marry an Italian. No, Italian girls' not good enough—he hadda go outside. What that does, it always happens—thins the blood. Weakens the stock. Makes the man less in his mind, his fortitude, you know? What he has to be a man with.'"

"Poor Cavicchi," Farrier said, laughing and shaking hs head. Hinchey paused the tape. "Hafta feel sorry, the guy. His father marries a Jewish girl whose family came from Florence, moved down there from Zurich fourteenth century or so. Generations they're bankers 'n' brokers for Medicis, and Borgias. Then the war comes, First World War; they pick the wrong side and they're ruined. What's left of them come here, she's still a little girl. Marries Giovanni Cavicchi, why not? All she's ever known're people with Italian names and this's America, the melting pot—what the hell is wrong with what? Turns out—everything. Here's her kid now, crowding sixty—even *he* can't live it down."

Hinchey restarted the tape. "And Carlo again," he said.

"But you say that, along with me for Nunzio here, the Giro-lamos, when Rocco and his people are having their wars with Brian G. and them, the Girolamos at the same time as I am asking you, they are also doing that. Because Rocco's not agreeing if the Gal-laghers are done with, should be Nunzio in charge—bastard Rocco, he thinks it should be him."

"Now Cistaro," Hinchey mouthed.

"Yeah, that's how I remember it. Me and Hugo, matter of fact, way we were lookin' at it . . . well, that he was lookin' at it . . ."

"Hugo Bottalico . . ."

"Right, yeah, Hugo Botto. I was still with Hugo then. Well, I wasn't with him, really, not that way that you would mean it. I, I did some things for Hugo before I went in the service. You know, little stuff, like you do for someone when you're still really just a kid, an' what they're doing's testing you, giving you small things to do, seein' how you handle it. You think you're the hottest stuff there is

but really, all you really are's a real stiff dick that won't let the big kid it's on think about a single thing in the whole world except a place where he can put it, hot, tight an' wet, 'stead of usin' his own hand."

There was laughter on the tape and then Cistaro's voice continued. "Yeah, we all know that's how it is because we know how we all were—at the age where the only thing in the whole world that you can think about is pussy. Anyway, then I decide to enlist. My father was all over me. He don't like what he sees as the way that I am headin', wants me apprentice with him, learn stonecuttin', all right? Always tellin' me it's an honorable trade, 'good honest work, always 'll be needed,' and ... well, you know, it wasn't like I thought he was wrong, or like that—I didn't wanna do it.

"I seen the kind of life he had, how hard he hadda work, outside, in all kinds of weather, and what he got for it, and ... that just wasn't what I wanted. So I then decided what I really needed most was some time to think about it, by myself. Or maybe just some time to maybe grow up a little—first some time to learn to think, and then after that, to think. Anna service—that seemed like it'd be the best place to do that, get myself figured out.

So that was what I did. I signed up the navy. But before I went to do it, along with tellin' this to my parents naturally, about needing time to think, I also went to Hugo, told him what I'm gonna do. So he won't think, you know, I'm now agreein' with my father—because he knew what my father said, what my father thought of him, and of me doin' things for him—he's not the kind of guy that I should be workin' with. Because he'd been good to me."

There was quiet on the tape and then there were murmurs of assent from several speakers.

"Sure, you know, so like I said, I went to Hugo, and I told him, so his feelings wouldn't be hurt. Said 'I'm goin' in the service, gonna be a navy guy.' And he, you know, gave me his blessing, and that meant something to me."

Carlo's was among several voices saying *"Sure"* and *"Course it did."*

"And what he then said to me, this's Hugo, I'm talking, he said that when I'm back again, I get through with the service, 'If I am then still alive, and have things that you might do, things that another man would do, I hope you'll still come and see me and that sometimes now and then we may do some things together.' Which I knew by that he meant that I would work with him and be like sort of junior partners with him, and that when he was ready to hang it up, retire, I would then take his place. Well, I took it that way, anyway, and, well, you know, I was kind of honored by it.

"And so that's what I was doing back then, four years later and I'm now back from the service, when Nunzio had you saying to me I should join with him and you, and Rocky and the guys with him were saying I should join with them, and both of you're telling me with what I know, explosives and the other stuff, the service, either way it's guaranteed that whoever gets me will be the ones knock Brian G. off and become the bosses here.

"And I did not know what to do. So again I talked to Hugo. Since I'd come out of the service I'd once again been doing a few things with him, nothing really major but still bigger'n anything I did for him before I went in, and he said to me himself, he's becoming an old man, and it's a natural thing for an old man to slow down—'You know, I hope you stay with me, all right?' So I had the idea still that I am going to succeed him, and this would mean that I would have my own small operation—not like with Nunzio, where you would be above me, or with Girolamo, where the boss would still be Rocky.

"But the thing with Hugo was that he wasn't, really, slowing down. His was always a small operation of course, mostly the furnishing of advance money and safe places to keep goods and so forth until they could be sold. Or if you wished, to sell them for you, sixty-five cents on the dollar, no matter what he got. And then of

course the money-lending. The airport and the Navy Yard were his territories.

"Now I saw it didn't have to be this way with what he had. If he had had the kind of operation that you and Nunzio and Rocco had, or even Brian G., then what Hugo had for himself would have been the basis for a much bigger one. A bigger operation and a much larger organization to run it. But he didn't have partners or people under him, and even though what he had said to me before I went inna the service made me think if I came back that was what we would become, and that in time when he retired, his operation would be mine, I began to see that what he did about retirement was that—he talked about it.

"And so I therefore went to him and told him about you and Nunzio, and also about Rocco, and asked him what I should do. And he told me I should stay with him, and again when he was somewhat older that this operation, 'and it is a good size for an operation because the man who runs it can do almost all of it himself—with one other person he can trust, which is about as many as one man in one lifetime can expect to find, and need not concern himself about betrayal as he would working with many.' And so I saw that if I expected to become richer before I was as old as he was, I would have to make a change."

Hinchey paused the Ampex. "Now this's where Carlo comes in and really puts it to him," he said. "I give it to the guy—he's good. Carlo's been around a while and he runs an operation full of very hard guys. When he wants to know something, he wants a straight answer. He's not used to having people bob and weave on him, and that's just what the Frogman does. I think that's what he does, at least. Maybe you listen, you tell me." He touched the Play button again. "Carlo now," he said.

"You say that. But you didn't come with us. And you didn't go with Rocco. Instead you went with McKeach. Why did you do that? When I had spoken with you, you had said that Girolamo also

wanted you to join him, and that what you thought you had to do was decide whether you'd be better off with him or us, or if you simply stayed with Hugo as the broker for a bunch of amateurs. Nothing about McKeach to me. Not a word of him."

"Cistaro," Hinchey mouthed.

"McKeach was not McKeach then, when you talked to me. McKeach then was Brian G.'s man. Very powerful, but still, one part of an organization—very dangerous, as we all knew, never to be insulted, but he did not have an organization that he ran and made decisions. He enforced Brian's decisions.

"When he came to me, this'd changed. It was right after Brian G. went down. I know some people—cops, I know, believed Bernie G. would take his place, but no one I respected did, and I didn't either. I thought, 'Now that Brian G. is gone and leaves his organizaton and the man who managed it for him, McKeach, the man who managed it for him will have it for himself.' And when he asked to talk with me and said we should get together because if we did that then with what he had left from Brian G. and what I had with Hugo we could make it possible for business to continue, while Nunzio—you—and Rocco's people fought with each other, and then when you had settled that, we would be the other organization in a city that is big enough for two.

"That made sense to me, the best sense I had heard, and so I said that I woud join him. And that is what I did."

Hinchey mouthed, "Carlo."

"Again, you confuse me. You said that you remained with Hugo because he made you believe that if you stayed with him long enough that when the day came he retired you would have what he had made. But then after Brian G.'s death and our war with Rocco began and McKeach then came to see you, you said you would associate yourself with him to form an independent organization—when you could have come with us. Or joined with the Girolamos. And Hugo was still in place then, when you joined up with McKeach."

The tape ran and made no sound. Farrier raised his eyebrows. Hinchey said, "Here it comes, now. Cistaro here."

"*Yeah. Well, tell you how that came about. What'd happened, see, was this. My wife Madelyn and I, I'm still livin' with her then, hadn't been married that long, and what can I tell you, huh? We're still in love. So these two young guys that dealt with Hugo every now an' then, freelancers—like most the people Hugo did his business with, you know? Hugo's organization was basically a bunch of people who weren't organized, didn't have a gang that they knew they were a part of, so when they needed something, just did something or they're getting ready tah do something, they came and they saw Hugo. And these were two of them, just a couple of young Irish guys worked on the docks, I guess, and I therefore also knew them. And my wife's then just found out for sure she's pregnant, with our first. This would've been our daughter, Suzanne, and the baby's not for at least seven months but she wants a washing machine. Right off, she's gotta have one. And a drier. Both of them. So, and you know how they are, they got one in the oven, they decide they rule the world. You don't get for them what they want, when they want it, well good-bye, that's all she wrote; go stick your dick in somewhere else.*"

There was knowing and appreciative laughter on the tape.

"*So I talk to Hugo about this, and he says, 'Here's what you do. Get ahold the Ryan brothers, tell 'em what it is she wants, I said get 'em for you onna cuff. And then when it falls off of a truck I loan you my station wagon and you get a friend of yours to help you, pick them up and take them home, an' hook 'em up? Guarantee it you're a hero, finest husband ever lived, and when you get home at night she'll have a cold beer in her hand for you an' your dick out of your pants before you can get your coat off.'*

"*So this sounds good to me and that is what I do, get a couple guys McKeach knows help me muscle the units around and I borrow Hugo's car. This big green Olds Vista Cruiser, had this little*

*windshield inna roof like the railroad cars with two decks in 'em.
'Yeah, we got the washer. Got two very nice units for you. Go down
the Navy Yard,' they tell me, 'sometime after nine o'clock. Building
Seven. Maytags'll be onna dock.'*

"So we do that, me and these two other guys McKeach knows.
And maybe I should also mention this's Friday, Memorial Day
three-day weekend. So these guys're all around, but places like the
Navy Yard no one is around—because they've all gone away someplace for the long weekend. Anyway, this's plus McKeach himself,
he also comes, because the two guys he's sending with me, they don't
have a car. I guess they cracked theirs up or something, means
they're gonna need a ride, and McKeach says he is free that night
and what he'll do, he'll drive them.

"We get them inna car, just barely, the two Maytags—hadda
put the backseat down, filled up the whole back. And what I do, I
then drive Hugo's car with the machines in it, an' have McKeach
and his two guys follow me in his car—which they would've hadda
anyway even if they had their own car—because they're both
pretty big and there's no room for them inside of Hugo's Olds. And
anyway I dunno how much weight the springs in Hugo's Olds can
take before they break, in case I hit a pothole, something, with the
Maytags inna back.

"And so we do that. Take it our first house we'd just bought then
in Tuttleville, me and Madelyn, this part of Hingham down there
over by the dump that used to be there then with little houses and a
sandpit there, now it's all filled up with big ones, and we get the machines out of Hugo's car and in the house, and hook 'em up—and
it's just like Hugo said. Madelyn's as happy as a little pig in shit,
'cause she has got two new things she can tell her friends she's got, I
just got them for her. That always made her very happy—didn't
matter what it was, when I bought her things, 'cause that was all
she cared about, having things were new. Especially if all her
friends, they didn't have one yet.*

"*And then we mashed up the box the drier came in and put it in the washer box, and put that back in Hugo's Olds. See, there's all these markings onna carton that I don't know what they mean; even where this washer came from. All I know is that I got it free, over at the Navy Yard, from two guys that I only seen once in my life, I'm not even sure their names, so I'm pretty sure it's hot. For all I know there's something on the box that if the people own the units get their hands on it again they may not then know who stole it, but if that box is at my house then they'll be able, make a pretty good guess who's got 'em. So I'm gonna take the box back into Inman Square over there in Cambridge, which's where I'm meetin' Hugo. He told me he hadda meet some guy he knew there, give his car back to him there. And also ask him he knows some place I can dump the box, so it don't come back to haunt me.*

"*So I go in this place where he was, leave his wagon parked outside, and he's in there, like he said, with this guy that I don't know. And I tell him my problem. And Hugo says when I meet him, 'Yah, I know where you can take it. You just follow me in your car and I'll show you exact place.'*

"*So I do that and where he goes, we go this big construction site out by Fresh Pond there, they're puttin' up this huge motel. Apartment complex, something. Very dark, lots of equipment—huge bulldozers, crane. Wonder no one steals that stuff, they just leave it all around. Must be worth a lot of money. Put it onna flatbed, something, just haul it away. Must be no one does, I guess, but then I don't know.*

"*So anyway, I follow him in there, I'm expecting him to stop and show me, I'm supposed to dump the carton, I'll then get out and help him do it. Pull it out the back his car and leave it there, 'til someone buries it 'long with all the other shit they got there just lyin' around. And he does stop, but then the lights on his car don't go off, so I don't know if this's it or if maybe this's not the place, he's just lost or something. Trynah get his bearings. So I wait. But nothing happens. Well,*

I'm not sitting there all night, so after a few minutes I get out of my car, go over to his, and he's still in the driver's seat, and I see that he is dead. Someone shot him inna head."

There was a brief period of soft laughter from several people on the tape.

"Right. Well, I dunno who did this but there's one thing I do know and that is someone has shot Hugo, and whoever this person is, he knows that I work with Hugo, so if he's still somewhere around there and he sees me there with Hugo I am liable, get shot next. So I'm not hangin' around there. I get the fuck out, and two or three days later, Tuesday, Wednesday, I guess, I find out that I was right. Because the people who're working the construction site go back there after the weekend, they find Hugo in his car, but they don't know it's him. They don't find out it's him for another couple days, because apparently what happened after I got out of there, whoever shot him in the head also set the car on fire while he was still in it. Some kind of stuff burns very hot, like homemade na-palm, maybe, and just totally destroyed the thing. Not only just the boxes, which after all're only cardboard, few slats onna bottom, re-inforcement, but everything 'cept Hugo's bones—just his bigger bones're left. Anna paper said that even then they still weren't sure, not completely anyway, if it was even him that died—just that they know he's missing and the Olds'd been his car, so what they hadda do was they were only calling it 'a tentative ID.'

"And so then, after that, I decided I'd better get myself some backing there, because then with Hugo gone you could say I was alone. No one to protect me. And that's when I joined McKeach."

"Now Carlo," Hinchey mouthed.

"McKeach was in the box."

"Cistaro."

"No, not when they found the car. See they didn't find the box at all. Least the paper didn't say it, that they'd found a box. Box wasn't even mentioned. Box'd burned completely up."

"Now this's Carlo again," Hinchey said. "First you hear him, he's laughing—but you can tell he's impressed. What I can't figure, is it the story he just heard, or Cistaro tellin' it? I think it's Cistaro telling. I think they all knew the story all along, 'm I right? Sort of Gangland's Greatest *Hits* Night? That McKeach went and hid in the Maytag box while the Frogman went into the Inman Square Tavern for Hugo, knowing that when Hugo came out he'd take them to a safe place to shoot him. Where did Cistaro get the extra car he used to follow Hugo's Olds? It had to be McKeach's, 'cause McKeach was in the box.

"Nick and McKeach had the guy set *himself* up—got him to pick his place to die. And *that's* what these hoods here're enjoying so much—hell's bells, they're lapping it up. This's an old story to them, their version of Mother Goose Tales. They've heard it all told before."

"Sure," Farrier said. "They like their war stories just as much as we like ours. It's like the Church's oral tradition, the deposit of faith—doesn't matter if no one can prove it, if everyone knows that it's so. What keeps the faithful faithful."

Hinchey frowned but said nothing and pushed Play again. The laughter came up.

"*Well, no, not when they found it, he wasn't. McKeach's never there when they find someone. That's how he's lived so long.*"

"Cistaro," Hinchey said.

"*McKeach is a reliable man. You can depend on him because for him it isn't work, he has to force himself to do. Or something to be feared. I've never seen him so juiced as when he's done a guy. Never. I've often thought, 'Tonight the woman who is with him is in for a very long hard ride.' You must know this. You've used him yourself.*"

"Carlo."

There was a gruff chuckle on the tape. "*Yes, I imagine she would be at that. A very reliable man.*"

Hinchey shut off the Ampex. Then he turned back to Farrier. "Okay," he said, "what do we do?"

Farrier showed surprise on his face. "'Do'?" he said. "'Do' about what?"

"About one of our top-echelon informants confessing that he conspired, and was an accessory before and after, in the murder of Hugo Bottalico. And is therefore to be charged as a principal in the commission of murder in the first degree, committed in furtherance of an ongoing racketeer enterprise. Which you know and I know is murder, by the *other* prize pigeon, one of the few kinds of activity we're not allowed to sanction. Or overlook when it's done. Grounds for dismissal. And prosecution. Of *us*."

"Nothing," Farrier said. "What you've got on that tape is an uncorroborated story Cistaro told last fall about an event that he alleges happened over thirty years ago. I will bet you a beer that if we go back now and review the evidence and the reports of the cops and the docs and forensics specialists who investigated that case, we would find that they did a good job. And that when they concluded—in pre-DNA days—they weren't even sure who the victim was, much less who did it, they reached the right result.

"Think we can do better now? Yup. We can dig up the big bones and establish conclusively that they're what held Hugo upright and he was guest of honor at the roast. We can prove that the navy taught Nick the Frogman how to use everyday substances to make basic napalm at home, and that it burns at temperatures high enough to consume all but the biggest pieces of an individual carbon-based life form. We can prove that Nick and McKeach shared a motive for wanting Hugo to say goodbye. And that will be just about all we can prove to establish this murder case—all the rest would be, as sarcastic judges like to say, 'nothing but mere speculation.'

"Now," Farrier said, tilting back in his chair and clasping his hands behind his head, "Brother Stoat and I're dining this evening with our prime top-echelon informants. His career and future depend at least as much as mine on the success of this case against Carlo. Shall I ask him to set an extra place, so you can share your views on this sensitive matter with him, before our guests arrive? I can tell you your views on it won't make him happy, but if you say so, I will do it."

Hinchey frowned. "I can't," he said. "I'm on a panel tonight up in Salem, regional Fathers for Justice. Agreed to it three months ago."

"Then you should do that," Farrier said. "And let the past bury the past."

19

THE AROMA OF DARREN STOAT'S signature chicken cacciatore filled the condominium at Number 7, 4 Gaslight Square in
Framingham at 6:38 that evening when Farrier arrived, as usual,
about forty-five minutes early for a dinner with Cistaro and Mc-
Keach. Cheri had suggested the policy to him when he first described to her his misgivings about Stoat's fitness as an OC
squad chief. "Honey," she said, "if he looks to you like he's just
not up to it, and he's not just plain stupid, think how *scared* he
must be, for the very same reason. He has to *know*, and also
know you feel that way. Have to face it, hon; you can stand
and sling the shit with the best of them—you just *became* Soot
Barillo—but even when you're bein' a completely different person, you're no good at all at hidin' what you think. That's why
you were so good under cover—you got *into* the character, *became* the guy they asked you to pretend to be. And so people
who met you as him, believed you *were* him—you *were*.

"You think he's not up to it, dealin' man to man with your favorite gangsters? Then count on it, darlin'—he *knows* that's
what you think. And that's makin' him more nervous'n he was
to begin with, which was plenty, when you first saw him and decided, 'he's too nervous for this job.'"

"Oh, no," Farrier said to her, "I'm not goin' down that road. The only reason Darren Stoat's uncomfortable around me is he knows I was a candidate for that job myself, and far more qualified. And he also knows I know the only reason that he got it, and I didn't, was because one of the SOG brass hats he'd been playin' footsie with for ten or fifteen years made him a present of it. Well, nothin' I can do about that. If he knows I think that, he's right. No way in the world I could ever convince him otherwise."

"No," Cheri said, "of course you can't. I wouldn't want you, even try. You could never bring it off. But what you *can* do and you *should* do, because he'll be so grateful for it, is make it as easy as you can for him to deal with these hoodlums. *Then,* when he *gets* the big promotion, he'll thank you for your help and do something nice for you."

"He could do that," Farrier said. "He could also resent me for seeing he was weak, and think my carrying him was a way of showing contempt. Not that he'd admit it—he'd just bury me, and then if someone asked him why, give some other reason. But I'd be buried just the same. No, he'll always have power over me; what I need is something that'll make him afraid to use it, except to do me good. I need something *on* the guy."

"Well, at least give nice a try," Cheri said. "Why you think I never did my imitation of his wife—high-hat phony bitch, can't *stand* her—when we're at someone's house who also knows her? That ever occur to you? Well, if it didn't, now you know why. Don't need to *always* be a wise guy—now and then it pays to give someone a break."

"You know, Darren," Farrier said, heading for his usual before-dinner place on the black leather couch, "if the liberal crazies ever get control of Congress and abolish the FBI, I dunno what guys like *me*'d do, make a living for myself, but *you* would have it made. Way that you can cook Italian, all you'd ever have to do's get yourself an SBA loan, open yourself up a restaurant—in no time you'd be a rich man."

"All my years a bachelor," Stoat said, closing the door behind Farrier. He was clearly distracted. "Either you learn to cook or you starve. Get you a beer?"

"Yeah," Farrier said, sitting down. "Beer'd be fine." Then he got up again at once and with no apparent purpose wandered after Stoat, but heading for the dining room instead of following into the kitchen. For his destinaton Farrier idly chose the Hitachi TV on the pass-through counter with the video image of Margie Reedy reading New England Cable News.

"... Jamaica Pond in Boston early today, two men in their forties, one of them a former well-known college basketball star, were gunned down in what police say appeared to be still another brutal drug-related shooting."

A view of the walk at the northerly end of the pond replaced Reedy's face on the screen. Fluttering yellow plastic tape black-lettered "POLICE LINE—DO NOT CROSS" placed about three feet off the ground linked the clump of trees where McKeach had hidden in ambush to the cement bench upright of the bench beside the place on the sidewalk where Walters and his bodyguard had gone down.

Farrier snickered. "'Another *brutal* drug-related shooting.' Don't you just love it? 'Brutal shooting'—ever hear of 'a nice *dainty* little shooting'?"

"Can't say's I ever have, no," Stoat said, turning away from the refrigerator with two bottles of Harpoon lager and setting them down on the kitchen counter behind the television. Then he frowned. Farrier expected him to say something, but he didn't.

On the screen a sandy-haired compactly built man wearing glasses, a tweed jacket and a blue shirt with a blue knitted tie began speaking into a handheld microphone. "'Walterboy' Junius Walters, sixties stickout point guard for the University of Kansas Jayhawks"—the screen flashed a black-and-white photo of Walters releasing a one-handed jump shot —"and his associate and friend, Aladdin Stephenson, jogged into a hail of bullets at peaceful Jamaica Pond just after sunup today, thus..."

As he continued talking, three brown ducks, one mallard and a Canada goose swam into the frame on the pond behind his left shoulder and the four trees. Quacking furiously, one of the brown ducks reared up on the water, spreading its wings and prompting the cameraman to edit the reporter out of the picture and zoom in on the fowls. "While his Bronx teenage pal Stephenson never made it to college, Aladdin too was something of a b-ball legend, making *his* name in the slam-dunk world of New York playground hoops."

Stoat opened the beers and put one of them on the pass-through counter. "Guys who got shot—they any concern of ours?" He opened a cabinet to his right and brought out two pilsner glasses, setting one next to the beer on the pass-through.

The cameraman remembered his mission and the reporter's face was on the screen again. "... Ron Gollobin, for the New England Cable News. Back to you, Margie."

Farrier picked up the beer with his left hand and poured it slowly into the glass. "Names never surfaced on my watch," he said. "Which doesn't mean if they'd've lived a while longer, they wouldn't've. My guess'd be the reporter's probably right—New York out-of-towners hornin' in on the drug trade. That's black gangbangin' stuff, not OC, way *I* look at our bailiwick at least. Not OC *yet* anyway; may be headed that way—boundaries're nowhere near as clear-cut's they used to be. State Police Special Investigations Bureau—drew that assistant DA shooting back a year or so?" He shuddered. "Horror-show case that one is—Jim Dowd, the SP boys, probably had a fat file on these guys. Good, let 'em have it. Our practice's always been, leave 'at shit to them and DEA. Stay as far's we can away from it." He tasted the beer. "Or the locals."

Stoat emerged from the kitchen, heading for the chair closest to the door. Farrier following his lead had reached the living-room area when Stoat said, "You can shut that thing off, you want. 'Less you want it on."

Farrier hesitated, then continued toward the living room. "Nah, leave it on, I guess. Case they give the scores and weather. Jeez, Sox've been amazing, haven't they? Swore, I got assigned here, 'Okay, so I'll go to Boston. Guys give their left nut to go there, I can handle it. Eat the lobster, take up skiing? Maybe dive the *Andrea Doria*. But one thing I'm *not* gonna do's become a Red Sox fan.'

"I was a kid, I'm a Cardinals fan. All I know 'bout Boston's we beat 'em in sixty-seven. Orlando Cepeda, the Baby Bull. Lou Brock. *And* the greatest clutch pitcher ever—Bob Gibson, mowin' 'em down. But this year's Red Sox? I dunno. Bunch of castoffs, rejects, but give the bastards credit: they don't seem to realize when they're licked. Cheap hit, steal a base, take advantage of an error, other pitcher hangs a slider and be damn if they don't win. Exciting club here, for change."

Stoat collapsed heavily into the chair. He sat with the bottle of beer in his right hand and the empty glass in his left on the arms of the black leather chair, staring toward some point on the wall above the couch. Farrier went back to his initial place and sat down again, just to the right of where Stoat's gaze seemed to be focused.

"Darren," Farrier said, "'re you okay?"

Stoat clearly heard him but seemed reluctant to shift his gaze. Then he shook himself out of his deep concentration; frowning, he began to pour the beer into the glass.

"'Re you okay?" Farrier said. "'Cause if you aren't, you know,

I can always find some way, get in touch with Nick and Arthur, tell them not to come—you don't feel right."

Stoat, shaking his head, filled the glass. "It isn't..." he said, filling the glass and setting the bottle on the coffee table between them. "It's personal, really. Isn't how I feel so much as I don't know what's going *on* in my life.

"Lily's back in Memphis. Her first husband, Wally Weymuss, finally died. Last Sunday. Hardly unexpected, man his age—he's eighty-*four.* Not that he'd been sick, either—he was at a yearling quarter-horse show somewhere outside of Fort Worth, had a heart attack and died. He'd arranged to have his lawyer call all of his ex-wives when it happened, he died. Lily was his fourth and then he had himself another one after that. And divorced her too, I guess. Number Five, I mean.

"So," he said, morose, "she got this call, like I said, and she told me she was going back down there to Memphis. For the funeral. And I just said to her, 'My lord, Lillian, what in *God's* name you want to do *that* for? You and Wallace're divorced, years and years ago. Hell, you were only married to him less'n four years, you divorced him. *We've* been married almost *nine* years, and you're single three or four years before we even *met.* Must be close to eighteen years, maybe nineteen, since the last time you've seen him; what the *hell* makes you think now you have to go his funeral?'"

He shook his head again, his eyebrows high and eyes wide, and he drank some of his beer. He softened his voice and exaggerated a drawl. "'Well, but he was my husband, Darren. For a while he was my *husband* and I was his wedded *wife.* We were one flesh, like in the Bible, an' the *Bible* tells us that when two people cleave *together,* a man and a woman, that they then become as one flesh—and that is what, the eyes of God, no man can put asunder, and I guess the Bible's right.

"'I just feel like I belong there, ought to be there. Wallace was my *husband,* and we *cared* for each other; and that even though he *did* make me so crazy we did have to get divorced, and it was quite a while ago, in some ways he's always remained a *part* of me, *inside* me, in that respect, and now he's dead, I just feel like I should go. And be there. It's the proper thing to do.

"'And all Wallace's other wives—Rosalie, you recall she was his first, his wife, she came first, she went and had this conference call set up the other day when she first heard the sad news down there, that Wallace had passed away, so we all could talk. And take counsel with one another. And we talked and, well, the more we shared our feelin's with each other, the more we saw that way down deep we all felt the same. Wallace finally left this world? We were all part of his life, and we should be there to see him off and say farewell. To Wallace. They all feel the same as I do, and they're going to be there too. All of us, one pew of all of Wallace's wives together, to say good-bye to him.'"

He paused and studied Farrier. "Now does that sound right to you, Jack?" he said, his face and voice both mournful. "Does that make any sense to you, that stuff she said to me?" He drank some beer.

FARRIER LATER AT HIS OWN HOME that night, before he had fully sorted out the meaning of McKeach's call and Cistaro's late arrival at Stoat's by himself, was struck again by the intensity of Stoat's gaze. "Never *saw* him like that before," he said to Cheri. "Didn't know he had it in him, this total *focus* that he had, like he's counting my pores or something and this is the most important thing, most *vital* and, well, *significant,* thing, maybe, he's ever done in his whole life. Seeing how I'm now going to react to this information he just gave me. And he says to me, the voice of doom—'Do you think that's right? Tell me, do you think what she said's right?'

"Thing of it is," Farrier said, "well, I know he's testing me, but I don't know what passing is. What it is I'm s'posed to do. One part of me thinks what he just told me's true, and he really is just as devastated as he certainly looks to be, but he thinks maybe I'm laughing at him. Maybe I think he's a fool. In which case his life is probably over, but if there's even a little bit of it left he's going to use it to destroy me, revenge for my destroying him. Don't ask me how I got this power over him, if I did, but apparently I did, and now how I use it's truly life-and-death to him.

"And at the same time the other part of me is saying he's making all this up, that Lily's at one of her suburban ladies' stock-and-bond seances, doping out the markets, and she'll be home by eleven. And if I'm not sharp enough to see how ridiculous this all is, the idea that she'd actually fly back to Memphis for the funeral of this old goat she and at least four other women married for his money, so they can now all cry together 'cause they now think they should've gotten more; if I *don't* laugh my ass off, then he'll know that either *I'm* a perfect asshole, or else that I'm convinced that *he* is—and the *very* first thing that he's going do tomorrow, when he gets back to his office, is get in touch with SOG and torpedo my career.

"So now, how do I call it? Because one way or the other I have got to make a choice here, I'm juggling live grenades—drop it, make the wrong choice and I'm going to be paying for it the rest of my life.

"And I am literally saved by the bell. So I think, for a while, anyway."

THE YELLOW PHONE MOUNTED on the wall next to the refrigerator rang in the kitchen. "*Unnnh*," Stoat said, exhaling heavily and leaning forward to put his glass on the coffee table. "This's probably Lily." He heaved himself up out of the chair and started toward the kitchen. "She's been down there four nights now and called me every one of them. 'Just to see how you're doing, don't want you to get too lonesome.' Making sure I'm at home, not off somewhere *enjoying* myself, even though I told her last night not to call because I'd have you and the lads here so I wouldn't really be able, talk." In the kitchen he grabbed the phone off the mount and said shortly, "Stoat." Then he said "yeah," and then "sure," and put the phone down on the counter.

"For you, Jack," he said to Farrier, coming back into the living area, saying as he stood up with an inquiring look on his face, "Didn't give me a name. Think it may be Nick—never heard him before on the phone."

Farrier took the phone cautiously. "Yeah?" he said.

"Jackie," Cistaro said, "is Arthur there?"

"No," Farrier said, "of course he isn't here. You guys always come together."

"That's why I'm calling, from the lobby, my apartment." Cistaro said. "Didn't pick me up yet. See him this after, over the Spa. Rico's droppin' me off, get my car there—he's gotta do somethin' with Max. Arthur says he's gonna do a few things, then go home. Grab a nap if he can. Said he's up fairly early today, couldn't sleep for some reason. And I know he's lookin' forward this evenin' with you guys. Says, 'I *can't* fall asleep over dinner.' But it's now after seven; he still isn't here. Called where he's been living—him an' Dorothy—didn't get no answer there. Thought maybe he went directly there."

"If he did he's not here yet," Farrier said. "I haven't heard from him either. You know how he gets—somethin' happen to spook him, he's halfway to Canada now?"

"Come *on*, Jack," Cistaro said, "don't kid around about that stuff. That's your department, knowin' if anything's happened to spook us. You're the one's s'posed to be Paul Revere, make the call, let us know if we oughta take off. You didn't do that. So then, why would he split? You ain't heard of nothin' goin' down?"

"Not a whisper," Farrier said. "And since anything federal'd clear through me first, and the staties're supposed coordinate with us when they got a party planned, if there *was* something I definitely would've heard. Look, there's nothing, all right? Either he's havin' car trouble and he isn't near a payphone or else one of you got screwed up. Calm yourself down. Get in your Beemer and come over here; we'll have a drink, wait for him. He goes to your place? He'll find out you're not there. He'll stop, make a call, find out that you're here; *he'll* come here and then we'll all eat."

"Okay," Cistaro said, "I will do that. But I will tell you, I'm worried. This isn't like Arthur at all."

"WHICH IT WASN'T," FARRIER SAID to Cheri. "But tell you the truth, when I hung up the phone I wasn't really too worried. Well, I was *concerned,* I was *very* concerned, but not about Nick and McKeach—I was concerned about me and my boss. What'm I gonna say to him, his crazy wife's antics? How the hell do I know what they mean?

"But then I decide, 'Hey, maybe now, thanks to the Frogman, I could be off the immediate hook—I can play for a little *time* here. First see try to find out he *wants* me to say'—see, I'm havin' in mind what you said—'and then when I do find out, well then, *say* it.'"

"YOU WERE RIGHT," FARRIER SAID to Stoat, hanging up the phone, "that was Nick. He doesn't know where McKeach is." He started toward the living room.

"Well, why'd he call here?" Stoat said dully. He had his left hand pressed to his forehead. He lifted the hand away. "Arthur's not here. They come here together, one car—so it draws less attention from the neighbors. Arthur said that: 'Less cars in front, fullah shady characters, looks like a Mafia sitdown.' Nick should know that; *he* isn't here." He coughed. "Whyncha bring in a couple more beers, while you're at it?"

Farrier returned to the refrigerator and took out two more bottles of Harpoon. He opened them on the counter and headed toward the living room. "Probably just the first thing that came into his head," he said. "You know how it is, you get frustrated. He called Arthur at home and no one answered there, so then what's the next thing he can do, he wants to find out where McKeach is?"

He put the bottles on the coffee table. Stoat immediately picked one up and poured it into his glass. "No McKeach cell phone," Farrier said, sitting down on the couch, "call him up in his car or his own jacket pocket. 'Too easy to eavesdrop,' is what he says. 'Any kid with a scanner could do it.' Guy's *paranoid* on the whole subject. He'll have nothing to do with the things. He won't even let *Nick,* or any their people, have one of those things in their car."

"I should probably turn off the heat under that stewpot," Stoat said, putting his glass and the bottle on the coffee table as he got up. He headed for the kitchen. "Had it on simmer since before you got here, but enough's enough. Stay hot for a while anyway. It gets cold, they're really late, I'll just heat it up again. Won't take long."

"Good idea," Farrier said. "Better'n having the sauce turn to red library paste."

"It's still surprising, though," Stoat said from the kitchen, "that Arthur won't use them at *all.* Think as conscious as he is of security, he'd *want* people be able to reach him. Tip him off, something went wrong."

"Oh, but that's exactly what he's *afraid* of," Farrier said. "If they had it for that they'd use it for *other* things and then they'd get him in trouble. 'Might use the damned thing to call me, I dunno I'm on it; I listen. Then I talk and he listens to me. Cops tapin' him? Cops're tapin' me too. They get him, he is stupid? Can't help that. They get *me,* even though I'm smart'n careful, 'cause *he's* stupid? I don't like that. And I *can* help it. Catch anybody usin' one of those things to call me, I'll find out where he is and go and shove his fuckin' cell phone up his fuckin' *ass.*

"'*Yeah,* they're convenient—that's why they're so dangerous. You get so you're always thinkin', "Ah, whatsa risk, there're *thousands* of calls every minute. What're the odds they get me? They're not gonna catch me, I use this thing once—they don't even know where I am. And if they did, they did tap onna mine, what possible good could it do them? It's not like I'm sayin', 'Let's talk about business,' when McKeach picks up the phone. And even if they did luck out, wouldn't do them any good— they wouldn't know what we're talkin'. Nah, know what you do? You worry too much. It could only happen, a fluke."'"

Stoat, massaging his forehead again, used his right hand to lift the glass and drink some beer.

"'So they get overconfident, you know?'" Farrier said. "'But what they forget is that flukes do happen—now and then even dumb cops catch a break, and I personally don't feature goin' to jail on no fuckin' *fluke.*'"

Stoat sat down in the chair.

Farrier shrugged. "What can I tell him? He's right. But tonight the result is, Nick's lookin' for him. He calls him at home and he can't find him there; where the hell else can he call him? Nowhere else; there's no other number. You know how it is, dunno what's goin' on, you got to do something, so what do you do? Call someone else, is what you do. Where else can Nick call? He calls here." He drank, leaving his glass half full.

"I suppose," Stoat said, flopping his left hand onto the arm of the chair. "What the hell do I know about anything anyway; why anyone does what they do? My wife's gone to Memphis, to her first husband's funeral." He imitated Lily's voice.

"Very well, too, I thought," Farrier said to Cheri later; "I think you would've had to agree. Not quite as *mean* as the take you do on her, but his version had *spite*; really captured her whine—"'I jes' *thank* it's ma *place*, to be *there*.'"

"I thought her place was to be where *I* am," Stoat said. "*I* am her husband now." He drank some beer.

"Well Jesus, Darren," Farrier said, "I mean, she wouldn't argue you that. She's probably just got some female-solidarity idea in her head—if all the others're gonna be there, and she isn't, they will've made her look bad." He picked up his glass and drank beer. "Like she didn't love him as much as they did—she was just after his money, and once she'd gotten all she could, had no more use for the guy."

"Then they'd be right," Stoat said sorrowfully. "That *is* why she married him, and it's why she's gone back now. The old boy still had *years* of income due him, well into the next century— from the deal when he sold all his funeral homes. She thinks he might've left it to his ex-wives, but only the ones who show up at his funeral, and that's why he had his lawyer call. Put all of them on notice."

Farrier chuckled. "That likely?" he said.

Stoat shrugged. "It could be. She got him to marry her, after all—must have some idea what made him tick—if *tick*'s the right word, for what she allowed him to do. Money's what makes *her* tick. Money's the reason she does everything, everything that Lily does."

"*Welll,*" Farrier said, "I know she talks a lot about it, money. But look at what she *does*—her field is stocks and bonds. She's only talking about what her work is, same way's we talk about the Mob."

"*Nuts,*" Stoat said forcefully. "Not the same thing. You didn't marry Cheri because you thought if you did you'd have a better shot at the Mob. You married her because you loved each other, or lusted each other—something. Same reason why I married Lily—I was lonely; I was horny, and I wanted to spend my life with her. But *she* married *me* for my money." He finished his beer and began refilling his glass from Farrier's second bottle.

"Not sayin' I was a great catch. I didn't have anywhere near as *much* money as she would've liked, but she's shrewd. Crafty. Her *assets* were gettin' stale. She knew that Miss Memphis year of hers was gettin' further 'n' further behind her, while *her* behind was becomin' bit *bigger.* An' besides, she'd already cashed in on the act once, when she married the rich undertaker.

"Now don't get me wrong. Lily's still a fine-lookin' woman, as she was when she married me—best-lookin' one ever glanced *my* way. But like they say about expensive cars you can get for a price, she'd been 'previously registered,' and that's the *reason* I's able to . . . get her." He drank some beer and reflected.

He nodded. "Rich man in the market for a beauty-queen trophy wife, he's lookin' for one steppin' fresh off the runway, slippin' out her little swimsuit right into his bed. Not an eighty-two, eighty-three model. And she knew it, too, better'n I did. By the time I met her, she was lookin' to settle. I may not've been quite what she'd had in mind, but I was the best deal in sight.

"A good secure job, a good pension plan, too. Plus I did have *some* money at least. Never'd made what you'd call major dough, but I never spent any either. I'd never been married; never had to pay alimony, child support. I'd never *had* any kids to support, braces and tuitions to pay for. And I hadn't been like you, going off with the guys, even though you were married, doin' glamorous things that cost money." He paused, looking at Farrier speculatively. "*You* probably had a Harley," he said. He drank some beer.

Farrier grinned. "No, I didn't," he said. "Always wanted one, though, and I would've, I guess, dough hadn't gone in the divorce." He sipped his beer.

"Uh huh," Stoat said. "Well, all the same. Scuba diving and skiing, all of that *guy* stuff; I never did any of it.

"I did used to play tennis," he chuckled bitterly. "Back when I lived in Alexandria, before I moved to Foggy Bottom—cut down the *commute,* put more time in on the *job*—two evenings a week, and three sets on Sunday mornings. Me and another young single guy; he was an economist, had his Ph.D., Indiana, worked for Agriculture, and he had no social life either. Then. We weren't very good tennis players, but in a way *that* was good—meant we could really compete." He drank.

He glanced at Farrier and smiled. "Rick also cooked, for the same reason I did—it was that or starvation; so we competed in cookery too. It was nice. The complex we lived in had six lighted courts and four more in a bubble. But for some reason, *careers,* probably, not many who lived in it played. Never a problem, getting a court. So we could play nights, if it rained or was windy, anything like that. And then after we showered, make something for dinner, or on Sundays, for brunch. Unless we went over to Georgetown, to Clyde's, that was *the* place to be then. 'Alla broads go to Clyde's'—it was true, too, good-lookin' women, though fat lot of good that did us. But we'd watch the Redskins game there and have brunch. With so many other people you could hardly move. But it was nice." He nodded, musing. He drank a swallow of beer. "Yeah, very nice."

Then he put the smile away and looked at Farrier with something close to scorn. "You're now thinking, of course, 'Uh *huh,* oh *yeah,* I can imagine: a couple of *fairies,* swappin' their *recipes* after their *tennis,* swappin' *spits* after dessert.'"

Farrier prepared to reply but Stoat's expression dissuaded him.

"I'm sure that's the first thought that most people had, if they saw us together more than once. So was Rick. We used to joke about it ... but it really wasn't funny. Our real reaction was 'fuck 'em,' but that's not a viable way to respond to people even if they do look at you funny. Not if they live in the same building with you. Next thing you know they'll be stealing your newspapers, deflating your tires. Spray-painting *fag* on your windshield." He drank.

He took a deep breath and exhaled it. "I dunno—might've been better, we'd been queer. Might've been happier if they'd been right. But they weren't—we were just friends. All we had in common besides tennis and pretentious cooking was hard work and ambition. Nothing sexual between us.

"Rick's hard work paid off before mine did. He got promoted and reassigned to run a new section. Met a woman there he *sort of* liked. She in turn *sort of* liked him. Only natural—just by looking at her you could tell she was female, without any question, but other than that she was *sort of* like both of us. Just the same as us, really, another member in good standing of the wall-paper people; we seem to fit most rooms all right, without ever really standing out in any of them. Beige lives.

"The kind of people," he said, smiling crookedly at Farrier, "that people like you, all you hotshots—when you see us for the tenth time we *sort of* bother you. You seem to remember meeting us, somewhere, but where, when or why it was, you can't quite recall. It's very irritating." He drank some beer, then emptied Farrier's Harpoon into his glass.

Farrier returned his gaze but said nothing.

———

"WHAT'M I *GONNA* SAY?" HE SAID to Cheri later. "In the first place, I don't want to make the guy feel bad. Like you said, I want him to feel good. And if I'd wanted to see him torn down, made into a total zero, how could I've improved on his own work? He was doing a great job himself. I couldn't've made him feel worse. So I didn't say anything, and after he'd stared at me for a while, just resenting the hell out of me, you could feel it, he got up and went into the kitchen again. I wasn't sure this was such a great idea, he was drinking them so fast, but he seemed steady enough—he fetched *us* a couple more beers."

"ELLEN BLENDED IN JUST LIKE *we* blended in, and pretty soon she'd blended all the way into Rick's apartment, living with him. And why not? They were meant for each other. And guess what? She played tennis too, also not very well. They were nice to me about it—people like us always are, nice to others. They didn't want to make me to feel bad, and I didn't want to make them feel bad, by *acting* like they'd made *me* feel bad. People like us have very complicated lives. So for a while the three of us played and had meals together. All spring, in fact, well into June, but I can tell you, it was forced. Now instead of Rick playing tennis with me, and my having dinner with Rick, *they* were inviting me to play tennis, and I was having *them* over for dinner.

"What *Rick and I* had done had been fun because it was effortless—just by being ourselves we furnished the entertainment in each other's lives. Rick said, 'We're each other's videos.' Whereas what *Rick and Ellen* were now doing was very self-conscious. It *did* require effort, a great deal of effort, on their part, making room in their life for me, and that was the end of the fun. Three really isn't much of a crowd, but it seems like one because it never works—not very well, very long.

"I moved to Foggy Bottom in July. Naturally I didn't want to make them feel bad—I was still who I was, after all—so I said it was because I was fed up with wasting six percent of my life, ten hours a week, fighting the traffic, morning and night, the *miserable* Fourteenth Street Bridge. It was true, but it wasn't the reason.

"Then that November I went back to Knoxville for the twentieth homecoming reunion of my college class. There was a football game, of course, which I didn't go to—because how on earth can you meet anybody, much less look for a woman, which was why I was going, by sittin' in a stadium, watchin' a damn football game?" He finished his fourth beer and refilled his glass.

"See, now finally I had a *plan*. When I was in college I'd had a few sort-of romances, never really went anywhere, and then I graduated. The years went by, and I didn't meet anybody to have a romance with, and—see, I *knew* I was lonely, which was at least something. Lots of lonely people never do figure what is *bothering* them, go to their graves still kinda wonderin', 'Something was *wrong*—what *was* it?' And I'd read in the alumni news that this one I'd dated'd gotten her graduate degree in nursing, and that one'd had her third kid . . . well, I suppose at first I didn't realize I was doing it—but I was trying to follow their *lives,* in those pathetic little dispatches, thinking that the husbands Tom and Chris and Buddy, well, they could've been *me*. Tried to imagine what they looked like, how they acted. I was playing make-believe.

"I guess my logic must've been that since by then I'd spent seventeen *years* as a single man in Washington, a town *alive* with single women, *yearning* to get serious, *teeming* with them, if I'd heard right, and I hadn't managed to have even *one* relationship; but I'd at least *dated* three or four women in college, the answer must be that I had to *know* I had something in common with a woman before I could even talk to her. Like I did when I was in college and the women were in college. And in Washington I hadn't had that common ground. So the thing for me to do was go back to Knoxville sometime when I knew women of my vintage'd be going back there too, and, who knew? Maybe one of my old, ah, *flames* would turn up, and, well, why not? It happens—turn *out* to've been *divorced*. And be even *better*-lookin', and we'd *reignite* the flame." He sighed, and drank.

"So I flew down in time for the Weekend-Kickoff Gala cocktail reception and informal dinner Friday night, and of course I recognized hardly anyone, or saw one single woman there. There were two other *guys* I knew, majored in finance with, both looking *great* and doing very *well*—like people at reunions always *are* doing, because those who're doin' *terrible* don't go to the reunions. Their smug little *wives* were with them, and one of our professors, by himself.

"Perfectly nice fellow, always neat, polite and friendly. Must be pushing seventy by now. Took a real interest in us students, back in my day, at least, but back then too he always came to our events by himself. Showed no evidence of family then and no signs of any now? I'd always assumed that he was gay, and now, by God, I knew I'd been right.

"Since he was alone that night, I assumed he was between boyfriends—although I'm actually not sure whether a gay man with a boyfriend on the faculty down there'd even *dare* to bring him to an alumni shindig. Anyway, I figured he probably had nothing else to do that weekend, a situation I was all too familiar with, and so to make a few easy brownie points with his colleagues he'd volunteered to be a faculty rep at one of those boring reunions. Him I wanted to avoid. I was there to look for women, not to fraternize with fairies."

He drank some of his beer.

"BUT HE WAS DRINKING IT SLOWER," Farrier said, telling Cheri. "That gave me some hope I wouldn't be putting him to bed and dishing dinner up by myself by the time the lads arrived."

————

"But it was like avoiding swine flu—he made very sure on Friday night that I'd be at the cocktail party and formal dinner Saturday, so it was clear I'd caught a bad case of old professor, and I was going to have him next to me at every damned event I attended until I left for the airport Sunday afternoon. And I couldn't figure it out, what the hell my attraction was. Did he think *I* was queer? Could've been—like I said, I'm sure people have. Or was he an FBI buff? You're familiar with that breed, I'm sure."

"Oh yeah, God love 'em," Farrier said. "Them and their opposites, the people who despise you for it. The ones in tie-dyed jeans an' Max Yasgur's Farm tee shirts. Woodstockers with sixties hangovers, hate you for chasin' their draft-dodgin' boyfriends all the way to Canada."

"But the reason didn't matter," Stoat said. "I was *beside* myself.

"I thought about trying to change my airplane reservation— just skipping the second cocktail party and dinner dance Saturday. But since I had one of those tightwad-specials, three-weeks-in-advance reservations, I didn't know if I could. And anyway, why? As usual I had no plans in Washington, *that* Saturday either. I figured the hell with it, 'I paid for this disaster fair and square, might as well at least get the drinks and dinner.'

"That night the professor arrived with a date, and a very presentable one. Lily, it seemed, was his teaching assistant. If you went by the dress that she nearly had on, he clearly was *not* homosexual. It was sleeveless, what she called 'lettuce green,' jersey or something, I don't know fabrics, very soft and clingy, with a high stand-up collar and a very deep vee neckline. She still looks darned good, for a woman close to fifty, but that night, in that light, she looked *sensational*—could've passed for being in her late twenties. My two classmates were at *least* as impressed as I was—their wives didn't like her at *all*.

"They needn't've worried. I still don't know for sure whether my old professor's queer—I'm surer now that he is—but he wasn't *with* Lily. He was trolling her for me, at her behest. She'd obviously ingratiated herself with him; she's good at that—beguiling older men's not her *only* speciality, but it may be her best. She enlisted him to be on the lookout for a second husband for her, and by interviewing me the night before he'd found out enough to make her think I might be worth a look-see.

"She seemed to be very impressed that I was FBI, and she knew enough about how the bureau works—and what my place in it was—to make me ask her if she once considered applying for a job. She was vague about that, but of course she hadn't. What she'd done was spend a couple hours at her computer in the library, swotting up on the Bureau to make me think, 'My gosh, she's smart'; and then three or four at the beauty parlor, so she could bowl me off my feet that night.

"Obviously it worked. I was back in Knoxville the next weekend. She came to Washington the weekend after that. And so on and so forth, her different strokes for different folks more than adequate to turn me into her little lapdog. We went out a few times with Rick and Ellen, three or four, not many, but enough to make it clear to them that if I was going to have Lily around all the time, there'd be no further need of them and their compassion." He sighed again. "Too bad. I could use some of it now." He drank some beer.

"Ah, cut it out, Darren," Farrier said. "This's a *temporary* thing. All marriages go through them. You think it's all over, world's come to an end, whole happy life's been destroyed. You wanna know somethin'? People get through those periods. You'll survive, believe it or not. Six months from now if I ask you about it, you'll look at me like I'm crazy. 'The hell're you talkin' about?' The way that I see it, worst thing that can happen? Turns out she was right about Wallace, he did what she suspected, she comes back with a new source of income. And the *best* that can happen's exactly the same thing—she comes back with a whole bunch of money.

"Your masculine pride's not involved in this, Darren. Try not to *get* it involved. Lily's spending a few days with four other women anna corpse. She's not between the sheets with her former husband, hummin' 'Auld Lang Syne' in bed. And when her trip's over, she's coming back right here, not runnin' off with him again—his runnin' days're over; he is dead.

"Look at the bright side. If what you say is true, money's what's on her mind, when she comes back she'll be happy. A happy woman's the best kind to have. The reason she's happy don't matter." He drank.

Stoat was glum. "Well, I hope you're right. She really *needs* money about now, more'n I can spare without damage."

"You two got financial problems?" Farrier said. "How can that be? You said it yourself, you don't exactly throw it around. You never did anything costly, I know about. This place's nicer'n what Cheri and I've got, but like you say, we're comin' from lot different circumstances. You haven't been married before and *divorced*; got no *kids*, don't drive flashy *cars*, you don't wear flashy *clothes*, you don't blow a wad on *vacations*, and the stock market she plays 's been up, never higher. Where the hell've you spent all the dough?"

"This past year or so, she's been branching out," Stoat said. He emptied his bottle into his glass and sat back in the leather chair. "She started playing the commodities markets, Chicago Board of Trade. You know, like Hillary Clinton says she did, buying some kind of commodities futures. Big money fast. Says she invested ten grand and made a big profit. She's not really sure how she *did* it, or *where*, or what *in*—just that some guy named Red who her husband Bill knew. Red said she did, so she must've. I dunno whether she bought cattle futures or maybe it was pork bellies—which I guess means bacon. She most likely doesn't know either, but a few months after that, Red gives her another call, and now she finds out she *sold* all her contracts. Hillary still isn't sure *what* she sold or to who—all she knows is she nets ninety grand on the deal, and this makes her think very highly of Red. Much more highly now'n she does of her husband, gettin' blow jobs from a pudgy White House intern.

"*But*—and this's how you can tell, if you didn't think so before, how much smarter Mrs. Clinton is'n we are—where I suspect *you*—and I know damned well *I*—would at that point've said, 'Way to go, *Red*. Now what you do for me is do that again. Buy some *more* stuff for me, anything looks good to you. Only this time buy ten times as much—,' Mrs. Clinton didn't. Mrs. Clinton says, 'Thanks, Red, cash me out.'

"Lily's pretty smart, but she's nowhere near as smart as Mrs. Clinton, and she doesn't know Red. She also doesn't know as much about commodities as Red does, or as she *herself* does about stocks and bonds. She went into metals, big time. And what's worse, she did it on double leverage. Borrowed money on stocks that she owned, what they're worth at the time—much more'n she'd paid for them. So she was betting those stocks wouldn't go down.

"Then with that borrowed money, she bet *again*. She didn't exactly buy metals *futures*; she bought *calls*, which're options to *buy* metals futures. Her theory is that if she borrows a dollar she can buy a dollar call, which will be worth at least ten dollars three months from now—the price of the metal will've gone up at least eleven, so the person with the option saves a buck buying it. She then sells those calls and buys her pledged stock back, leaving a bundle for profit.

"The trouble is that for her to win, at least two things have to happen her way. But to lose, and lose *big*, only one has to go against her.

"The metals market has to keep going up, so the options to buy it three months from now will be worth something. If metals go down, she will lose. And the stock that she pledged has to stay at least even. If it goes down before she pays off the loan, she'll have to come up with more stock. But what'll she use to buy some more stock? All her cash's in metals futures. She'll either have to start selling her other stocks, or borrow against something else. Like this place." He drank some beer.

"Oh, no," Farrier said, interrupting. "I wouldn't care if she's *swimming* in shit, I wouldn't let her do that. I've been strapped for cash a good many times, had to borrow so much it scared me. But two things I know—no matter how broke you may get, you never touch where you live, and the *only* time you touch your pension is to finance the place where you live."

"I agree with you," Stoat said. "And she can't get at my retirement. But the reason there's so much in it is because unlike you and most people, I *didn't* tap my retirement account for the down payment on this place. I was willing to, but I didn't want to, and she didn't want me to either. So I agreed to make the monthly payments and furnish the joint. Furniture—the stuff I had in Washington was *cheap*, and *old*, and worn out. Wouldn't've been worth the cost of moving it up here—gave it to a battered-women's shelter in Bethesda, took the tax deduction. And *she* made the down payment, twenty-seven grand, twenty percent of the purchase price—on the condition the place would be in her name. I had no objection; we hadn't known each other that long. If it didn't work out, she'd be where she didn't really want to be, but at least she'd still have her money—and like I said, I needed new furniture anyway.

"So, even though I'm the one who's made all the payments, these past thirteen months, my name is not on the deed."

"So," Farrier said. He finished his first beer.

"So I can't stop her from hocking it," Stoat said, getting up.

"End of last year she opened up a line of credit, sliding limit." He picked up the empty beer bottles and headed for the kitchen. "Lets her borrow up to the amount of market equity we've got in this property—which the bank's appraiser told us, this surprised me, is *lots* more'n we paid for it. Boston real estate market's gone nuts.

"Up to now we haven't drawn on it, the equity. Had no plans to at the time we took it out. Her argument was that the banks were competing to offer very good deals, one point over prime rate, and if the day ever did come when we needed it for something, maybe fix up the bathrooms, put in a hot tub, when we put the place up for sale—as we surely will someday—to make it sell faster, or to put a down payment on a new place someplace else while we're waiting for the sale on this one to go through. All we'll have to do's make a check out and we'll have it. No hassle, and a very good rate." He paused one beat. "And the clincher was," he said, "the interest that you pay on it's just like the regular mortgage—tax deductible."

The Hitachi showed a young man in a yellow slicker standing on a wharf around midday, holding a microphone, his dark hair ruffled by the wind. There was a battered dark green fishing trawler tied up on his right and a white one tied up on his left. "What New England fishermen are saying is that unless foreign pressures on the cod fisheries can somehow be reduced, this important species will fairly soon become extinct."

Stoat took two more Harpoons from the refrigerator and put them on the counter. "Sounded reasonable to me, then," he said. "It sure doesn't now. She made it very clear to me, 'fore she went to Memphis, that if dear old Wallace didn't make thoughtful provisions for each of his dear former wives, what she's going to do is write one of those checks. If it comes to it—which it will, once she starts—right up to the limit of our current equity."

"Which'd be?' Farrier said.

"In the current boom market," Stoat said, opening the beers, "with low mortgage rates, she guesses it'd come to at least eighty grand, and since that sort of thing is her stock in trade, my guess'd be her guess is right."

"So if one of those two things you mentioned goes wrong, and she loses her bet on the options, she can put you in the hole for eighty grand," Farrier said.

"Already did," Stoat said, coming back into the living room. "Go wrong, I mean. The wheels started coming off the Russian wagon a year or so ago. The country was broke, had to raise cash. They've got some of the world's richest mineral deposits, so they did the obvious thing and started digging faster, flooding world markets with metals. Now all of a sudden Lily's call-prices on metals futures're higher'n the price of actual metals. The calls aren't worth anything, and there doesn't seem to be any real prospect they will be, two, three months from now." He put the beers on the coffee table and sat down again in the chair, crossing his legs.

"But you've at least got those sixty days to think of something else," Farrier said, leaning forward and refilling his glass.

"No, we haven't," Stoat said. He uncrossed his legs and leaned forward, taking the other beer and refilling his glass. "The stock she hocked was a five-thousand share lot of Advanced Extrusions, at the time worth eleven bucks a share. They invented, and patented, a new and much cheaper way to make the heavy-duty molded fittings that secure the electrical wiring harnesses in motor vehicles. So they don't flop around and chafe, short out. Revolutionary—enabled General Motors to cut the average cost of manufacturing passenger vehicles by about three bucks and quarter. Times hundreds of millions of cars and trucks every year? Pretty easy to see why that stock took off. And AdEx was just *one* of Lily's *many* brilliant investments—she bought at the initial offering price of four and three-quarters.

"Of course it's also pretty easy to see why AdEx's now *down* almost half last year's peak value. This year GM's been on strike and so AdEx earnings're down. GM'll go back to work, so AdEx's still one to hang onto—closed yesterday six-and-a-half. But five thousand times six dollars and a half is thirty-two thousand five; the loan she hocked it for is for fifty grand. She's got until Monday to cover."

"So she needs seventeen-five," Farrier said.

"Not exactly," Stoat said. He put the bottle back on the table and drank some beer.

"Well, twenty grand then, whatever," Farrier said. "They want extra margin, have her sell some other stock. But whatever you do, don't hock your house."

"Ah, she won't do it that way," Stoat said, his face a map of misery. "She says even though real estate's looking very strong now, the stocks in her portfolio will appreciate at least twice as fast in a year as this condo will. More likely, she thinks, they'll triple." He paused one beat. "She includes AdEx in that calculation."

"So borrow more on the stocks then," Farrier said. "Makes more sense'n risking your *house.*"

"I agree," Stoat said, "but she won't do that either. And maybe I didn't make it clear enough—when she says the contents of her portfolio will triple in the coming year, she's including AdEx in her expectations. 'GM strike won't last forever,' she says. 'Six months after it ends, AdEx earnings'll be back at least to where they were, probably higher—answering pent-up demand, and the price'll go up again.'"

"So?" Farrier said.

"So she's not planning to sell AdEx to offset the loan," Stoat said. "It's the whole fifty grand she plans to pay back with the equity line." He took a long drink.

"Jesus," Farrier said. "So that means unless you find some other way to come up with fifty grand, you're going *way* back from where you started when you bought the house, far's paying off your mortgage is concerned."

"Damn betchah," Stoat said. "We shopped around and got a twenty-year eight-point-five mortgage. I've paid in roughly thirteen thousand on it. I figure about half of that's been interest. So if she does what she says she plans to do, by the end of next week we'll be about a hundred-and-fifty-one thousand in debt—instead of the hundred-and-one we are this week, or the hundred-and-eight we owed when I started making payments." He drank some beer. "You can see why I don't want to do that."

"It'd amount to..." Farrier said, drinking some beer; he coughed. "What it'd amount to'd be that after making payments for the past year, you haven't gotten closer to payin' off the mortgage. You haven't even treaded *water,* stayed in the same place—she's puttin' lead boots on your feet, sinking you further, a *lot* further. Transferrin' the money *you've* been puttin' into, and'll have to *keep* puttin' into, the house, *out* of the house and into *her* stock account."

"Precisely," Stoat said.

"Which is, of course, in her name," Farrier said.

"That's right," Stoat said, "her name sole."

They sat drinking beer and considering the matter, oblivious to the Hitachi and the young woman with short dark hair in the navy blue suit with a white blouse and flowered scarf standing with a microphone brightly lighted for TV against the blue surrounding evening next to a small white wooden sign outside a three-story brick building. In the center of the sign there was a blue and gold Commonwealth of Massachusetts seal above black block letters reading "STATE POLICE BLUE HILLS DIVISION."

She said, "State Police still aren't commenting on what sources say was a series of arrests made late this afternoon and earlier this evening at a number of locations, at least one of them in nearby Randolph and throughout Norfolk and Bristol counties. Reports that what's involved is a *truly* bizarre story—an elaborate scheme involving as many as a dozen people, some of them terminally ill, many of them cancer patients, to obtain painkilling prescription drugs using counterfeit prescriptions. Norfolk County District Attorney..."

"So," Farrier said at last, "the metals options she bought are worthless and they're going to stay that way. It happens. Lily's a smart investor, made a lot of good deals, but every smart investor makes a bad deal now and then, and this's one of hers. Too bad, but it's a bad deal she made, not you.

"So, let her cry in *her* beer. You forget about it. What *you* need to do is stop her from fobbing *her* bad deal off onto *you*. To do that you need someone who will lend you twenty thousand dollars—*not fifty*—to cover her margin account. For as long as it takes for this AdEx stock to bounce back, which she says will not be long. After which she's going to withdraw the twenty grand from her account and give it back to you, and you in turn are going to pay it back to the guy who loaned it to you."

"She won't agree to that," Stoat said, grieving, shaking his head. "She'll say, 'No, I won't do that. I'm writing the check.'" He drank some beer.

"And at which point you will say," Farrier said, grinning at him, "'If you do that, sweetheart, *darling*, then I hope you've either got some income stream that you've been keeping secret from me, or else come fall you won't mind moving. Because I've made my last payment on this house that I don't own, and I ain't gonna make no payments whatsoever on that new loan for fifty grand. So, unless *you* start making those payments *I've* been making every month that you're now gonna piss away, you'll be in arrears in thirty days, and in default before foreclosure—Veterans Day'd be my guess.'" Farrier grinned. "Think she'll write that big check then?"

Stoat's eyes showed some life and he managed a small smile, but he shook his head again. "You're brilliant, Jack, you're brilliant—and you've got an evil mind. No wonder you get along so well with the crooks and the hoods and the gangsters. But you're overlooking something. I don't *have* a banker who'll give me a twenty-thousand-dollar unsecured loan until the stock market improves. Federal employees credit union won't give me that kind of money. They'd tell me either to withdraw it from my retirement account or use it for collateral—both of which would amount to withdrawal and neither of which I will do.

"And I'm not from around here; I don't have the kind of long-established personal reputation, family ties, that if I'd stayed in Tennessee where I grew up and my family's always been, I could maybe call upon to get a private personal loan. I've been sort of a nomad. I don't have anybody here who's got that kind of money, *and* either knows me well enough, or owes me big enough to do me that big a favor."

"Sure you do," Farrier said. "They're on their way here for dinner."

Stoat's eyes opened wide and his mouth hung open. He closed it, licked his lips and swallowed. "Jesus H. Christ, Jack," he said. "I can't take *money* from those guys—the only reason I don't say which felony it'd be is because I don't know which crime to call it. Extortion? Soliciting bribes? Corrupt practices? Any one of them, for *damned sure*—probably at least a dozen more. *Hell,* the two of us here—*we've* probably already committed a crime, and a serious one, conspiracy, minimum, you by suggesting I do such a thing and I by even considering it. One overt act now and that's all it would take—guilty as Lucifer, the pair of us."

He shook his head vehemently. "*No, no, no* and *no,* Jack—I couldn't *possibly* do that."

"Darren," Farrier said, "you're forgetting something. We haven't committed a crime at all, and we won't have if you take my advice. It *isn't* a crime if nobody knows about it. It never *becomes* one until someone finds out. The only way *anyone* ever *finds out* is if someone involved in it *tells* them. Who in this scenario of *yours*———"

Stoat shook his head again vigorously, saying "*No*" again.

"On the contrary, *yes*," Farrier said. "The idea of floating a loan from the lads has been on your mind for some time. It isn't new to you, and it did not come from me. All I had to do was *hint* at it, and you knew exactly where I was going. Couldn't *wait* to denounce it, because the temptation's so strong. It may *scare* you some—I don't doubt that—but it doesn't *surprise* you at all. The idea of floating a loan from the lads didn't come into this room tonight out of *my* mind, my friend. It came out of yours.

"But, since *you* had the idea, and you *are* tempted by it, enough to invite my opinion, let me put on the finishing touches. If there's no crime unless somebody tells, who in your scenario's gonna do that? Certainly *we're* not gonna tell—not unless we lose our minds. And what would make Nick or Arthur tell? It'd be against their interest too, to make such a claim. In the first place, no one'd believe them. And if anyone ever did, all we'd have to do'd be let it be known that we're about to get them indicted for all kinds of bad acts. Then say, 'What do you expect? They're *criminals,* for Pete's sake, pulling the usual criminal dodge—telling lies about us to stay out of jail.' And that would be the end of them."

Stoat licked his lips. The Hitachi showed various views of a BMW 328 sedan being driven at high speed along a mountain road while a male voice-over assured listeners the car cost less to buy than the road to build. It was 7:41. The doorbell played "Dixie." "*Annnnd . . . showtime,*" Farrier said.

20

"I HOPE YOU DIDN'T TELL HIM you've done it," Cheri Farrier said. They were in the kitchen of their condo on Adams Street. She was at the refrigerator in her emerald green silk robe trimmed with white ostrich feathers. "At *least* once, that I know about."

Farrier sat at the table trying to make himself believe that the glass of milk in front of him would put him speedily to sleep. He had had a third mug of black coffee and waited for an hour and a half to pass before very carefully driving home from Framingham, so he was wide awake, but he still had enough Chianti in his system to be amused by anything she said or did that he could take as a sign of advancing age. "*No*," he said, "I didn't tell him about our small transaction with the Frogman." Cistaro had, but he saw no need to mention that.

"*Your* small transaction, you mean," she said. She emerged from the refrigerator with a liter bottle of effervescent Evian water and, as she turned toward the counter next to it, kicked the door closed with the clear plastic gold-flecked spike heel of her mule, also ostrich trimmed. "I wouldn't've gone on that trip, agreed to it in the first place, if I'd known where the money was coming .from." She poured the sparkling water into the twelve-ounce double-highball glass of ice and Martell Five-Star cognac she had prepared there.

"Not much you wouldn't've," he said. "The minute, the *minute,* I got home that night with Andy's fax to me from Santa Fe, how he'd run into Hammer on a detail, San Diego, they'd had a few drinks'n decided to try round up the old gang from Buffalo, reunite at that fabulous place Dennis found at Longboat Key, you started worrying what to pack. I hadn't've come up with the necessary, you would've probably divorced me."

She sat down at the table opposite him, the robe blousing open on her breasts. "Well," she said, making a halfhearted effort to cover herself and then giving up on it, "I would've at least *said* something, like there had to be some other way we could get three thousand dollars without asking *them* for it. Get a cash advance on the Visa card or something."

He chuckled. "Be serious," he said. "Our highest *limit* then, any one of the four cards we had, was twenty-five *hundred,* and we maxed it every month. Never *saw* a zero balance. 'Til we agreed you'd use Mastercard and I'd use Visa so we might not kill each other. It was *routine,* every month, one of us'd have a charge disallowed—the other one already used up all of the two-three hundred bucks that we'd paid the balance down the month before. Maybe we could've gotten fifty bucks—that wouldn't *quite*'ve done it."

"Well," she said, "I suppose we could say it wasn't as *much*— only three thousand. Three thousand isn't that much money— so there's that difference, anyway; that's a *lot* less money'n *twenty* thousand would be. And we did pay it back."

"Honey-chile," he said, leaning toward her and lifting her chin with the first knuckle of his right forefinger, gazing into her brown eyes, "when you ain't *got* it, an' you cain't *git* it, 'cause no damn bank on God's green earth'll lend you one thin *dime* more'n you already *borrowed,* 'n' haven't paid it *back, ain'* no difference between three and twenny—*any* sum of money you got to have so much you borrow it from *those* guys, *is,* a *lot* of money."

"And it was a long time ago," she said, pushing his hand away. He sat back, pouting a little, and tugged at his trousers. "My lord, how long ago was it? Two years, three years, that long? I know it was at least *three*—every time I go to get something in the dresser I have to look straight at that picture of us outside the shack where they filled the tanks, the one of you with a hard-on in it. I still even had blond hair then."

"Got one now, too," he said. "The hell with this milk; not gonna make me sleep. Leave your drink here and let's you and me go in the other room and fuck."

"It's pretty late," she said, thinking it over. "I hafta be at work early in the morning. That judge who passed away, you know him? He had a funny name, Dienstermacher, something like that, German, I suppose, Horace Dienstermacher."

"Never heard of him, my life," Farrier said. "Come on, let's go to bed. And do it."

"Well, maybe *you* never did," she said, "but a boatload of other people sure did. Yesterday afternoon—I guess it was on the noon news. He'd dropped dead in court. A lot of people must watch that—we had a flock of orders come in, and a good many of them were for the big *dis*play pieces, too. Law firms, mostly; whenever it's in the news that someone died that was widely known in the legal profession, anywhere on the South Shore, Randy says he always knows he's gonna have a banner week. They all seem to really go for the showy stuff. Lots of football mums, and stock. Snapdragons, glads. And roses, very big blankets of roses. Randy says sometimes the flower car for one of those dead legal guy's funerals, all those big rose blankets, looks he won the Kentucky Derby, collapsed in the winner's circle.

"But he just eats it all up, Randy does, and you can't blame him for that. He was on the phone taking the orders almost the whole afternoon. And when he wasn't doing that, he's almost rubbin' his hands, is how good he felt. So he's gettin' up at five-fifteen, take the truck in to the wholesale market. Pick up all the stuff he's ordered to make the sprays and bouquets, and he'll be back out at the shop by six-thirty.

"So that we can then get to work, gettin' them all put together if we're going to deliver them the funeral home, twelve thirty. Means I'll have to leave here by six-fifteen, which means get up five-forty-five." She paused. "What time is it anyway? Lemme see your watch. We've just *got* to get ourselves a clock, put in this kitchen. This must be the only kitchen in the whole damned *world,* in the whole damn *universe,* doesn't have a clock in it."

"It's a little after one-fifteen," he said, rolling his left forearm over so that she could see the Tag Heuer, "and if you'd just forget about Randy's dead judge now and put your mind instead to thinking about my sergeant major, by one-twenty-five I'll have you 'bout as close to paradise's any goddamned judge *I* ever met is liable to get." He stood up.

"Well, I suppose," she said, standing up and gathering the robe about her, taking a long swallow of her drink. She grinned at him and took his hand. "After all, it *has* been almost eighteen hours since we last did it. Wouldn't want to lose the knack."

"Absolutely not," he said.

"You'll just have to tell me all about your dinner with your pet gangsters, you get home tomorrow night."

"Well," he said, "we'll see. I may only have one tame gangster left now. Other seems to've gotten loose and run away."

CISTARO CAME THROUGH STOAT'S FRONT DOOR a plainly worried man. "He isn't here?" he said to Farrier standing by the couch as Stoat shut the door behind him. Farrier shook his head. "Course I didn't think he would be, since his car's not out in front." He let Stoat take his black leather coat. "And he hasn't called, either? You haven't heard from him?"

Farrier said "Nope. Phone hasn't rung since you called. And we've been here all the time."

Cistaro shook his head and started toward the leather chair to the right of Stoat's. "I tell you guys, this bothers me. This bothers me a *lot*." He sat down.

Stoat, closing the door to the closet in the hall, said, "Can I get you a drink?"

"You better believe you can," Cistaro said. "What I'd like to have right now is a tall glass with about three ice cubes in it and then the rest filled up with vodka." Then he snuffled and smiled as Stoat went toward the kitchen. "Well, maybe not filled all the *way* up, that might not be such a hot idea, but you know what I mean—what I want is ice and vodka and no decorations, little something for the nerves."

"You got no idea where he is?" Farrier said.

"Nope," Cistaro said. "Like I told you onna phone, I see him today, this after, I was over at the spa there, Rico's droppin' me off so I can get my car. He's gonna shadow Maxie onna a piece of work that *he's* got, where he has to go to Canton and then go over Randolph, and this's gonna take them all the rest the afternoon. But since there's no reason me to be there, I am pickin' up my car. That way I can then go home and do some stuff before it's time for Arthur come and pick me up, and then we both come out here. So we can have dinner, you guys."

"And everything seemed to be all right with him?" Stoat said, handing Cistaro's drink to him. To Farrier he said: "Cacciatore'd cooled off more'n I expected, so I just turned the heat back on underneath the pot there. Wasn't quite as hot as I like it to be, I serve it. It should be ready in fifteen minutes; then I figure we should eat—whatever you think, huh?" Then he sat down and drank some beer.

"Absolutely," Cistaro said, before Farrier could reply. He drank some vodka. "Ahh, that's good. That hits the spot. Much better. I was thinkin' comin' over, see, I'm afraid I might get lost—never drove here by myself. Way we always did it since we started comin' here—as opposed the guy before you, him livin' up in Salem there, would've been way out his way, Arthur came to pick me up, so it made sense then we both drove—but with *you* now, livin' out *here*, well, made more sense Arthur'd stop and pick me up. 'Cause then it's *not* out of his way—it's right *on* his way, in fact. See, where I live where I've been livin', inna Towers, Chestnut Hill, since I move there, eighty-eight. But it turns out I *did* know the way, remembered it all right. But while I'm doin' this I'm thinkin', 'I could use a drink right now.' So this one here, it sure tastes good."

He looked at Farrier. "But no, I didn't see a thing. Or didn't notice anything, I guess, is what I'm trying, say. As far as I could see. Of course this now's just from lookin' at the guy, but I've known him a long time, over thirty years or so, that we've been doing things together, so I think that I *would* know, I'd be able to tell, if he had somethin' on his mind that was botherin' him. An' there just *wasn't*, I could see, anything like that at all.

"Nothing on his mind," Farrier said, reaching for his own glass.

"Well, business, naturally—he was always thinkin' about that. But nothin' *else*," Cistaro said. "And Arthur *never*, all the time I've known him, kept a thing that was botherin' him to himself. Never. The first thing he does is talk about it, work out in his mind what to do about it—and the second thing, he does what he has worked out. And if he decided *you* were the cause of it, *boom*, right off, he'd be in your face about it. Who it was didn't matter—he would go right into action. No holdin' the guy. 'Cause that's just the way he is. It is not his style to wait."

"Well, you're right about that, all right," Farrier said.

"And like I say," Cistaro said, "I knew he was particularly lookin' forward comin' over here tonight, because, well, we aren't sure about the date yet so you can't move on this right now, but him and me, we kind of think we've got a case you're gonna like. And the reason that I say this, and I'll tell you what it is, is that this's so far off the beaten track for you guys—and way off the beaten track for *us,* too—that you're not gonna . . . well, I don't know, you might have trouble believin' it."

He paused for their reaction. Both Farrier and Stoat frowned. Farrier shrugged. The Hitachi replayed the taped report from the young woman with the short dark hair wearing a blue suit and standing with the microphone outside the Blue Hills Division barracks of the Massachusetts State Police. All three of them ignored it.

"Right," Cistaro said, "okay, let's try it this way. You remember when Steve Martin, the comedian who I guess he now thinks he's an actor, in the movies? I mean, like I guess Robin Williams? Every now and then he used to be on television, 'Saturday Night Live.' May still be on, for all I know—almost never tune it in now.

"Anyway, he'd be one of these two real blazing assholes that're always, you know, going out to places seeing if they can find *dates,* and pick up girls. And although of course they couldn't actually say it on TV, at least back then, of course what they're doing is they're trying to get laid. Which of course is when any man who's ever gonna act like a total asshole does it—when he's horny and he doesn't have a woman and he doesn't wanna pay for it, so he's out trying to get laid.

"And one thing that I really remember about this is that they would both, both of them would wear berets. Like they thought this was really cool—as soon as women saw those hats, they would just go wild. And then what they would do, these two guys playing assholes, one of them was Martin—Steve Martin like I said, not that in his real life he is an asshole but he would be acting like one—one of them would always say, 'cause this's what the act's *about*—'We are such wild and crazy *guys.*' All right?" He looked brightly at them, first at Stoat and then at Farrier.

Farrier shrugged. "All right by me," he said.

"Well, okay then," Cistaro said. "These two guys we heard about that I'm telling you about—only you've now got to promise me, and I mean both of you, that nobody's gonna act on this until we give you the go-ahead, probably next month, but I'm not sure about that and it could be that it goes two. Now do I have that?"

"Oh, positively," Stoat said. "You got a problem with that, Jack?"

"Works just fine for me," Farrier said. "I'm the soul of flexible. Got to get myself a haircut 'fore too much more time goes by. Maybe get my good winter suit cleaned and pressed, and put away. But otherwise on most days I can always make room on my busy schedule, almost anything worthwhile. Mostly lately, all I've been doing's listening to my tape collection, *Evenings at Carlo's?*

"Funny . . ." he said as though musing, "funny how when you get something that you thought you always wanted, and then when you finally get it—and you'd know this, Nick, 'cause you are *on* it, heard a tape of you today, tellin' Carlo all about the night Hugo got you your first washer and drier, and then you picked him up in Cambridge . . ." He hesitated one beat.

Cistaro was impassive.

"Well, anyway," Farrier said, "then you start to think, 'My God, what have I got here? These guys're vicious *animals.* Did I really want this thing?' But anyway, that's what I do most days. So, for anything worthwhile."

Stoat got up. "We should eat," he said.

"Amen to that, brother," Farrier said. "That okay with you, Nick, we don't wait any longer, see if Arthur's showing up?"

"Oh, *yeah*," Cistaro said. "I am personally hungry. No, all I say 's I am worried about the guy; and where he is; and how come he isn't here, and so forth; but we've all still got to eat.

"And anyway, Jack, I was saying, there's also another thing on my mind when I am thinking about Arthur, and you'll know what I mean by this, Jack, is that Arthur now and then ... well, put it this way—from time to time he has been known to go and do a thing that he has been thinking about, thinking maybe about doing it for quite a while, you know? But he did not see any need, any reason or whatever, he just never got around to telling me about it. Or anybody else, either, as far as that goes.

"And then one day he would have just decided that, okay, the time has *come*, the time has come to go and *do* it. And then he would go where he had to go to do it. Just, you know, *disappear* on you, he'd vanish, and you wouldn't see him for a while, or hear from him, either. But you didn't dare touch anything that was his, any operation, because you didn't know when he'd show up again, just as unexpected, take it back and most likely shoot you for trying to take it over.

"One day there he'd *be* again, right where he'd been before, doing the same thing that he always'd been doing, and you would say hello to him and he would say hello to you, just like he'd never been away. Maybe some time later he'd tell you something about it, drop some hint or something, that would at least give you some rough idea of where he'd been and what he did. And maybe he wouldn't. In fact usually he would not. And you'd just never know where he'd been or what he did, and the reason would be because he didn't want you to."

"I'm going out in the kitchen," Stoat said. "Open the wine and dish out the food. Keep talking—place isn't that big. I'll be able to hear you."

"Right," Farrier said. "And this's also something that I think that you'd know, Nick. The worst thing you could do, the absolute worst thing that you could do, was to react, when he'd disappeared like that and've *been* gone a while, and then he had come back, was *ask* him where he'd been and what he'd done."

Cistaro nodded vigorously. "Absolutely," he said, "that is absolutely right."

"Well, I know it is," Farrier said. "Fogarty told me that when he was first getting me ready to take over from him as, what, as liaison to you guys, and he said he got it from DeMarco. Al De-Marco'd had to learn it for himself, find it out the hard way, but *when* he did, he remembered it; he never forgot it. And when the time came for *him* to leave, when he retired, he'd handed it down to Fogarty. Passed it down to him. Which was that you never *did* that, ask McKeach, or even not exactly *ask* him, but just indirectly say something to him, *tell* him that he'd had you worried, or that he'd even pissed you off, when he pulled that shit of his.

"Because if you did that, one thing it told him was that what you'd thought when it happened, he was missing, not around, you didn't see him and nobody else had, either, was that maybe he'd pissed someone else off that you didn't know about, and as a result he was now in the trunk of a stolen car someplace, with a couple in the head. You know—dead."

"Oh, Jesus, no," Cistaro said. "You got that right—never, ever ask him. Because to him that means you'd actually been thinking—*worried*—that maybe he couldn't take care of himself. That if anyone came after him they might actually get him. That it would be him that then got clipped and not the other guy. No, he prides himself on that. That if anyone came after him he would *always* know about it, before the guy could make a move, and take care of it himself—the other guy would always be the one who said good-bye.

"Because Arthur thinks if *anyone,* even his friends, ever even *thought* it, that he *could* get taken out, and then that kind of thinking got around, then that would be the beginning. People would get *used* to it, you know? *Used* to the idea it could be actually done. And if that idea ever did get started, then sooner or later some dumb bastard would actually *try* it. And he *might* even get lucky, just get off one lucky shot, and then if that should happen, he would in fact be dead. So, he saw it as a threat.

"There were a few times when I almost made that mistake, myself. When I thought that maybe something in the paper or I maybe heard from someone, that explained me where he'd been and, you know, what he might've been up to.

"Like, I remember one time when he was gone there, that time back in the late seventies, seventy-seven, seventy-eight, in there, one of those years anyway, I know it was in the spring of, and he was gone for quite a while, too. Long time, six-eight weeks, maybe more. And as usual he comes back and he didn't say a word. So you now knew that that meant all he wanted you to know was just that he'd gone *away,* and he'd been away a *while,* and now he was *back* again and that was the *end* of it. And what I remember first I noticed that he didn't have a tan, so you knew that it was not that he'd been down south someplace, wherever he'd gone. But I still did not know where.

"And then that whichever year it was, seventy-seven, seventy-eight, sometime in July or August, now, good while after he came back, there was this item in the paper where they said police in Ireland, or else maybe it was coast guard or the army, Irish army, coast guard that I'm talking about here, not the British army there. Anyway, it said that they had gotten wind of someone shipping arms over there in this big fishing boat that came from here, from Boston. This big oceangoing trawler you could go all the way across the Atlantic in, very easy, any time. And basically what these guys'd done was pick up guns in Canada, and the plan was they were then going to land them on the Irish *coast.*

"And what it was, the IRA would then've *come* down from up where they are, up in *Northern* Ireland, come down and pick up the guns, and then smuggle them *across* the border, back up there to *Northern* Ireland, Belfast probably, I guess. And they would then use them to kill British soldiers with. And also to kill Protestants, of course, naturally, those crazy bastards all still then fightin' with each other, no good reason whatsoever. Like whichever *church* you went to, it could get you fuckin' *killed,* Christ sake, and nobody'd even be surprised.

"And this thing in the paper said that what'd happened was the guns'd *gotten* there all right, been landed on the coast, but that then apparently somebody over there that either was involved in it himself or else he knew some people were, they caught him doing something else, with a bomb, I think it was.

"He had some explosives with him and the feeling was I guess that what he'd been plannin' was to go blow up the queen, Queen Elizabeth I mean—she went out in public somewhere. Or maybe it was Princess Di, I'm not really sure on that. All I'm *really* sure of is that it was someone in the royal family. Anyway, it was about as serious as it could get unless he'd actually *done* it, them catchin' him with that in mind, and so they didn't needah tell him he's goin' away for a *good long* time, for havin' *that* idea in mind.

"And so to save his own white ass he told them about the guns. Who was involved, at least in Ireland, once they'd gotten there, and where it was they had them stashed, and that was how they grabbed them.

"And like I say now, this was in the summertime of that next year I read this, when Arthur'd gone away inna spring, the year before, and come back in the spring of that year, and so after readin' it I naturally think, 'Now I know where Arthur was when Arthur wasn't here. He was on the deep blue sea, takin' arms to Ireland.'

"And so the next time that I see him I say, 'Hey, Arthur, my Irish friend, now I know where you were when you're not around last year and this. Too bad that guy on the other end wrecked all your hard work.'

"I'm just kiddin' him, you know? And he gives me that *look* he had, you know, when he's irritated? When something that you maybe said irritated him? And he says, 'The hell're you talkin' about?'

"And I say then, 'This spring, Arthur, when you're gone, six weeks, a couple months. Now I know where you went and what you were doin' there—you were takin' guns to Ireland, and from what I see the papers, everything that you did, your end, seems to've worked out pretty good. Isn't your fault, some asshole got himself grabbed and turned rat—you did a good job.'

"He just *flared* at me, that horrible look that he gets on his face and his eyes, they've got this look in them that some of the guys I trained with—I trained *under*'s what I mean, back when I was in the navy; they're career UDT men, underwater demolition teams. And they had it too, I mean. 'Thousand-yard stare' was what I heard one guy call it. These guys were stone-cold killers.

"Now I don't mean I never, I mean, I was trained to do that too, that was how I got to know them, learning how to do that stuff, and when I had to do it, well, that was what I did. But I never, I don't think I ever, had that look in my eyes they had and that he gets. I thought he was gonna kill me. I thought I was gonna die.

"He backed *me* off with that look. Even *me*, I'm on his *side*— *did* things with him. *Been* with him thirty *years*, more—even *I* backed away. '*Hey,*' I said, 'now don't get mad now, I was only foolin' with you, *teasin'*, for the luvva Mike, givin' you a little shit. Like I could've said, you know, all along I was afraid you'd gone and joined the Program.'

"Well, as you well know by now, Arthur isn't famous for his sense of humor. He is not well known for that. He's got one—if you tell a joke he gets he does think certain things're funny, and he'll get on a guy and ride him, although I think he has to be in a good mood that day. Because as you can see, I'm here tonight and talkin'; he must not've killed me yet."

Stoat had put two bottles of Antonori Chianti Classico Riserva and three wineglasses on the pass-through counter. He put three plates of chicken cacciatore on the counter. The Hitachi segued from a Bell Atlantic "Wild Things Are Happening" ad featuring cartoon monsters into the 8:00 P.M. rerun of the 6:00 P.M. Channel 5 News. "Gentlemen," he said, "dinner is served. A bit overcooked and a little late, but dinner is served nonetheless."

Cistaro and Farrier moved to the table, Cistaro taking his usual seat and Farrier going around his customary place at the end of the table farthest from the kitchen to the chair McKeach had occupied opposite Cistaro. Stoat brought large serving dishes of linguini and more cacciatore from the kitchen and set them at the center of the table. He put a plate of food and poured a glass of wine at each place, and as they began to eat proposed a toast: "to our absent friend, Arthur, whom we hope to hear from soon."

"Hear, hear," Farrier said, and Cistaro said "*Yeah.*" They clinked glasses and drank.

"Because," Cistaro said around the first forkful of chicken in his mouth, "even though I was just sayin' I have known him to take off like this without givin' any warning, what makes me nervous this time is that I know he's never done it without havin' some good reason, and therefore without knowin' tonight what it could've been that made him do it, I still have to think there is one, and I don't know what it is. That he might've heard something, you know? Heard something that I didn't, but that he would assume I did, that if he did so must've I, and therefore without callin' me or anything like that, that he would just take *off.*"

"Well, how could that've happened?" Stoat said. "Where you and he 're partners, and've *been* partners for so long? How could it've happened that he'd hear about something that would frighten him enough——"

Cistaro, now chewing his second forkful of chicken as he used both hands and the large serving pieces to lift linguini to his plate, shook his head and said, "No, un uh, no, not 'frightened.'" He swallowed as he replaced the serving pieces in the large dish. "Arthur now, he would be *pissed,* he heard you say he was frightened.

"Frightened's one thing I would doubt that Arthur's ever been. Frightened is what he makes other people. No, if he did hear something and that was why he cleared out, the reason that he wouldn't contact me first before he left?" He continued to eat while he talked, twirling linguini onto his fork in his soupspoon, cutting meat from the chicken breast with the knife in his right hand and delivering to his mouth with the fork in his left.

"Well, first," Cistaro said, "it could have been something that he knew would not be something that would concern me. See, while it's true that as partners for a very long time now we have had a number of interests that have produced income for both of us, we have also, each of us, had a few interests of our own, that we kept separate. He had some things from when he was with Brian G., all right? That he kept when Brian went down and after we got together. And also some other things that came out of those things, you could say grew out of what he had with Brian G. And there were quite a few of these.

"Just as when we got together, I had quite a few things going that I had, I was with Hugo. And after that some other things that just in the normal course of things, that grew out of those things, too. And so when we got together, he kept those things that he had had before we did that, and likewise I myself kept those things that I had had before.

"Now I realize when you say it, I'm explaining it to you now, it sounds pretty complicated, but it's really not at all. Or at least to me and Arthur, don't seem that way. See, that kind of independence we still kept when we joined up, that was very important, to me especially. If I had've gone with Nunzio, all right? With Nunzio Dinapola who was the Boston Cosa Nostra guy before he died and Carlo, Carlo Rizzo took his place? He was the guy who you hadda go and see, if you were a made guy and you wanted to do something, before you could do it. And if he said you could, you could, and if he didn't then you couldn't.

"Well, he always wanted me to join, both of them wanted that—he had Carlo ask me, Nunzio did, I dunno how many times, and I would always tell him No. I mean, I would be polite about it, no use pissing someone off, he's tellin' you he likes your style, the way you go about things, right? And so he'd like you, work for him. No, you don't want to do that unless for some reason you have to, and then of course you got no choice.

"But still I would always tell him No, and that was the biggest reason. Havin' to get their permission before I could do things, which if I became a member I would have to do. But if I didn't, then what I'd built up with Hugo and what I'd made out of it, that was mine and it would stay mine—unless I joined up with them. Became a made guy, LCN. At which point it would become from then on an interest of *ours.* Well, no thanks, I don't think so.

"And as far as Arthur was concerned, well, he didn't have the problem that I had with *Nunzio,* with *Carlo,* because of course he's not Sicilian or Italian like I am, and unless you are one of them you're not eligible. You can do work for them, as Arthur has, as he has no doubt told you. Lots of times when they've asked, the order came direct from Providence. And at least one time that I heard about, it came from New York. Hadda go to Florida, Arthur's got a reputation, and he don't mind travelin' to do a job—if the money's there. That could be where he is now—off on a hurry-up job. But even though he couldn't join I know he never would, and for the same reason I had. Arthur works for Arthur. He is no one's employee."

Cistaro took a second piece of chicken and another serving of linguini from the serving dishes. "So Arthur may've heard something about one of his private interests that may have caused him to hit the road, but wouldn't affect you?" Stoat said. "And that's why he didn't call? Get in touch with you somehow?" Farrier cut and chewed industriously, pausing now and then for wine, as though having found a nice rhythm he didn't wish to break.

Cistaro nodded. "Right," he said. "If hit the road is what he's done—he's not just doing something else. And then when he gets where he is going, he'll then find a payphone and call me sometime when he knows where I'll be and it isn't where I live— he'll assume my phone is tapped and whoever put the tap on's looking for him, tracing every call I get. So if he called me there then they might not know what *building* he was in, but they'd at least know what *town,* where he was, and to start looking, be- cause that's where the call came from. When I get *that* call, I will then know.

"But by then, if he's gone because something *he* had just went wrong, then probably tomorrow sometime, or the papers come out tonight, I'll probably already know what it was that made him go. Because even though we both have things of our own the other guy is not involved with, I know what things he's got, or most of them, anyway, and he knows most of mine. So one of his has gone haywire bad enough for him to screw, it'll make the papers." He swallowed and snorted. "Wasn't for da fuckin' Broons, I'd probably know right now."

"The Bruins?" Farrier said. "What the hell've the Bruins got to do with it?"

Cistaro was laughing and shaking his head as he worked on the chicken. "Ah fuckin' Broons're playin' ah fuckin' New Jersey Devils tonight, is what the fuckin' Broons've got to do with it. Game didn't start until seven-thirty, but WBZ's got this god-damned pregame warm-up show, I guess it starts at seven? I dunno when the fuck it starts—all I know is by the time I re-member Arthur with his fuckin' old shitboxes, those old cars he's always driving? Well, to him it didn't matter they're old, made him look like he's retired from the insurance business? Only things he cares about're that they run. And the heater works; same thing with the air conditioner—if it's even *got* AC. He don't insist on AC, a couple of his old cars *didn't*; that's how old they were. I used to tell him I'm surprised he didn't ever have one that burned coal instead of gas. He laughed at that. But if it's in it it should work. And the radio. Hasta have a radio and it's on *all* the time.

"There was this one car, years ago I'm talkin' now, a big grey fifty Mercury, looked like a giant bathtub someone'd turned up-side down, then put a setta wheels on it. Got it for two hundred dollars, someone settlin' an estate. Anna radio quit on him. Hadda new one put in that cost him a hundred-fifty, 'most as much as the whole car did, 'cause it was the cheapest model that they had, at the first place he went, and he wanted it done fast.

"If he's in his fuckin' car, that radio is on. He is not listening to music and he's not listening to talk shows. He's got BZ on, WBZ AM, ten-thirty AM dial, all news all day long. One of the things they must do is monitor the scanners, and also must have people call them out around the various towns, because once some cop makes an arrest he thinks should be a big deal, seems like they're on the air with it before he's shut the siren off. Which's why when he's in Boston any time he's in his car, Arthur always has BZ on—it comes on with the ignition.

"Same reason he's got bank accounts all over everywhere— that's what he's been doing sometimes when no one knew where he is; drivin' all over the country, opening these bank accounts, nothing that attracts attention, two, maybe, three thousand dollars. I dunno what names're on 'em, whose Social Security numbers or anything like that, but I know they exist—I got no idea how many. Different names on different licenses; I know where he got those, but also, different names on different *passports*; where he got them I don't know. And this small gym bag of hundreds that he keeps in some safe place that he keeps changing all the time. I got something like that myself—escape cash. Just in case some cop does something that could mean something that we wouldn't like at all."

"Mean something like get arrested?" Farrier said.

Cistaro nodded. "Exactly," he said, bringing a forkful of pasta to his mouth. "But by the time I think of that, I don't know where he is tonight, 'Where the hell's Arthur? Did he maybe hear something on the radio today, tonight, that would make him take off? Maybe he did. I'll turn on BZ and see.' But of course the time I do that, some asshole is on the air talkin' about hockey."

"Would it be on CNN?" Stoat said. "Either CNBC or that? Lily has CNBC on all the time, on the big set in the study, where she is, she works at home, and I know it's also news in addition tah the stock market. CNN's got two channels, I think—one's headlines all the time."

Cistaro shook hs head. "Nah, I doubt it," he said. "If it was one of Arthur's private actions gettin' sideways on him, I doubt it would be big enough to get on CNN." He finished his second helping and drank some wine. Then he sat back in his chair, contentment on his face, and clasped his hands over his belly. He shook his head. "Hafta hand it to you, Darren—for a redneck cracker boy, best a man'd hope from you's a good seat at a NASCAR race and some Elvis gittar music, no chance of a decent meal 'less you go for ham an' grits, but you sure do cook up one mean Italian meal." He beamed at Stoat. "How come you took it up?"

"Waal," Stoat said, "Ah figured if Italians do it, cain't be awl *that* hard."

Cistaro sucking at his teeth said "Uh huh" and studied him for a moment, deciding whether to take offense, before shifting his eyes to Farrier. "You been talkin' to this boy, Jack? He learn this new fresh talk from you?" Farrier smiled. "Yes, you have, Jack, I can tell. You've been tellin' him bad stories about the Italian people, puttin' bad thoughts in his head."

He grinned, but there was no fun in his eyes. Nodding slightly—"'Bout how we're all, what did you call us? 'vicious *animals*,' last time we're here? Now I ask you, is that nice? Is that any way to act? Undermine me with my friend here, when I'm tryin' tah help you out? I tell you, I don't think it is, and that just for doin' that, doin' to me what you did, I might decide to make you *wait* a while, before I give you the names and addresses of those two evil faggots, payin' unscrupulous foreigners to rob graves, steal valuable artifacts and national historic treasures, ancient Greece and places like that, and import them for snooty rich folks who display them in their homes."

"*Really?*" Stoat said. "Snooty rich folks around Boston?"

"Absolutely," Cistaro said, nodding but keeping his eyes fixed on Farrier. "Snooty, rich, and very well-*known*—'prominent,' I think you'd say, 'prominent Boston physicians.'" He paused, smirking. "Suppose I could be mistaken, but isn't that against the law?"

"It certainly is, and very much so," Stoat said. "We sent out several directives when I was in Washington, heads up to all field offices alerting them to this traffic. Administration's told the State Deparment to emphasize to other heads of state we intend to take this outrageous conduct—'looting' and 'smuggling' were the terms we used—'most seriously.'"

"That's what I thought," Cistaro said. "Something like that, I imagine, you made an arrest here like that, *that* would get on CNN, I bet, no doubt at all of that."

"Oh yes, I would think so," Stoat said.

"And Washington would like that, right?" Cistaro said, now looking back at Stoat.

Farrier cleared his throat. "Washington would love it," he said evenly, regaining Cistaro's attention. "And since the man who has the secret and his friend, the absent man, have strong reasons of their *own* to *want* their friends from Washington to speak *highly* of them there, and to seek cordial treatment for them, should they get their tails in *cracks*, the man who has the secret would act in his own best interest if he imparted it promptly." He paused one beat. "He would *not* want to get them mad, any more than they would want him to get mad with them."

Cistaro stared. Farrier looked at Stoat and indicated Cistaro by moving his head.

Stoat nodded and said, "You do *know*, of course, that I was only, you know, joking, when I said that. What I said about Italian cooking. Being easy."

Cistaro, still looking at Farrier, blinked and shook his head. He curled his lip but nodded. "Oh, sure," he said, making a dismissive motion with his right hand. "No problem. I understand. Could say I asked for it, I guess. And what you were sayin', Jack, you *know* how anxious me and Arthur always are, we can ever do you a small favor. All you got to do you know, is let us know, you know?" He snickered.

"Well yes, of course, I do know that," Farrier said. "As a matter of fact this evening, before you got here tonight, Darren and I were discussing how he has a small financial problem right now, and how it's been on his mind. How it distracts him from his work. And I said he shouldn't let it. I was *sure* that if he mentioned it to you and Arthur, that you'd immediately say to him, 'Well, we can take care of that for you.'"

"I see," Cistaro said. His smile showing only his four upper front teeth, the tip of his tongue protruding for a moment, he talked to Farrier but studied Stoat. "And would this be a loan you're talking? Or did you have in mind a gift?" Stoat squirmed.

"Oh, a loan, of course," Farrier said. "Just a short-term loan, sixty, ninety days." He paused. "A gift, you know, under the circumstances we'd be uncomfortable with that. People might look at a gift the wrong way—interpret it as something else. So no, no gift, a loan."

"Well, a reasonable amount," Cistaro said, "if this was a reasonable amount that you two're asking here, we would have no problem with that. And I know that I can say that, even though for some reason, Arthur isn't here tonight. But I know he would agree.

"So, how much did you have in mind? Three grand or so, like we duked you a few years back, Jack, you and the bride could get some R an' R, a little sun? Something in that neighborhood?"

Stoat could not prevent his mouth from dropping open or his eyes from darting away from Cistaro to Farrier. Now Cistaro looked at Farrier too.

Farrier smiled. "You know, Nick," he said, "I'm glad you brought that up. Because Darren I think had some slight *reservations,* guess you'd call them, about asking you this favor as I'd recommended. And I was just going to remind you of that, how you and Arthur'd done me a somewhat similar though smaller kindness a couple or three years ago—though I wouldn't say exactly, I don't think I'd say you 'duked' me because to me that would connote a *gift*, you two made a gift to me—whereas I of course did pay you back. In full. And promptly."

Cistaro grinned at him with the gleeful malice of a man observing at the effect of his new evident wealth and confident satisfaction on an old and envious adversary. "But without any vig, wasn't it?" he said pleasantly. "I recall it, we charged you no *juice*, *no* interest. An' you kept the three large 'til your wife found a job—which was what, pretty close to a year?"

He smirked. "So that part, I guess, you might call that a gift. Put it this way—we duked you the *interest.* Six hundred dollars a week. For, if I get this right, now, forty-six weeks, would it've been? What's six hundred times forty-six? You're good with numbers, Jack, what would that be? That one you can do in your head?"

Farrier scowled at him. "Twenty-seven thousand, six hundred dollars," Stoat said, his voice dull, his eyes dead on Farrier.

Cistaro nodded and swung his gaze back to Stoat. "That's what I figured it, too," he said, his face calm, his voice pleasant. "Now how much did *you* have in mind? As a loan, of course—I don't think you'd want to call it a gift either. Want to think of me and Arthur as giving you *presents*," he nodded at Farrier, "any more'n your sidekick here would."

Stoat, despairing, said nothing.

"Oh, for Chrissakes, Darren, *say* it," Farrier said grimly. "No wonder you're so pussy-whipped." Stoat remained silent. Farrier looked at Cistaro. "Twenty thousand," he said, savagely. "You keep that much in your jockstrap—which you wouldn't *have*, a jockstrap, and nothin' to put in one, if you didn't have your ass insured with us."

"*Twenty* thousand," Cistaro said, chuckling once, still looking at Stoat. Stoat, pale now, swallowed and licked his lips. "Almost seven *times* what you had, Jack. And yeah, I know, you say short term, but—and all of us know this, Darren, especially me and Arthur, the kind of business we're in, but also, as now you and me both know, Jack knows this too—these small financial problems often take a little longer'n we expect them to, 'fore they work themselves out. Financial problems, I mean. 'Check's inna *mail*,' but the check doesn't *come*. 'Have it for you *Monday*.' 'No, see me on *Friday*.'

"So let's say, we're just talkin' now like you're one of our regular *customers*, 'stead of who you really *are*. If you *were* just like anybody else, you'd want to know our terms before you got yourself involved. And we'd *want* you to know them. Truth in lending. Although naturally I'm assumin' here that what you got in mind is you want the *Jack's* kind of loan, the *special* kind we made to Jack. Which is good because of course, be considering how close we are, the four of us, that'd be the *kind* of loan that me and Arthur would *prefer* to make to you. Like Jack says," indicating Jack with his left hand, "since you got him vouching for you, Arthur and I both consider you as much a friend of ours as *he* is—too, in every respect.

"But at the same time let's be honest—if I loan you twenty on the terms we loaned to Jack, and you keep it"—now looking at Farrier—"how long was it, did we say, Jack? Forty-six weeks, right?" Farrier nodded. Cistaro looked back at Stoat. "If you keep it that long, let's say, as we know of course you *won't*, but since we're all just talking here, that would be..."

Stoat with his eyes wide and not realizing what he was doing started forming the syllables with his lips as Cistaro said, "That's it, Darren, you have got it, and my God, I agree, because if we've both got it right now, that'd come to a hundred and eighty-four large. Are we all sure we're up to this, all four of us can live with it afterward, if Arthur and I really do go ahead and do for you a hundred-and-eighty-four-grand favor? You're sure that won't, you know, *change* the way things are between us?"

He turned to look at Farrier and then he put his head back and laughed. Then he reached his right hand over the dishes on the table and patted Stoat on his left hand. He looked at him again with glee. "Well, don't you worry, Darren, 'cause your friend Jack is almost right. I don't have that much cash with me right here in my jockstrap, but I do have it where I can get it— right outside here in my car." He got up. "No need to see me out," he said. "I won't even put my coat on. I'll leave the door partly open and be right back in a *flash*."

"WHICH HE WAS," FARRIER SAID to Cheri shortly after 1:30 A.M. when they had finished having sex. "Darren'd remembered Fifty-six has news at ten so he'd turned on the little TV again. And just as Nick came through the door the female anchor finished telling us about the two big black guys getting shot down, and then the male began to tell us how the Massachusetts State Police around six o'clock tonight began arresting all these poor bastards who've got cancer but they're not gonna let that get them down—they've still been able to drag themselves out there and con many druggists out of all the happy pills and painkillers you could possibly imagine.

"And not only have the Staties arrested all these crooked invalids, they have also bagged the filthy crooks who put them up to this vile trade and then sold the dangerous stuff to poor innocent construction workers and naive warehousemen along with their doughnuts and morning coffee.

"The Staties said they suspect two of the people they grabbed 'may be connected to organized crime,' and since one of them is

Rico Garza, who's the Frogman's legbreaker and the other one's Max Rascob, who's McKeach's bookkeeper, my guess is the cops're right."

Cheri sat up in bed hugging her knees and thought about that for a while. At last she said, "Did that mean Darren didn't get his twenty grand?"

"Are you kidding?" Farrier said. "Nick tossed it onto the coffee table while Darren was helping him on with his jacket. 'You guys just remember now, don't you forget the nice guys who gave you that nice little package. I sure hope you got lotsa friends inna State cops. I think me and Arthur may need them.'

"Then he said, 'I'll be in touch.' And he went off into the night."

"Will those two guys you mentioned, you think they will talk?" she said.

"I don't know," he said, "I don't know them. Like I said I'm not sure I know now what anyone will do, or if I ever did, or I want to. Not, at least, anymore. Or if any of those guys ever knew what I'd do. None of us figured on this. I may have to go back being Soot."

"Could be worse," she said, "you were good."

Epilogue

WHEN DOWD ARRIVED AT THE YELLOW two-bedroom bungalow hidden in the woods south of Wareham Road, Route 6, on Marconi Lane in Marion on the evening of May 8, Ferrigno was in the kitchen making coffee and Rascob was in the living room watching the Channel 5 Evening News.

"They have it on yet, the decision?" Dowd said.

"Just the headline," Rascob said. "Said this judge wouldn't let him out on bail either, but they're going to appeal again. You were at the hearing?"

"Yeah, wasted my whole day there," Dowd said. "Never got put on the stand. Everything I could've said I already testified to, twice before. But the AAG said I hadda be there, in case Al Castle thought up some new reason why the Frogman should get bail, so I could knock it down."

The male anchor with grey hair said, "And security was again tight in the state Supreme Judicial Court today as well-known attorney Alfred Castle argued that his client, accused gangland leader Nicholas Cistaro, should be freed on bail."

"Here it comes," Dowd said, "Henry, come in here—this'll interest you."

The same sandy-haired reporter who'd been at Jamaica Pond, now wearing a blue blazer, stood holding a microphone on the brick plaza outside the New Courthouse at Pemberton Square. "Thanks, Chet," he said. "Associate State Supreme Court Justice Francis Keating today, sitting as a single justice, upheld Superior and District Court rulings holding alleged organized crime kingpin Nicholas "the Frogman" Cistaro without bail. Noticeably angered by attorney Castle's argument that since Cistaro, a Vietnam vet Navy Seal, has no prior record of convictions, he must be allowed bail, Justice Keating said, 'The fact that this guy's amazing good luck ducking the police finally ran out is not sufficient reason to give him a fresh chance to join his pal and business partner, Arthur McKeon—the notorious McKeach—on the run. This gentleman's charged with every major crime in the book except child molesting and treason. No way am I letting him out, so he can bolt for the border, too. He's a menace to society. Decision affirmed—bail is denied."

"Well, maybe there's some hope after all," Ferrigno said. "Maybe now that gangbangers out on bail've killed four or five people would've testified against them, the courts're catching on."

"Yeah," Dowd said, "but the reason any of those judges held him was because we nailed him on the Walterboy murders. Without Murder One on the Frogman's grocery list, guarantee you he's on the street. Now you see, Max, why we grilled you on what happened at that midnight meeting at the Spa, night before those guys went down?" He paused. "And I still want his driver, you know," he said. "I haven't forgotten that little item— who chauffeured McKeach to his rifle party."

Rascob shook his head. "Nickie's bad enough," he said. "And I still say it wasn't his idea—those two're strictly McKeach's project. All Nick did was say 'Okay, fine by me.'" He paused; then staring directly at Dowd he said, "More'n enough lives'll be ruined by this, like mine with Jessie—those at least McKeach don't find me first. Some kid who's still got a chance to shape up, have a good life and die happy? I won't drag him into this. And if you knew—or you *know*—who it was, you wouldn't want me to, either. So, *I* have forgotten who drove the car. Got no plans at all to remember."

Dowd thought about that for a while. Then he cleared his throat. "Well," he said, "the driver I'll think about—you may have something there. And as to Nickie, yeah, I sort of know how you feel. But our law says if you say okay to a plan to knock off a few guys, your okay is enough to get you in the shit, along with the guy with the rifle. The law moves in mysterious ways."

"Yeah," Rascob said morosely. "Too bad McKeach moves so much faster."

"Oh, we'll track him down," Dowd said at once, but without the confidence he wished he felt. "Canada, Ireland, Iceland? Doesn't matter, we'll get him. He's gettin' old now; don't move so fast. Time's on our side with this guy."

"Right, *time*," Rascob said. "Same thing with me. About all I've got on my side. My only hope is that his time runs out, he dies before he gets me. If I could've chosen which guy you catch and which guy gets away, I would've said, 'Leave Nick get the jump. He'll understand why I hafta to do this. But *McKeach*?" He laughed. "Somehow I don't think McKeach ever will."